ALICE MCVEIGH was born of American diplomat parents in South Korea. She lived in Southeast Asia until she was a teenager, when her family returned to the Washington DC suburbs. She attended Indiana University School of Music, graduating with distinction in 1980. Later that year she moved to London to study with cellist William Pleeth. Alice is currently a freelance cellist playing with numerous orchestras, including the BBC Symphony and the (period instrument) Hanover Band. She is married and lives in Kent.

By the same author
While the Music Lasts

GHOST MUSIC

Alice McVeigh

ORIEL

An Oriel Paperback
First published in Great Britain by Orion in 1997
This paperback edition published in 1997 by Oriel,
a division of Orion Books Ltd,
Orion House, 5 Upper St Martin's Lane,
London WC2H 9EA

A CIP catalogue record for this book
is available from the British Library.

ISBN 0 7528 0920 2

Typeset at The Spartan Press Ltd,
Lymington, Hants
Printed and bound in Great Britain by
Clays Ltd, St Ives plc.

For Simon, and all other springtimes

Chapter 1

Last week, Warren Wilson died.

Natural causes, it said in the paper, though that didn't fool anybody. No, the truth lapped round the music world as everyone knew it would, while people wondered whether it had been preventable, and how Isabel would take it – if she could take it at all.

Warren – a clean-cut, narrow-chinned fellow, with his poetic fervour and his mania for Italian frescoes. Not a joiner, never a leader, but not gloomy either, just quiet. Quiet, competent and sensitive, the kind orchestras, on the whole, could do with more of. A decent sort, who got on with his work without it ever really mattering to him. No, his life was Isabel – Isabel and Giotto and Yeats, and I always thought that the latter two would be enough for him, though it seems now that I was wrong.

And it got me thinking about that business three or four years ago, and whether it didn't explain, if not everything, at least a part of everything. And, because I like to look for connections, I thought I'd go back to my old diaries, and try to understand – the real along with the surreal, in the light of later evidence.

Definition of an orchestra: a combination of the unlikely and the insufferable, attempting the impossible. Ninety-odd musicians (some of them very odd indeed) carrying their pasts on their backs. Each musician laden with the baggage of his past, each in secret preparation for the joint assault on the North Face of the Eiger.

Beethoven. Sibelius. Brahms. Auditions; rejections. Performance nerves and intensely public failures. The heroism – the heroic insanity – inherent in focusing every sorrow of the soul into the belly of a cello or the bell of a horn . . . Everyone alive is a victim of his past, and we all deal with what we only partly understand. But musicians carry more baggage than most, and sometimes it feels as if the music itself is haunted.

The tale is maverick and strange, the cast large, though I've trimmed off all the fat that I've been able. A story of passion, loyalty, deception – and a cello without a name. A story of a man fighting his feelings, and an orchestra fighting to survive.

I was the orchestra manager, an observer rather than a participant, and thus, I flatter myself, a little clearer sighted than most. Judge for yourself, from the shadows of your own past. Then write and tell me everything I still don't understand.

Pete Hegal
March, 1999

CHAPTER 2

The assistants at London's auction houses possess a style of singular pomposity. The specimen assisting William was bald and benign as an egg, sporting a double-breasted suit and a double-barrelled name. They were processing down a line of cellos – mainly overvalued or in poor condition. The few famous cellos were far beyond William's pocket.

'I suppose there's a – ah – slight chance that this one might suit,' the assistant said, lifting the last cello. 'Charming Italian instrument, though unnamed. It is however rather under full size, while you are – if I may say so – strongly built.'

William glanced at the proffered cello. He was well built indeed, and had never played a smallish cello. However, the gleam of the varnish somehow appealed to him. He examined the one-piece back under the sharp spring light.

'When was it made?' he asked.

'Our experts think it possibly dates from about the year 1800. Edward himself suggested 1800, and you'll find Edward very rarely mistaken ... It's in very decent condition, though not immaculate – you observe a minor crack along the belly.'

'Seems solid enough,' said William. 'It's for orchestra touring that I need it. I want to spare my best cello as much as I can.'

'Indeed. Indeed.'

'And there's no clue as to the maker?'

'There is, as it happens, some Italian scribbled inside – rather hard to decipher. If you utilise a – ah – dental mirror, you can just make it out ... I don't know whether we kept a record. Edward would know, but he is, unhappily, at lunch.'

William wondered whether the unknown Edward was always unhappy at lunch. 'Who owns it?'

'The cello was the property of a gentleman amateur, a doctor by profession, I believe. His daughter – or possibly his niece – is now perhaps getting on a bit, and has elected to dispose of it . . . One moment, if you please.'

And he hastened to intercept a second visitor, who was drifting vaguely but tenaciously towards the most expensive violins.

William, left alone, plucked the strings. The cello seemed to glow still more persuasively at his touch . . . What an unusual colour it was, a dark glowing brown, like night dismantling the embers of a sunset. It wasn't set up properly – an ancient bridge – but some instinct propelled him into wheeling out the spike and pulling his bow across the strings. The sound . . .

The sound – hoarse as a voice long rusted with disuse but innately, warmly sensual – effloresced through the length of the room. The assistant paused; his client swivelled, ears funnelled by the sound.

Unwillingly, William put the cello down. If the cello could give like that! There was more potential than he had suspected. Unnamed! Who knew who might have made it? Better not to alert the dealer; better simply to observe how much was bid. He might be lucky, perhaps. Whatever the market value, there was quality about it.

He turned back at the door for a final glance. Was it his imagination or had it really shone in his hands, soft as a claret- coloured jewel? Because when he looked again, the gleam was gone.

A week later, Will first brought the cello into orchestra. It caused a flurry of interest in the cello section.

'Rather a characterful scroll . . . Doesn't look Italian to me . . . positively shoddy, I call it . . . They're making cellos exceptionally dark this year.'

'A very odd colour indeed,' agreed John, the principal cellist.

'I've never seen a colour quite like it. Was it very expensive?'

William twirled the cello around, varnish oily under the stage lights.

'I paid nearly ten thousand, but I think it was a bargain. Only one dealer bid against me.'

'Unnamed, Italian,' mused John. 'Well, let's hear it.'

William handed the cello to his section leader with a smile. 'It's all yours.'

Later, people said they hadn't heard anything like it – years afterwards some said they'd felt a strange and vibrant presence. A very long time afterwards, so long that it might have been imagined, one or two who were there that day claimed that the cello flamed into life, the colour firing redly as the sound opened out. But at the time they didn't have the words. At the time – this was the crux of the thing – they were all too startled, William not least of all.

'What a rich sound! . . . Loads of projection . . . Must have been made by somebody famous, whatever they told you . . . Of course, there *are* a few cracks . . . long crack under the soundpost, wasn't there? No, it's only the wood grain under the lights.'

And John handing the cello back: 'Quite a find, Will. Well done you, spotting that.'

'Beginner's luck,' said William.

'However, it does feel – strange – under the hand.'

'I know what you mean. Malleable.'

'Yes, malleable. Almost fluid.'

But the others had lost interest and moved away. The sound of the Italian cello, newly rebirthed, still quivered in the resonances of the hall's secret chambers, but it was soon drowned by niggling human worries. Two of the back-desk cellists resumed their dispute; John meditated on his upcoming solo; while William was quietly engaged by his old suffering, one part of his mind playing over and over the immovable bass notes of loss.

*

William had been a member of the Royal Sinfonia for only a few months when he discovered the cello. A still-striking man in his fifties, he was regarded as something of a mystery in the orchestra, partly because of the circumstances of his arrival. He'd first accepted the post at Christmas – only to change his mind the next day.

During January and February, the vacant cello position was filled, in turn, by a 'friend' of the leader's, who was decorative but useless, by an irritating lad fresh out of music college, and by an aspiring soloist who possessed an uncanny knack of blasting in early.

By March, John McDaniel had suffered enough. He had auditioned ninety-five snatches of unaccompanied Bach, of wildly varying degrees of authenticity. He had endured ninety-five excerpts from *Don Quixote*, and ninety-five dogged, if deeply felt, Haydn cello concertos. He rang William, then still belonging to a rival London orchestra, and begged him to reconsider.

The post was only cello five, true, but he could match William's current salary. The cello section, admittedly, possessed the usual number of crazies, but Will needn't sit next to any of them. Will could trade David Schaedel – notoriously the most arrogant principal in London – for his old mate John, and every effort would be made to accommodate him. He would make an old friend very grateful – at least, for God's sake, think about it. Take some time, and think about it. And William had thought about it, through a long week of indecision and misery, until he saw his way clear.

Nobody in the Royal Sinfonia was told the reason why he had joined, though gossip hinted that Isabel Bonner, a violist in his previous orchestra, had more than a little to do with it. There were rumours too about William's invalid wife: he had deserted her; she was worse; she might even be dying.

Rumour licked like a flame around first one orchestra and then the other. But William behaved so discreetly that rumour, baulked of substance, was quietly scorched to ashes. Even the most avid gossips were snookered by William's stillness; even the most intrepid admitted defeat.

Those women obviously attracted to him he discouraged, just as he resisted any overtures of especial and particular friendship. Which was considered curious, since he'd been so identified with the effervescent Piotr in his previous orchestra. Yet over the months William had become accepted by the Royal Sinfonia: a cellist, handsome although reserved, who was reliably cool, even-tempered, self-possessed.

Upon returning home, William took the Italian cello out of its case. It was a flinty November day, the kind of day when the sun never entirely creeps from beneath its shell, and he needed every light in the music room to dispel the house's well-scrubbed gloom. He checked the cracks on the cello's belly; just smoothing the soft tactile varnish with his fingers.

It was only a cello, he thought, attempting to reassure himself. Only a cello without a name, without a pedigree, possessing a strangely compelling sound. It had been kept in the attic of a lady whose father had played, doubtless with gentlemanly inconsistency, in the middle of the century . . .

He laid it beside his English cello, a Lott, which looked even larger and more stolid in comparison – a small Italian street-lad mocking a stentorian country vicar.

William went into the kitchen, which the cleaning service had left as impeccable as in the old days. He put the kettle on while considering, without interest, whether to microwave something or to make a small salad for dinner. The trouble was, he didn't feel hungry; he hadn't felt hungry ever since his life had been turned quietly and viciously upside down . . .

Coffee mug in hand, he returned to the music room, mechanically adjusting a photo that the maid preferred at a clever angle on the mantelpiece . . . Isabel, he thought, and wondered that recollection could so distort his heart. Just to hear her voice on the telephone – but he knew better. Isabel, after all, was the reason he was running away.

He picked up his Lott cello, which nestled against his broad chest like a long-familiar lover. Its voice, comfortingly familiar, warmed his muscles as he stroked out the sound. A Bach sarabande dipping into the secret cry of Isabel, the sinewy tenor voice smoothing over little spurs of pain. Bach under his fingers, drowning the silence of the clean empty house.

CHAPTER 3

We will meet, and there we may rehearse most
obscenely and courageously. Take pains, be
perfect. Adieu!

Shakespeare

(from Pete Hegal's diaries)

The same week Will bought the cello, young Janice arrived,
and it didn't take me long to spot trouble.

Now I didn't hold it against Janice that she was gorgeous.
Small and delicately built, she had long waving blonde hair
with a silvery cast to it and the most deeply lashed, clearest-
streamed brown eyes I'd ever seen. Her beauty altogether gave
an impression of a peculiarly yielding softness – almost, of
corruptibility. Oh, I enjoyed looking at her – until I recalled
that certain other members of the orchestra might enjoy it too.
Until I recalled that this pliant goddess was on trial for a job.

Now orchestra trials, as is generally known, are like
absolutely nothing else. Though now an orchestra manager
(read escapee), I had served my time in the second violins, and
had never forgotten the sheer sweated torture of the whole
business.

The first hurdle is the audition. Never will I forget the horror
of entering that warm-up room and hearing the most brilliant
violinist I had personally encountered tossing off the most
teeth-grindingly tricky segments of the Sibelius violin concerto. The whole clashing, I need hardly add, with strands of
an ill-advised Brahms, a slightly shaky Beethoven and a fiercely

accomplished Tchaikovsky . . . In short, a serious psyching-out battle was in progress.

The rest of us auditionees merely tuned up, bashed through a bit of Ševčík and exchanged twitchy smiles, while wishing with genuine fervency that we were dead. The audition itself was positively civilised in comparison.

After the audition, I was one of the lucky four invited to attempt a trial period with the orchestra.

How can I describe the sensation of being informally interviewed by literally dozens of people? Or the rictus that affixes itself to the corners of the mouth, or the experience of being perched next to the principal during a concert, confident that my every error was being noted and might be taken down in evidence against me? How to communicate the humiliation of stumbling accidentally into the leader's room ('You'll find that "Orchestra leader" *is* written on the door')? Or the exhaustion inherent in attempting to jolly along ninety jaundiced and judgemental strangers in the space of one ganglion-tangling fortnight?

I still recall the phone call with which my appointment was confirmed, the dizzy certainty that I'd done it, I'd beaten three really sensational finalists for the rank-and-bile second violin post. (More or less by default, as I later discovered. One girl had refused to sleep with the section leader, while the young sprig from Cambridge had jarred the effete sensibilities of the principal oboe. The third – a really brilliant prospect – had been decreed altogether too rowdy after mischievously slipping fourteen sugars in the principal second's tea.)

Poor Janice, I thought feelingly. Poor girl, to be thrown to the anacondas of the horn section, the predators of the percussion. I hoped she was tougher than she looked, and knew ju-jitsu. I hoped she had imbibed, as with mother's milk, the Truth about Trumpets. (If you want the truth about trumpets, ask any string player. Hell, ask a trumpeter; they're shameless.)

I watched Janice before her first rehearsal. She was listening to principal cello John McDaniel, who was waffling on about the orchestra chess club – sadly, about the only side of orchestra life which still held any fascination for him. I noticed that she had a habit of slowly opening her eyelids and fixing her gaze – a look of almost languid, almost unbearable sensuality. The second trumpet watched her too, running a finger around the edge of his collar.

William Mellor was passing; John, never a ladies' man, seized on him with relief.

'Janice, you must meet William. Will is one of our most distinguished cello players.'

'Janice, hello.' William spoke with no more than his usual courtesy, but the impact on the girl was remarkable.

'William Mellor? Didn't you once lead the cellos in the Orchestra of London?'

I felt sorry for William, who had whitened at this further evidence of the dead past signally failing to bury its head.

'I didn't usually lead,' he replied. 'Felix Price generally—'

The girl interrupted, eyes shining. 'I used to love watching you when I was a child. I watched you through every concert.'

'Well, there's a testimonial, Will,' observed John. 'Without even realising it, completely unconsciously, you managed to inspire the next generation.'

'I'm astonished I didn't put them off, *en masse*, for life.'

There was sudden colour in Janice's face, adding rose to the silvery effect. She said, 'I remember feeling as if the music could still reach you, touch you, even take you by surprise. That's what I used to imagine. I used to imagine – lots of things.'

'Whereas Felix would only be dreaming of his roses,' observed John, well pleased with his own wit. 'That's what you meant, eh, Janice?'

Janice dropped her eyes. William was smiling politely, but something had clearly touched him on the raw. And while John wandered out into the hall, William remained, head bowed, as if grief – or premonition – had pricked him with an invisible sword.

*

Ten minutes later, Leszek slunk in, scowling, and leaned down to shake the leader's hand.

Leszek, our principal conductor, had just turned forty. Striking rather than handsome, he had burned-out, socketed eyes and a body – lithe, vibrant, and sinewed – to match. His eyes swivelled impatiently around the orchestra, checking for the most crucial players, resting without interest on the trial cellist at the back.

'*Job*, Scene II,' he ordered. ' "Satan's Dance." '

Suddenly there was an atmosphere in the concert hall, the same subdued but unmistakable excitement as when a famous actor takes the stage, as if the very air molecules were speeding in anticipation. It was a tribute to the actor in Leszek, and to that factor – inexplicable but undeniable – that people call charisma, for lack of a better name. His thin, nervy hands summoned first the cellos – the minutest thrill of threat – then gathered up the threads of the other sections out of the ether . . . The dance gathered in his fingertips, and then exploded.

Leszek glowered maniacally down at them; the syncopated menace of the score nerving his stretched frame. He had willed it: he had plucked them up and carried them away; the mute struggle for supremacy – man versus orchestra – was over almost before it started. He had a genius for spurring an orchestra into playing better than it could play, and could ride any group, however sullen . . . The invisible waves of antagonism only inspired him; and what drove him was the battle – the battle, against the odds, for the soul of the music.

While William's instrument played the dance without his assistance, every note, every rhythm. The cello glittered under his fingers; as if there was an invisible understanding between the end of Leszek's baton and the glowing, smouldering, subtly alien cello.

William felt the hall darken then blaze; the stage lights shrink then glow again, round and lemony false as a child's portrait of a moon. The sound swelled, then shrank back while his fingers flicked over the strings . . . His bow, precise and perfect, negotiated the white and silver notes, which he was too blinded to see properly.

Dizziness gripped him – and with it, real fear. It was a brain tumour; it was schizophrenia; it was a judgement on the almighty ruin he had managed to make of his life. Oh God, let the end come quickly, nothing drawn-out and painful, nothing that would test what remained of his courage . . .

Instead the spangles slivered away, disappearing down the minute cracks on the stage. Leszek glanced down the ranks of strings to stare at the Italian cello, which had seemed only a moment before so darkly radiant. It lay mute, lifeless in William's hands: mere wood and varnish, the crack dull as ash down its belly.

William took resolute hold of his imagination. What had happened must be nothing more than nerves, overwork, and the manipulative business of musical stimulation. He fastened his eyes back on his music, where the notes had resolved to black again, and ceased to dance.

CHAPTER 4

Jesters do oft prove prophets.
Shakespeare

(from Pete Hegal's diaries)

To put it in context, let us momentarily consider the orchestra, that vital, organic, monstrous, man-made creation.

At the top there perches the conductor: overpaid, over-stressed, oversexed, and over the top. In theory, the conductor's tenure is at the whim of the players' board, the trustees and such uncontrollable factors as the Arts Council current predilection (or lack of it) for symphonic style. In practice, he's a rampant dictator with an inflammatory ego of South American proportions.

Beneath the conductor – a very long way beneath in terms of salary, prestige and nefarious influence – we observe the orchestra leader and principal players, who browbeat their own sections and generally the orchestra board besides. The Royal Sinfonia had at this time the full palette of principal types, from the famously extrovert Eddie Wellington on the horn to the well-meaning if lustreless John McDaniel at principal cello.

Below these scions of the establishment slink the rank-and-file members; and skulking somewhere around the bottom of the totem pole such humble serfs as orchestral librarians, lesser-crested dogsbodies and orchestra managers, i.e. me.

I knew you would object. Being an orchestra manager,

surely, is not such a bad deal. Near the action – in on the foreign tours – but out of the direct line of fire. The manager doth protest too much, you thinks.

Well methinks differently.

For a start, the hours are foul and the pay is chronic. Worse still, conductors, orchestra boards, principal players – even the lowliest serf in the double basses – all spend the better part of their waking hours bending your jaded ear with their complaints. If things go right, it's luck, it's a one-off, it's just deserts, mate. If things are screwed – well, bugger me, let's murder the manager: that's what he's there for, lucky sod, doesn't have to work for a living, does he?

Does he, heck. Though I have to admit that, in the increasingly far-off days when I myself decorated the second violin section, I too dreamed of revenge. I admit it: beneath the drooping façade of even the mildest player lurk day-dreams of darkest fantasy. I daresay the average concert-goer wouldn't credit what goes on in most second violinists' minds, but thumbscrews, boiling oil, and those bone-crunching medieval stretching racks generally come into it somewhere.

Indeed, the farther down the orchestral ranks you get, the wilder the imaginations tend to become. It's not generally the principals who dream of revenge. No, they're too busy mobile-phoning their accountants and number-crunching VATs on to their last film session. What energy they have left over – and, by the results, it can't be much – is wasted on attempting to look intelligent when bullied by conductors. No, behind them, far behind, are the ones whose diaries – centuries from now – will put Pepys squarely amongst the also-rans. These are the souls whose spirits rise above their serfdom, who charge in early to rehearse with their string quartet, whose artsy black-and-white photographs disclose a world of weirdest fantasy, whose imaginations would make Picasso and Tolkien (should they happen to still be with us) gnash their molars in impotent despair.

I find now that when I look down at the heaving swells of a toiling orchestra – the roll of waves and the hiss of spray – I feel gleeful as a child missing school. I've been there, you observe, I've done that; I have even, God help me, got the T-shirt. I've succumbed to the great moments – and I've endured the endless, back-blistering three-quarters-of-an-hours. I've been lifted up by geniuses and suffered any number of fools, not particularly gladly, but there you are . . . I can even recall the exact moment when I knew I'd had enough.

It happened seven years ago – I was thirty-two – and I was assisting in dismantling Prokofiev's 'Classical' Symphony in the Royal Sinfonia's second violin section. Further, I had just been informed by my principal that I'd been rushing the beat – which was not only bare-faced cheek but untrue to boot, the comment being applicable, if at all, to the horny-handed son of toil beside me. I picked up my violin, fantasising that it was loaded, only to hear the orchestra leader piping up about the second violin section's unendurable heavy-handedness.

Now this, between us, was purest apple-sauce. The leader was one of those leaders who secretly feel that what most composers really had in mind was a continuous violin solo, the extraneous violins being, to all intents and purposes, painted on the backdrop. Notwithstanding this, and with a smugness indescribable, my principal assured the leader that the matter had already been attended to, meaning yours, the undersigned. Upon which my odious, and indeed malodorous, desk-partner dared to chuckle at me.

That combination was what did it. I suddenly felt, as I hoisted my violin back on to my shoulder, what an absurd position it was to make a living. And (still more bitterly) what a scurrilous profession it was that enabled a blameless soul to be publicly excoriated without recourse to defence lawyers, affidavits, witnesses and the awful paraphernalia of British justice. It would not be going too far to say that I seethed. I will say it: I seethed. Deep in the heart of the second violin section, I seethed like a dried-out, plugged-in water kettle.

And, as I seethed, the truth dawned that I was not formed by my maker to sit in the middle of the second violin section for the rest of my natural.

That there are people, millions of them, so inclined is undeniable. There are stalwart men and women – bless them – who ask nothing better, who positively thrill to the sensation of being one of ten or twenty violins playing (almost) exactly the same part at (very nearly) the same time. More power to their elbow, say I – particularly their right elbows – and I hope they have a fine day for it. However, I, Peter Christoph Hegal, suddenly recognised that I was not amongst them, and became simultaneously seized with the determination to escape.

People have often told me since just how lucky I was. This is because there is absolutely nothing people enjoy more than telling you how extraordinarily lucky you were, and how (whatever it was you did) it's become most frightfully more difficult since. The subtext naturally being that, in these more enlightened times, a grade A buffoon like me wouldn't get a foot inside the interview room door. But are these self-same people ever lucky themselves? No, they were born to struggle and endure.

However, I was genuinely lucky with my advice on this occasion. That same afternoon I went to the Toadster, Leszek's world-famous predecessor. I've often thought since how frantically Leszek would have fried me around the edges, Zimetski being the sort who considers it a crashing honour to be conducted by him and giving precious little scope to any opposition view.

The Toadster, however, was of very different metal – a great conductor, and, still rarer, a great gentleman. Already past eighty, health failing, he looked at me and smiled crookedly.

'So. You've had enough, my young friend.'

I intimated that such, sadly, was the burden of my tale.

'Fancy having a go with the stick?' he joked.

'Certainly not,' I said with a shudder. 'No, what I'm after is a lowly office job. Something to keep cheap wine on the table and the bailiffs at bay, but – and this is my point or drift – nothing to do with shoving a bit of wood under the chin while simultaneously sawing away with accumulated horsehair.'

'Not any good at accounts, are you?' he inquired wistfully, but truth compelled me to shake the bean. I had heard about the difficulty of squaring the orchestral accounts, and, familiar as I was with red ink in my private life, had no desire to encounter yet more acres of the stuff in my work. At this point the Toadster seemed struck by a notion.

'Actually there might be a vacancy in personnel coming up shortly. Auditions, publicity, that sort of thing. Might that interest you at all?'

'Maestro,' I said – which is not a word I use often, as it goes to conductors' heads like pink champagne – 'you have saved a human life.'

'Also a fair amount of horsehair,' observed the Toadster.

Thus I worked my way up, through auditions co-ordinator/ assistant under-librarian to lesser-spotted assistant orchestra manager all the way up to the dizzy immortality of (plain old unadorned) orchestra manager. My rapid rise did not surprise me, as I had early mastered the two crucial qualities for orchestral management: the ability to tell when a player's malingering and the nerve to tell him so.

Having said all that, I hadn't meant to listen to Leszek's Vaughan Williams in today's rehearsal. Much though I enjoy the feeling of being above the fray, start listening to conductors, and the next thing you know you're an unpaid, unhonoured and unsung resident psychologist/hand-holder/ orchestral balance expert. However, though not inordinately fond of V.W. as a general rule, *Job* is one of his gutsiest works – thick and over-fussed, as you would expect, but also imaginative, even astringent. And I just happened to be passing when I heard Scene II announced.

I entered on an impulse, just in time to see Leszek turn to

ignite the cellos. Then 'Satan's Dance of Triumph' snaked and shuddered down the length of the hall.

Entranced, I watched Leszek, diabolical in black, stoking up the double basses like so many gigantic kindling furnaces. I'd never heard the dance sound like that – I'd never heard the Royal Sinfonia sound like that, nor any other orchestra either. The ignition came from Leszek – must have – but at the same time there was another focus, another pattern. I half-closed my eyes and the air subtly took on another form. Half-awake, half-dreaming, I saw a constellation take shape, erupting silver out of the lower strings. I couldn't tell which until I opened my eyes again, and then I could see – or thought I could see – a haze of dust, like silver, settling around William Mellor's dark cello.

Now some people might have wondered if they were going crazy, but I'm of German descent – both sides, no prisoners – and not prone to fits of craziness. Instead I watched the silvery dust fade with the dance; then I sauntered backstage to organise the break-time coffee.

I had not deliberated long (Trick of the light? Hyperactive imagination?) when Leszek swept backstage, swishing his baton as if he wished there was a whip attached to it. There's an elemental force to Leszek, a force hard to describe. He moves – not as beautiful women move, with conscious grace, but with animalistic purpose, a cat, sublimely unmoved by its own perfections, centred upon its prey.

'Pete,' he said, without preamble, pronouncing it, as is the East European preference, rather like 'Pit'. 'Where the hell is Edward Wellington?'

His very appellation concisely demonstrates the imperfect fusion between the two men's souls. Eddie Wellington is the Duke, has been the Duke since music college, since his first imperious horn blasts powered him into the ranks of horn principals fifteen years ago. Nobody calls him Edward except his mother, and even his mother only does when he deserves it.

'What, is Eddie missing?' I inquired, caught off-guard.

Leszek only tapped his foot. His are little feet, usually booted, and seem to spring when he walks, not with adolescent sexual emphasis, but silkily, a Latin dancer.

'I'm sorry,' I added hastily. 'I'll check at once. Have you called the break?'

'They do not deserve a break,' said Leszek, his lower lip protruding. 'But I have given them one. It is, most lamentably, the rule.'

He turned on his boot and disappeared down the hall towards the conductor's room.

I swept up my mobile and pressed the Duke's number.

'Is that the Duke?'

Eddie's native cheerfulness, never easily repressed, bounded forth like a rewarded spaniel. 'Deuced kind of you to call, old bean. Honoured, believe me. Not even old Lenny's checked up on me yet.'

'You sound well enough.'

'Oh I *sound* well enough,' he reassured me, 'I sound fine, but I pulled a back muscle installing the new bird-bath and my fifth vertebra's a goner, if vertebra is the word I want.'

'Sorry,' I said, 'but by a goner, you mean—'

'I can't get up today, and whether I can get up tomorrow is a moot point, a very moot point indeed. I'm on the cordless now, flat on the old disc brakes. However, you'll be pleased to know I got hold of young Spragg – you know, J. Spragg's lad. You won't have any complaints about his horn-playing, I can tell you. Whether he can keep his hands off the merchandise is another matter.'

'Eddie, you should have called me about this,' I said, trying to keep the peevish note from my voice.

'I meant to. Slipped my mind, to be honest, and by the time I remembered I thought Spragg minor would have spilled the beans. Stale news, old hat – in short, yesterday's papers.'

'I'll check with you tomorrow,' I said severely.

Whether he detected the tone of resignation in my voice

remains doubtful, however, as he merely said, 'Pip pip,' and rang off.

I made my way to Leszek's room, gathering a precautionary coffee for him *en route*. There was always the risk that he would chuck it at me, but the odds were that he wanted one. Most of the players were laying siege to the coffee, quipping, quaffing and flirting – yet some seemed strangely quiet, as if the dance had ripped some level of protection away.

I knocked on Leszek's door, and entered upon his growl. You'd imagine a man of Leszek's finicky build to have a lightish voice, but Leszek's is low – oceanic, I thought suddenly, the Vaughan Williams still echoing in my veins.

Leszek was seated at his desk, a single light shadowing his face. All bones it looked, all angles. He was supporting his head on one hand, and the look he raised to me was unfriendly.

I placed the cup of steaming coffee before him.

'I've just spoken to Eddie Wellington. I'm afraid he's ill.'

'Ill? Ill? What, is it genuine?'

'Afraid so,' I said, having deliberately selected an economical-with-the-truth policy on the bird-bath angle. 'Is there a problem? Are you unhappy with the horns?'

Leszek brought his fist down on to the desk, a crunching blow. I winced as if it had been my own hand, but Leszek never regarded physical pain. I have known him to conduct when he should have been in bed – even, arguably, when he should have been in hospital.

'It is all unsatisfactory! I am unhappy –' he stumbled over the word – 'I am unhappy with everything!'

I felt increasingly bewildered. The troops had excelled themselves; and Leszek, for all his moodiness, was not accustomed to deny the players their due.

'The orchestra—' I began.

'Hang the bloody orchestra!' he said, and the British construction sounded perverse in his accelerated Polish accent. 'You – you will never understand!'

His eyes were crazy, reddened – and he was wrong, I did understand. I realised with sinking heart that he hadn't slept, that he'd been on the cocaine, that the cycle was starting over again. I knew Leszek, I sometimes thought, better than any of his wives had ever known him, mainly because he simply didn't trouble himself to act for my benefit. And I knew when Leszek's eyes got that thin red tinge that man is born to trouble as the sparks fly upward – which is, incidentally, about the only line in the Good Book really relevant to orchestral management.

The trouble with Leszek is that everything is a balance – between health and illness, fury and delicacy, his superhuman passion for sound, and the all-too-human failings of the creatures he conducts. And he never believes that he can do it again. Even when it's at its best, with the audience on their shoe leather and the orchestra waving their bows like back-benchers with their order papers, even then there's the inner blackness of fear that it will never be this good again. He suffers the most when he performs at his best, which is why there are moments when he seems to be raging at the music, even at life itself. The strength of his perfectionism is what corrupts him – and makes him dangerous.

There are very few methods that work on Leszek in this mood, but overt stupidity is one of the few. Contrary to what you might expect, the stupidity of others confirms his own brilliance, and inclines him towards stability. I kept a weather eye on the coffee and gave it a go.

'I'm puzzled,' I told him, with a manly frankness that became me well. 'I thought *Job* sounded really workmanlike.'

'You thought it what?' he inquired, and I saw that he was smiling, that his complexion, from a dusky brick, was already easing cool and dark again.

'Not at all bad, I thought.'

'Not at all bad? Not at all bad!'

'Only my opinion, mind.'

'You – you . . . it was unbelievable; it was possessed! You

Germans! No imagination, no soul, no – no nothing! Work-manlike, he tells me, workmanlike – pah!'

He flung himself out of the room, and I followed, well pleased. Only a handful of virtuoso managers world-wide, in my opinion, could have weaselled Leszek into tamer mood, perhaps not so many . . .

William Mellor detained me as I emerged from Leszek's cell. It's always hard to tell what William's feeling, but he's a feeling soul, that's certain, and I had a notion that he'd been through a good deal recently.

'Sorry, Pete,' he said, taking a deep breath. 'I'm afraid I need to lie down.'

'Headache?' I quipped. 'Insomnia? Dizziness? Period pains?'

Once I retire, I plan on going into medicine. Homeopathic medicine, perhaps, or whatever else requires the least training for the meatiest profit.

'You can call it dizziness,' said William, with the faintest of smiles.

'Feel free to use my office.'

Only then did I remember the silver dust, stars speckling his shoulders. A moment later I passed his cello case while corralling the herd back on to the stage. The cello looked almost liquid, a dark gleaming russet like some semi-precious stone . . . I just fingered the strings. My nerves must have been a bit tattered at the time, because I imagined it hot to my touch, as if the cello was burning burning.

CHAPTER 5

The bow is bent and drawn: make from the shaft.
Shakespeare

There were times when Margot awoke in her parents' house and felt nineteen again. The walls, then ice blue, now greeny yellow, still sloped, and the descendants of the same birds scrabbled and gossiped on the roof. Thin curtains still failed to keep out the sun's earliest fidgetings, and their cascading patterns still reminded her of an old nightmare about a tidal wave. She was six, and dreaming of a wave curled taller than a skyscraper. She was ten and longing for ice-skates for Christmas. She was forty-two and her only remaining dream was being well.

The recollection of her illness – her two illnesses, though she sometimes forgot that they were separate, and not ineluctably tied together – always startled her. It was as if her life had been assigned to some other person, someone like her to look at, but whose feelings and certainties were separate from hers. Inside she was well, she had always been well – or perhaps she had always been ill, and only realised in her mid-thirties, when the blow fell.

Inside, she could still play tennis (although erratically) and chase her young son Sam up the stairs. Inside, she was uncorrupted and incorruptible, unchained to anything as clumsy as a body, and wheelchairs were still something old people used to stop themselves from falling. In her dreams she was always riding, riding bareback on a pony whose dense, close-fitting coat slicked chestnut hairs on her jodhpurs and smelled of horse sweat. In her dreams she was always riding away.

One morning Margot awoke with that comforting horse-tang in her nostrils, only to realise that the smell was actually bacon; her mother's traditional Sunday fry-up sidling under her bedroom door. Bacon: a smell so tied to childhood that the combination of nostalgia and recollection almost suffocated her. Bacon and ponies, her mother Olivia's strident tones – and the aching sensation of loss twisting her stomach. What was she doing back home, at her age, and in her condition, when she had a house and husband of her own?

It was a question her mother, usually so forthright, had never asked her. No, she had accepted the merest slivers of information, shaken her head darkly, and been ominously silent.

William had misbehaved, was all Margot said. Odd age at which to misbehave, but then, he wouldn't be the first. Men: men were always the problem. Olivia knew about men, ought to, at sixty-four; at sixty-four there could be no excuses. Sixty-four years of dealing with masculine wiles and im-portunities, sixty-four years of sharp-nosed watching and waiting, sixty-four years of pessimistic churchgoing, of pray-ing for the sinful, warring souls of men.

Oh, Olivia had seen it coming, or so she maintained. He'd a fine eye on him, William, and a fine leg. There was in short something about him, that indefinable something which Olivia's favourite screen actors shared; and perhaps in some secret part of herself she'd always considered William to be more attractive than Margot deserved, and felt in retrospect complacent, even vindicated.

Moreover, Olivia had never quite forgiven William for installing her, soon after her last attack, in an expensive asthma clinic. *That* hadn't been suffered long; Olivia had seen to that. Chest troubles or no, she still had spirit enough to make her objections felt, and her infuriated smashing of an art deco table remained one of her most satisfying memories.

The experts' verdict had been unanimous. 'Unsuited to residential care . . . signally lacking in group-orientated sociability . . . better off in her own home.'

Margot delicately tested her limbs, as she did first thing every morning. There was still no guessing what her legs might do, though she felt in reasonable control at the moment. Her anger at William seemed to have lifted her, animating her nerves to greater stamina, and lending assurance to her wasted muscles. Her anger sustained her, as if the illness, recognising the imposition of an alien grief, had momentarily loosened its grip.

Margot levelled herself into her wheelchair. It dazzled in the clear light, the sun focusing on its smooth chrome lines as lovingly as on a sports car. Handsome, silver and solid, it dominated the room, drowning out the threadbare carpet and weathered furniture . . . She had brought so little with her: the wheelchair, a couple of well-travelled suitcases that had previously been William's. She had brought her wedding ring too; it lay small and insignificant, flanked by grander presents, in the centre of her jewellery box. She noticed that shopladies sometimes paused before addressing her as Madam, eyes drifting to her newly defenceless left hand.

It had started with a phone call from a woman without a name.

'A friend,' she had described herself, adding, without taking breath, 'someone what has suffered the same as you.'

A patient given her number by the local multiple sclerosis support group, Margot had assumed, but it hadn't been; no, it was the phone call she'd known would come, the call she'd been dreading for more years than she could remember. She had longed to put the phone down on the woman's hissing viciousness, but instead had heard her out, had even listened to her own voice, level, testing: How often? For how long? How had the neighbour known it was William? And then the girl – darkish, youngish, over-made-up, legs displayed 'like a hussy'. Single. Why would such a girl still be single, Margot remembered wondering. Divorced, more likely, and maintaining a secretarial existence in one of the rain-streaked cement flats that flanked the Barbican like rows of serried graves. Her name was Isabel – and, with that name, the last puzzle pieces slipped together, snapping her heart.

Isabel. A name on an orchestra programme, a face, spoiled and haughty, glimpsed at the back of the violas. A name which had provoked a wan smile from William. What had he told her? Something about beauty being an excuse for folly. A girl cursed by her own beauty, burdened with it. And the obvious subtext: not William's type. Flamboyant, over-emotional, promiscuous, unstable – what conceivable set of character-istics would be less likely to appeal to a man like William, whose entire philosophy was based on relationships of part-ners, of women as equals?

A girl lacking in self-respect, reaching, searching – and yet . . . five minutes on the telephone and nothing left but to throw the form book out of the window. A name, a grind of metal like a car crash – and Margot realised that she had known for a long time, had known even as she'd denied it to herself.

The German conductor's face bent over hers and Will's voice, quiet, too quiet, as he made the introductions; a flutter from the girl like a frighted bird momentarily alighting on Hochler's arm. A girl with a trick of beauty, a face abused by beauty and William's unnatural stillness behind her wheel-chair – she had known, in that instant, everything.

'Thank you for calling,' she had told the caller finally, in a voice that sounded, even to her ears, tremulous and exhausted. 'Forgive me; I must go . . . Perhaps, some day I – perhaps. Goodbye.'

She remembered the woman's displeasure, cheated of her justification, robbed of her drama. And she remembered staring at the slim grey telephone until it merged with the striped wallpaper and dissolved.

Margot heard her mother's clashing cookery pans,

heralding impatience for her appearance at breakfast. There was nothing subtle about Olivia; she had discarded subtlety, along with colours, in her early fifties. That her endless combinations of black, white and grey rather suited her cropped hair and dogmatic features was probably irrelevant; even her preference for cacti seemed vaguely symbolic of a nerveless and uncompromising mind.

But Margot, dressing herself with slow endurance, was still in a mood to remember.

She had known he would deny it, of course. William loathed scenes, upheaval; his first (and very English) reaction to anything hurtful was simple avoidance. There was no risk of his admitting it, but the next few days had proved a slow torture of wondering whether, having weighed his conscience against his passion, he might not choose to tell her when she could least bear it.

Possibly he understood her fear; at any rate, he was kinder than ever, more courteous, and immeasurably more distant. Horrible though a scene would have been, she felt his gentleness like an insult, an ache that she could neither touch nor bear. Margot even began to fear his polished thoughtfulness, which left her so little to despise, which demolished her dried-out anger at its roots. She was conscious of her anger rotting beneath the soil, withering in its juices, denied enough light to express itself normally.

There were times too when she hated life for loosing this second illness upon her. At these times she didn't blame William, indeed she could have adored him for his painstaking deception, for his courageous refusal to acknowledge something so obvious to everybody. These were the times when continued silence seemed the only answer, when anything was survivable as long as it was never put into words. Though she'd known too that this could not last.

Some days she grieved for William's unhappiness as much as for her own. Here, after all, was no wilful mid-life adventurer. William was also a victim – a victim of her illness, of Isabel's misery, of his own startled and startling feelings.

What had frightened her most was the strength of the attachment, and the effect it had on William. At first, she felt confident that it would pass, given time and satiety. The fact that it didn't terrified her, though she'd never been able to believe, even in the darkest hours of the most airless nights, that he would leave her. She'd known William too long and too well for that; she trusted his natural code, his hatred of being the focus of gossip, his innate sense of truthfulness, of justice.

No, the worst she could imagine was that he would stay, a patient, shadowed creature, sap dried and feelings stiffened into a meaningless courtesy – and in truth, that had almost happened. What she had never conceived was that the time would come when she could bear the waiting no longer, when nerves sliced through the back of her fear, when her own sore and aching pride cried out, enough.

'Quite ready, dear? Need a hand?' Olivia, outside her bedroom door.

'I'll be out in a moment,' replied Margot, hair still tangled and face night-pale. She wheeled herself over to the mirror where her blunted weapons lay: comb, powder, muted lipstick, an almost undiscernible shade of blush. Odd to think that Isabel, so incomparably more beautiful, would doubtless have so many more aids and artifices, would know so very much more.

No one had believed that she could leave William. Her son Sam had voiced the universal reaction with the sophomoric understanding of a typical twenty-five-year-old. 'All relationships go through tough times, Mother. You don't simply give up on a good marriage, not without trying.' While her mother-in-law Vera had phoned to suggest, 'He's so desperately sorry, my dear. Why don't you—' In the background Margot could hear her father-in-law objecting that he was 'never told anything' – which, she knew, was at least partly true.

Her friends were sympathetic, but secretly they thought her over-reacting, even 'kicking up a fuss'. Margot had watched them shaking their heads as they drove away. ('Well naturally it's a shock, but what else could you expect? Will's only flesh and blood . . . In his profession, the miracle is it hasn't happened before, *if* it hasn't. Margot's naïve if she thinks otherwise.') Along with the inevitable codicils: 'It's not as if she's young any more, or likely ever to be well . . . What does she hope to gain by it?'

Self-respect, thought Margot, running her comb through her still unruly curls. Nothing more grandiose than that. She hadn't wanted to punish Will – or not much, at any rate. She hadn't wanted to live with Olivia again, though the rich contradictions of her mother's outsize character could prove a welcome distraction. No, life had worn itself down to a choice of startling simplicity. To be herself, truly herself – or to be the victim, the patient invalid, the selfless, bloodless charity-working angel everyone thought they knew. To be herself, not taken for granted, not – for once – to behave beautifully.

She had done no more than what, in an able-bodied person, would have been considered perfectly understandable, and that she had done it, under such different circumstances, vindicated her courage. People thought her illogical, even unbalanced, but she knew better. She knew that she'd never had a choice, not once she perceived the whole truth about what Isabel had done to him. Now she was herself again, and as free as when she'd run along the Cromer sands with a younger Sam, as free as when she'd unwrapped her new ice-skates at Christmas. William's crazy love had crazily set her free.

'I thought you were never getting up. Your bacon's gone cold long since and I finished the sausages without you. Thought I heard you stirring hours ago.'

I was stirring, thought Margot, drawing her wheelchair up to the kitchen table. Stirring for years, roots pressing beneath the soil, pushing, reaching. But I never knew.

'You were always slow in the mornings,' continued Olivia, pouring her a cup of tepid tea. 'Even as a girl. Had to beat the door down to get you to school on time.'

In that same white bed, gone cream with age and tiredness.

'Woke up in the middle of the night, I did – three, it was, because I heard the clock chiming – thought I heard burglars. I came down the stairs with the poker, quiet as you like, but it must have been the wind. I told you about the time I had burglars.'

'Yes.'

Over and over, time after time – the trauma and the police officer and Aunt Emmeline's exquisite necklace . . . 'An heirloom,' Olivia had termed it after the burglary, though she'd never worn it before.

'Cat got your tongue, Margot?'

No, Mother, life's got it; life came in the night and tore it away. Now I've gone dumb and sweet with sorrow, sweet and sickly as food we can no longer force down.

'The bacon's lovely,' said Margot with an effort. 'Thank you.'

It was, she thought ironically, what William might have said, but then, hypocrisy was no one's birthright. Olivia pushed the *Telegraph* towards her.

'There you are. Orchestra of London in financial crisis.'

'William's not in the Orchestra of London any more.'

'No doubt they'll be in a similar state. They're all alike, these orchestras.'

They're not alike, thought Margot, heart speeding. This one's got Isabel in it . . . She searched the photo for Isabel, but she wasn't there.

CHAPTER 6

'Tis one of these
odd tricks which sorrow shoots
out of the mind.

Shakespeare

(from Pete Hegal's diaries)

The next week I spotted Janice outside the rehearsal studio,
alone and palely loitering.

'The name's Bond, James Bond,' I said, materialising above
her. 'Have you any worlds that require saving? Or are you free
for a drink?'

'The horn section are taking me to the pub once they've
finished rehearsing. Would you like to come?'

'It would represent the height of my current ambitions.
However, I won't have enough time. I'm taking Leszek home
at six, as his Maserati is being serviced. At the moment he's
disembowelling the librarian, so I'm steering well clear.'

'It's extraordinary what he does with *Job* – the dance
especially.'

She had interested me strangely; I asked her what she meant.

'I expect you'll think it's only imagination.'

'Try me.'

'I thought – I thought the stage seemed filled with tiny lights,
specks like snow that rose and spun, poised themselves in air,
then disappeared.'

'Where did they come from?' I demanded.

'You think I'm crazy, don't you?'

'Perhaps we're all crazy. However, you haven't answered my question. Given snowflakes, whither the snow?'

'Perhaps Leszek – conjured them up, somehow.'

'The devil in Leszek,' I observed, 'is a fellow to reckon with.'

Then I asked Janice whether she'd take the job, if it was offered. The girl's cheeks were feather-dusted with pink again.

'Of course. I've always dreamed of playing in a London orchestra.'

'And it's not such a bad band, either,' I said tolerantly. 'There is Leszek, of course, but, face it, most conductors are barking, the good ones anyway. "Let Hercules himself do what he may, The cat will mew, and dog will have his day." Not my own, Shakespeare's.'

'What about the cello section?' she asked me, skimming her feathery blonde hair through her fingers. Was she quite as bland as she seemed, I wondered, or was her pliancy a mere device, a characterisation subtly calculated to appeal to the maximum number of colleagues in the shortest possible time? With an effort I disciplined my mind upon her query. The cello section. What could you say about the cello section?

'The cello section is composed of a subtle blend of Mary Poppins, Piatigorsky, *Julius Caesar* and *Nightmare on Elm Street*, but the point to bear in mind is that you needn't spend time with them, not unless you want to.'

'What do you mean?'

'Avoid them, is my advice. Cross the road as soon as you see the whites of their eyes. Evade questions like, "Know any good places to eat around here?" Ankle off, standing not upon the order of your going.'

'I meant, why *Nightmare on Elm Street*?'

'Well, just look at them! There's John McDaniel, a cello principal with no interest in music. If you want to oblige John, rather than applauding his most recent, rather pedestrian cello solo, you will allow that the Madagascar defence, as demonstrated by Kasparov, is fundamentally unsound.'

'Is it?'

'Haven't a clue. There may not even be a Madagascar defence, though it rings the faintest of bells. Then there's Felicia, whose formidable energies are channelled into a thousand useless directions. There's the mad Czech – escaped during the cold war and hasn't practised since – and Terence, who last missed a note at the age of six, while demolishing the Boccherini at his infants' school. Or so he says.'

'What about William?'

'Oh, I'll grant you Will – but who knows what he's doing here? Will's probably spying on behalf of the Orchestra of London, which he only resigned from in February . . . Nor can I omit to mention the four other whizz-kids at the back, Terence's partners in crime. Not surprising John's so invertebrate, considering all the invisible knives protruding from his spine. "O conspiracy, sham'st thou to show thy dangerous brow by night, when evils are most free?" Hello, chicken,' I added, this last to the orchestra librarian, who had just emerged from Leszek's office. She was in the grip of some powerful emotion, however, and ignored me.

'The trouble with cello sections,' I continued, 'is that they really haven't got quite enough to do. All those razor-sharp techniques, honed against cliff-hanging studies and Hail Mary showstoppers and what's their role in an orchestra? Playing Tweedledum to the viola section's Tweedledee. Not good enough, is what your average hot shot, sick-as-mud, would-be-principal cellist thinks, and perhaps, who knows, he may be right.'

'You mentioned William Mellor,' Janice ventured.

The second reference struck me as a bit strange. I didn't know William well back then – hardly at all, in fact – and I failed to see what interest Janice could have in him. Her eyes glowed too, almost metallic, as if something inside had been quietly kindled.

'You seem most awfully interested in Will.'

'I admired him tremendously as a student. Just watching him leading used to inspire me.'

' "He is the brooch indeed, and gem of all the nation." I call him Hamlet.'

'Why?'

'Because he is himself o'erridden by black clouds, and divers ghostly things. Why, just last year—' I caught myself at this point, on the cusp of breaking one of my personal rules. 'But still, shouldn't gossip. Not pukka. Not cricket.'

The girl flushed. What an easily bruised creature she was! I hastily added, 'It's just that Will hates being talked about, hates his new image – since all that business – as some kind of ladykiller. He isn't what people think he is, Janice. That much I can tell you.'

At that moment the advance flank of orchestra members spilled out of the rehearsal, led by the ever-impatient brass. Will Mellor was one of the last to emerge.

'Are you absolutely sure you want to join this orchestra?' he asked Janice wryly.

She laughed. 'Well, you did, didn't you?'

'*Touché*,' he said under his breath. Then something impelled him to address her again.

'Janice, are you trying to escape from anyone – or anything?'

'Escape? I don't think so.'

'This orchestra in Germany – the orchestra you're currently with . . . Are you happy there?'

She nodded, looking slightly puzzled, and Will continued.

'Because escape isn't possible. We might imagine it is, but it isn't. We think: a change of place, a change of people – but it doesn't work, it doesn't answer. We carry our burdens with us, it's either one shoulder or the other . . . Think long and hard before leaving a place where you've been happy, Janice.'

'Ready, Jan?' asked Eddie Wellington chirpily and Janice was carried off by the horns, leaving William and me behind her.

The next morning I found John McDaniel fuming. Leszek had asked to hear Janice play – an unprecedented request, though his attendance at auditions was not uncommon. John had just been obliged to ask her to reaudition at the end of the day's session, and was feeling far from gruntled about it.

'She took it quietly, thank heavens, though I've no idea what Zimetski thinks he's about. He really ought to make at least an effort to follow his own procedures! And what about the two other candidates? Oughtn't I to call them back so Leszek can vet them as well? I can't understand it. It's not according to procedure at all.'

I had a sudden vision of John in a tax office, gently but firmly informing some businessman that his accounts were so poorly kept as to be, conceivably, open to misconstruction. And I thought, as I've thought before, that John would have made an excellent civil servant, or solicitor, or any number of things other than a principal cellist, for which he was too pedantic, too fussy even, to be quite suited.

As for Janice, there was something disquieting about her – even her stillness had an unexpected, elliptical quality. I'd never seen an allure so subliminally yielding, so overtly sexual – and yet, at the same time, so controlled. Even her soft little exclamations had a scripted quality. Perhaps she was an actress, I thought – or simply a vessel into which people could pour their own interpretations.

'Leszek might have a more personal interest in Janice,' I observed.

John peered at me. 'Oh, I've thought of that. She's not a bad-looking girl. But what can I do?'

When Janice entered, Leszek was hunched over his desk, six drained cups of coffee before him and only a single light bulb burning. He glanced over his half-rimmed spectacles and waved an airy hand in her direction.

'One moment please.'

The atmosphere of the room was dense and cavern-like. There were piles of scores, a few framed photographs of Leszek with famous soloists, and a quantity of books on music, many though by no means all in English. At length Leszek glanced up, shoving his loop of loose hair clear of his eyes.

'I hear that you play this Schumann concerto. I think you are too young to play Schumann, and not crazy enough. Now is your chance to convince me otherwise.'

The girl smiled and a vague weirdness filled Leszek. This room is so airless, he thought; really, I should have something done about it . . . Then Schumann flooded the room, while Ashkenazy and Perlman looked down benignly from the wall. At the end of the second section Leszek abruptly stopped her.

'This passage,' he said, tapping the page. 'What colour is it?'

'What colour?'

'Think! Is it blue? Is it purple?'

'Red, I think.'

'Red, yes, good! Red, then. Which shade of red?'

'A true red, nothing added or taken away.'

'Yes, yes, precisely! You are not crazy enough, not yet, but still perhaps . . . How old are you?'

'Twenty-eight.'

'Twenty-eight. You still have time to become an artist. Why did you choose to play, of all instruments, the cello?'

She paused. Vexed at her hesitation, he crunched his fist on to his desk.

'For the lower strings, of course! What other reason could there be? The violin sounds more beautiful at the top and the viola has more character in the middle. What earthly purpose is there in the cello except for the rolling glory down below? Think, think! Why do you bother, except for that? Why do you sweat for hours, days – whole decades of your life spent over strings made out of catgut! The life, the entire sexuality of the cello is in the G- and C-strings; the rest is only for the composer's convenience. Yes? Yes? You agree?'

The girl nodded, the light just missing the swifter gloss on her hair. Leszek looked at her with a ferocious seriousness, drew her to him, and kissed her.

37

He hadn't planned to kiss her; on the contrary, while she had played he'd been racked with irritation. In an impersonal spirit, of course, he had considered her admirable to look at, but where Schumann was concerned, such considerations took a poor second place to Leszek's musical judgement. The girl had talent, yes, but there was nothing really startling about her playing; he felt half-starved, as he always felt when he heard a good attempt, a solid effort, at something by Schumann . . . There was so much there! Idealism and aspiration, decadence and desperation – so much to unearth! There wasn't time enough on earth to do it justice.

The thought was like despair, and something very like despair drew him to her so strongly that he couldn't oppose it. There was a startled moment when he felt weak holding her, light-headed, even shivery, as if swimming in some strange energy like air. Something was controlling him; while heat shot through his entire body like a finger of sunlight.

Breathing swiftly, he released her, one hand shielding his face, intensity, dizziness slowly draining away. The girl stood where he'd left her, unmoving, but still with that fluid colour. Whatever possessed me? thought Leszek. I go crazy, I go insane – like Schumann himself I go insane.

'I'm sorry,' he muttered. 'I do not know how such a thing would happen.'

'Yes,' she said. What a curious, rosy voice she had: a cor anglais with a shadow on it. She was watching with a certain seriousness and Leszek felt a wave of something – was it heat, scent? – wash over him. He struggled for a normal tone.

'Thank you for playing. I will see you – I will see you tomorrow.'

And she left, taking the strangeness with her.

CHAPTER 7

Dear William,

I'm sorry to sound harsh, but I don't want to see you – and for several good reasons.

First, the MS is better than it's been in ages. No one knows for sure, of course, but if there *is* a psychological constituent involved, and if I'm improving without the stresses of seeing you, then surely it's not very selfish to think that perhaps we should continue apart.

Secondly, I simply don't see what's altered. I know you've switched from one orchestra to another, but this means nothing if your feelings are the same. We've both seen the scars these kinds of events leave on other people – how do you suppose our marriage to be immune? Considering this, your suggestion still seems almost impertinent, and unworthy of us both.

Margot.

(Isabel to William, scribbled on the back of a card)

Please see me, if only for a moment. I've heard that Margot's left. Warren told me this last, but more lurid rumours also abound. Someone told C. your wife was dead, but that isn't true. Is it? Is it true? I never thought that I would long for it not to be, for if it is true, I know you'll never forgive me.

(Unsigned).

(William to Isabel)

My dear,

Please don't write; it only makes things worse. Believe me, it's over for good – for your own good most of all. God bless you.

W.M.

(William to Margot)

Dear Margot,

I read your response with a complicated mixture of feelings. Delighted about your recent improved state of health, and relieved to be communicating – yet so frustrated that I could hardly finish it. Your arguments seem, on the surface, so eminently reasonable as to be uncontestable – but I think nonetheless that we both know better.

We know how your disease gored and tattered the relationship, until it became the second child we never had – an unmanageable child with which we had to struggle continually, a wearing-down process, waves against stone. We know how the marriage broke down physically, even before your illness – how it became hollowed out, a weakened thing. Until anything might have crushed us – but, as it happened, it was Isabel.

When I realised what was happening I tried to feel guilty. I did feel guilty, of course, but not as much or as strongly as I deserved to. I'm ashamed to say that there were even times when I thought it would be better out in the open, except for how my own behaviour would have appeared to others. I knew too well what all our acquaintance would have said – and doubtless are saying, now the folly and absurdities of my middle-age are evident to everyone.

Margot, I can't blame you for leaving – how could I? – but I do blame you for supposing Isabel solely at fault. She was certainly wrong for ever thinking of me, but my own weakness was the principal trouble, and the slow subsidence in our marriage my only excuse . . . But now I find I miss you. I miss my old life – our companionship, my old orchestra, my friends. The truth is that I lack the emotional energy to find a role in a new orchestra. I feel deadened, only half-alive – I look at my face in the mirror and read defeat.

You may suppose that I deserve no better. But I beg you instead to remember the good years, the good times, and to try to give us both a second chance.

William.

CHAPTER 8

He is a dreamer. Let us leave him. Pass.

Shakespeare

At forty-two Eddie Wellington had been principal horn in the Royal Sinfonia for almost two decades. Generally light-hearted, when he played he seemed to expand, the nobility of the music entered into him, and his cherubic features took on semblance of seriousness. Yet even then he was famous for his muttered asides, for he was an artist at dismantling tension with humour.

His friend Lenny was nothing like him. Where Eddie was open and irrepressible, Lenny was laconic and morose; while Eddie suffered waves of depression and delight, Lenny was consistent and cool. Yet theirs was one of the historic French horn partnerships, having first begun in music college.

'Name of Lenny, Lenny Denver.'

'Eddie Wellington, no relation, at your service. Seems you've drawn the short straw, supporting yours exceptionally truly. Do you know this piece, and, if so, are you any good at holding hands?'

'If you mean, am I a poofter, no,' replied Lenny with mournful emphasis.

'I didn't ask that,' said Eddie reproachfully. 'I would not inquire, on so short an acquaintance, into so personal a detail. Besides, I can always tell a poofter. I was referring to the task set before us, i.e. to murder this Bruckner, as foreshadowed.'

'I dunno about shadowing anybody,' retorted Lenny, 'but I know this symphony from soup to nuts. The bit you want to clap eyes on is top of page three. That is the bit you want to worry about, sunshine, not holding hands like a blinking poofter.'

'I ask,' said Eddie passionately, 'only for a modicum of support in facing triumph and disaster, treating said impostors just the same. For this I get termed a blinking poofter?'

'Also,' said Lenny, pessimistically flipping through the pages, 'that little lot there. You want to take a shuftie at that, in my opinion, before asking for whom the bell tolls.'

It was not until the third movement that Lenny spoke again.

'Correct me if I'm wrong, E. Wellington,' he observed, 'but that was all just so much flannel, wasn't it? About not playing this piece before?'

Eddie straightened. 'Brother, if you are looking for flannel, you have come to the wrong place. Flannel is not the speciality of the maison.'

'In that case, squire, I reckon you are not holding up that horn for the purposes of decoration. No, in that case – and, mind, it's only my opinion – you are a horn-player.'

Whereupon Eddie, to hide his extreme gratification, duly fluffed his next entry. By the end of the rehearsal, long before they had downed their first celebratory pint, they were friends, a partnership so satisfactorily complementary that it had continued beyond Eddie's all-conquering march through music college and into their fortuitous reunion in the ranks of the Royal Sinfonia.

Eddie was head of the panel when his friend auditioned for second French horn.

'Friends,' he said apologetically, 'you see before you an embarrassed man. You see, I am not capable of listening with unbiased judgement to the bloke that is on the other end of that horn. That fellow – I allude to the gloomy blighter – is like a brother to me. Time after time have we sat in music college, while conductors miscued our entrances and besmirched our exits. Day after day did we, magazine between us, surmount our mutual boredom while the strings were goaded into underpinning their passagework . . . I hear you ask, can I judge this horn-player against others we have heard, and against those horn-players yet to come? And I say no, I must decline. For honour—'

'For God's sake put a sock in it,' said Lenny with quiet exasperation and proceeded to play a near-immaculate finale to the Mozart concerto. And the rest, as Eddie liked to remind him, was history. Through Eddie's early conquests, and Lenny's scantier and less durable involvements, they had stuck together, as finely attuned as their major thirds in Haydn symphonies, spiritually closer to each other than to their partners, inseparable on tours and holidays alike.

During the first years of their partnership, the orchestra was under the benign eye of its founder, the skies were uniformly blue, and women the only doubtful consideration in an otherwise perfect world. Under the Toadster, the Royal Sinfonia had been indisputably the greatest orchestra in London. Eddie had enjoyed fifteen glorious years of working under a master of inventiveness, a witty and passionate exponent of his craft, someone who made the exploration of every score into an adventure.

Eddie had loved those days. How well he remembered the little twitch of lip with which the Toadster observed, 'Spare the horses till the concert, Duke. I'll tell you when to lead the charge.' Or the way the Toadster seemed to stand still taller and bonier as he glanced with inquiring affection towards his horn section, trusting them to shape the phrases, controlling their excesses – for Eddie was a master of excess – with the merest flicker of an ironic eyebrow. Under the Toadster, Eddie had been given chance after chance. Concertos came his way, and he was hauled to the front of the band, miles from Lenny's tacit support, close enough to have wiped the delicate crystals of sweat from the Toadster's upper lip, but always comforted by the twinkle of faith accompanying his cue.

There would never be another Toadster, Eddie thought sadly. The orchestra hadn't yet made up the ground lost by his death – nor recovered the whiphand over its rivals either. Instead it had veered disconsolately, wind and orchestral board permitting, from one temporary conductor to another, finally alighting on a Pole of imperious temper and Paganinian profile called Leszek Zimetski.

Though he had lobbied for a British candidate, Eddie had tried to make the best of Leszek's appointment. He stopped to congratulate his new leader in the Barbican hallway.

'Nice going, sport,' he observed, clapping Leszek between the shoulder blades. Jaw stiffening, Leszek whipped round to tower over the stocky horn-player.

'And you are?' he inquired, in the silky tone Eddie was later to recognise as inherently dangerous.

'E. Wellington, colloquially known as the Duke, at your service.'

'You play the horn, is it?'

'The horn, as ever was. I lead the cavalry on your left-hand flank – reading, that is, from left to right. You gave us a good ride in the Beethoven, though – and it's only my opinion – I found the last movement a trifle on the nippy side.'

Vain was Lenny's restraining touch, vain too Pete Hegal's warning glance.

'Mr Wellington, I have only one thing to say to you – one! – and it is this. Touch my back again and you are a dead man. Good day!'

Yet there would probably always have been an uneasy chemistry between Leszek and his principal horn. Their notions of phrasing and line too often differed; their concepts of dynamics and tempi seemed constantly at odds. It wasn't that either was quantifiably right or wrong, but their gut reactions seemed in basic and intractable opposition. Time after time they clashed – with a bruised Eddie always emerging the loser. Concert after concert would find Eddie careering through a symphony, playing solos of unsurpassed beauty, only to watch the other principal players saluted by Leszek without so much as a nod towards himself . . . His playing went unacknowledged, his team unrewarded – beyond an occasional black look.

Such lack of sympathy was enough to cloud even as sunny a temperament as Eddie's. It became his continual, obsessional ambition to play so brilliantly that the pressure became irresistible on Leszek to indicate the horn section, and, when this happened, Eddie would shoot to his feet, eyes glowing, a small boy given a birthday present. Although Leszek, whose charm didn't extend to forgetfulness, still rarely smiled at him.

Yet beneath all the vaunted self-confidence was a very young Eddie, the Eddie who longed for the Toadster's trusting wink, the Eddie who had ceased to enjoy his playing, who wearied of the constant battle to impress a man of such dazzling talent and equivocal temperament.

'I hate him!' he told Lenny.

'He's a conductor. Show me a conductor and I'll show you a bastard. Correction – a very rich bastard.'

'You don't understand! . . . It's my section. I built it up, I knitted it into a unit, I welded it and polished it and smoothed down the edges, and all for what? To be ignored and ridiculed and have my individuality ground down into his personal mould. Do you know what he wants from us? Nuts and bolts. Well, nuts and bolts to him! That isn't my way.'

'Great. You don't need his approval. He can't play a real instrument, can hardly play the piano, even. He's a conductor, end of story, finish. Forget about him.'

But Eddie couldn't. He was conscious, as perhaps even Lenny wasn't, of the mesmerising certainty which sometimes lifted Leszek into greatness. He felt cheated, in a sense that no one else could comprehend, to have the faith and happiness of working with the Toadster hauled away and Leszek substituted. Perhaps, subconsciously, he even blamed Leszek simply for not being the Toadster, that magical, almost fantastical creature.

Perhaps Eddie could have borne it better had Leszek been consistently unkind, but Leszek's mercurial nature was legendary. 'Ha!' he would say, passing Eddie with a pretty girl. 'Wine, women and song! Remember the saying – wine is great and song is wonderful – then there is trouble in the middle!' Only the next day to scowl at Eddie as if unable to recall anything beyond the fact that the fourth horn had not been present for the start of rehearsal – a calamity for which he seemed to hold Eddie responsible.

'No, he is consistent,' Lenny observed. 'He's consistently nuts. It startles me, in this day and age, with psychiatric counselling for everything from grief to parking tickets, that he hasn't been shut away years ago. Paranoia, persecution mania, manic depression . . . They could chuck away their books and take a dekko at him instead. He's a one-man case study.'

'But Lenny, he's a good conductor,' objected Eddie, on whom logic and sarcasm were equally wasted. 'Sometimes even a great conductor.'

'Not poss. He ain't dead yet.'

Respect and hatred made a combustible combination, though Eddie sometimes managed to forget Leszek altogether and, as a man might fantasise while making love, imagine that the Toadster was conducting him, the Toadster with his kind crooked mouth and worn, sunken eyes – the Toadster as he was in the end, face tautened and gaze diluted, but still waggling his finger and twinkling across at him. And sometimes he would be overwhelmed with old and rotting grief, and the sound of his horn would punish the hall's farthest echoes with a swelling despair.

Leszek alone seemed to understand the meaning of this sound. The orchestral timbre used to warm to greet it, in instinctive response, but the Duke's sound – that distinctively gutsy, earthy sound – seemed to stir the bitterest depths of Leszek's spirit. He would glower at Eddie as if itching to smite him, eyes sparking, lips thinned, but the Duke's eyes were closed; the Duke had escaped – and perhaps his escape hurt Leszek worst of all.

CHAPTER 9

Hence! Home, you idle creatures, get you home:
Is this a holiday?

Shakespeare

(from Pete Hegal's diaries)

Touring; now, I could write a book on orchestral touring. Percussionist spends night as deadbeat on Prague streets. Leader captivates flute extra (who, after succumbing, is never booked again). Timpanist lays siege to room occupied by estranged amour (since remarried, but not – and this is the point or nub – to him). International concert torpedoed by previous night's partying in room of principal bassoon. (Critic: 'Equally inexplicable was dodgy ensemble in the winds, and a general listlessness amongst the lower strings. Never in living memory has a touring orchestra with so intrepid a reputation given so lacklustre a performance.')

The catch is that no outsider would believe it. No, they observe the Royal Sinfonia delving into Debussy or Stravinsky, perfectly attired for a Victorian state funeral, and the images (if any) that arise of their non-musical lives are blameless and middle-class – taking the kids to school, grabbing a coffee across from Moorgate station, travelling home from the concert on the District Line. The dark side of the moon stays hidden, and an excellent thing too, for how many corpulent society matrons would sponsor Australian tours if they were aware that the orchestra would subsequently be blacklisted by Qantas? And how many corporate executives (many with their own secrets to hide) would welcome revelations of late-night shindigs where their company logo might be in evidence?

These thoughts rambled across the surface of what I'm pleased to call my brain as I automatically went through the inevitable rigmarole of tickets and passports at Gatwick. The orchestra was off on its usual May tour of Madrid, Seville and Barcelona. What dramas and disasters might await us there, I had no notion, but there was bound to be something.

Janice was beside me on the flight to Madrid – no particular surprise, as I'd wangled the seating order personally. I tried to kid myself that this was no more than natural civility towards a youthful trialist, but, even at the time, I knew it wasn't. Something about Janice absolutely fascinated me. There was something abnormal about her beauty, a birth defect that was, paradoxically, the lack of any defect. She made me feel intrigued, unsettled, almost skittishly alive.

We discussed Germany, where she'd been working; then she asked me what Leszek was really like.

'Leszek's straight Shostakovich – bantering in spite of a blackened soul, jokes over the body in the back room. And always that secret undertow of threat.'

'Do you always codify people by composer?'

'Sometimes. I'm Beethoven, myself, due to my innate weakness for heroism.'

'Are you? And which composer is William?'

'William Mellor?' I repeated, suddenly sober. 'Will's not easy. Why did you pitch on Will, particularly?'

'Perhaps because he looks a bit sad.'

'Well, there's his wife, of course.'

'Is he a widower?'

I shook the bean. 'She's got MS, had it for years. But she's not got it all that badly . . . No, she left him, Margot left him, three months ago.'

Janice was silent – perhaps shocked.

'I suppose you could say that it was Isabel's fault. Met Isabel, have you? No reason why you should have, of course.

48

She's a violist in the Orchestra of London. However, Will was crazy about her, crazy . . . I can't see it, myself. Not that she isn't stunning to look at – but she's fatal. She always struck me as fatal.'

'What a difficult situation for him,' said Janice.

Always the right answer, I thought, with some misgiving. You couldn't call it charm; it was too effortless for charm – like a foreigner whose English too closely brushed perfection. Which was, had I only known it, a genuine insight . . . but later I'm afraid I forgot about it.

'And then,' said the waiter, 'it was finished, yes? The clouds were blown clean away.'

'We missed it all,' said Pete, with a wild regret. 'We only heard the thunder from inside the concert hall.'

The orchestra had emerged, pale and blinking as released prisoners, into the rain-freshened air. It was late, the concert not having started till ten, but Madrid was still alive with tourists, filling the restaurants, besieging the bars. Laughter flooded the streets from the downmarket venues, while a more discreet enjoyment radiated from restaurants' lit alcoves.

In one such establishment, a covey of orchestral revellers had forgathered, with Pete amongst them. It was midnight; and the group had dined wisely if perhaps too well.

'A toast!' Pete bellowed. 'Marry, a toast, i'faith! To the Armada, to the hounds of Spain, to Queen Elizabeth the First and to this brave company!'

'Well put, squire!'

'To the Royal Sinfonia, and all who sail in her!'

'Aye!'

'Sirrah!'

'And death, disorder and destruction to the nefer— to the Nefertiti – to the nefarious collection of government and arts administrators that contrive to screw us up year after year!'

'And death, disorder and destruction to the Orchestra of London!' added the second trumpet. This allusion to their arch rivals loosed another ragged volley of cheers. Pete drank to the confusion of the Orchestra of London with relative composure however – darting a lizard-swift look out of his big sleepy face towards William, to see if he minded.

But William had turned to Felicia, hand resting lightly on his wineglass, while the brass players resumed their meandering dispute.

'. . . heard it all before, haven't we?'

'Don't see why it shouldn't happen. Almost did a few years back, didn't it, when the Philharmonia –'

'All the more reason for people to realise –'

'Listen, sunshine, the Orchestra of London hasn't got a hope, not a prayer, not a snowball's. We're talking meltdown here, pure, unadulterated meltdown, with no preservatives added. And if the Orchestra of London plugholes, we're laughing.'

Lenny lifted an eyebrow, inquiring, 'What makes you think that our good friends are in quite such dire trouble?'

The combatants paused, then burst forth in a spate of simultaneous explanation.

'They've lost the Faversham sponsorship, and their conductor's rowed with their main recording company . . . Piotr gave Nancy the low-down, and Nancy told me . . . They've got nothing left to bail themselves out with . . . There's no doubt about it this time.'

Lenny smiled sceptically, his resemblance to a dyspeptic runner-bean commensurately increasing.

'I hadn't heard about the Faversham trust. But there's no reason why their government grant shouldn't tide them over. They do a few more tours, shake down a few bankers – even take out another loan, if they have to. The truth is – and you can paste this on your hat, Toby – that orchestras don't die, they just fade away.'

The second trumpet objected, his faith reinforced by cheap and plentiful Rioja and the vocal support of his colleagues. Lenny had mistaken the case – got hold of the wrong end of the stick entirely. No, this was the goods, the end was nigh, blood on carpet, *et tu Brute*. The Orchestra of London was tearing itself to pieces while simultaneously being gunned down by the Arts Council. Plus, their new principal conductor – the one who'd sautéed Roger Ash's goose – German bloke, you know, Karl Hochler—

William, startlingly, seized Felicia's hand. There was a strange swift brightness in his eyes, a steepness in his voice.

'Come on, Felicia, let's dance.'

Felicia stared in mock astonishment.

'My dear creature, I don't dance – never have and never will. Get one of these young things to stand up with you. Angela, Janice – you're young and foolish, get up and dance.'

Angela pulled William to his feet before he could object. Orchestral politics bored her, and she was in that exalted frame of mind which attends too many glasses of red wine and a vague but tangible undercurrent of sexual stimulation.

Angela was the orchestra's harpist: slight, single and pretty, with sensational hair like an autumnal waterfall. An Irish witch, the trumpets called her, though she was generous, open, and warm-hearted to the bone . . . Moreover, Angela had been intrigued by William Mellor almost since his arrival in the orchestra. During their Copenhagen trip, she'd put herself in his way often enough for him to notice her; though failing to rouse him beyond his usual civility. Sometimes she thought him too old, and sometimes too sad, though she still failed to argue her attraction away . . . Dancing, she thought she read amusement in his eyes.

'You're thinking about Copenhagen,' she accused.

'The music's too loud to think about anything.'

And it was loud: a skinny Spaniard with a heartbreakingly ugly voice encircled by accompanying guitars and castanets . . . Angela imagined other diners were looking at them, and perhaps they were: her long burned hair spangled as a banner, William's subject to every strobe light, altering its shade of silver with the separate gyrations of each flickering candle.

Space seemed to contract as people finished eating and wandered towards the platform. The dance floor became a confused medley of body heat, strobe lights and incongruent nationalities, with a group of moustached natives gatecrashing a party of Canadian tourists and an unlikely handful of Japanese.

As the music sped faster the dance subtly altered: there was a keener stroke to the guitars; the singer grew more guttural, the air hotter. Angela was aware of the heat, of William, of sulphurous lights jangling in her head like bells. The swiftening hoarseness of the singer jump-started her pulse, firing his eyes to admiration.

Then one of the Spaniards took to the middle of the floor, inspiriting the company with sizzling energy. The rest formed a circle around him, clapping in rhythm. Angela's hair flew redder and wilder, the guitars twanged hotter and thicker, then she was flying too, tossed from dancer to dancer, while castanets clashed syncopations against her swift-beating blood. And when the music crashed, strobes switching from pitch blackness into light, Angela was thrown breathless into William's arms. And she'd been wrong: he wasn't old, no, his eyes were young, and the two most beautiful things she'd ever seen.

Chapter 10

Foolery, sir, does walk about the orb like the sun,
it shines everywhere.

Shakespeare

'And, while we are on this so-lamentable subject, I asked you later, if you recall it, for a light sound, like a memory of a memory. A ghost of a memory, as if behind a closed door. And so – and so – you tear in like a tiger on its prey – fangs, blood, fur everywhere! What do you think of in this place?'

'I was still a bit upset about messing up letter E earlier,' admitted the Duke. 'Thought I went a bit over the top, to be honest, but somehow I just couldn't help it.'

Leszek's fingers plucked at his black jeans, as if he was pulling out hairs on Eddie's head. 'Well you had better learn to help it before you become completely wayward, completely lousy! Mr Wellington, this is a warning, an official warning. Do not forget!'

It was a subdued Duke that propped up the Madrid bar late that night. Surrounded by carousing double basses, he sat in a gloomy oasis with Lenny.

'Sometimes I think it's only a matter of time before he murders me. He's going to string me up by my thumbs; he's going to pull out my fingernails. He's going to get me, Len; he is, I know it.'

'No, he ain't. You're the one who gives him what he wants. You're the one that makes him feel like gale force nine, expected soon . . . Fact is, he bullies you.'

'Yes,' said Eddie, gulping down his drink. 'I feel bullied.'

'He bullies you – you in particular – because you care too frigging much. I've told you once, I've told you a thousand times: the boy don't want anyone to care. The boy wants his show all to himself. Reason he can't deal with you is because you won't let go of the music.'

'How could—'

'Yeah, well, most of us got that scorched out of us years ago. It's ashes, ashes and gut-rock professionalism, most places you look . . . But love is different; love ain't a containable emotion. If Leszek thinks he can choke that out of you, the boy ain't thinking.'

'Len, do you think he meant it – about the warning?'

Lenny hesitated. Warnings, in his experience, came in two varieties: the off-the-cuff shoot-outs that Leszek specialised in, and the genuine prelude to disaster. The ritualised system of warnings was the only method by which the players could be fired, but the process was long and tortuous, and rarely pursued to its conclusion. Leszek had probably not been serious – why would anyone want to lose a principal like Eddie? – yet there was something strange about the way he reacted to Eddie, something instinctive, irrational.

'Reckon we'll have to see if he puts it in writing,' said Lenny at last. 'Though, even if he did, it wouldn't be your first warning, nor your last, probably . . . I'm off to meet the Sandman. Tomorrow, or so they tell me, is another day.'

An hour later, Eddie was slouched over his drink, eyes reddened, lip pugnacious. He and Ian, his third horn, were among the few revellers still on the premises, some few of the others having gone to find somewhere livelier.

'I can play the horn,' he told Ian defiantly.

'You wouldn't kid me?'

'The *Telegraph* once wrote I had a luminous sound. Luminous, the *Telegraph* called it, meaning full of light.'

'Reminds me of a joke I once—'

'You're a good pal, aren't you, Ian? You and Lenny and –

and – and everybody. A good section, good mates. I'm good too, aren't I? Not past it, am I? I can still play the horn, don't you think?'

'Hell,' said Ian, amazed. 'You're not blinking forty-five, are you? You'll see us all out. They'll have to forklift you out of this job, feet first, in about twenty-five years . . . You'll be playing the horn in your bathchair.'

Eddie gulped down his whisky so fast that it lit up the back of his throat. 'Oh, I can play the horn,' he said softly, and Ian was too tipsy to notice tears in his eyes. 'I can play the horn; I'm not what some people like to call very lousy on the French horn. I'm bleeding luminous, I am; I'm full of light!'

'Yeah,' said Ian. 'You have another on me.'

So Eddie, rightly or wrongly, had another drink.

CHAPTER 11

And those things do best please me
That befall preposterously.

Shakespeare

(from Pete Hegal's diaries)

It was a beautiful dream. I was snorkelling nude over the Great Barrier Reef. The sea was warm as suede and the lights shifted erratically, filtered and layered by the dark emerald shadows of fishes. I was just uncurling a sea anemone when suddenly a grey shadow intervened, surging between self and sun.

Having seen *Jaws* my heart bungee-jumped. However, instead of mucking up a perfectly delicious dream with sharks ('so hackneyed, darling, so Hampstead') Black Beauty emerged.

B.B. was naked too, and naked to some purpose. Slim and chocolate coloured, she had glowing copper overtones and wide-flared nostrils. Her eyes were decadent, her hair was charcoal, and her full lips were curved in a smile. A smile of such intent that my interest in the reef's flora and fauna became indefinitely suspended.

At this juncture I woke up, and, needless to say, I woke up cross. A pounding on my hotel door roused me, along with Eddie Wellington's voice outside my door.

Now the Duke has a thousand good qualities, but abstemiousness does not rank among them; his voice was sludgy, and my first thought was that he'd locked himself out of his room.

'Go away!' I moaned, but the dream was already gone, gushing past in a swirl of surf.

'Iss important!' he bellowed.

I staggered to the door. Eddie was there, as foreshadowed, and as foreshadowed, he was drunk. He had passed the first stage of lustful effervescence, and was well beyond the determination, which generally followed, to claim all men as brothers. He wore his little-boy-lost look and his shirt-tail protruding over his trousers.

'Lost your key, have you?'

He produced it waggishly, and I began to feel annoyed.

'Then what the hell's the matter?'

I suppose I expected the usual: traumas about being deserted and alone (though Lenny never deserted him; where was Lenny?), ravings about the deathlessness of Mahler and the misery of being misunderstood. Instead, Eddie's face crumpled like a soufflé.

'Are you mad at me?'

'No,' I lied.

'I can play the horn. Ask Lenny or anybody.'

'Now tell me exactly what's happened, omitting no detail, however irrelevant.'

'It wasn't my fault, so help me God and little sunflowers.'

'What? What wasn't your fault?'

'It was Oscar,' adding with an acute sense of injustice, 'I never meant to do it. At the rising of the sun, and the tumty tumty tum, we shall remember them,' he further explained, closing his eyes as if the light hurt them. I shook him, but Eddie, all too clearly, had shot his bolt. I turned back inside my room and dialled reception.

'One moment,' said a woman. I waited, registering footsteps, voices testy in the background. Eddie wandered in.

'Mind that table,' I warned him. He hit it anyway, and plumped down abruptly on the bed. I watched him, thinking: here we observe one of London's leading French horn players, too sozzled to steer accurately round a small table.

'Yes?' asked reception wearily.

'Pete Hegal here, from the Royal Sinfonia. I was wondering—'

A crackle of hysterical Spanish, then the hotel manager put himself on as understudy.

'Mr Hegal, how extremely fortuitous. Come down immediately. There's been trouble.'

Eddie rocked himself back and forth on the bed. I glared at him, uselessly, and willed myself to face the worst.

'Is anyone hurt?'

'I would be most obliged if you would come down at once.'

I slung on the clothes I had abandoned only a few short hours before. 'Listen, Eddie,' I said. 'You've got to go to your own room.'

'Can't.'

'Why can't you?'

'Because I can't.'

It was exactly like arguing with a toddler, and I felt too impatient to bear it. I pushed the Duke into my bed, turned off the light, and shut the door on him.

It was two-thirty by the time I reached reception. Subdued music still filtered through the sound system, an assortment of stars were operating through the French windows, and the indoor fountain continued to trickle soothingly between bar and reception. However, if from this you infer that all was serene, you infer wrong. The bar looked as if a rhino troupe had selected it for a modernist interpretation of *Romeo and Juliet*. Furniture and bar stools were overturned and in some cases dismantled; blood-red wine competed with chipped gin bottles on the ruined carpet, and smashed glass was everywhere. I turned to the manager.

'Did you see what happened?'

'There is such a thing as criminal damage. Criminal damage, Mr Hegal!'

'Yes, yes, no doubt,' I returned, needled by the fellow's tone. Granted, he had every right to be annoyed, but it should still have been obvious that the bloke just parted from his most promising dream in years was not one at whom the finger of blame should have been pointing.

'I have called the police,' he continued. He had found a talking point, but suddenly there were confused noises without.

'They return!' cried the manager, and adroitly barricaded himself behind reception. The night staff were taking cover in all directions, and closing the manholes after them. I turned towards the entrance in time to eyeball the most battle-stained trumpeters, horn-players and double basses I'd ever seen. Oscar had blood on his nose, Toby a crude bandage on his cheek and Geoff was limping. Some few of the others, though physically tolerable, looked as if they'd not so much drunk Rioja as swum in the stuff. I gestured grimly towards the remains.

'Which of you was responsible for this?'

At which point there appeared on high – or, to be exact, on the balcony of the floor above – a heavenly vision. It was the Duke, feet dangling precariously over the fifty-foot drop, waggling his hand at us like the Queen from her state coach. This guest appearance was greeted with every evidence of enthusiasm by his colleagues, none of whom stopped to consider that a fall from such a height would almost certainly kill him.

'Stop!' shrieked the manager. 'Stay there!' I ordered, in the same breath.

Eddie's feet sashayed back and forth over the abyss. There was a contented smile on his face, which didn't surprise me, because the Duke only really feels himself when he's the centre of attention.

'Eddie,' I said urgently. 'Eddie, listen, don't be a fool. Do you want to die?'

'Not going to die,' objected Eddie, and then chuntered on in this vein for some little time. 'No, never, not me. Not me, no thanks, not going to die, not me.'

'Silly sort of thing to ask . . . Course he isn't . . . German nerd,' were some of the more intellectual criticisms raised from the floor.

'Send somebody to grab him from behind,' I told the manager, interrupting his spirited attempt on the world record for hairs-pulled-out-in-moments-of-crisis. While Oscar, the principal bass, reminded Eddie in a high, rather peevish voice, 'You still lose the bet, sunshine.'

'No, I don't.'

'*Au contraire, cher frère.*'

'Wrong country, toad.'

'Who are you calling a toad, reptile?'

'Listen,' said Eddie, and I saw with misgiving that he actually had his French horn with him, that he had swiped it up and was waving it gleefully. He had the distinct look of a principal horn with every intention of favouring the company, but on this point, as so often, opinions seemed divided. Half the gang seemed wholeheartedly in favour of an impromptu horn recital, as the perfect end to a perfect evening, while half expressed cordial dissatisfaction with the scheme. Personally I strung along with the latter view, and not only on the basis that the horn is, on the whole, an instrument best appreciated within the context of the entire orchestral palette of sound.

'Duke,' I said, faking a calm authority. 'It's a quarter to three a.m. If you attack that horn, you could wake most of central Madrid. Which is why I expressly forbid you to touch the mouthpiece of that horn. If you do so—'

Eddie frowned dangerously. 'I can play the horn,' he objected. It seemed to be an *idée fixe* with him, if *idée fixe* is the phrase I want.

'Play it, baby, play it . . . Drag the bugger back to bed where he belongs . . . Let's hear it, Duke . . . Play it, Duke, play it!'

'Eddie!' I shouted, just as Siegfried's horn call resounded across the fake-marble hall. It surged out of the lobby and into the night street; it swept with natural exuberance up through the first floor, clear through the second floor, and (I later discovered) as high as the fifth. It sang as no horn had ever sung before, with a perilous and bell-like clarity and abandon, over and over, while the light bulbs seemed to judder in their sockets and the boys formed a makeshift male-voice chorus below.

Usually well-informed sources tell us that, at the Second Coming, seven angels will sound seven trumpets – and, without doubt, a good deal of stirring noise can be extracted from seven trumpets, whether blown consecutively or in tandem . . . However, it wouldn't surprise me if God, having heard Eddie Wellington in Madrid, didn't clap His hand to His brow thinking, blow Me down, why didn't I think of seven horns in the first place? Because that was what it sounded like: as if the seven last trumpets had decided to kick-start the Second Coming well ahead of time. It sounded like seventeen horns, and seventeen pretty well-nourished horns at that. It was a sound vital enough to wake the dead, and it certainly woke somebody, because somebody set off the hotel fire alarm. The alarm merged with Wagner in a fashion that only Charles Ives devotees could truly have relished.

Suddenly, all was bedlam. Extras swelled from every porthole like auditionees for *Ben Hur*. Terrified guests were being urged to return to their rooms by staff, while the boys cheered and passersby clustered bemusedly at the lobby windows. Everyone seemed to wish to know where the fire was, and why some horn-player had been first to blow the alarm, while distant Spanish police sirens edged ever closer.

And if you imagine that the Duke at this point mopped his fevered brow while modestly accepting the plaudits of such colleagues as happened to be still speaking to him, you're wrong, because the Duke was still playing. He was up against stiffish opposition by then – the alarm, the sirens, the babble of commentary and even the occasional scream, but you could still hear him, the Duke's almighty horn drowning the sound of God's gnashed teeth.

I noticed two young second violinists being consoled by Felicia, who was looking perfectly foul in a yellow and purple dressing gown. One of the sozzled trumpeters came down in such gulping hysterics that his colleagues doused him with a fire bucket. His yowls were, however, equalled or even exceeded by a few of the other hotel guests, at least one of whom appeared to retain but a tenuous grip on sanity.

The moment I'd been dreading occurred with the anarchy at its height . . . It was then that I spotted Leszek, fully and even nattily dressed, poised at the top of the broad central staircase: Leszek, with ash-reddened eyes and sharp, twitchy hands, glaring down at the Duke as if he was a troop of Midian and the time for mere prowling long since passed. I saw him weaving his way through the tumult towards the sound of the horn, towards Eddie's perspiring face and tight-clamped eyes, while I recalled that sickening fifty-foot drop and rushed to intercept.

I was beaten to the Duke by a hitherto unsung hotel waiter. He it was – tall, rangy, and seriously moustached – who hauled a winded Eddie away from the abyss, and pinned his mighty chest to the ground.

The police swarmed in, just as someone managed to disconnect the fire alarm. For a moment there was a comparative hush, disturbed only by an informal round-table discussion between Oscar, Toby, the assistant hotel manager and any number of standees. I noticed that Lenny had detained Leszek, enabling me to reach Eddie before him, but before I could unload even a tithe of my own feelings, the Duke absorbed an earful from the hotel manager. My Spanish is lousy, but still, I think I caught his drift.

'He says,' I translated, 'that the long walking tour on which he was hoping you would join him is now off, and that your presence will be superfluous at his upcoming birthday party.'

Eddie seemed neither surprised nor discomfited by these revelations, but then, the Duke is one of nature's philosophers. He looked like a man who had not only an extant headache, but a headache on its way that would knock all headaches, past and present, into a cocked hat, but there remained a certain serenity about him, the air of a man who, in the teeth of fervid opposition, had done his best, and could live with himself.

'That's three hundred pounds Oscar owes me,' he said contentedly. 'I told him I could do it.'

CHAPTER 12

What meanst thou by that? Mend me, thou saucy fellow?
Shakespeare

Pandemonium still reigned as William reached the stairwell. Hotel patrons were still emerging on to the staircase while earlier guests trickled back from reception. There was clearly no fire and William was doubting whether there was any point in his going down, when he observed Janice being besieged by a trumpeter in urgent undertone. She was holding her cream silk nightrobe around her throat, and her face was flushed, though whether with embarrassment or vexation William couldn't tell. Then he saw her turn and say in carrying tones, 'Thank you, no,' but the trumpeter remained undeterred.

'Just one little drink . . . Wouldn't kill you to have one drink in my room, would it? Not married, are you?'

A little thrill of irritation propelled William forward. 'Listen, she's on trial already. Nobody needs more pressure than that.'

His intervention, mild as it was, was clearly resented.

'Nothing wrong with asking, is there? As you should know better than most.'

William stood aside to allow Janice to pass, while the trumpeter pounded furiously up the next flight of stairs. His heart thudded erratically. What had possessed him to interfere? He hadn't the authority, in any sense . . . But the look Janice had given him stirred his brain, rushing memories along the synapses.

Thoroughly awakened, he continued downstairs. At the

reception he encountered Angela, who was surveying the scene with a connoisseur's enjoyment.

'Hello, Will,' she murmured. 'Come to view the remains?'

'Was it the basses or the horns?'

'The horn-player was the Duke, as you'd expect . . . Only Eddie has a temperament so exuberant that he can't combine it with alcohol without risking melodrama.'

'And the riot?'

'Ah, there you have me.'

They were so evidently surplus to requirements – for the ambulance had just arrived and the police were leaving – that they made their way back up the stairs, both absorbed in their own thoughtfulness. Angela was concentrating on William, on his quiet breathing beside her, among the swirling river of guests and staff, strangers and orchestra members. There was such steady purpose about him – she felt a sudden impulse of purest bewitchment.

'Wait,' she said, on the landing. William leaned forward, breath warm in her hair.

'Don't even think about it, Angela,' he told her, so softly that she wondered afterwards if she had dreamed it. 'I'll see you at breakfast.'

'Do you never feel lonely?' she asked, as he turned.

'You know better than to ask that.'

Angela watched him as he moved down the corridor, stopping at his door to fish his key from his trouser pocket. She thought, he's right, of course. Looking at his strong bowed shoulders and his handsome bent head, she thought that she had never seen anyone look lonelier in all her life.

CHAPTER 13

You blocks, you stones, you worse than useless things!

'Tis the infirmity of his age and yet he hath ever
but slenderly known himself.

Shakespeare

(from Pete Hegal's diaries)

We accomplished a smooth transfer to Seville the next morning. Leszek travelled on his own; and I frankly dreaded meeting him at the concert-hall for the afternoon rehearsal. I knew he would blame me, in part, for what had happened; Leszek's invariable attitude being that to be present is to be guilty.

At the concert-hall, my fears proved well founded. Leszek looked as if he'd spent the entire night mud-wrestling with sleep. His hair was lank; his face was wan; that dreaded knifeline bisected his brow. He snapped my head off, twice before his coffee and once after it, and damned all Spanish coffee in between.

Elgar's First Symphony was on the menu, and – for sheer human interest – I chose to keep an eye on the rehearsal. Turned out to be young Janice's moment of trial sitting with John McDaniel on the first desk of the cellos. She looked composed and quite ludicrously pretty, mermaid hair contrasting with eyes darkened to mystery by stage-shadows.

The Duke appeared altogether less salubrious in the horns, as did any number of brass and percussion players, and I didn't feel overly perky myself. Before my dry and aching eyes lines of correspondence leaked into each other, ink gone runny at the edges. My throat felt sore too, and I was just determining on a staid and early night when I suddenly became aware that practically everyone was looking at me.

Well, they weren't, of course. I'd happened to station myself near the back of the cellos, and that was where attention was really riveted. Leszek had just bludgeoned his baton down on his music stand, and manoeuvred his eyes – part-grey, part-green, part no colour seen on earth – towards the fag-end of the cello section. Everyone was looking, and even John had pinkened faintly, a child caught misbehaving at school.

'Barbarians! Vandals! Carrion! Look at me! Yes, you, look, *look*! I will *not* be ignored!' snarled Leszek.

Now human nature is so curiously constructed that – even if innocent – it tends to feel vaguely guilty. I dropped my eyes as if I'd only just dismembered the body, but secretly I was mystified. The section had sounded together, or as together as a section can sound where the back persists in playing louder than the front; the intonation had been exemplary, and, though distracted by nerves and dulled by exhaustion, I'm sure I would have noticed anything markedly out of order.

'Stand up!' snarled Leszek, gesturing at the back of the cellos, but, naturally enough, nobody dared. Felicia was there, looking disdainful; she'd switched positions with Janice for the session. Then John asked, 'Whom do you mean?'

I felt Leszek shudder, as if chilled with fury. 'You, I will talk to you later. You four. Yes, you know who I mean! Now, we have it again. Again, I said! Letter K!'

I glanced towards John, wishing to convey sympathy and support, but he seemed maddeningly philosophical about the prospect of being skewered between Leszek and the four young Turks.

Meanwhile Leszek was attacking the last movement. Leszek conducts Elgar with a purely Eastern European flavour – it isn't Elgar, no, but his conviction is such that it still over-powers; and some voices emerge with exotic unexpectedness –

the coaxing whine of the cor anglais, the threatening, widening swell of the double basses . . . The second time Leszek exploded there was a still-grimmer silence.

'Trumpets! Geoffrey! You are deaf, or only stupid? You are behind! Behind, behind, always behind!'

Geoff lifted bloodshot eyes from the principal trumpet part. Some people, I know, maintain that Geoff is an alcoholic, but the truth is that he simply prefers a near-constant stage of superficial inebriation to braving, unfortified, the stomach-constricting tension involved in his job. Accepting the rebuke, he nodded, making a wry face towards his troops.

Leszek remained unmollified. 'And why? Because you do not listen! You are behind even the horns, and that I would not have believed.'

'Perhaps we could try the entire passage again,' proposed the leader, but Leszek was too entrenched to pay attention.

'Do you hear me, Mr Wellington? Yes, you! I am talking to you, to your section! How do you dare to ignore my beat!'

Eddie stood up in patriotic, even noble vein. It is a far, far better thing, he seemed to be telling himself, although it wasn't. 'It was me, Leszek. The boys were fine.'

'Siddown,' hissed Lenny beside him.

The Duke's loyalty to his section did him no service with Leszek. 'But you, you are the first! Am I always to suffer? After last night, I had thought at least – and do not think that you are so blameless either,' he snapped, rounding on the first violins. 'On the last page you were sharp, sharp, sharp! My ears have pins in them, from you, from the flute, from – from almost everywhere! I wish that I was dead before I hear an orchestra make such hash of this thing. It would be better to be dead, dead or deaf, so that I can be left at least with my imagining of this music. There is – there is a *soul* here, a soul in the music! Are you all deaf to miss this soul? Journeymen, hacks, machinery! You are an old car that no one can steer! You are an old and lousy car, you do not listen, you do not care. Dead! You are worse than dead: you are dead in soul, worn out, moth-eaten, lousy!'

There was another silence, one which even the leader was too experienced to break. An uncomfortable, tingling silence, the tuba player afraid to turn the next page of his thriller, eyes averted, as from a disaster.

Why, he's miserable, I thought suddenly. I believe he means it, about dying. A release from his disappointment; honourable discharge from a mission ambition had stripped of all but the most meagre meaning. Escape, from the crushing burden of critical consciousness. Escape.

At that moment Leszek's eyes, hotly scouring the horizon, bore down on Janice and something – who knows what? – made him pause. I realise now that she'd been gazing at him for some time. I have a clear recollection of her almost Grecian profile lifted steady towards his, at the same time as the remainder of the orchestra was looking absolutely anywhere else.

At any rate, Leszek glared down at her, putting both hands to his temples as if they suddenly hurt him – and I stopped breathing. He would demolish the girl in front of everyone; the mind juddered at the thought of what he might do. I had a vision of self lurching forward to protect her, of her face glowing seraphically as she thanked me . . . Instead, fight seeped from Leszek like breath from a balloon.

'Gentlemen – gentlemen and also ladies,' turning with sudden dignity to the trumpets. 'I apologise, I, Leszek. I am not – I am not quite myself. You understand, I have the migraine. You will excuse me, if you please.'

He didn't apologise to the horns. They were left stranded, while the trumpets sat embarrassed and redeemed, very nearly stupefied.

'Again! Letter K,' said Leszek, and the game went on.

Janice averted her face until I could see no more than a corner, and I had to crane in order to see even that. What had she done? What wand had she waved, this frighteningly self-possessed creature, to halt the shark's feeding frenzy? In a daze I heard Leszek call for the break and stride off to the conductor's room; automatically I handed out my own announcements ('No valuables to be left in the dressing rooms, all large instruments to go in the van, and will anyone planning on demolishing a bar tonight please identify themselves now for police and criminal evidence purposes. Not at all, Duke, thank *you*.')

Felicia strolled up from the back of the cello section. 'Well, that's a mercy,' she remarked.

John looked up, politely vague. 'Sorry?'

'Leszek didn't hang about to lacerate the back of the section after all. I suppose it slipped his tiny mind.'

'What *did* happen at the back?' I asked curiously.

'More than should have, I expect, and less than he imagined,' she said cryptically, while John spotted Lenny putting down his horn and hailed him.

'Well?' asked Lenny.

'Knight to Queen six. I've been thinking about it the last hour and a half, and it's the only move.'

'Well bugger me.' Lenny returned to his seat, where he altered a chess piece, and stared down at it, looking still less rollicking than usual.

I couldn't resist joining Janice, who was putting her cello in its case. What I wanted to say was 'Will you marry me?' though I contend against marriage on principle. If you take it at all seriously, it rules out so many options – and there's no point, is there, in marrying and not taking it seriously . . . But there was something so divinely captivating about her as she stood there, having felled Goliath with a single inspired glance.

The Bard, as always, put it best: 'Art thou some god, some angel, or some devil, That mak'st my blood cold, and my hair to stare? Speak to me what thou art.' Later, of course – but more of that anon.

CHAPTER 14

This is the very ecstasy of love.
Shakespeare

Janice was greeted by Terence when she returned to the back of the section. A portly, verbose, oleaginous creature with complacent little rolls of fat on the back of his hands, he wasted no time in justifying himself.

'Leszek was most unfair to snap at the back-desk cellos. The fact of the matter is, I was simply trying to explain Gerhard Mantel's basic theories on bow position ... More of a kindness, really, when you consider what I'm up against.'

'He wasn't very pleased.'

'Victimisation, I call it. Trouble is, by rights I shouldn't be at the back anyway. I really see myself, longterm, as a front-desk player – and so does John McDaniel, though he wouldn't admit it.'

'Wouldn't he? Why not?'

'John doesn't want to admit that I'm a threat to him, ability-wise. Not that I'm egotistical, not at all, but, in the long run, recognising one's true worth is the first step towards fulfilling your inbuilt human potentiality. All the self-help books agree on that. Step one: identify true potential. Step two: decide on long-term career goals. Step three—'

'I'm afraid I don't read those sort of books.'

'No? You owe it to yourself, if you're really serious about getting ahead – though women, of course, needn't bother too much. I mean, you could always play cello as a hobby, and have a few children ... But my case, you must see, is rather considerably different. Where I sit in the section is of crucial, indeed critical, importance. And the bottom line is that I feel much freer, much more myself, sitting at the front of a section than back here between the dregs and the double basses. Fact, I assure you. I play better at the front, as well.'

'Really.'

'Of course, there needs to be back-desk players – and there are; I mean, there's no immediate shortage – it's just that I don't really fit in. It simply doesn't feel like *me*, somehow. My short-term goals are frustrated, and my constructive suggestions ignored . . . Now you – I've happened to notice – play rather decently at the back. Horses for courses, I suppose.'

It occurred to Felicia, who was listening, to suggest that Terence might fit in rather better if he ceased throwing himself from side to side like a seasick mariner and resisted the impulse to play louder than everyone else, but she remained silent, curious to see if he could goad a reaction out of Janice. She was an odd girl, a deep girl. Who knew what went on behind the mask of her beauty?

'No doubt,' said Janice smoothly – but that was all.

It was always a good deal easier, of course, to figure out what Leszek was thinking. His equanimity restored by an excellent concert, he collided with Janice on his way to his Green Room, sweeping her up like a leaf on the wind.

'You again! Are you crazy enough yet to do the Schumann justice?'

He was conscious of a scent – what was this scent? – along with dizziness. Rose quartz, he thought; her cheeks were clear and pink as quartz.

'I doubt it,' she said, smiling. 'I made a terrible hash of the scherzo.'

'This does not matter,' Leszek said, in a really astounding reversal of his usual policy. 'The notes cannot be replayed, the pulse can no longer alter. Poof! An instant – an eyelash, first down then up – then a concert is finished, finished forever! It is tedious even to recall it; it is deader than mutton . . . Come with me.'

Janice – and Leszek! John McDaniel started at the sight, while Angela paused, case half-covering her harp. Leszek! Leszek ushering Janice into his dressing room, and closing the door behind them. When had such a thing happened before? piccolo inquired of clarinet, and trumpeter of trumpeter. Never, was the answer. Never, sunshine, not since the dawn of time.

Leszek was wandering around the room, undoing his tie, pushing back his hair, pacing as if the adrenalin of the music, once whipped into peaks, needed time to die down again.

'This Walton, it drives me crazy, crazy! I need spurs to ride it, and a better horse. The viola solo – what can you do with such a player? He is a Clydesdale, he should instead be pulling hay . . . This work needs vibrancy – light shifting, exploding . . . And never are the trombones together, no, this one is ahead, another behind; I see their eyes over their trombones, doggy eyes; they know it, they hear it; it has happened again. Then I need to shape the horn solo, but no, he goes his own way. Half the time he plays with his eyes closed, this fellow, this Wellington. And always he drives me crazy . . . There are people,' Leszek added, ceasing his perambulations, 'who are lousy in any orchestra. They should play concertos only, and their families should starve, without a toothbrush . . . Which German orchestra did you say that you play with? I have forgotten.'

Her voice caressed his ears strangely.

'Regensburg.'

He struggled for his usual energy.

'Regensburg, so . . . And were you never in Munich? Did you never meet a conductor in Munich called Jorg Otto Steiner? No? Such a beat that man had! He cut pies in the air, segments, crusts flying everywhere! I knew him in Vienna, we had the same professor . . . He is crazy, completely crazy, and a very lousy conductor, but I love him. I wish he was dead so I could tell the world that I love him like a brother.'

The girl smiled faintly. The very air in the room seemed different, he thought – sultrier, heavier: summer air with sulphur in it. He wheeled on her, struggling through air like water. 'What are you thinking?'

'I was thinking that you looked better now than you had earlier.'

'In what way better – not so angry? You think I am always angry – but this is quite untrue. Sometimes I can be most charming. You would be surprised, I think.'

'I suppose I meant better looking, more attractive.'

Leszek seized her chin. Her eyes were endless – starry, gold-brown. There were minute waves in them, fragments of ether like light filaments. He felt unspun by their closeness, their endlessness, by some heaviness in the atmosphere.

Leszek's lips closed down on hers. Sensation shot through him like a current, vibrations from the most passionate moments in the Walton symphony. Her suppleness, the silky texture of her skin, her strange flowing colour . . . He pressed into her warm pliancy and she did not resist. It was delirium: he was gone; he was falling. There was a drumming somewhere, but he was almost too lost to recognise it.

The pounding was on the door, accompanied by Pete's world-weariest accent: 'My apologies, Maestro, but there are members of the local press corps here.'

He whispered to the girl, 'Tomorrow. Meet me tomorrow.'

'Yes.' A breath of honeysuckle.

Leszek stalked to the door, throwing it open.

'Gentlemen, I am at your disposal,' then to Janice, curtly: 'Good night.'

'Who's that?' inquired one journalist.

'An orchestra member requiring discipline,' replied Leszek, meeting Pete's gaze without blinking. 'Come in, gentlemen, please. I am quite at your disposal.'

Hell to pay, thought Pete, though he also felt disquieted –

jealous, even. Sometimes he wearied of being the court jester, longed for the leading role. And why not? All gravediggers secretly fancied a go at playing Hamlet. Inside yet subtly excluded; the orchestral manager's fate . . . It'll end in tears, he predicted, but who's to say it wouldn't be worth it? Janice, with her air of corruptibility, her ability to charge the air. She was a poltergeist, a grown-up poltergeist.

Whistling, Pete made his own way back to the hotel.

CHAPTER 15

Tell me in sadness, who is that you love?
Shakespeare

(from Pete Hegal's diaries)

'Of course,' said William, 'things feel different here.'

Will and I were ensconced in an overpriced if atmospheric café just around the corner from the palace. The pace of the tour had slackened delightfully in Seville. We had already performed two concerts to discreetly appreciative audiences – and I'd almost forgotten how it felt to have eardrums assaulted by fire alarms, hotel managers and the cry of the Duke's wild horn.

I'd spotted Will emerging from the palace, and wondered to see him on his own. The Royal Sinfonia has its fair share of loners, but Will wasn't one of them. His preferred role seemed to be that of a stabilising influence in a gaggle of sportive spirits. You would find him the single sober soul among the brass, or smoothing the double basses' exodus from a pub at closing time. But in Seville, I don't know why, he looked lonely. There was something about the set of his shoulders which struck me particularly.

'Hello, Will. Fancy a drink?'

'You don't think it's a bit early?'

'On the contrary. The percussion will have the jump on us by hours.'

'I don't pretend, at my age, to keep up with the percussion.'

'And nor do I, except for purposes of comparison. This place looks tolerable.'

And it was tolerable, so much so that we stayed two hours, while horse carriages clopped past on their usual route to the Maria Luisa gardens and the sun suffused the sky with porcelain pink and skimming violet.

We began by discussing the board's refusal to suspend the Duke after Madrid, and Leszek's well-known blind spot where Eddie was concerned. Then Will made his comment about things feeling different.

'How do you mean, different?' I inquired.

'It's the freedom, I suppose. The childlike sensation of being looked after, of being allocated spending money and having plane tickets confiscated. We hand over the reins of our lives on a tour. Nothing's our problem, nothing's our fault.'

'It doesn't feel like that for the management,' I retorted, remembering the ninety-odd plane tickets in my hotel room. Will carried on.

'And children don't feel guilt, or not the way we do. Guilt is at least partly learned; so our sense of guilt seems to dissipate as well. We're made over new, in a new country.'

William Mellor belongs to an unusual category of cellist – older distinguished, sub-genus diplomat – but when he smiles he looks much younger, and very handsome. His father's Welsh, but I refuse to hold that against him, nor the fact that he attended Winchester on a music scholarship.

'Perhaps I'm just jealous,' I mused. 'It must feel delightfully liberating to have all responsibility lifted off your shoulders.'

William seemed to have stopped listening. The streets had grown more hectic with twilight. Carriage-horses were trotting off homewards, while a guitarist with a husky smoker's twang was peddling songs from table to table.

'Do you believe in ghosts?' Will asked, eyes glowing.

This time I really did look askance. William's a relative newcomer to the Royal Sinfonia, but nothing had yet suggested that he suffered from manic depression, hallucinations, drug addiction, or any commoner disorder. Still, there were darting slashes of colour beneath his cheekbones, while his hand – a cellist's hand, broad, steady and masculine – moved uneasily against the table.

'What, have you seen a ghost?' I joked.

'No, but I think I'm playing on one.'

'What!'

'You know Bud,' he went on; and I admitted it, fogged. Bud's the stalwart soul who hoicks the larger instruments around for the band. He's a good-natured, muddle-headed fellow, with a monstrous pot belly and tiny black eyes like raisins in suet. William continued.

'Is Bud fond of practical jokes?'

'Bud? Bud isn't capable of even recognising a joke, whether practical or impractical. He's a kindly soul, but with all the finesse of a cricket bat – and about as much sense of humour.'

'You know him better than I do, of course. But otherwise – Pete, the cello I'm playing here in Spain isn't the same cello I gave Bud to transport.'

'What! Whose cello is it?'

'I'll tell you what happened. I put my Lott in the case at home, played the concert on it, then left it in the locked room at the hall with the others . . . But when I opened my case in Madrid, I found that my other cello had replaced it – without my consent, or Bud's collusion, or the collusion of anyone else that I can think of.'

'Your second cello being—'

William hesitated a fraction before answering. 'I bought it recently at auction. It's a curious, characterful instrument. Sometimes it sings, electrifyingly, and sometimes it's completely still, as if it's waiting, longing for some cue . . . It behaves oddly around Leszek – and it behaves oddly around Janice.'

'The trial cellist.'

'And Leszek.'

'How can you tell?' I inquired sceptically.

'I can tell,' said William, with a quietness infinitely more convincing than any protestation would have been. 'It simply takes over. I'm not playing it, no, the cello plays me . . . And then, when Leszek passes, it – moves, it quickens. Sometimes it glitters, and lets loose dust, like grit off the heel of a star. And sometimes it feels warm, as if it's been running, and pulses under my hand like a child.'

I was shaken. He had suddenly reminded me of that day in London, when Leszek had been conducting *Job*. Silver-grey dust and a cello still warm to the touch.

'O all you host of heaven! O earth! What else?'

'Don't you believe me?'

'I was there,' I reminded him. 'I was there, for Satan's dance.'

'The dance, of course. I thought my fingers would never stop dancing. It was terrifying – terrifying and exhilarating at the same time. For a moment I thought I was going mad.'

'You went to rest in my office,' I remembered.

'Even John McDaniel's noticed that there's something about it. He played on it once – the thing simply bloomed.'

I thought for a moment. 'Could it, might it respond to how you're feeling?'

'Not obviously.'

'But say, for the purposes of argument, that you fancied Janice. I mean: everyone else does, why should you be any different?'

'But I don't think I do. It's just that the air around her is subtly different from the air around other people. Something about that girl disturbs the air.'

'Take Leszek, then. Perhaps he inspires you. Perhaps there's some kind of – of psychic power involved.'

'I have lost the ability,' said William with energy, 'to be inspired by Leszek or any conductor. I've been in this business for thirty years and I'm tired. Tired of the travelling, the in-fighting, the internal politics – tired of the struggle for recognition and the consciousness of defeat. I've played everything I want to play and travelled everywhere I want to travel. I'd retire tomorrow if—'

79

'If what?' I prompted. Dusk had dipped into night and Seville's pavements wormed with tourists, lanky American students, British honeymooners; while exaggeratedly casual local youths pretended not to eye up the talent. William's face twisted in the half-light.

'It doesn't matter.'

'You can't stop there. I am hooked and intrigued. What stops you retiring – money worries? Family commitments? This crazy cello?'

William took a deep breath.

'I've stopped believing in escape. I tried escaping once, and it almost killed me ... No, I'm staying in this orchestra, where there are people who like me, who respect my playing, people who – without even realising it – help me to get by. The routine of work, the imperative to be in a certain place at a given time – this is reassuring, subtly restorative. It fosters a false but nonetheless comforting purpose in being alive.'

'Your former friends ... Wasn't one of them called Piotr?'

'I might have guessed,' said William with resignation, 'that you would know Piotr.'

'Oh, I wouldn't say I knew him, exactly. I met him at a party. I was with my former girlfriend – and he seemed to be alone.'

Will was silent.

'This was recent, was it?' he asked finally.

'Maybe a month ago.'

'He didn't mention me, I suppose.'

'I have to admit that he didn't. He amused me, though, very much.'

'Piotr amuses everybody,' said William quietly, and I was struck by the sadness in his tone. I remembered Piotr vividly – the errant lock of black hair slipping over his face, that tilted eyebrow, his self-mocking air – and thought again what an unlikely duo they must have made. Will traced the pattern left by his glass on the table.

'I saw her,' he told me. 'Not long ago.'

I didn't have to ask whom he meant. The conjunction of names, of circumstance – but I found myself holding my breath all the same. The idea of Will's choosing to confide in me was a heady one. I didn't dare even prompt him, in case he changed his mind.

'It was in the lobby of the Barbican, before one of the children's concerts. I was early, and somehow not in the mood for backstage gossip, so I decided to read on one of those leather sofas. You know what a wilderness the Barbican can be. Imagine it: mid-afternoon, student clarinet quartets in the distance, grey skies, and that fountain spewing endless khaki-coloured water into the pool.

'I saw a stranger, not pretty and not young, throwing bread for the ducks. Her dogged trick of standing, her straggling hair and her tired raincoat impressed me with a strange empathy. Watching her, I felt suddenly thick with grief. I had to restrain myself from weeping; I had to bite my lip to distract myself with physical pain.

'Then I saw Isabel, wearing a leather jacket I didn't know, wandering among the concert brochures. She glanced at her watch, seemingly waiting for someone, possibly – well, it doesn't matter who. I would have left, except that movement would have rendered me more conspicuous. I resumed my book instead, though the words littered themselves together in my mind. Nerves had dried up my misery; instead of being dead I longed to be invisible, and I could feel my heart testing sharp against my ribs.

'Her footsteps, which had been so casual, so irresolute, were suddenly arrested. I turned a page, but my eyes refused to obey the ordered lines. No, they would rise, against the background of student clarinets and cries of feeding birds – they would rise up regardless, to see what they'd always used to see.'

Here William paused. I cleared my throat.

'I've met Isabel,' I said. 'She is – achingly beautiful.'

'Yes,' he agreed, rousing himself. 'Though she's altered. For the first time the shadow of middle-age had touched her. For whatever reason she no longer looked purely youthful to me. Perhaps it was her stance, the too emphatically sexy jacket, the angle of her head – who knows what divides the young from the rest of us? She's only thirty-five but we've altered her, corrupted her. She looked defiant but frightened, longing but unsure. And her eyes searched mine, though what they were searching for I didn't know.

'Conventionalities were useless; words were useless. I shut my book, and rose to leave. Isabel, however, moved closer. I've never heard her voice like that; wouldn't have recognised it, even; it sounded so dead.

' "I'm not here any more. They think I am, but I'm not. My body's here, that's all."

' "Yes," I said quietly.

' "You sound as if you understand."

' "I do understand."

' "You killed me," she said, with sudden passion. "You've killed almost all of me, but you botched the job. You might at least have had the nerve to kill me properly!"

' "Perhaps I'm not accustomed to killing people."

'Colour rushed into her face, softening it; suddenly her beauty looked as terrifying as I'd remembered.

' "I thought you were different. I was so sure with you. You were the only one I was ever sure of."

' "I always told you I was the same as the others."

' "But I never believed you."

' "No. I know you didn't believe me."

'I felt dizzy with remembering – the texture of her hair, the smell of her skin. She half-swayed towards me, and every instinct in my soul pulled me towards her. Every instinct, from compassion and feeling to lust and the desire to dominate – but we're not, thank God, composed entirely of instinct. At least, I forced myself not to be.

' "No," I told her, almost harshly. "Not again. No."

' "Hold me, William," she whispered. "Just for a moment – I feel so alone."

'I said goodbye and left her there. I didn't look around but I know she remained, because I couldn't hear the sound of her tall heels clipping away.'

It was dark by the time Will finished, and I found myself lighting a cigarette with uncertain fingers. For the first time I realised what must have driven him to Isabel: the sensual power, the impulsive courage. Indeed, I felt suddenly sorry for her, despite all I'd heard to her disadvantage.

'Poor girl,' I said, clearing my throat.

William acknowledged this with a gesture.

'Piotr told me she was a witch.'

'Oh, she is a witch. But he never did her justice.'

And I suddenly remembered the curl of Piotr's lip, the bone-dry anger in his eyes. A different betrayal, I thought: Piotr had also suffered a bereavement.

Suddenly I noticed a couple wandering down the street, which was thinning at last.

'Leszek,' I observed. 'Leszek and Janice, no less. Well, well. You live long enough, you see everything.'

William followed my gaze, though without interest. He looked exhausted, and I recalled his words about retirement. Besides, he couldn't be expected to share my frisson of intrigue where Leszek was concerned, having belonged to the orchestra for so short a time. He roused himself politely, however.

'I thought Leszek was married already.'

'Oh, he's been married – thrice, as of even date. However, as his principal passion is music, the others never seem to last long . . . Why young Janice is more the question. Perhaps she's so determined to get the job that she'd do anything.'

'I think she's looking for something more complicated than that,' said William.

I remembered what he'd said before – about Janice and the unnamed cello – and I knew that he was remembering it too. And a shadow of foreboding crossed me like a northerly wind.

I thought about William's former band – the Orchestra of London. By all accounts it was in complete financial and emotional crisis: the third horn's death, the embezzlement scandal, Isabel's breakdown –and the blood was still fresh on the floor from Karl Hochler's palace coup. Recently there'd been other leaks from the front line: sponsorship withdrawals, salary cuts, tour cancellations – the bad news seemed almost endless. But the precarious position of our rivals suddenly seemed no cause for jubilation; instead, fate's finger seemed poised over every London orchestra, and William's arrival like the spreading of the plague.

Leszek had stopped to examine a restaurant menu across the way. I watched him against the lit window, his aquiline, lean-lipped profile. Janice was smiling at something he said; they might have been any good-looking couple, the man perhaps no longer young, but otherwise unremarkable. We watched them enter, just as the guitarist hove into view again, strumming some sad Spanish song.

CHAPTER 16

O, speak again, bright angel! – for thou art
As glorious to this night, being o'er my head,
As is a winged messenger of heaven.

Shakespeare

Leszek installed Janice in her seat with a flourish, well pleased with himself. His motives for singling her out, while not purely altruistic, were not in his view ignoble either . . . It was surely a kindness to take an aspiring cellist under his wing – nor would it be such a bad thing if she returned to London enthusing about how generous and amusing the great Zimetski could be. Later, something might perhaps come of it . . . But for now he must lay the groundwork. The girl was delicate, and artlessness was part of her appeal. He would capture her gently, amazing everybody.

During the main course, Leszek tried to describe his reaction to the first movement of the Walton symphony.

'The recapitulation affects me in such a fashion that once I saw a vision. It was the most extraordinary thing, a horse soaring into the clouds.'

'What, Pegasus?'

'No, he had no wings. He was crashing on towards the sun as if his own power was enough, like a glory . . . That was in Dresden, I think, or else Berlin. I was transported that whole tour, the concerts effortless.'

'Why that tour particularly?'

'Ah, well.'

He watched her colour alter out of the corner of his eye.

Really, she was captivating, never the same complexion for two moments together!

'I didn't meant to pry,' she said softly.

'Not at all; these things happen. It was some years ago, after all.'

'Don't tell me if it upsets you.'

Leszek sighed, preparing himself like an actor in his dressing room. So many times had he reworked this tale, and each time he told it better, with a more shadowed yet stricken grief . . . Remembrance, he had heard once, is not painted in too bold a shade; memories come in soft pastels. It was in that spirit that he had created the story of his lost love – misunderstandings, reconciliations, a dash of scarlet, a slash of purple – the whole relayed with a combination of subtle nuance and sudden, divinely timed silences . . . It was artistic; it was untrue; it was sublime.

The effect of this embroidery on women was magical, combining their impulse to heal, their fascination with danger, and their real sorrow at the (completely fictional but not inartistic) death scene. So powerfully drawn was this fiction that there were times when Leszek imagined his grief was genuine; there were even times – so complicated a creature is man! – when his grief really was genuine. Where, he sometimes asked himself, did art end and humanity begin? Where did imagination ellipse into near-remembering?

'I was young, remember,' he began. 'And my wife was then forty, the sort of age when a woman sometimes feels she has to choose. She decided that my career was stifling her artistry – she was an actress, of sorts – and that we would be better apart. It was a kind of test, perhaps, to see what would happen, how I would behave, whether the future together would be possible. We did not divorce, you understand; we lived apart. Until it happened.'

She was watching him with an intensity he did not see.

'You met someone,' she suggested.

'I fell in love elsewhere.'

'You often fall in love.'

Leszek leaned his elbows on the table. 'Often? I am never out of love, not since I was a boy.'

It was hypnosis; he was being towed on a band of light out of the centre of her bronze-brown eyes.

'When you were a boy,' she echoed.

Leszek continued, suddenly demolished by the music of his own voice, mellow as a tenor sax, rising and falling, altering shape with each cadence. His script mislaid, forgotten, instead he was recalling something real, something so fundamental to his consciousness that he'd believed it buried long decades before. A scent teased at his memory, delicate as origami, and Leszek was lost in the persuasiveness of its music.

'I was in school in Poland when I first fell in love. Mikhail was in my class, the cleverest, handsomest creature, very blond, very soft brown eyes, eyes like a fawn – very unlike myself. I would not only have liked to look the same, but longed in fact to be this creature, this Mikhail. We went everywhere together – he so beautiful, and me with too thin torso and my too long nose, because my nose grew before the rest of my face decided to agree with it. I was very conscious of that, as you can imagine.

'I spent lessons thinking of ways to divert Mikhail, and much of my spare time amusing him. Often we would stay behind to play trios with the music teacher, for I was learning the violin and Mikhail the cello, although –'

A cloud over his voice, and a soft prompt. 'Although?'

'No, I have forgotten, it does not matter . . . We even had a language, Mikhail and myself, a secret, magical language which was ours alone. Always it was Mikhail and Leszek, though others would tag behind, putting themselves forward in hopes that Mikhail would notice them, and give them too the slow slow smile that burned through me.

'One day – I recall this as if it only just occurred – we emerged slightly later than all the others. A game had commenced, a new game, a game with a ball; I forget now how to play this game. The others turned towards Mikhail like flowers towards the sun and called out, "Mikhail! Come and play!" And, still smiling, Mikhail detached his arm from mine and joined them.

'If I live one hundred years, I shall never forget that moment. Not: "I will come if Leszek also plays," or (as I had hoped): "Leszek and I have no desire for such childish games." No, the betrayal was complete, endless. One moment he was mine, the next everyone's – accepting the ball, running into the sun, the light bending to caress every silvery hair on his arms.

'They sprinted to the other end of the field, these boys, perhaps seven, perhaps eight, but the only one I saw was Mikhail, his image pressed on my brain, running into the sun with the ball in his hands. I watched without moving until the sun slurred his hair, and what had been a wash of colour disappeared before my eyes. Then I went into the empty schoolroom, leaned against the windowpane and cried out to my soul.

'You will say, and so? – and I know that many people might have forgiven Mikhail this. Many people might have thought: he was only a boy, of course he preferred a game with a ball. Perhaps he intended me to join as well; perhaps he did not notice that the invitation had been for him alone, perhaps he did not even think, my Mikhail. But I am made quite differently from this. Not that I loved no longer – I loved more than ever, my soul was pure love, pure wretchedness – but for me it was over. Something – something that I had until that moment refused to recognise – had suddenly come home to my soul. Something I could not even – but I cannot explain this, never . . . You must simply believe, that this was not the whole, that there was something still worse beyond it, that there was an illness, a perversion. And from that moment I could be with Mikhail no more.

'From that day onward I was alone, because if I could not have Mikhail I would most assuredly have no other. A few other boys approached me with offers of comradeship; these I

88

scorned. I applied myself instead with such ferocity to my work that I outshone Mikhail, I outshone everybody. I was sent for by the teacher and asked if I wanted to carry on, or whether it would not be more amusing for me to attend the class above.

'That was the moment. Mikhail on the one hand, still puzzled, hair scorched by sunlight – and on the other hand: glory. I did not hesitate, though the memory of his smile gripped the sides of my head. I left, leaving Mikhail behind me forever.'

Janice was watching him strangely – very strangely, he thought later – when Leszek remembered whom he was addressing.

'I hadn't meant— I don't know where all that came from!' he said, almost laughing in his embarrassment.

'No. You were going to tell me something different, I think. Something more recent.'

'Exactly so, yes.'

Yes, I was going to lie. I was going to lie but your eyes delved the truth out of me. I was going to lie but you opened me up instead, thumbing over the pages of my most secret heart.

'I suppose you needed to talk about it. I wonder why.'

Because you have his eyes, thought Leszek suddenly: those clear brown eyes of a monk or a madman; why did I never notice this before? His soul juddered at the completeness of it. She was feminine – almost unbearably feminine – but the tossed glittering waves were the same, that tidal, slow-burning smile. She must know, she must realise . . . Or perhaps she did not realise. So straight, so complete, sitting with that flexible erectness, as if, at only a touch, she might melt into someone's arms. It was a pleasure to look at her, and yet –

He could only watch, marvelling at his super-awareness, the tensile fibre of his nerves registering everything: pleasure, anticipation, jealousy, even fear. It's over for me, he thought: only I would rush out to greet my nemesis.

'Is anything wrong?' she asked.

Leszek touched her arm, feeling more sure than ever, and more surely crazy. Her eyes reflected candlelight back at him, almost metallic, the soft fluorescent centres like the core of a star. Her gaze consumed his and (almost as swiftly as if it had been struck from his consciousness) he forgot what it was that he'd momentarily remembered. If he had recalled it, things might have happened differently; if she'd let him remember – but she was too clever for that, and too surely prepared.

Leszek poured some more wine. 'But enough of the past. We will have instead a little toast. To the orchestra – and to the future!'

He put a hand on the soft resistance of her thigh, and, bent on this sweet giving flesh, missed the shadows jarring the corners of her eyes.

Chapter 17

There's language in her eye, her cheek, her lip,
Nay, her foot speaks; her wanton spirits look out
At every joint and motive of her body.

Shakespeare

'You can't carry on feeling guilty indefinitely. Besides, she left you, didn't she?'

'I don't see it that way, or not entirely.'

'You mean you've decided to suffer. Well, I've no sympathy for you. It's an addiction; suffering is an addiction – just as living intensely is an addiction.'

'I agree, of course. However, I suffer from other addictions.'

'You mean sex.'

'I don't have to answer that,' William replied, with a smile.

'You don't,' said Angela, 'have to answer anything.'

Earlier, William's room had seemed full. Fourteen musicians had been with them, on the floor, on the bed, chatting, drinking and enjoying Angela's jazz tapes. But it was past one-thirty, and William and Angela were alone.

It was a test, thought William. She was testing his psyche against her thumb, just as she had during the fire alarm in Madrid. She didn't realise that it was too late, and that the reflex with which he responded to her suggestiveness was just that – a reflex – and meant nothing.

'Finish off the food,' he suggested. 'It won't last.'

'I'm not hungry, thanks.'

And what she was hungry for suddenly unsettled her. She glanced at his still-powerful shoulders and thought, I'm in danger of becoming obsessed. Not my style at all – and it would only embarrass William.

'I'll help you clear up,' she offered.

'There's no need. I can do it in the morning.'

'You look tired,' she said, although she had meant perhaps to say something different.

'I am tired.'

Tired of being away, tired of the struggle. An old dream – or was it one of Isabel's? – rushed back to him: a sunlit Sussex village, an Irish setter chasing ducks in the quiet shadows of late afternoon. It was true, he was tired, and sometimes it struck him as an ending tiredness, though he recognised this partly as sickness and partly as despair.

'Do you want me to leave?' she asked.

'I think you ought to leave.'

'Because of what people might think about you.'

'No. Because of what I might think about myself.'

His soberness might have unnerved some women – others, perhaps more passionate, might have felt challenged by it. Yet there was a masculine energy in Angela that responded far more deviously. William might be 'down' – depressed being a word she instinctively loathed – well, she could cure him; she could cure anyone. Her instinct – part maternal, part predatory – was to resume the attack.

'You don't believe that you deserve to be comforted.'

'We discussed this before, remember.'

'Oh, I remember everything – about that tour, at least.'

And so do I, he didn't say. The dance in Madrid had brought it all back . . . The vivacity in her small, spirited body, hair as copper as a river at twilight, Irish accent mocking against a background of castanets. It wouldn't work, he wanted to tell her, but the will was lacking. He wished she would leave; he wished sleep would come; he wished for death, but without any real fervour. He thought: the strength's gone out of me, this time for good.

'Where did it happen? Was it Paris?'

'Copenhagen,' he replied, with some reluctance. 'And it didn't happen.'

'Copenhagen, of course: you'd only just joined. You said you didn't have what I was after. I think that's the rudest thing you've ever said to me.'

'I only meant to be truthful,' he said. William had a loathing of rudeness, of insensitivity. It seemed sinful to him – more so, perhaps, than more overtly sinful things. He added, 'I only meant that you are far too attractive – and I am far too old.'

'It isn't possible to be too old.'

'Even if it isn't, I'm not in fit state. Imagine I made love to you—'

'I have imagined it, ever since. I've imagined it over and over again.'

'So much so that you avoided me altogether afterwards,' he said, attempting lightness.

'I did avoid you, feeling almost afraid – not of you, exactly, but of what you made me feel.'

William refused to look at her, his fingers drumming a counter-rhythm on his thigh. He felt moved, and surprised, and surprised to be moved. He reached for sure rationality again.

'But that's only because – because of what's happened to me, and what people say . . . I've noticed it ever since things changed in my life. I've become a curiosity, a talking-point. I never was before.'

'Because of Isabel. You think it's because of Isabel.'

'Yes,' he said, less steadily, 'and what she represents.'

'Say her name. Go on, say it.'

William said with visible effort, 'Isabel. What Isabel represents.' Her name on his lips hung resonant in the air, three syllables like small shining bells.

'You're shaking,' said Angela. 'You're almost shaking . . . You're terribly tense, Will.'

'It's only tiredness.'

Angela's heart reverberated; she could feel it, punishing her for punishing him.

'No, even the angle of your head is tense. What you need is a proper massage.'

'What I need is sleep.'

'Just lie down on the bed.'

'I'll be all right tomorrow.'

'You can be all right tonight.'

William submitted. The idea of a massage was appealing – appealing too was the rough warmth in Angela's voice.

'Fine,' he said humorously. 'But if you expect this to lead to anything of a more athletic nature, I warn you, you'll be disappointed.'

'The Irish never expect – they dream, instead. And sometimes they write bloody good poetry.'

Her hands, lightly starred with freckles and misleadingly fragile in appearance, roamed over the muscles in his neck, unbottling the knotted tendons of his upper back. They were smaller, more insistent hands than Isabel's, yet somehow recalling those darker, longer hands . . . He found himself surrendering to her sureness, drifting, weakening. How blissful it was to be stroked and pummelled, to feel wine glowing through his bloodstream and Angela's palms convulsing his shoulders.

'My dear girl, you're no novice at this,' he murmured, half into his pillow.

No, thought Angela with a rush of elation – but the outcome never felt so uncertain before. She transferred her efforts to his legs, enjoying their muscular solidity. His thighs gave the first intimation that she might be winning. They tautened, gathering power under her fingers; Will stirred.

'Well, that's me made over new,' he joked, half-turning on to his side.

'Not quite . . . I haven't finished the shoulders.'

Hoisting herself astride him Angela attacked his back again, making swirling motions with her small white fists. With every

94

moment he felt her will driving more surely into him, the stubborn purpose of her desire. His mind ordered him to refuse, to move away, but his blood sped ever more traitorously, waters rising towards a riverbank.

At first he failed to identify a certain sound; then he knew. Her naked crotch was crunching across his trousers in rhythm with the motion of her hands. A moment later he recognised the sensation of a small tight breast tingling against the nerves of his palm. And then with exquisite, almost unbearably sensuous timing, the points of her breasts began to caress him, brushing across his arms, the awakening surface of his naked back.

How long had it been since he felt a woman's nipples harden along the line of his skin, or that empowering furore in his groin? Had he really been guilt-smothered for so long? And he knew in that moment that Angela had defeated him, as perhaps he'd known she would, had even willed her to. Suddenly he was no longer capable of extricating himself, of saying something casual and slipping away. He hadn't realised how all-pervasive his loneliness had been, the extent of his isolation . . . He might despise himself for his sudden longing for the sensation of his body inside hers, for the ticklish static of her smooth hair between his fingers – but the truth was that he lacked the will to hold out any longer; it was surrender.

He twisted around to face her, gathering her body powerfully to his. His lips closed over hers, as he ran the tip of his finger thrillingly along the open line of her soft shoulder.

But when the moment came the name on his lips was not hers, no, it was the long-lost cry of the damned. His lips on Angela's breast and a deep surge of 'Isabel' as if the end hadn't come and never really could.

Chapter 18

O Madam, my old heart is cracked; it's cracked.
Shakespeare

'More chicken?' Vera inquired. 'The breast is very tender.'

'Thank you, no.'

William's mother Vera sat irresolute, carving knife still hovering with a slab of chicken on it. Very tender, thought Will, and felt suddenly sick with grief.

'You didn't like the bread pudding.'

'I loved it. I simply lack the space I had when I was younger.'

Vera looked critically at him. 'Space! You're peaky, is your trouble.'

'Oh, let Will alone,' came from the direction of the settee, where his father sat in aggrieved possession of delicate health. 'Happen I'll have more roast potatoes, if you've left one between you.'

William gathered the remaining potatoes and delivered them to Hugh.

'Peaky,' scoffed his father, neatly dissecting a potato. 'What rubbish women talk. Why, you're twice my size.'

'And always was,' said Vera, in subtle revenge for the last potato.

'Height isn't everything. Suppose we ring the grandson.'

'That's the third time you've suggested that.'

'Save me breath, then, why don't you, and ring him?'

'I'm not best pleased with Sam,' said Vera.

William paused, wineglass halfway to his lips. 'Why not?'

'You ask that, on the first of our family anniversaries that he's not been here!'

A stillness descended upon Will. That's got nothing to do with Sam, he wanted to say.

'Thought it was agreed,' came in irritable tones from Hugh. 'Thought it was Will's idea, but then, nobody tells me. Speak up, boy! Was it your idea to come on your own or not?'

William smiled – a smile that would rise, irrepressible, at the notion of being addressed as 'boy'.

'It was an idea I agreed with,' he said, compromising with truth for the sake of peace.

'I don't know; nobody tells me. Here, Vera, there's no gravy on this. Asked for gravy, didn't I?'

'No, you didn't, but there's plenty left, for Will's hardly had a drop.'

'Don't understand,' grumbled Hugh. 'Thought it was your notion. *I* said you'd be better sorting it on your own, you can ask Vera, ask the dog, ask anybody. Take a holiday, the two of you, drag Margot off to Buenos Aires and come back brown and straightened out, like bread out of a toaster. Don't see the point, otherwise. Isn't any point, is there?'

William looked affectionately at his father. Hugh was a fine-looking old gentleman, short and feisty, with a mobile face and square-turned jaw. His manners could be extremely winning, particularly towards shopgirls, his grandson Sam, and his tiny great-granddaughter. When he fancied himself nervous, however, he tended towards sulkiness. He was sulking now in his favourite settee, though he couldn't help brightening at the sight of the remaining gravy. His wife had grown busier during his speech, hands fussing over the condiments.

'You said you wouldn't mention – that – on our anniversary, Hugh. You promised me you wouldn't.'

'Aye, and you promised me we'd be ringing young Sam.'

'I'll ring him myself, if you like,' said William, rising from the table. His mother looked at him, marvelling, not for the

97

first time, at his powerful shoulders, the reserves of strength in his deep eyes and fine carriage. He was like Hugh yet not like him, the same design on an altogether grander scale, stronger and surer and more serene.

It must all come right, Vera thought, with an unquenchable surge of hopefulness. Whatever had been the cause of the split between William and Margot – and after so many years, whoever could have imagined it? – no one could resist William for long. It must be Margot's sick fancy – a function of her illness – nothing more than that.

As they did the washing-up, Vera washing, William drying, she submitted this theory to him. William shook his head.

'No, Margot's well enough. She's just angry.'

'Angry at you? Why? Why is she angry?'

'Must you force me to say things that will hurt you?' he asked.

Vera seemed to shrink. 'Just say it's not to do with us, Will. Tell me that, at least.'

'Believe me, absolutely nothing. Margot's very fond of you, you know that.'

'And very fond of you.'

'Perhaps,' said Will, his throat constricting, 'it would be as well to get hold of Sam now.'

'You don't even seem to blame her!' exclaimed Vera.

'No,' said William, half under his breath. 'I don't blame her. How can I blame her? In her place, I'd feel the same.'

'You mean, with her illness you would feel the same. If you had her – you know, her physical troubles.'

William was conscious of a sudden longing to transfer some of his burden to someone else's shoulders. Margot's illness! It was his illness; he was the one infected! Yet his habitual self-control reasserted itself, steadying him. It would be purely selfish to tell his mother, and he'd been quite selfish enough already. Though part of Will derided himself for cowardice, for enjoying that proud warming glow in Vera's eyes when she

98

looked at him, the look that must surely disappear if she ever learned the truth.

'I'm not who you think I am,' he said, so softly that she misheard him.

'Oh I know it isn't your fault,' she said, squeezing his bicep fervently. 'You needn't tell me that; Margot's who you need to tell. Do you really feel up to talking to Sam?'

From the sitting room came unmistakable rumbles of discontent. If Hugh had one policy he adhered to more strictly than another, it was that, when he had a grievance, he gave it utterance.

'It's a conspiracy. It's "don't tell Dad, or else he'll kick", or it's "needn't upset Dad", as if I was on the milk and water already, and gaga and deaf to boot. I know you're talking about me!' he shouted, a spasm of irritation. 'It's a flaming conspiracy, is what it is. Yes, a flaming conspiracy,' he added to the dog, enjoying the sound of the words in his mouth. 'A flaming conspiracy it is, and don't you go telling me otherwise.'

After the ritual of washing-up, William rang his son. In the background he could hear Vera rushing the tap to make a noise, attempting to procure him a modicum of privacy.

'Sam, hello.'

'Hi, Dad. How are you?' To his father's ears, Sam's voice retained that husky uncertainty of adolescence.

'Everyone well?' William asked lightly.

'Mostly, yes. Little Emma's been ill, but I think it's just excitement from her birthday.'

'Was she pleased with the presents?'

'Pleased? Can't drag her away from them. You were very kind, Dad, too—'

William, unable to bear the taste of gratitude, interrupted. 'You only care for birthdays when you're young. Have you finished your meal?'

'Yes, ages ago. Is Grandad asleep, or is he on about his nerves?'

'He's not asleep,' said William cautiously. He could hear Hugh's muttered objections. He wasn't allowed anything, and it was his right to talk to his only grandson – the implication being that William had been too incompetent or careless to give him more.

'Mother said she'd like a word with Grandma,' said Sam. He said it casually, but William was silent. 'Still there, Dad? Doesn't matter when.'

What about me? William wanted to ask, but found that he had lost faith in the obedience of his voice. Margot wanted his mother, not him, she wanted – he could feel it – to destroy his mother with some part of the truths that he'd just spared her. And he had given her this right, he had done it, with one year's craziness he had sealed the world's end.

'Dad? Dad? You still there?'

William drew breath. 'Yes, Sam. Still here.'

'Look, I'm sorry about all this. It doesn't feel – right – not being there on the day. I'll do what I can, believe me. I'll do everything I can.'

But underneath Sam's stubbornness William heard the breath of doubt, of worry that it was too late, too late for him, for Margot, too late to avert the gathering threat of the virulent, fisting summer ahead.

'Is Grandad there now?' asked Sam, after a pause.

'He's been looking forward to it. All yours,' he told Hugh, who was springing towards the telephone.

'Hello, hello? Young Sam, is it? Thought they'd never let me on. Wanted to call you hours ago, but it was "Don't be silly, Dad" and "Have to finish the dishes." All sorts of excuses . . . My nerves? Same as usual, rotten. Still, I can't complain.'

Vera came up to William and hooked her arm into his. But he could so little bear sympathy that he gently disentangled himself.

'I think I'll just take a short walk. I won't be long.'

The feel of flint-grey air on his face, sun just retreating over the hills – and the recollection of other years, other family occasions, slowly dissipated. Loose asphalt gritted under his feet while his tears were drained by a gusting wind, promising rain.

Where was Isabel now, he wondered, watching the street-lights gather from dust pink to rusty yellow as the light deepened around them. In her Barbican flat – or playing a concert? In Gloucestershire with her family? Sitting in some restaurant with Karl Hochler? And he felt the past grip his soul more securely than ever, as he headed back beneath the sloping rain.

CHAPTER 19

Thou rememberest
Since once I sat upon a promontory
And heard a mermaid on a dolphin's back
Uttering such dulcet and harmonious breath
That the rude sea grew civil at her song,
And certain stars shot madly from their spheres
To hear the sea-maid's music?

Shakespeare

It was an illness he longed to possess, a disease he had learned to worship. Leszek's nature veered naturally towards excess – he had adored each of his wives, at least temporarily – but his infatuation with Janice went beyond any previous example. He was besotted, sublimely unconscious of public opinion, blinkered to commentary, ridicule, even overt contempt.

'Hormones. It'll never last,' said Lenny, but it did last. Lasted long enough for John McDaniel to feel disquieted, even guilt-stricken.

'Janice is still a guest in my cello section, after all,' he told Felicia.

'Guest, my foot. Fixture, more likely.'

'I feel – responsible for her.'

'She's as responsible as he is. How old is she – twenty-eight, twenty-nine?'

John shook his head. 'I don't think you quite understand how a delicate young girl, innocent of this corrupt profession—'

'My angel, you're more innocent than she is.'

'—could be carried away by the glamour of the conductor mystique. I've heard about this before. Some conductors – especially dramatic, dynamic conductors like Zimetski – simply fascinate young women. They don't see what they're really like, as we do; they're simply swept up and carried away . . . And Leszek's a good conductor – on his day, a very fine conductor indeed.'

'Rubbish. Janice's behaviour gives a whole new meaning to the term job-hunting. Leszek's the one I feel sorry for.'

William also noticed a change in Leszek. Always rangy, he appeared still more sinewy, as if the girl were subtly devouring him; generally tense, he seemed strung to a higher pitch than ever, his eyes more febrile, his performances more driven. He gave an impression of a man obsessed by a physical or psychological hunger, and his performing edge was terrifying.

'Tiger's on the warpath again,' said Pete to William in the pub.

'Warpath? A strong wind could topple him.'

Peter uttered a coarse expression.

'I doubt it,' said William.

'Frustration, d'you think?'

'I could be wrong.'

Pete struck a thespian pose. 'Is love a tender thing? It is too rough, too rude, too boisterous, and it pricks like thorn.'

'Tell me, Pete, do you know any poetry besides Shake-speare?'

'Not poss. Poetry ended with Shakespeare.'

Not that it was the first time Leszek had caused catspaws of gossip to riffle through his orchestra. Angela, the lively harp player, had been taken to dinner; a divorcée in the flutes had been singled out for admiration; and two of the younger second violinists had been invited for an occasional coffee. But his interest in Janice was of a different order altogether.

They met in his office before every session, and came together in every rehearsal break. Gossip pursued the pair like detectives: Eddie's wife spotted them leaving a Knightsbridge restaurant, Felicia met them at the English National Opera, and they were observed countless times heading off at speed in Leszek's red Maserati.

'Find out more,' the tuba-player urged Pete. 'You've got opportunities.'

'I'faith, I can cut a caper. But if I sauntered into Leszek's lair without knocking I'd have a new career as top soprano opening out before me.'

But Pete still heard more than most, though his Shakespearean sense of honour prevented him from distilling it. He heard snatches from Leszek's study, comments in passing: mainly Leszek's, for Janice's voice seemed to dissolve in air. And what he overheard disturbed him profoundly.

What did Leszek mean by agreeing that 'he' was out to get Leszek – that 'this fellow' was a nefarious influence on the rest of the orchestra? Janice's responses were too soft for Pete to discern, but Leszek's paranoia – for such it seemed – troubled him.

'Do you think music more a salvation or a curse?' Leszek asked him one day.

'Save thee, friend, and thy music: dost thou live by thy tabor?' returned Pete, but without any zeal. Leszek slammed his desk drawer shut.

'You are only a fool, like all the others!'

While the more Pete reflected on the situation, the more uneasy he became.

'I'm sure they talk about me,' he told Will.

'I doubt it.'

'He even looks at me oddly.'

'He probably imagines enemies everywhere.'

'Yes, but what if I get the boot?'

'He might sense disapproval,' said William thoughtfully. 'It's an odd thing – so many affairs occur in orchestras – yet each time it's as if such a thing had never happened before.'

William kept his own encounter with Leszek to himself. The night when Leszek had stopped him outside the Barbican to say: 'William Mellor, is it?'

'Yes.'

Leszek's eyes were so socketed, such human hunger in them!

'You have been in love, I am told.'

This time William was silent. Leszek laughed sharply.

'The English! They can speak of anything but love.'

And William, goaded: 'I have, yes.'

'How are you so sure?'

'I knew.'

'Would I know also?'

'Of course.'

Leszek, moving closer: 'And were you completely sane?'

William drew breath. 'No, I can't say that. Perhaps it isn't even possible.'

'You are truthful. I had heard you were truthful.'

'No, only honest. They're not quite the same.'

William watched Leszek depart, shocked by this insight into his conductor's feelings, reminiscence fluttering whitely over his own scars. What an odd attack to make! Desire washed over him, the recollection of being 'not completely sane'. The vivid imprint of Isabel's every movement, the way his ear latched on to her voice in a room crowded with voices, the sensation of burying his face into her wild black hair.

Perhaps you're never sane again, he thought: perhaps once lost we're lost for good. But he recalled Leszek's sunken eyes with unease. Surely there was something obsessional in the business, as if the girl was somehow consuming him . . . He remembered her gaze outmetalling the stage lights, colour slashing the angles of Leszek's face. And he shivered, remembering, as if picked clean to the bone.

CHAPTER 20

A mote it is to trouble the mind's eye.
Shakespeare

Eddie Wellington parked his car and wandered into the house. It was a rather chaotic, rambling old place in Sidcup, over-cushioned but comfortable. His wife Joyce was cushioned and comfortable too, a marvellous cook, a cook whose very security was bound up in her comforting rolls of pastry.

'Is that you, Eddie? . . . You're back early.'

Only because I nixed the pub, thought Eddie, who had in fact prepared her for a later return in case he went out with the boys. He wandered into the kitchen, where he moodily sampled a pastry crumb and got hopelessly in Joyce's way.

'Had a good rehearsal?' she asked, rescuing the pastry. Really, Eddie at forty seemed to grow more and more childlike. His lower lip protruded exactly like young Harold's when distressed.

'Rotten.'

'What was wrong with it? Leszek?'

'Partly Leszek. Partly me. I played rotten.'

'What did Lenny say?'

Odd, thought Joyce, how her attitude towards Lenny had altered. When she'd first come to know Eddie, she had distrusted his comrade-in-arms, but time had mellowed her opinion. It was as if Eddie, burdened with twice the personality of most people, required twice the accustomed level of support . . . Acolytes, students, horn associates, ex-colleagues: all committed in blood to the Duke, who needed the reassurance of their admiration more than most of them would ever imagine.

'Lenny said it was OK.'

'So it must have been OK, right?'

'Not for me. For me, for OK read terminal.'

'What did Leszek say?' she asked.

'Nothing.'

'But surely Leszek would have said if it was bad! He doesn't specialise in consideration where you're concerned, surely?'

'No, but he's got other things on his mind. He's got the hots for this trial cellist and today he conducted like some kind of lunatic . . . Joyce, tell me something. Do you ever just feel that it's all too much?'

'That what's all too much?' inquired Joyce, still intent upon her pastry.

'Being alive. As if the weight of your soul's too heavy to carry. As if you can't bear it – and somehow you have to put it down.'

She looked at him with concern. 'You must have a temperature.'

'It's a perfectly normal question to ask, isn't it? Isn't it? At least think about it – take it seriously!' he cried out, in immortal despair.

Joyce wiped her hands on her apron. 'Now, Eddie, you can't be well. You go lie down and I'll bring you some aspirin. Hardly surprising you catch things, when you're cooped up in the same room as that stressed-out maniac, hour after hour and week after week.'

Eddie looked sadly at her. 'You don't understand. Nobody understands, not even Len.'

Joyce felt a momentary spasm of her old jealousy towards Lenny. Really, they were like boys, she thought, egging each other on, drinking all hours, living on the edge of their adrenalin-spiked nerves. Horn-players! Even at music college it had been the same. Heroes playing out their fantasies against the music – knights errant poised on the breaking point, fighting fear with tomfoolery and alcohol, bragging against the dying of the light.

'So you had a bad day at work,' she said, all sweet reason. 'You can live with that.'

But I can't, he thought. And anyway, doesn't she see it's gone beyond that? A bad day at work! He made one last attempt.

'It's such a struggle; you've no idea. The notes start dancing in front of your eyes – they grow tiny eyes, sometimes, or funny little accents like the Froggies go in for. They dare you on, rushing you to your doom, and then they leave you, still mocking, hanging over an abyss . . . That's what it feels like, sometimes, as if the very notes are laughing at you, for daring to take them on, for daring to care enough. It's a game, don't you see, that you're bound to lose, that nothing can compensate you for losing . . . Then the sweat pours from your fingers and you wonder that you ever loved it, that the sweet surging power ever thrilled you, that the sound ever echoed back to you over the empty seats in the concert-hall . . . That's when I know I can't take it, when nothing but drink can lull the pain. Though there are worse days still when I wish I could die, go out on a high note, clear as a horn call and the high breakers of the sea, simply keel over . . . I even imagine it sometimes: Lenny's thin face looming over mine and the last breaths squeezing, the end of a long illness, and nothing but sweet peace beyond! Do you understand what I'm telling you, or is this just craziness? For God's sake, don't just stare at me!'

'I'm getting the doctor,' said Joyce, stepping towards the telephone, but he caught her wrist.

'No, you're not!'

'Eddie!'

'Mum, can I have a Mars bar?' This from Harold, seven, long eyelashes, sticking-out ears, swinging into the room.

'No,' said Joyce automatically smoothing her apron.

'Why not?' Harold inquired, without affront.

'Because it'll spoil your dinner.'

'It won't. Why will it spoil my dinner? It won't even meet my dinner. It'll be out of my stomach before my dinner ever gets there . . . Dad, my teacher hates me.'

Eddie, who had turned away, halted. One of Harold's preemptive strikes, he thought gloomily. One rotten school report on its way. Joyce was also concerned.

'Don't be silly, darling. Mrs Allinson doesn't hate you.'

'She does,' Harold persisted, still addressing Eddie. 'She picks on me.'

'What, out of the whole class?'

'Out of the whole world! Yesterday it was my homework, today she fussed and yelled at me. Even the other kids are sorry for me. "Whatcha done to Allers?" they asked me in the break. But I haven't done anything, I'm just alive. Being alive is what I done.'

'I've done,' Joyce interposed.

'Doesn't matter, does it? Not when I'm snipped to pieces by a hating teacher.'

'Mrs Allinson—' began Joyce, but Eddie cut in fiercely.

'You just tell your teacher, son, that she can look for a victim somewhere else. Somewhere else is where she can look, because you're not going to take it any more.'

'Eddie!'

'Yeah,' said Harold, hopping from one foot to the other. 'I'll tell her! I'll tell her that from my dad, who's twice as big as her.'

'She, Harold, she.'

'My dad won't have me picked on, not by anybody! Right? Right, Dad?'

Eddie lowered himself to Harold's level. 'Listen to me, Harold. Your whole life – forever! – people will try to cut you down to size, make you seem ordinary, even pick on you just to make themselves feel better. But remember, you don't have to let them. You don't have to let anybody do that to you! If you've got an outsize soul, people are bound to be jealous, even teachers. They'll want to – to contain you, to console themselves for being puny in comparison. But it doesn't matter, don't you see? None of it matters! They can try as much as they like but they can't do it, because, in the ways which matter, you're actually bigger than they are. Think about that, Harold, because if you don't believe in yourself, nobody else will. Do you understand?'

'Yeah. 'Course I do. Dad, when you were seven, were you bigger or smaller than me?'

'Just exactly the same size,' said Eddie, though he couldn't in the least remember.

'Good-oh. I'm going next door to tell Tom.'

Eddie watched him go, while Joyce attacked.

'The things you tell that child! Do you want him to turn into a dysfunctional adult?'

'Yeah. Just like his dad,' said Eddie, and trundled away, feeling strangely better.

Joyce remoulded the pastry, so satisfyingly malleable, between her hands. She was a motherly, sensible woman – as Eddie's women had always tended to be – and she consoled herself with the recollection that most musicians were moody, that the situation with Leszek was difficult, and that a good meal would cheer Eddie amazingly. She wondered if the oven had been pre-heated long enough, and whether the filling might not use a touch more pepper. Her face was pink and her fingers sticky, but she had the cook's creative flair and knew, in her soul, that what she had created was a minor masterpiece.

CHAPTER 21

Peace, peace, Mercutio, peace!
Thou talkest of nothing.
Shakespeare

Olivia, who disapproved of any lack of activity, but Margot's especially, tried to bully her into attending a local Conservative meeting.

'You spend altogether too much time mooching about the garden and reading books you've read before. It's high time you did something useful with your life.'

'I don't care for politics, Mother. I never did.'

'Nonsense. All intelligent people are interested in politics. Your late father simply adored it.'

He hated the Labour Party, thought Margot, but perhaps it amounted to the same thing. And she allowed herself – perhaps hoping for diversion – to be transported to Margaret Thatcher Hall.

'Welcome, ladies and gentlemen, members and guests, friends and allies! And a very special welcome to our own current – and future – Euro MP, Edwin Narbold!'

To sycophantic applause, Edwin Narbold took the floor. He was a stocky, slightly dandified man with a reassuring, if somewhat stagy, northern accent. A white carnation adorned his buttonhole, and his black eyes were badger-bright.

'How delightful it is to see so many of the faithful gathered together,' he began.

Margot almost laughed: the faithful! Yet there might be something in it. Glancing around, she recognised in a dismayed heartbeat the uninspiring backbone of middle England. Bankers and pensioners, salesmen and businessmen, pillars of their churches and staunch, not to say bloody-minded, upholders of local footpaths . . . Some of them might have been unfaithful in their fashion but most lacked imagination enough to stray as far as the nether wing of the Party, or to the rival supermarket in the next village.

Perhaps even infidelity could be a life-affirming act, thought Margot recklessly. Perhaps what William had done was to prove himself still open and alive, open to newness of experience, open even to pain. After all, it's when the gates close that the soul atrophies.

'. . . and Europe matters. Indeed, Europe matters now more than ever. I venture to suggest – I venture to maintain – that Europe will never matter more than it does now. Dear friends and fellow Conservatives, I tell you that now, now is the time for us to communicate with our fellow Europeans, to get our message across! If our message – nay, our mission – fails, then we risk drowning, either in the backwaters of socialism in our own country or in the encroaching tide of socialism from Europe!'

Here Olivia interrupted with applause, carrying some few of the faithful with her, though Margot remained motionless, locked in her inwardness.

Messages. How many times had she failed to communicate with William? How many messages had been returned to sender? We reached a stage in our marriage where we were living by rote: falling into patterns of behaviour, even habits of thought. We both forgot there was any other way, until William was shocked into living again. Life is such a complicated disease!

'. . . but the real European disease – and the real disease here in Britain – is complacency. As Conservatives, we cannot afford to be less than supremely vigilant – against Brussels' complacency, against Brussels' bureaucracy, and, most of all, against Brussels' tragic and terrible – I will say it again – tragic and terrible waste. And let it not be forgotten . . .'

Waste. Of course it was a waste. A waste of a young and emotional girl, as well as a long and honourable marriage. It was my fault too, thought Margot. I'm not stupid; I should have seen. I was busy re-reading my favourite biographies and fretting about whether or not we needed a new fridge-freezer. I was too obsessed with charting the course of my own symptoms to pay attention to William's. If we don't deserve what we have, life will tug it away from us. And love too can be a kind of vengeance.

Sound, waves of sound; Olivia nudged her sharply.

'Really, Margot, you're intolerably rude. Don't you realise that everyone in the room applauded Mr Narbold except for you?'

Margot noticed with a start that the Euro MP was now seated, while the chairman gushed forth her speech of thanks.

'*Such* an honour for our little group . . . so shining an asset in Europe's howling wilderness . . . what I really must call an *awesome* grip of the issues facing us as "true blue" Conservatives . . .'

I didn't mean to seem rude . . . The trouble is that I seem to spend my life wondering, at the moment. As if I were an alien creature dropped in the middle of a strange country, attempting obedience but preternaturally observant of every inconsistency or stupidity.

'— for we all know it can be only a matter of time before he rises to *really fabulous* things in the Party we have the *honour* to call our own.'

And then, while the attention of the audience was elsewhere, the Euro MP suddenly shot Margot a secret smile as if to say: yes, it's all rather a bore, really. And: I'm real, despite the trappings, believe in me.

And because no man had looked at her, really looked at her, since her illness, Margot was too nervous to risk a smile back. But inside, another barrier had silently fallen, and throughout the tedium of the remaining speeches and the ensuing tea ritual the moment stayed with her – warming her, an obscure comfort. It even remained, strange as it seemed, while Olivia drove home.

'– wonderful address, though Hilda was quite diabolical, even worse than usual. The way she accents her words! "In the Party we have the *honour* to call our own"! She imagines it well bred, but really, it makes me feel quite seasick. I shudder to imagine what Mr Narbold must think of us, with a chairman like Hilda, and a building as dingy and down-at-heel as Thatcher Hall.'

There are worse things than illness. I could be blind, as I used to be, or dead. I feel more alive now, in spite of the pain. I feel more alive because of it.

'I don't suppose he noticed.'

'Nonsense,' said Olivia tartly. 'Mr Narbold is far too clever not to have noticed. You mean, I suppose, that he's far too polite to comment.'

'If you like.'

'But I don't like, Margot, not at all. I think it makes us look second-rate, and as Mr Narbold – Edwin, he asked me to call him – as Edwin said, presentation is one of the main issues on which we fall down. Standards, it all comes down to standards. Standards in public life, standards in private life—'

There's a victory in still being here, in spite of everything. The real illness – love – hasn't beaten me yet.

'Margot, I don't believe you're even listening. Really, you get vaguer all the time.'

But there's a natural hierarchy of thoughts . . . Your idea of vagueness is really just a different order of priorities.

'Well, I don't know why you bother to come to meetings if you don't trouble to listen.'

As if it mattered. It doesn't. It doesn't matter.

'Mother,' said Margot, and stopped.

Olivia glanced at her. 'Well, go on. If you wish to apologise, I'm listening.'

I can't apologise for trying to work out my life. Think of me as an adolescent, still feeling my way towards who I am and who I ought to be. One day perhaps I can explain, but not now, not tonight.

'I was – only wondering. Do you think Mr Narbold will keep his seat at the Euro-elections?'

'Well, that's a good question, Margot, a very good question indeed, and I'm glad (and a bit surprised, to tell the truth) that you seem to appreciate its significance. It all hinges, doesn't it, on the support he gets from his agent, his own efforts locally, and what Central Office does (or, more likely) doesn't do. But my own feeling is that the result will prove to be a good deal closer than does our constituency the remotest credit. As I said to Hilda last Tuesday – though she's sadly ignorant, as you know . . .'

Too many speeches, thought Margot, dipping her hand out of the car window. Life was far simpler than politicians imagined. So many manoeuvres and schemes – so many complications – so many restless people, reaching, searching – and it all came down in the end to such simple things. Feelings: the night air in her fingers. The colour of spring.

CHAPTER 22

Feeling so the loss,
I cannot choose but ever weep the friend.
Shakespeare

In the interval of a Barbican concert, John McDaniel sought out young Janice.

'Your trial's been extended again.'

'Thank you.'

'Don't thank me,' returned John, with determination. 'It's not my doing . . . I don't feel it's fair that one trialist should get three times as long as the others. It's not right and it's not according to procedure; and that's exactly what I told Leszek.'

'Of course it isn't,' she said, in soft distress. 'But what can I do? He's put me in a bad position as well.'

John became conscious of a strange, dizzy scent; he shook his head vaguely, saying, 'I know – I know it's hard on you too. Tricky business altogether.'

Upstairs, Angela braced herself to encounter William. Not having been alone with him since Seville, she felt almost embarrassed.

'Angela, hello.'

'I didn't mean to disturb you.'

'You don't disturb me,' said William, closing his book. 'You take me out of myself.'

'Then you don't feel I've stolen your soul?'

'I'm in no position to object on moral grounds.'

Tenderness washed over her. He belonged to someone else – to two other people, perhaps. Yet she couldn't help asking.

'What were you thinking just now?'

'I was thinking,' he said slowly, 'about friendship.'

'In a philosophical sense?'

'Not exactly. About one friend in particular.'

'Anyone I know?'

'I don't think so. He's a cellist in the Orchestra of London. A silver-tongued risk-taking anarchist with a loop of dark hair continually falling over his forehead. Piotr.'

His voice was not like a man recalling a lover – yet not unlike either. A textured voice, baritone to bass.

'You loved him,' she said gently.

'Love – perhaps. What does love mean? He made me laugh. He needed me. He isn't a – strong person. Angela, you mustn't imagine him strong, only clever – and even then, not as clever as he pretends. A gambler, crammed with prejudice and conceit, acidic and untrustworthy but, beneath it all, the most honest soul I ever knew. Yes,' he added, in a lower voice, 'the most honest soul I ever knew, though he'd have hated to admit it.'

'You never see him,' she hazarded, because there was so much sorrow in his voice. 'Did you disagree? Did he – misunderstand – something you said?'

'He thinks I betrayed him, and, in some complicated way, perhaps I did betray him.'

'Which you regret.'

'I couldn't have done otherwise – so how can I, logically, regret it?'

'But it's got nothing to do with logic. You miss him; you probably miss him all the time. And the feeling that you – disappointed him upsets you.'

He put his head in his hands.

'Oh, Will, I'm so sorry,' said Angela feelingly.

They were recalled to play the second half of the concert. In silence they moved down the stairs, and she watched as

William unlatched his cello case. When he touched the instrument he started, then grasped the cello's neck more firmly.

'Is it all right?' she asked.

'Yes. I'd imagined I'd got my other cello here, that's all.'

'Nice playing cello, is it?' asked Angela, admiring the curling grain of the wood.

'You don't play it,' Will said lightly. 'Generally speaking, it plays you.'

CHAPTER 23

So quick bright things come to confusion.
Shakespeare

(from Piotr's private files)

I don't care a fig what anyone says – not even that rather dishy junior minister who's just been caught *in flagrante* with his Peke – this government's gone beyond a joke. What earthly use is there in being an anarchist if anarchy is embedded in the very seat of power? It takes all the delicious perversity out of the exercise.

These reflections – plus a good many doodles – emerged from my attendance at a recent Orchestra of London board meeting. As the newest board member – and I blush to recall how many drinks I purchased in the cause – I feel it my duty to make my presence as obtrusive as possible. And, while I would be the last to boast, I feel obliged to admit that since my appointment the orchestra has succeeded in losing a third of its revenue, all of its reserves, a quarter of its sponsorship, and half its clarinet section. Not a bad little haul for a life of sweat and toil, I think . . . And when you consider that, just prior to my elevation, we'd managed to lose Roger 'Trashy' Ash and almost a quarter of a million pounds, the latter due to embezzlement on a really inspired scale, the damage could be said to be complete.

Indeed, so diabolical was our financial state that informed opinion expected every week to read of our demise, probably in the small print at the back of the *Evening Standard*.

(England collapse to 53 for 8 . . . Orchestra of London office stormed by bailiffs.) Things had reached such a pass that the Royal Sinfonia and the other beasts of the jungle spent most of their waking hours eyeing up our assets and wondering how best to spend the monies soon to be released by our disbandment. However, what these doomsayers failed to recall was that I, Piotr, was now, if not at the helm, jolly near it – and that the Musicians' Union, by its very nature, is largely composed of good-hearted mugs.

We negotiated our first union loan shortly after my arrival in February, and our second following our (fiscally disastrous) Japanese tour. The lawyers were dubious, and the chairman edgy, but my view was that if the debts of whole shards of Latin America could be written off, then our piddling little loan could probably be written off as well. If push came to shove, I remember urging – though my reception was far from enthusiastic – we could all busk, while Karl Hochler made himself useful passing round the hat.

Still, no one knew better than yours, the undersigned, that we were in trouble, if not in terminal decline, and it added a little frisson to my loneliness to think that I might soon be retiring to one of those bijou cardboard residences near Waterloo – assuming of course that I failed to drink myself to death before the blow fell.

Since William left me – not that we were ever together except in a deeply spiritual sense – my loneliness reached such epic proportions that I started giving the matter serious consideration. Until the middle of a film session, in between wiggling the headphones on and off the bean, I reached an earth-shattering decision, and this was it. You jolly well can buy love, and not only at London's more amusing gay bars. You can buy a dog.

Dogs were specifically created, it seems to me, in support of this thesis. You toddle along to any self-respecting dogs' home, eye up the talent, and, for the most modest of outlays, walk away with the surest love on earth. Four legs good, two legs bad, was my conclusion, while the conductor of the day just failed to marry his beat with the clicks on the soundtrack . . . And on our next parole I duly presented myself at Battersea, wearing a pink-and-yellow tie calculated to stir all but the most balanced canine into a frenzy.

I ignored the puppies on principle. Youth is overrated in practically every respect, and puppies never get left on the shelf. Anyway, I didn't see myself with a winsome puppy, all warm tongue and wiggles and no self-respect; what I wanted was a dog, a real dog, and preferably a dog on death row. Possibly, with the future of the orchestra in the balance, I felt a certain kinship there.

There was no immediate shortage of no-hopers at Battersea. There was a homicidal near-Alsatian and a suicidal Pomeranian, a terrier mix with battle scars and a Labrador that singlehandedly renewed my faith in ghosts. But none of these specimens of man's inhumanity to dog spoke to the inner Piotr, and I was turning towards those still on the appeals bench when I spotted the thinnest Irish setter I'd ever seen. He had steady gold-brown eyes and a burnished auburn coat which had been made to last several seasons too long. There was a certain constraint about him; he had the air of a Bastille aristocrat waiting for the next tumbril.

'My dog, I believe,' said the Scarlet Pimpernel.

The grubby elf at my side replied, 'Wot, the red one on the end?'

'*Exactement*. The Irish setter.'

'Bru-us, 'is name is. 'E 'asn't been well.'

'And nor would you be, my good peanut,' I observed, 'in a cage the size of a refrigerator, surrounded by the pong of dog and an emotionally disturbed Alsatian cross. Wheel him out. Is he a widower or an orphan?'

''E was found off the M25. 'E's 'ad stomac-tic trouble.'

'Off his Pedigree Chum, eh?'

'I think 'e's all ri' now.'

Once I was able to see him steadily and see him whole, the

specimen of doggedness under discussion was terrifyingly thin. You could watch him ventilate through his ribcage and his pins had diameters like cocktail-sticks. When I patted him he almost fell over, though of course that might have been shock.

'I'm not calling him Brutus, mind,' I warned the sprite.

'We allus 'ave one called Bru-us.'

'Well, this isn't it. Your casting agent will simply have to look elsewhere. The dog under advertisement will be known to intimates as Anton, after Chekhov.'

'Check-off ant-on?' she inquired doubtfully. 'Well, 'e's your dog. I'll jus' give 'im a li-il brush for you.'

Anton submitted to her attentions with a wonderful air of resignation. I felt more peaceful just looking at him, at his noble head and gloriously deep-sunken eyes. Negotiations concluded, I tipped the elf, warning her, perhaps unnecessarily, not to spend it on drink. I was already leading Anton to the car when I stopped in shock, remembering.

It had been William's fantasy to own an Irish setter. I had blinking well gone out and bought William's dog.

A gigantic spurt of antic rage rose up inside me, misery for every dog I'd left behind, sorrow for every loving, trusting creature left caged by life – and, most of all, sorrow for William. Remembering, I was tornadoed by a lethal swirl of frustration and regret. If only I'd held my tongue about that business in Stockholm! If only Will possessed the customary, cavalier attitude towards his bit on the side! If only I'd never met him, never learned to play the cello, never been catapulted – red, crumpled and screaming – into such a petty, paltry, scurvy and disastrous world!

Grief unspun me in that car park, and with it a killing, ruinous rage. The recollection of William's quizzical irony, his lifted eyebrow, that sidelong amusement in his deep dark eyes — And if William had been there in that moment, I think I could have murdered him – for having been my friend as much as for leaving me, for holding out his friendship and then taking it away. My only father, my only brother –and if he'd been there in that moment with his strong cellist's hands and his crazy human eyes I'd have ended his misery and mine there and then: roll the credits, sound the synthesizer, put the kettle on, and marvellous acting darling but I still don't understand the motivation of the scrawny little fellow with the Russian name.

Love is a debilitating disease. Better off out of it, better off growing senile in docile conformity, taking note of government health warnings and slowing down before traffic junctions – complacent against the dying of the light, unless it might occasion a stoppage of play at Lord's.

Gradually I became aware again of earthly noises: commuter trains, the deep-fry sizzle of passing wheels on asphalt. The car park returned to its normal dimensions, my blood pressure evened out; and I became aware that I was being observed by a quietly attentive canine. Anton, *né* Brutus. My dog.

I invited Anton on to the back seat, which he inspected, seeming to feel that the tumbril was well up to standard. His enormous eyes – not even Will's eyes could be as large as his – examined me speculatively, as if wondering whether I had it in me to do a good clean job of it. He moved his tail sideways – the word wagged would give quite the wrong impression – when I stretched out my hand. I handed him two dog biscuits, of which he sampled one.

'You're a cheap date,' I told him, noticing the dark red sheen on his coat. 'Stomactic trouble,' the sprite had confided; meaning that we had our work cut out inspiriting the gastric juices. Well, I could live with that. The day after the booze-up before, I'd been known to experience stomactic trouble myself.

Anton looked trustfully up at me. You can buy love, I thought; I thought, that basket's too small for his spindly legs. And I drove the dog home.

CHAPTER 24

O day and night, but this is wondrous strange!
Shakespeare

Eddie, for some reason, felt restless and uneasy. Of course, he was now past forty, and he'd read that men in their forties generally suffer career crises and marital upheavals (this from nosing through his wife's magazines in the bath). However, search though he might, he could find nothing in his feelings that equated to anything so apparently normal, almost predictable, as a mid-life crisis.

He still adored music; he loved playing the horn; the orchestra was still his life. Nor did he seem to fit into any of the neat categories dissected by the omniscient editors of *Women's Wednesday*. He doubted whether he was the genesis of such articles as 'Has your man got a wandering eye?' or 'Four easy ways to deal with your partner's bad temper'. While he was confident that he was not personally responsible for 'Lotharios – and why we love them', or 'Women's sexual empowerment – stand up for *your* rights'. He didn't even lust after young women – or no more than he always had done (in the flesh he found them vaguely alarming). His marriage seemed, to him at least, to be just fine. His attempts to seek his wife Joyce's advice on the matter only startled her.

'What do you mean, am I happy? Happy in our marriage?'

'Well, are you?'

'Why, aren't you happy, Eddie?'

''Course I am. I just feel . . .'

'What do you feel?'

'I don't know what I feel!' His doggedness troubled Joyce – so many scandals, so many tales! Leszek and that young second violinist, the leader and that piccolo player – why, even Lenny . . . Eddie had once told her (though he'd later derided it as 'practically nothing') that Lenny had spent every night on one trip with a voluptuous extra trombone. Joyce had stayed awake marvelling that Lenny, who could scarcely tolerate most women, could have managed such a feat.

Perhaps, thought Eddie, escaping to his tool shed, it was really only Leszek, Leszek's baleful influence, Leszek's multi-coloured eyes swivelling towards him like the muzzles of separate guns. Recently he'd felt afraid not only of Leszek's firepower but of Leszek's weakness. There's nothing more dangerous than weakness, he realised, in sudden revelation. You can appeal to strength, but to weakness even appeals are terrifying.

That there was 'something wrong' with Leszek, that there had been something wrong since Spain, did not admit of a doubt. Some said he was back on cocaine, some said it was neurosis, plain and simple – and some people blamed the trial cellist, young Janice.

Rumours about Leszek and Janice had started in Spain, and had threaded through the orchestra the way rumours always did, a complicated ritual of implication, suggestion, and doubtful coincidence. She was holding out on him . . . She was playing him along to get the job . . . She had submitted in Spain, but later rejected him . . . All that was certain was that Leszek seemed still nervier when she was absent, and that they had been seen talking – he gesticulating, the girl with that fluid colour – at the back of the Barcelona concert-hall.

And it was certain too that her trial had been extended again against John McDaniel's fairest judgement, and that the chances of anyone else succeeding to the cello vacancy were looking increasingly slender. Gossip observed acidly that it wouldn't be the first time a good-looking player had side-slept her way into a major orchestra . . . And besides, with Leszek's record, who could really be surprised?

But Eddie only knew that Leszek, having gone through a few weeks of unusual calm, was firing again like a bush fire in high wind. He seemed to delight in punishing Eddie, in mocking his high-flown phrasing, his passionate, billowing sound. And Shostakovich Tenth was on the Promenade programme that night. Performing his favourite Shostakovich under Leszek would be lethal; the struggle between his love and his great sweeping hate would completely undo him. It had been quite bad enough in the rehearsal, with his soul swelling against Leszek's ever-tightening musical leash. In concert . . .

At the recollection of that debilitating dress rehearsal, Eddie felt so restless that he raided his wife's bathroom cabinet. Didn't Joyce used to keep something – beta-blockers, Valium, Rest-in-peace Herbal Remedy – on the top shelf? He searched with growing panic, upsetting a conglomeration of unused hair treatments.

'What exactly are you looking for, Eddie?' asked Joyce from outside.

'Toothpaste,' Eddie replied, sulky as a child because what he wanted wasn't there.

That evening, as the orchestra tuned up around him, Eddie found his breath ominously shortening. He glared at his music, pugnacious as if it had challenged him.

'I can play the horn.'

'Whazzat?' inquired Lenny, wiping his keys.

'Boiling hot tonight,' replied Eddie.

'It is and all.'

Janice smiled over at him from the cellos – a curiously intent smile; a smile that quickened the pulsebeat in Eddie's stocky neck. It was as if – as if there was a line of heat swelling the air between them. Flu, he thought morosely; most likely he was getting the flu. Then dizziness overruled.

Eddie lowered his head between his legs. The floor was unexpectedly dirty, discoloured in the places where generations of horn players had emptied their horns. He tried to focus on the blotches, the swirl of woodgrain under the chair . . . She had golden eyes, Janice; tiger's eyes, with endless black pits in their centres . . . I can play the horn, I can. I can play the horn.

Lenny's voice, from a distance: 'What's up, Duke? You lost something?'

Only my nerve.

'Stone me. Look at young Janice's outfit. Might as well be a swimsuit.' This from Ian, the youthfully lascivious third horn. Eddie didn't look up. I can; I can. Light washing over him; his whole consciousness glittering with light. He sat up shakily.

'I don't care much for young Janice.' Lenny to Ian.

'You got no eyes, boy, is your trouble.'

Watch me, listen to me. I'm full of light.

'You all right, Duke? You look a bit green around the gills.'

Leszek ascending the platform with his coiled and feline stride. Seventeen, eighteen, nineteen . . . Light closing over him, Eddie was counting the rows down the left-hand side. The Emperor had arrived, the only question now was who would be thrown to the lions . . . Twenty-five, twenty-six, twenty-seven . . . A woman in row twenty-eight held her head on one side exactly as Eddie's mother had used to – inquisitive, alert to his every misdeed . . .

Mother: Watch me, listen. I am swimming in light.

Leszek's eyes scoured his troops, he lifted his hand, and then, like God, like Michelangelo, the music crashed out.

Eddie's gently perspiring fingers worked the keys, the breath from his great cavernous chest subtly modulating the volume. True, he had almost lost it, but now he was safe, cradled by the rushing glory of the music. Waves parted over his head; he gulped down deep breaths of clear sea air. He closed his eyes and it was the Toadster again; it was spring again; he could play the horn.

CHAPTER 25

Here in her hairs
The painter plays the spider and hath woven
A golden mesh t'entrap the hearts of men.

Shakespeare

The Shostakovich had blown the ill weather away. Left behind was a mild and dreamy night with a zephyr blowing, a night coquettish enough to masquerade as evening. Half the flower boxes behind the Royal Albert Hall were still in bloom; and Janice was leaning back beside the stage door, waiting for Leszek.

''Night, Janice!'

'Now Jan, don't practise all night.'

'See you. Good night, good night!'

They'd forgotten she was only on trial; they'd forgotten she was still there only because Leszek had insisted she must be. The orchestra, in its casual, thoughtless way, had decided that she belonged.

Pete sauntered by with a nod, Felicia with neat short steps, making no judgements, awaiting events. Eddie and Lenny left in fervent discussion, Lenny frowning while the Duke expostulated. Then Leszek appeared, and whirled her towards his Maserati.

Since Spain, Janice had seen many sides of Leszek – the quixotic raconteur, the steely career-conductor – but she had never experienced quite this mood of ferocious calm. His nostrils looked chiselled into his face, his cheekbones scalped his narrow skull.

'Where are we going?' she asked, but perhaps she knew the answer; perhaps his silence was all the answer she needed – that and his hand, lithe and hot, on hers.

Leszek was reasoning – with himself, against himself. Why should he be afraid of something so long in preparation, so cogently rational, so obscurely recognised? He was in love, and there was no one in his life left to betray. With Shostakovich still singing in his blood, what stirred this accusation in his heart? Tonight, he thought, and the quiescence of her hand under his reinforced his certainty.

They drew up in front of Leszek's house with a squealing of brakes, startling a thin-skinned man walking a dachshund across the road. Leszek's was a cream-coloured row residence, with lights left on all day because of nerves about burglars. Even from outside the front room looked suffused in rose, the underside of a seashell. He led her in, his arm punishing her slender wrist.

'Come.' It was the first word he had spoken. He turned her head towards him, admiring her corruptible line of profile, the delicate decadence of her lips. She had Mikhail's eyes, and Mikhail's trick of slowly lifting her curtain of eyelashes; above all, she had Mikhail's slow-burning smile. Perhaps she was Mikhail's ghost, come back to taunt him. Yes – Mikhail had died in Poland, and this strange alien creature had hijacked his passing soul.

'Janice,' he said, stressing the second syllable. He took her hand, turning it over as if to reassure himself of her reality, tracking the fine network of veins across her wrist. She smelled of honeysuckle, a soft curling scent that rose from the back of her ear, the flesh below her neck. There was nothing contrived about it: intoxication curved from the centre of her bones. He guided her on to the floor.

'Your pulse is charging like a trumpet section,' he whispered. 'I told you once that you were not crazy enough to play Schumann. Tonight, tonight I will make you crazy enough.'

His hand slipped up her thigh, unlocking the buttons of her skirt. His hair brushed her neck on its way to her throat, lips skidding to where skin metamorphosed into breast. In his temples was a fisting like an imprisoned creature, and a voice, not hers, resounded through his brain. And inside him an irresistible imperative, inevitable as the waving of the sea.

His last doubts rolled effortlessly back against the tantalising sensuousness of her skin under his fingers. And, for all her passivity, perhaps she felt the same, for she clasped her parted lips on to his, tasting the faint sweat that had gathered there during the concert, the drive, the waiting. Blood rushing through him, sure as a command: Come, come.

'Wait for me,' she whispered, as she slipped down the hall, and he paced as he waited, Satan's dance snaking his veins.

He saw her first some minutes later, watching him from inside the darkened hall, and he wondered for an eerie moment how long she had been there. He'd never seen Janice in a silky cream nightshirt, her white-gold hair furred across her shoulders. She was leaning motionless against the wall, arms behind her back, breasts pushing against the cream, with a curiously opaque look in her eyes.

As he switched off the lamp, the only light was reflected from her hair. She bloomed in his arms and he could have cried out from astonishment at the combination of softness, creaminess, warmth. He heard bells chime on the landing, a methodical bass accompaniment to a thousand brasher heartbeats. Perhaps death felt like this, he thought – and then he flew.

CHAPTER 26

Love is merely a madness, and I tell you deserves as
well a dark house and a whip as madmen do: and the
reason why they are not so punished and cured is, that
the lunacy is so ordinary that the whippers are in love
too . . .

Shakespeare

(from Isabel's diaries)

It's been months since I've written, months since I could bear
to. Instead I've been drifting, carried onwards by an invisible
current, all purpose torn away.

The orchestra tours Japan almost every year, but this time
memory dusted over everything like dry ice. We pretended it
didn't; we rehearsed, performed, went for meals and made
jokes, but the malaise still gripped us, a disease we couldn't
shake off.

It was especially bad for me – not that Mirabel's death hit
me the hardest, but because, in addition to having been her last
tour, that Far East trip was the last that I shared with William. I
kept remembering – the hall in Tokyo where he'd kissed me,
the Kyoto street where we'd wandered late one night – I
couldn't believe it still existed. It's as if I secretly think (and this
is madly illogical) that places I leave behind dissolve into some
form of suspended existence – or into no existence at all. In
Kyoto I was confronted with reality: that the street that had
disappeared for me that soft autumn night could still thrive
under such different conditions this July.

There was the same smell of fresh fish and dried seaweed, the same relentless businessmen and casual tourists, the same crush of motorbikes and passing traffic. The restaurant remained as well, and was open, but I couldn't go in. Suddenly it was too much: that it was still there when William wasn't.

In Osaka, where we stayed in the same hotel, the strain was almost unendurable. I don't think any of us could forget the party, admittedly rather a zany one, where Mirabel had sung that silly 'Desperado' song, acting out the verses with a cardboard sombrero and an umbrella for a gun. . . Unequal to confronting those particular memories, we left the hotel in small defiant groups, with false laughter, beer and bravado on all sides.

That party was the last time I remember talking to Mirabel.

'After Hong Kong, I'm going on to Aussie-land,' she'd told me. 'And I may never come back, so don't say I never warned you. I may curl up my toes on Bondi Beach and never come back again. It's either that, to be honest, or shooting Henry. What do you think, Isabel? Would I have a chance at principal horn if I was to shoot old Henry?'

Henry too I remembered, Henry as he'd been before the crash: heavy, blokeish, almost stolid – the longest-established principal horn in London. The contrast between Henry then and Henry now – paunchy, irascible, and very nearly alcoholic – was almost too painful to contemplate.

'We've gone to pieces,' I said to Caroline recently, when I went to inspect the baby. (It was a baby much like other babies: plump, smug and manipulative.)

'These funding troubles are very worrying,' agreed Caroline, with all the complacency with which she would have deplored the latest European dispute, or some instance in Tulse Hill where Gas Explosion Maims Six.

Worrying! I wanted to tell her, it's *Götterdämmerung*, the twilight of the orchestral gods. This time next year there may not be any orchestra to be worried about. Bang will go your precious maternity rights, bang will go your husband's job in the first violins. It won't be a Big Bang, admittedly – a gust of wind on the Thames and another orchestra sinks – but it'll be the end nonetheless, with the ripples widening outwards till the tide comes in.

The trouble had started with the discovery of that fraudster in accounts, but it's gone much deeper since. A clear case of embezzlement, decreed the court, but somehow the money was never recovered. Some of it was spent, some never traced, and some went to pay the lawyers. There remained too a deep reservoir of ill-feeling surrounding Karl's abrupt dethronement of Roger Ash. Some members took a long time to get over it, and some never got over it at all.

The reviews we achieved under Roger's immediate replacements were terrible. ('The way the Orchestra of London played last night, they were a disgrace to the title of orchestra, and a disgrace to the name of London.') After *that* particular concert – and mind, I'm not saying we hadn't deserved it – at least one recording contract was cancelled overnight.

The truth is that an orchestra can play tolerably even when the conductor's pretty poor. An orchestra can even play tolerably, given corporate determination and really herculean work from the principals, when the conducting on offer is unspeakable. But this redeeming spirit can't manifest itself when the will is lacking, and it was frighteningly lacking in the Orchestra of London.

There were disagreements on the board and apathy among the troops; the leader was off doing his celebrated impersonation of an international soloist and our schedules were gummed up with commercial rubbish . . . Of course, I was low anyway, had been low ever since running into William at the Barbican.

By the time Karl arrived that afternoon, I felt pummelled, reckless with unhappiness. I wanted to be comforted, gathered up somehow – but Karl isn't the comforting sort. He kissed me casually, his eyes approving my new jacket. Then he heard Dvořák from the concert-hall, and the competitor in him, never completely dormant, stirred to life.

'One moment,' he said. 'That must be Zimetski rehearsing the Sinfonia for tonight. If you have no objection, I would like to hear the start of this rehearsal.'

'I'd rather not,' I said.

Karl is naturally, perhaps even unnaturally, courteous, but at this a sharp little frown dissected his flat brow.

'Why not, so particularly?'

Then he remembered, and his smile made me almost hate him.

'Still, my dear?' he asked softly. 'But this is exquisite. It very nearly renews my faith in fidelity.'

It was on the tip of my tongue to tell him that he was wrong, that it was nothing to do with William, but after what had just happened, the idea of watching him play was intolerable. That I would never again run my fingers through his thick hair, never curl my hands around his rich, fleshy shoulders, never see him smiling down at me – this was painful enough without being forced to watch him play, with all the separateness that being in an audience automatically entails.

As so often, the flicker of antagonism between us seemed to excite Karl. Sometimes I feel his fascination for me springs from dislike – or because he can't reach me, not completely, as if William himself is part of my attraction for him, as perhaps he always was.

Karl pinned my arm to his side.

'Come,' he said. 'I find I have lost interest in this rehearsal. Besides, I have heard Zimetski's Dvořák before, and he rushes in a way I cannot bear.'

'You're hurting.'

'Of course. It is partly what you enjoy, and partly what you deserve.'

It was one of those times when things snap into focus, when even the smallest occurrences take on an almost symbolic importance. There was a woman in an ill-fitting raincoat feeding the ducks. They snapped at her bread and fled, bickering over the biggest nuggets, and I found myself thinking: what gratification does she get from feeding them? What do they give her that people don't? — Precious little, that was certain. What depths of loneliness there seemed in that little being enough! At that moment there seemed no limit to human loneliness. It encompassed the entire Barbican, the entire world.

We'd just reached the exit when we encountered the most enchanting girl I've ever seen.

She had exquisitely light brown eyes combined with a haloed mass of waves and a complexion so startlingly perfect that she left it innocent of assistance. She made me feel worn and effortful, too cleverly made-up, too expensively dressed. I couldn't have been more than six or eight years her senior, but suddenly my age ached on my shoulders, eyeshadow weighed down my eyes, gravity itself bore down on me.

'Has the rehearsal started?' she asked.

'Only just,' I responded, noticing the Royal Sinfonia touring stickers on her cello case. So – one of William's new colleagues. Someone who could talk to him, someone whose acquaintance with him could have only just begun. What a chance! I thought, and felt crazily, madly jealous of her. Just to be in the same cello section as William seemed reason for envy.

'What a lovely creature,' I murmured, as Karl lit his cigar. But she was too fresh for Karl – I know his taste, and a certain decadence is prerequisite. And William's taste? I wondered, before deciding that the question was absurd. William had suffered enough guilt to last him forever.

It was a stormy evening, in every sense. The wind banged against Karl's windows most of the night, the thunder drummed dustily –finally the rain came.

I first woke at three a.m., sticky with brandy and saliva and aching all over, but still with that athletic feeling of repletion Karl never fails to invoke in me. He was naked, curled noiselessly asleep in the half-light with his Rolex still on his wrist, the light from the bathroom accentuating the thin, taut scar across his abdomen.

His flat is enormous, three times the size of mine, and, unable to get back to sleep, I wandered around it, listening to rain careering down the windowpanes.

Karl's decor is modernist and masculine, featuring bold lines, angled chrome and soft dark leather. He has a few experimental paintings, each bought on a hunch that the artist will eventually justify his faith, though they never quite seem to . . . There's one emphatically textured painting that looks like a nightmare alongside a weirdly convoluted horse composed entirely of bits of wire. His favourite, however, is a small black marble sculpture on a pedestal in his hallway.

The first time I saw the piece I thought it horrible, but the longer I've known it the more it appeals to me. A girl in torn Spanish dress (Carmen?) lies provocatively on the ground, with a bull bearing down on her.

The bull is superb, not classical exactly, but not stylised either. He's a coiled, electrifying spring of power and ego, erupting from out of the earth he pounds. Beside him the girl looks tiny, alien and vulnerable but, head thrown back, passionately submissive to her fate. I forget the name of the artist, but the sculpture never fails to send little shivers down me. I've even dreamed about it, feeling as if fate – or Karl – is bearing down upon me in the last seconds of my life.

In one of the spare bedrooms Karl keeps what it amuses him to call his 'instruments of torture'. I used to find something perverse in Karl's fantasies – but there's something innately truthful about them as well. Perhaps other women are different (some of them must be) but Karl's ideas of domination don't worry me. I don't see any contradiction in regarding myself the equal of any man, while at the same time absorbing the limits of their sexual force – and even enjoying the surrender of the will.

Perhaps that's what Karl first saw in me, across the serried ranks of the orchestra: a silent cry of Hurt me, Take me. There must be something elemental here that scientists haven't located, perhaps haven't even imagined: the wavelength on which can be heard the cry of the seeking soul. Take me, I'm lonely. Hurt me, I don't care. Answer me – you know I'll match the jagged pieces of your long-since-broken heart.

Perhaps William gave me an inkling that intense sexuality doesn't need that spark of sadism and brinkmanship, that feeling could be sufficient excitement on its own. But William had faded too quickly, too sadly, leaving only an ache behind.

I fingered the straps of one of Karl's gadgets, thinking: William would consider it obscene, strapping me into this thing. Tiredness was beginning to wash over me, rain still hissing down the windows. Then I heard footsteps, and turned to see Karl enter, tying his purple silk dressing gown. We stared at each other, as shocked as strangers.

'What are you doing in here on your own?'

'Thinking.'

'What, does nothing tire you?' he inquired humorously.

'Oh, yes, I'm tired. I'm too tired to sleep.'

He ran his finger impersonally down the curve of my breast, asking, 'Do you want a drink? I'm having one.'

'No. Thank you.'

And what I want you can't give me. Instead it's a process of patching the cloth, the gaps breaching wider with every break, until at last the garment will take no more. Some day, I knew, he would notice the wear in the silk and throw me away – perhaps the surprising part was that it hadn't happened already.

Karl paused at the door.

'Isabel. Is there something you wish to say?'

No, I wanted to tell him, nothing at all, but I managed an automatic smile instead. He wouldn't notice, I thought – but I'd misjudged the elliptical, almost morbid nature of his sensitivities. Karl's smile suddenly tautened, flattening against his skull. He pulled me close enough to smell the brandy on his breath.

'He hates you now, you know,' he said, and the contrast between the raw power of his muscles and his conversational tone was surreal. 'That is the kind of man he is, this William. The very idea of your body now revolts him – the memory of your skin, your smell . . . Why do you pretend, when you know in your soul that he hates you?'

'I don't think of him,' I lied. 'Let me go!'

'Oh, I will – when I am ready. You tried to escape before, if you remember.'

Karl reached past me to put the tape on, the one that always makes him crazy, and I used this half-chance to slip from his grasp and down the hall. I knew that I couldn't win – the security system was on for a start – but still I ran, instinctively, hoping to reach the door before him.

But Karl was twice as fast, his breathing more elastic. He caught me at the door, whirled me around to face him, and hit me shockingly hard. He'd never struck me before; it was alien to his usual control mechanisms – even alien to his character – and it appalled me. My hand flew uselessly to the salty blood on the side of my mouth, while Karl dragged me unresisting on to the floor. Careless of hurt, careless of everything except his sudden, startling fury, he reared up, wrenching my arms backwards, teeth tearing at my shoulder, my breast, his body pushing into mine. He seemed impelled by something beyond pleasure – driven by some frustration I didn't understand – or only by his instinct to possess.

And I admit: part of me was glad to have reached him, to have goaded him into reaction. I also recognised his anger as punishment: for attempting some level of control, and for what I had been secretly thinking – about him, about William. It was as if he guessed everything, and suddenly couldn't bear it, had somehow to pound the thoughts from my body – as, perhaps, I'd even wanted him to.

Karl took me once more later that night, though by then even his stamina must have been almost exhausted. And the shadows on his face frightened me, as if there was something he too didn't completely understand.

*

At the beginning of May the Faversham sponsorship collapsed, spiralling the orchestra management into chaos. The record company's desertion had been worrying enough, but the withdrawal of Faversham, our mainstay, was still worse. There are always recording companies, said the knowledgeable gloomily, but sponsors like that come along only once a generation.

I overheard Piotr saying, 'I give us four years, five at the outside,' and knew that it was true.

A divide fissured the players – between those who refused to recognise our disintegration and those who, fitfully, fretfully, saw all too well. There were rumours about poachings: some of the wind players were supposed to have been approached by other orchestras. Resignation was in the air, but nobody resigned – or perhaps the rumours were only straws in the wind and no one had actually been offered anything.

It was three months since William had left, but Piotr still avoided me. I'd become accustomed to hearing his news third-hand. ('Piotr went off like a blinking Exocet in the board meeting. Doesn't half speak well, for a Ruskie.' 'Like all gays, he's a combination of sensitiveness and over-sensitivity, nerves and neurosis.' 'Piotr maintains his deceased lizard was a better conductor, but hell, he says that about everybody.' 'Heard about Piotr? Drink-driving. Banned, the silly bugger.')

I knew what the matter was, but the recollection of the New Year embarrassed us both. If he happened to catch my eye (and depending on whim) he would either roll his eyes, lift up his head with ineffable disdain, or stare stonily through me, with a miserable and unnerving hatred.

While I struggled with his behaviour, even agonised over it, our acquaintances inundated me with advice.

'Ignore him, he'll come round. You're two professional people, after all . . . You should give as good as you get; there's a cruel streak in Piotr, and he only respects courage . . . I think he hates women/is jealous of your impact on William/can't deal with latent feelings about his mother (his sexuality, his defunct lizards). That's what I think, anyway, you can take it or leave it.'

Which was all, however perceptive, of little use. So, being miserable and stung by Karl, I tried what I could. I called Piotr, and was stonewalled into hanging up. I wrote him a note, passionate with misspellings: he never mentioned it. I waylaid him in the corridors of the Festival Hall, but Piotr was eel-like and well-practised at escape.

'I have to talk to you,' I begged him.

'Sorry, state business in the nearest loo.'

'I'm serious!'

'But I'm not. Do you understand nothing?'

And after this, a sudden gust of fury, urgent yet still sardonic.

'Can't you accept that someone might detest you? Does the vote of confidence have to be unanimous? Believe me, there's nothing you can say – nothing! – that will make the remotest difference to me. I don't want to talk to you. I don't want to see you. If it was possible to murder you without causing you physical pain – for I am a tranquil, peaceful soul at heart – I would blissfully murder you, just to save myself the – the glissando of misery that seeing you always gives me! Can't you grasp how hopeless it is? We'll never be friends again – if, in fact, we ever were, if that wasn't always an illusion of your lurkingly sentimental female brain.'

'You told me once—'

'Then consider it unsaid, unspoken and unsung. Whatever it was, I take it back. Can I make it any plainer? You're wasting time and charm on yours, the undersigned. You're barking up a tree without a squirrel in it. You couldn't chuck a brick in this band without hitting someone with more sympathy for you than I've got. My advice to you is to give up, resign, call it a day, and throw in the towel. And after that, sod off.'

I'd hated Piotr for that, hated him with a fervour he would probably have appreciated, for anything full-throated made its way effortlessly into Piotr's heart, which was always softer than he pretended. Indeed, the only human creature to have found his way there was William, and in that lay the essence of his misery. By leaving me, Will had not only rejected the orchestra, he had rejected Piotr – by leaving me, he had left us both. And Piotr, who couldn't blame William, couldn't forgive me.

Piotr's tongue, never gentle, became more asp-like, and his presence on the board became an embarrassment. He was intolerable in rehearsals and insatiable in his private life; his leather-thin Paganinian figure (for he stressed black even more than previously) contrasted ever more sharply with his greenish pallor and Rasputin eyes. Although his hair was still midnight, he looked older than his thirty-seven years, and his long, nervous hands – very thin, very white, even whiter than his face – moved with a different rhythm somehow. There was a looseness about him, a disjointedness, almost a lack of co-ordination. As if he was always partly drunk, drunk on words, or music – or vodka, because in mistaken tribute to his Slavic ancestry, Piotr was reported to have developed a preference for that beverage.

Yet my fellow feeling for Piotr remained so strong that, after seeing William in the Barbican, I couldn't help telling him. We were fishing our instruments out of the storage area.

'I saw him yesterday,' I said.

Piotr's mouth twisted.

'Oh good,' he said savagely. 'I *am* pleased for you. That'll set him back nicely.'

'I think he – understands.'

'Of course he understands, woman! From the very beginning, he was the only one who saw clearly. God's nightshirt, when didn't he understand?'

'You know you can be heard, Piotr, clear down the hall,' reported Lucy with pleasure.

Once I'd calmed down, I wrote to Piotr again. I don't pretend to be a saint, but anger won't lodge in me; no, it passes through like a hailstorm, melts away and vanishes. I knew it wouldn't do any good, but I couldn't help writing; I knew it wouldn't make any difference, except to my own feelings – but perhaps that alone was worth something. I later realised that I loved Piotr because of William, because William had loved him. It was as if Piotr was partly William's son, and I had to love him, for being William's.

'Dear Piotr,' I wrote, 'your unhappiness eats at me also. Don't punish me. I'm sorry I hurt you. Isabel.'

Then something James Hilton wrote came back to me. 'If you forgive people long enough, you belong to them and they to you, whether either person likes it or not – squatter's rights of the heart.'

I thought, perhaps that's what he's afraid of – of being forgiven. And, in the end, I never sent it.

CHAPTER 27

You cannot call it love. For at your age
The heyday of the blood is tame; it's humble,
And waits upon the judgement; and what judgement
Would step from this to this?

Shakespeare

It was the beginning of August when Sam came. It struck William how long it had been since they'd been alone together, without the paraphernalia of children, spouses, dogs. Lacking the comforting ritual of such family gatherings, his son seemed to him like a young and rather judgemental stranger.

Sam, for his part, glanced around the front room, noting the spareness of it, its spartan, unlived-in quality. His father had a cleaning service, he knew; but did he tour so much that he lived nowhere?

'How are you, Dad?' he asked, once they were settled.

'Well enough,' said William.

'Been away, have you?'

'I turned down the Swiss trip, but I was in Spain for a week in May.'

Where I disgraced myself with a harpist called Angela, he thought, with a wave of self-disgust. And yet, at the time, he had thought it healing. Her slight, swift body, slender fingers in his hair . . . He pushed the recollection away.

'The house is awfully – tidy,' Sam observed.

'An agency. They do a good job.'

'Almost too tidy . . . Dad, I came about Mother.'

'I hope she's well,' said William quickly. This was more than

143

courtesy: he found that not knowing Margot's current state of health frayed his nerves worse than knowing it.

'Physically, she's not bad, considering.'

'You mean, she's depressed.'

'I don't know that I do mean that,' said Sam, considering. Sam had the literal turn of mind compatible with overseeing a scout troop and two church choirs.

'Then what do you mean?'

'She's just not herself.'

Not herself: what a curious phrase that was, once you came to examine it! Who knew which of the selves they contained was the real one?

'That can be a symptom of depression.'

'Are you saying that she's nuts?' inquired Sam dangerously.

'Not at all. Depression may even be a symptom of sanity. Many intelligent people seem to suffer it almost continually.'

'Listen, Dad. I have to ask you something. Is there anybody else?'

'You know there was.'

Sam made a gesture of impatience. 'Not that silly business. I mean now.'

William shook his head, with a sudden rush of affection for Angela. He would have found it hard to describe what there was between them, but it wasn't what Sam was driving at. She's looking after me, he decided. And – God knows why – she fancies me. That won't last, of course, but by then perhaps it won't matter. In her blunt Irish fashion, she's already helped to make me well.

'Was that a no?'

'No. Not the way you mean.'

'And you haven't been contacted by that woman again?'

Does it count if we met by accident? he wondered, remembering that day at the Barbican. Isabel's eyes beseeching him, and her beauty, worn out by love, imprisoned in her new leather jacket . . . Does thinking count, so many remembrances per day?

'No,' he told Sam. 'I left that orchestra, remember.'

'Nan says they're all alike.'

Olivia – positive and presumptuous, unsupportive and sometimes insupportable.

'Tell me, how's Margot coping with Olivia?'

'There's nothing wrong with Nan,' said Sam defensively.

'No, but she's a tricky soul to live with, I should think.'

'They get on wonderfully well. Of course, Nan's out a lot – does her work for the church, and the Conservatives, and so on. But there's no problem.'

Margot would have understood, thought William. Perhaps they should have lunch and dissect their relations, the way they'd used to. Perhaps that was what Sam was so tortuously leading up towards. When he was young, William too had imagined he'd all the time in the world.

'You want us to meet, is that the idea?' he asked Sam, amused. 'Are you vetting me for the privilege of seeing my own wife?'

'Well, I needed to know . . . If you were with someone, well, it would be different. Naturally.'

'And have I got through the screening process?'

Sam sighed. 'I don't think it would do any harm. Mum's been odd, recently: always tired and – and, well, still.'

'What do you mean?'

'Sometimes she sits for hours, pretending to read. Her mind seems elsewhere, somehow . . . She doesn't – fight – as she used to.'

'It was the illness she was fighting,' William reminded him. 'Perhaps she doesn't have to now.'

'I'm not sure she wasn't happier fighting.'

Olivia would quietly drain the life from a person, thought William acutely. Just coping with her mother's enthusiasms would probably exhaust Margot. He had a mental picture of Olivia holding forth while some politician she abhorred (and she abhorred most politicians) dared to inhabit the TV in her sitting room.

'What makes you think that Margot would see me?' he asked. 'She wouldn't before. Has she suggested it?'

'No, but then she wouldn't. She never mentions you at all.'

'What, never? This is confoundedly hard on the ego.'

'I wish you'd be serious, Dad. It *is* serious, after all.'

It's because it's serious that I can't take it seriously. Thank God I'm not in my twenties again. I'm glad to be nearer the end than the beginning.

'Well, Sam, shall I call her? Or do you think it would come better from you?'

'I don't know.'

'I can but try.'

Sam was silent. When he spoke, he didn't look at William. Instead he looked at the curtains, the floor, the mantelpiece.

'You do want her back, don't you, Dad? I mean, you don't want to be alone for the rest of your life.'

I could cope: I've had practice. It's lonely but possible, like swimming the Channel or running a marathon. There were even – though Sam probably wouldn't imagine it – other options.

'I was happier with your mother,' he admitted, 'but—'

'You must still love her.'

I love them both, but differently. How to explain that to someone like Sam? And he marvelled: how Isabel has changed me! Before her I loved my wife; I loved my son – and perhaps I loved Piotr. Now I'm open to every gust of love; they all flow over me, wash through me. I see the world with different eyes; I play the cello with different fingers. I ache with so many loves, so many warm and crazy desires! Perhaps love too can become a habit, like suffering.

'That was a question, Dad, in a way.'

'I still love your mother,' said William, 'of course I do. She'll always – matter – to me. Always.'

'And you'll call her?'

'If Olivia lets me.'

'Oh, I'll deal with Nan.'

'You're a good fellow,' said William, putting his hand on his son's shoulder.

At the door, Sam suddenly turned.

'I do know what it's like, you know. Really I do. There was a girl at college, complete stunner, tall, blonde, amazing legs – well, anyway, I was fair smitten with her until I realised she was just incredibly bad news. Took a few terms to figure it, but I did, though it hurt a lot at the time. I never told you that before. To be honest, I never told anyone.'

William said very gently, 'No, I would have remembered if you'd told me. I'm sorry.'

'Oh, there's nothing to be sorry about, is there? But I thought you'd like to know. See you, Dad. Keep your chin up.'

'Love to the family,' said William, but he meant it.

CHAPTER 28

But soft, behold, lo where it comes again!
I'll cross it, though it blast me.

Come not between a dragon and his wrath.
Shakespeare

(from Pete Hegal's diaries)

Looking back, the trouble was that I lacked faith in my own
instinct. There were quiverings on the breeze, but I never read
the wind right. There was sniping about the Orchestra of
London's possible demise, about Arts Council funding cuts.
There was Eddie's unease, Lenny's preoccupation, Angela's
uncharacteristic snappiness ... Most worrying of all, there
was young Janice's ever-increasing influence over Leszek.

At first I thought the change external. I would come in with a
coffee and find him leaning back in his chair, eyes staring, very
nearly asleep. Upon my arrival he was prone to leap up ('Ha!
and I had thought myself forgotten!') but even this modest
effort sometimes seemed to exhaust him.

Then there was his appetite. Leszek had never much cared
for food ('Pete, get me a sandwich – what kind? Any kind,
anything!') and had always been lean, a feline mover, his caged
tiger impersonation. But after the Spanish tour he seemed
ravenous; he seemed continually to be wolfing down sausage
rolls or great hunks of cheese – yet, despite this, he lost more
and more weight. His trousers were buckled ever more
shrewdly around his waist, while the muscles of his arms

tautened dangerously. He lost flesh in his face too: instead of looking like a contented enough sort of Siberian wolf, he began to look like a wolf who hadn't had a square peasant for a fortnight, and was beginning to feel the strain.

But strangest of all was his change of attitude. I made notes at the time, notes I thought significant enough to hang on to.

July 30: Leszek takes a call from his agent, detailing an offer of work with the St Petersburg Symphony, which he refuses. When I screw up enough courage to ask him the reason, he unexpectedly keeps his temper. 'You cannot do everything,' he tells me, almost sadly. 'You cannot even try.'

August 2: The principal clarinet, who was due to drop the flag on Sibelius' First Symphony with that endless unaccompanied solo, withdraws from a concert at the last minute. When I break this to Zimetski, he hardly even looks up from his papers.

'Who plays the second?' he asks vaguely.

'Pia, but she's got time off. There's the deputy, but—'

'Good, good, fine.'

August 4: Leszek didn't even go home last night. I entered his room this a.m. and almost passed out to see him still at his desk, staring eerily into the dark. 'I needed to think,' he said fretfully. 'I cannot think at the moment; nothing connects. Did you, Pete, ever feel like this?'

Thine eyes, sweet lady, have infected mine, I thought, and I asked him instead where Janice was.

'She was here – I think. I think she was here.'

'You're run down,' I observed. More than once, Leszek had near-decapitated me for less; now he only looked weary. The marine-coloured bruises between his nose and eyes were deeper and bluer than ever; his sloping, curiously coloured irises darker, as if swamped with blood.

'Have you ever been – obsessively – in love, Pete?'

For Leszek to ask such a question! It was contrary to everything between us, to everything he'd ever let me see. Luckily, I didn't have to struggle for an answer.

'Sorry, no. Lust is as much as I can handle.'

'What would you do?' he asked me simply, and I had an answer there too.

'Unload her. There was an Australian trialist, wasn't there, Greg somebody? Epic cellist, by all accounts.'

With a gesture he dismissed such childishness. Obsessions – well, not my style, to be honest. I'm too preternaturally observant to be able to throw myself into passion – a certain element of wilful blindness being the prerequisite for same.

I've often wondered what love feels like – crazy, full-throated, William-Mellor-type love – but without ever wishing to experiment with it myself. I'd felt much the same when Leszek got strung out on cocaine a few years back. I remember marvelling how some temperaments are always trying to fasten themselves on to something – cocaine, oblivion, women, the Russian school of violin playing . . . Besides which, it should never be forgotten that Leszek was a romantic. You have to be a romantic to get married three times, and never for money.

The orchestra had a recording session at EMI that afternoon. Leszek drove me in his Maserati, skidding below fifty only as an afterthought, and oblivious to black looks from pedestrians and traffic alike.

Upon entering, I overtook Janice, and asked if I could have a word with her. She paused, and I recalled how interminable her beauty was, how unreal. Players wandered by, towards the studio, the cafeteria, talking, joking, gossiping. They all looked curiously grey to me, as if Janice was the only one on colour film; the rest of us subtly lacking.

'I'm a bit worried about Leszek,' I ventured.

She was looking at me intently; there was an almost amber inflection in her eyes. Hunter's eyes, I thought.

'Are you? Why?'

Suddenly kitten-weak, I felt a terrible empathy for Leszek. All right, he was a single-minded, incurably neurotic Pole, but there was something unmanning about Janice – Janice, of all the trite Essex-girl names . . . She dropped her eyes and in that moment I knew – I don't know how – that Janice wasn't her name. Her real name was something else.

'Who are you?' I asked, idiotically, but the only reply I received terrified me. A splash from those strange loaded eyes, and my knees, the sides of my head, going shadowed and woolly on me. Instinctively, I backed out of the corridor and into what passes for fresh air in that section of St John's Wood.

Half an hour later, the backbone stiffened, I re-entered the studios. A single glance at the faces of the recording engineers told me that the going was soft to lousy.

'What the hell's up with Zimetski?' one demanded. 'He's carving like last week's warmed-up chicken tikka.'

'He didn't sleep,' I admitted.

'And so? Listen, even if by some miracle we get this in the can, they can't release it – no way, José. There's no hum, no zing, no grip . . . *Plume de ma tante!* Now he's murdering one of the horns.'

I caught up a spare set of earphones, while eyeballing the drama through the soundproofed glass. It was the Duke, of course – but I was careful to observe Janice as well.

'This is lousy! Lousy!' fumed Leszek.

(The recording engineer said audibly, 'Oh shit, he's noticed.')

'You, Mr Wellington – yes, you – look at me!'

Eddie, wounded: 'I am looking at you.'

They were mainly looking, Janice included. Experimentally, I half-closed my eyes, but there weren't any stars. No stars, no dizziness. Only Janice's sick-steady gaze: at Eddie, at Leszek – only those metallic eyes and nerves like acid corroding the bottom of my stomach.

Leszek said with snarling sweetness, 'You are ill, Mr Wellington?'

'No, I'm fine.'

'You are tired, you are drunk?'

'No, sir,' said Eddie indignantly.

I forget what Leszek said then, because that was when I saw it. A puffy haze, like gilded smoke – smoke, light or dust – straight from Janice to Leszek. I breathed in so sharply that the two recording engineers swivelled towards me, surprised.

'Did you see it?' I asked.

'See what?'

I could tell from their expressions that they thought I was loopy. But you must have seen, I longed to tell them: how could you miss it? Something fired from her eyes – and I suspected (though this could not be proved) it smelled like honeysuckle.

Suddenly nauseous, I swept off my earphones, letting Leszek and Eddie's voices drift into static. Through the soundproof glass the Duke's face looked mutinous, and the muscles on Leszek's neck as strained as marionette wire. I skulked in a corner, listening to the engineers lying about their sex lives and thinking about gold-coloured dust off the heel of a star.

'. . . four or five times. On the bed, on the chair, standing up, and then she— What? Shot his bolt, has he? Well, they might as well bugger right back to the first bar; I've heard riper crap from the Sudanese Virtuoso Chamber Players.' Through the mike, appreciatively: 'Nice work, team, lovely. I've just got one or two little patches . . . The section before letter R was a little untidy, perhaps, and the final crescendo just possibly a fraction early. What do you say, Leszek?'

During the break I wandered out into the battlefield. I found the casualties well scattered – Eddie being jacked up by Lenny; the seconds being hauled, arse over apex, by their principal – but I was in need of reassurance, so I headed towards William. Oh, I know: Will was a mess. His life was a mess, his marriage was a mess, his career was on the downslide and he was hanging on to the edge of control. But there remained an inner serenity about William. He still knew – always did – what really mattered.

Angela was perched beside him. Clearly, I was interrupting a flirtation – a flirtation so concentrated, at least on her side, that I wondered it wasn't remarked by everybody.

'I sometimes wish Eddie would give Leszek as good as he gets,' she told him.

'I know what you mean, but it won't happen.'

'You? You might know what I mean – but you could never do it yourself, you know you couldn't. You'd be too controlled altogether.'

'I'm not nearly as sure about that as you are.'

'Usually I'd string along with Angela,' I said, lounging against the principal double bass's stool. 'But today, between us, Leszek's up against it. No sleep, skipped breakfast, bolted his lunch and drove here like Damon Hill having a tough day at the office.'

I don't believe Angela heard me, though Will did, glancing over with sudden seriousness. Angela was fiddling with – nay, caressing –Will's hair, once almost black, now thickest, silkiest white.

'You need these bits trimmed, Will. It's almost curling.'

'I know. I haven't had time.'

'I could do it for you. I cut my brother's hair, until he got too trendy for me.'

I felt discontented, even annoyed (though this was un-reasonable – if Angela fancied Will, why shouldn't she have him?). But most of all, I was angry at Janice. I caught her gaze as I turned to go, and stonily dropped it. Bad news, for Leszek, for Eddie, for the orchestra – even, more obscurely, for Will. I didn't know who she was and I didn't know what she wanted, but that much I was sure of: she was news, bad news.

CHAPTER 29

Write till your ink be dry, and with your tears
Moist it again and frame some feeling line
That may discover such integrity:
For Orpheus' lute was strung with poets' sinews
Whose golden touch could soften steel and stones,
Make tigers tame and huge leviathans
Forsake unsounded depths to dance on sands.

Shakespeare

Isabel awoke after a few hours' uneasy sleep. Karl was away doing 'Turangalíla' in Prague – and, as her own flat was in the throes of redecoration, he had urged her to be comfortable in his own. Alone, however, she felt oppressed by a sense of silence and alienation. The dark colours, bare floors and luxurious textures all seemed to converge on a vague feeling of threat.

She retrieved a glass of water, examining her face in the mirror, as was her habit. Stress had thumbed dark coins under her eyes and restlessness sharpened the bones of her chin, but her complexion – naturally a soft tan – was unscathed, and her near-black hair still curved in a becoming mass around it. She felt as she had before, that her looks were not her own – they had been meant for someone sure and confident, programmed for success.

William, she thought, switching off the bathroom light. The recollection was like the smell of spring, the tang of something too sweet, too real, to bear. Sometimes she still found herself reaching for him, only to experience, along with Karl's tauter arm, an instinctive withdrawal. Sometimes she awoke forgetting the intervening months entirely, and, as memory overruled, felt blackness bearing down on her again.

Isabel returned to bed. Around her were night sounds: footsteps from the floor above, a car door slamming in the Knightsbridge street. Sounds from the building too – pipes hissing, even creaks from the structure itself, as if it was only held upright by the buildings on either side, and might collapse, given a wind from the wrong direction.

A sense of her own fragility bore down on Isabel. She wished Karl was back, she wished that someone was with her – almost anyone – simply to relieve her of the weight of remembering. She would have welcomed Karl's elegant hands, Karl's prick, in arousal so stocky as to seem nearly rectangular – Karl's sadism, his mocking suavity. She thought: I was never meant to be on my own. I need an audience to play to, a script to lean on. Perhaps the trouble with my life is that I've never been able to sort out the actress from the rest of me.

Isabel fished out her diary from the bottom of her travelling bag. She'd never brought it to Karl's before, and it felt wrong, even dangerous, to open it now. After all, her diaries, however chaotically maintained, remained the only place where she was completely honest, completely herself. And Isabel of all people was experienced enough to know the dangers of perfect honesty . . .

Most of her relationship with William was catalogued here, although at the point when he'd resigned from the orchestra there was a series of pages left blank. Each time she'd opened it since, she'd attempted to fill in the gap: and each time her courage had failed her. Yet she'd recently felt impelled to face up to what had happened, as if the act of choosing words would subtly rationalise her feelings, making acceptance possible.

Truth was a terrible force, a destructive force. Confronted with the truth, her first instinct was to escape. Confronted with the truth, she usually found she couldn't bear it. She had become an artist at avoidance, skilled at glossing unpalatable facts into acceptable patterns, expert at procrastination and agile in self-defence. Yet she was conscious too of an opposing force, a gut-rock determination to dig to the bottom of things – and even a fascination with the realities that she so instinctively loathed. She turned back to where the omissions started, to where the blankness of her life had first been mirrored by the blankness on the page.

'Recording this six months later,' she wrote. 'I can't pretend to have put it in complete perspective. As Piotr said at the time . . .'

No, she thought, go back farther – to Margot. Margot had struck the first blow, after all.

William and I had crashed back together with the New Year, but late in February Margot left him. My first reaction was shock – where could she go to, after all? – but then I felt such an uprush of release . . . It seemed at that moment an abdication, and only a matter of time and tactfulness before I could be crowned. I didn't know – how could I? – how William felt. I could only think: it's over, it's finally over. The sniping, the lies, the intangible but palpable disapproval of our friends – everything.

William took a week off work. I understood: naturally there were practicalities to be sorted, decisions to be made. What I knew was patchy. I only knew that someone had alerted Margot, making her determined to risk everything – also, more strangely, that she'd refused to see William since.

I supposed she was too angry. I didn't think of fear, that it might weaken her resolve for punishment. Looking back, I didn't understand much. I didn't know Margot, still don't. She seemed half a person in her chair – that's what the disabled complain of – sheer prejudice, a crazy, immature impression. She's real, a whole person, she exists, and when I think of her – oh, I still can't bear to think of her! It's easier to pretend she isn't real; a round face, all cashmere and curls, a doll propped up in a wheelchair too big for her.

At any rate, March opened with stalemate. William didn't

return my calls; Margot didn't return his. Their son Sam revolved between them, ambassador without portfolio, growing testier and less sure with every failure.

It was late the second week by the time I reached William. I was shocked when he became angry, or as angry as he ever allows himself to be.

'Do you really think, Isabel, that I'm in the mood to see you now?'

'Why not?'

'Sometimes I despair of making you understand.'

'But no one would have imagined—'

'No. Isn't that reason enough not to see each other?'

'William. You don't – you can't mean that.'

He must have heard the panic in my voice, because his – so dark, and usually so controlled – moved to soothe me.

'I don't mean never, Isabel. I mean for now. Don't call me, not this week anyway. Don't ask for more than I can give you at a time like this.'

His exhaustion reproached me; I apologised and rang off. A little flutter of nerves ruffling my happiness, and yet – it was so like William to feel guilty! I blamed myself for not recognising his shock, his sense of rejection; I accused myself of selfishness, hastiness, even ill manners. One of the clarinettists, seeing how low I felt, invited himself around after a Barbican concert – I thought I'd never get rid of him. And the worst part was that I almost weakened, that I almost felt there could be no harm in it – that sex could be a mere distraction, even a comfort, after all.

It was in an altogether humbler spirit that I approached William on his return. Piotr was with him, his gaze darting between us like a desert lizard on a wildlife programme. And not only Piotr – so many orchestra members were covertly observing, noses twitching for sensation, for news. It was as if that decisive blow, from the least expected quarter, had shaken our very foundations. We were fastidious as strangers while Piotr fooled about at being chaperone.

'Hello, William.'

'Isabel. I hope you're well.'

'Well you both look perfectly frightful to me.'

During the rehearsal I watched William's shoulders – I used to love to watch them, the serene power of his bowing, the quietness of his exertion compared with the cellists around him. But when we were finally alone I felt almost light-headed with nerves. Just as I had when it had all started: sure yet unsure, my powers and his powers of resistance invisibly clashing the air between us.

'Well? Do I live or die?' I asked him.

William was putting his cello away.

'You haven't grown less dramatic with time,' he observed, attempting lightness.

'Look at me.'

He looked, as if the sight hurt his eyes. 'I'd hoped you'd learned more self-respect over the last year.'

'Has she upset you so terribly?'

'You know she has' – very quietly.

Some impulsive desire – to be put out of my doubtfulness, at least – seized me.

'Do you want me to quit? Do you want to finish it, here, now?'

He paused. He seemed to be steeling himself, while I waited for the end with defeat in my mouth. I knew its taste; I recalled it on my tongue, the sweet-sour taste of surrender. Death in the mouth, and quiet footsteps heading out into the rain. But it wasn't death, or at least, not then.

'Isabel,' he said, very gently, 'you have to give me time. I don't think perhaps you realise – never having been married yourself – quite what a marriage is, how unreal its unravelling can feel. It's – like an amputation, part of my soul's gone numb without her. I feel dazed and wounded and afraid, afraid for her and for you, as well as for myself. Afraid of what may come, as if my every step might have disastrous consequences. It sounds absurdly self-important, but I feel as if every step I take might dent the earth.'

His tone terrified me. I'd felt so sure that our troubles were over! I said in a rush, 'William, let's go away.'

'Go away? Where? What do you mean?'

'Does it matter? Australia, South Africa – anywhere! America, perhaps; perhaps New York – somewhere no one knows us, or Margot – or anything! Somewhere we could start again.'

'How could we work in New York? Or in Australia, for that matter? What could we do? Be rational, Isabel. Try to think of real possibilities.'

His proximity undid me, and his sadness; I reached to caress his hair. He endured it, though I saw a flash of pain cross his face. Suddenly his patience, his correctness, simply maddened me. I wished I'd slept with that clarinettist – I wished I'd never thought of William in the first place. There had been years – years! – when I'd never noticed him – if only they'd lasted! I felt as if he'd set out purposely to torment me and shake up my life. Something of this must have shown in my expression because he said: 'Don't deceive yourself, Isabel. You could easily hate me, perhaps you do already. Love at its most intense is almost always mixed with hate anyway.'

I wanted to say: I do hate you, but I couldn't trust my voice: I was too completely miserable.

'Time,' he said, almost to himself, slipping his cello case on to his shoulder. 'I need time.'

How much time? I wanted to ask, but I realised he didn't know himself. I was half-crazy with fear and selfishness and sexual frustration. Part of me wanted to go abroad; part of me half-longed for him to end it; while part of me yearned for the childish, careless life I'd known before William. Oh, I knew that I'd simply slipstreamed from lover to lover – but to feel used up, drained, even dissected by such feelings seemed harder than anything my previous life had offered me. And I could only endure the waiting by pretending it wouldn't last.

Here Isabel paused. The night had grown still, though in the distance she heard the chromatic roar of a motorcycle, wavy lines of sound. She could leave it until the morning, she thought; surely, now she'd started, the truth would come easily. But she wanted to finish; she wanted to dig deeper, to dig the truth out of her character like an actress unearthing a role.

William withdrew from the Scandinavian tour, though it was only five days long. I was very disappointed; I'd promised myself that away from the persistent rain and still more persistent wind of an English March, we would ease back together again. I remember feeling absolutely desolate as the plane took off, as if I was leaving William behind me forever.

I didn't anticipate much pleasure from the trip, for the programmes were difficult and the schedule relentless. Older members maintain that touring used to be different – with time to practise, relax, even get the feel of a country – but that was in the unimaginable past, and alien to today's spirit of international competitiveness. Orchestras now commit hit-and-run raids, decamp and depart; touring has become a process of organised survival, armies on the march.

We had fifteen minutes in the Stockholm Hilton before getting back on the coach, but a lot of rumours can circulate in fifteen minutes. Roger, our conductor, had got migraine, toothache, cancer . . . the tour was cancelled; they'd roped in some young Swedish hopeful; we were about to fly back. Once on the coach, I asked the orchestra manager what was really happening.

'Karl Hochler's filling in,' Susan told me, as casually as if she didn't know the story. How Karl had picked me up when William had left me; Karl's suaveness – along with the faintest ripple of threat – when William had taken me back at the New Year.

Karl, I thought stupidly. Karl, with his meticulous accent, his subtle suits and his elegantly pointed shoes. The clean lines of his lips came back to me, along with the unexpectedly sexy hairiness of his forearms, the curling smell of his slim atmospheric cigars. Karl's little games, the tasteful decadence of his sexuality – except when it so rarely gushed into violence. And I felt a flicker of excitement – was it excitement or pleasure? – at the thought of being conducted by Karl again.

I saw him first from a distance, iron-grey hair lightened by sunlight, moving with neat, calculated steps, steps like a tango dancer. He was talking to Paul Ellison – looking back, they were probably putting the finishing touches on their *coup d'état*, though at the time I was far too self-absorbed to imagine it. Upon perceiving me, Karl awarded me a subtly intimate bow.

'My dear. What a pleasure.'

'Hello, Karl.'

'I had supposed that you were not coming.'

Because William wasn't? I wondered, and flushed. 'What's happened to Roger? No one seems to know.'

Karl smiled. 'Officially, Roger Ash is – most tragically – ill. However, it is only a short tour, I suppose – not much in comparison to a debut in LA.'

'Los Angeles!'

'Indeed, our mutual friend's conducting career seems to be on an upward curve – in some respects at least . . . They will like Roger Ash in Los Angeles. He has most precisely what the Californians like – a splendid presence, a foreign accent and a pronounceable name.'

'His beat isn't easy to follow.'

'No. He was once, I believe, in the possession of a lucid beat, but time has so distorted it that only the most professional ensemble derives any aid or comfort from it now. His presence, however, is most decidedly an asset, and no one postures with more assurance than he. In California, believe me, they ask for nothing more.'

His bantering tone brought everything back – the day when William had left me; the moment when Karl, with matchless insouciance, had evenly picked up the pieces.

There was a silence through which the harp's tuning sounded magnified, and suddenly I was lost in his eyes. His voice was still dissecting Roger's technique, but his eyes were communicating quite a different message . . . It was *Verklärte Nacht* all over again: sometimes, in life, things come full circle. I forced myself to say something, anything.

'Did Roger ask you to fill in?'

'No. We have the same agent.'

He was standing too close, or perhaps I just had that impression. I recalled the texture of his neck, the muscles of his back and thighs, the unexpected authority of his shapely, almost effeminate hands. This is crazy, I thought; this is transference – was that the word? I was so heartsore for William that my body was traitorously transferring all my longing on to Karl.

'I think I've met your agent,' I said, forcing myself to speak normally despite the yielding in my blood. 'Big woman, smokes cigars.'

'Yes, Irene is her name. Less beautiful but somehow similar in resonance to Isabel.'

'Much more beautiful than Isabel.'

'I defer, naturally, to your opinion.'

In another moment, I remember feeling, there would be no going back. There would be some dingy conductor's room, some battered leather couch, Karl's hands expert on my body – but suddenly David Schaedel, our principal cellist, was among us. David with his perilous ambition, his alertness for the main chance – the main chance in this case being the possibility, unspoken but tangible, of Karl's succeeding Roger Ash.

'Maestro,' David said ingratiatingly. 'Forgive me, a matter of some little moment. You observe, the cello section at letter G must divide into three different parts. I feel myself that only the first desk – perhaps the first player only – is required on the top line. The finesse required here, also here, is very great, and the register is high. Believe me, it is not the part for the average orchestral player.'

Isabel heard a night bus lumbering into the distance, the stirring of trees in the wind outside the flat, each tree reacting differently, like members of an audience to music. It would be easier when morning came, she thought; then the wind wouldn't sound so hungry . . . Tiredness warred with memory; it was almost three.

I'll just get over the next part, she thought. I'll have done it then, and understand everything. Once I've written it down then I'll be free. Though free of what, she could not have said . . . She poured herself a drink from Karl's cabinet, then picked up her pen.

Karl found me at the stage door after the Stockholm concert. 'Sorry to have kept you,' he said, slipping his camel coat over his shoulders.

'I'm waiting for my desk-partner,' I said swiftly. It was so feeble an excuse that I wondered later whether I didn't want him to believe me, even whether part of me might be still angry at William. Certainly there was the old energy in the air between us; while the evening was crisp, a foretaste of some Scandinavian spring.

Karl considered me for a moment.

'In my opinion, lying is not unlike playing a string instrument. You work too hard, you press with the bow – and it comes out harsh, defiant. If you procure the correct angle and let the arm flow, you will be better rewarded in your lies. You were waiting for me. I do not think this; I know it. Come.'

'I can't,' I said impulsively.

'Why not?'

'Oh Karl. You know the reason.'

He shook his head, patient.

'No, no, this will no longer do. Before, perhaps, but no longer. He is ten years older than I, this William; he has been devastated by the truly bizarre behaviour of his wife; he will never love you again. This is so clear; why do you force me to be brutal? He tells you, or so I hear, that he needs time. The world doesn't have enough time for what he needs. It's over, Isabel, and you know it; you send me signals, lightning flares over a night landscape. The very air has thinned, and vibrates between us. Listen! We are lit candles, you and I. Waste no more words. Come.'

It was a dream, and had a dream's carrying quality. What happened was bound to happen – who has control in a dream? And besides, one of my oldest longings is to lose control. There was a moment in the hotel room when I almost awoke, almost pulled back, but the deep knowing in his eyes held me, as it had always held me, from the beginning.

I relived Karl's smooth shoulders, his tight-crafted rear and taut abdomen, then still unlined by surgery. The phone rang in the night, but he didn't answer it, no, not when it rang again and again, in baffled irritation. He was inside me, filling me entirely, lips intent upon my breast; he was drowning out my sorrow with the tidal urgency of his blood. The phone rang like an alarm but no one paid it any attention: there was just the sound from the flickering television, and the twisted, breathing pulses of our twin lost hearts.

It was so simple, thought Isabel; it was as simple as tragedy. Margot left William after a neighbour's phone call. William avoided Isabel after an upsurge of guilt; while Karl took her again because their dark sides precisely matched each other. And finally Piotr – never to be discounted – finally Piotr took it upon himself to tell William what had happened. For whatever reason – out of misery or loyalty, truthfulness or blindest vitriol – Piotr told William, and made himself lonely forever.

The moment William returned, I knew. The first rehearsal after the tour, he quietly dropped my gaze and I knew. A breath of fear, a premonition I couldn't or didn't know how to answer. Piotr was off with flu, but I didn't have to ask Piotr either. I wrote William a note, which I left inside his cello case.

'It's not what you think. It was only loneliness. I only love you.'

He returned the envelope unopened at the end of the rehearsal.

'Your handwriting, I believe.'

It was the harshest thing William had ever done to me, indeed the only time he proved a desire to hurt me. Shock chilled my stomach, but perhaps it was partly fear. Some members of the orchestra were still practising, the leader and David Schaedel were lounging on the podium nearby, but it was too late to worry about what other people thought.

'William!' I cried out, stricken, but he was leaving.

Caroline tried to restrain me, but I ran after him. I caught William up, forcing him to turn around. I wanted to say: How can you behave like this, after everything? What could be important enough to make you want to hurt me? But when I saw his expression – dark eyes banked in suffering – then all I knew was sorrow, pity, the fiercest aching love.

'I love you!'

'I don't want to hear this,' he said, turning his head away as if warding off a blow.

'Don't you care any more?'

'I won't answer that.'

'William, if you leave me I'll die, I will. I'm not strong enough to bear this!'

'Perhaps,' he said quietly, 'you should have thought of that before you left me.'

'But I never – I never left you!'

'Besides, I could no more touch you after—' He broke off, breathing more swiftly.

But you did before, I longed to say; you came back afterwards. But I knew in my soul it was different. Last year, William had told me it was over, before I had – exhausted, drugged, and utterly miserable – let Karl do what he wanted with me. This was different, as even I had to admit . . . What lunacy had overtaken me in Sweden? At that moment even the thought of Karl's fit clever body sickened my memory.

'It was physical,' I protested. 'It meant nothing – I felt nothing for him!' But still I knew it wasn't completely true. What I meant was: Karl is my dark side; he answers my darkness with his own darkness. I always guessed he would destroy us; I knew he wanted to.

'Please. Don't trouble to explain,' said William, grasping control. 'I know you, after all – I ought to, by now. I know your insecurity is so profound that, having possessed him once, you had to reassure yourself that he was still part of your collection, even the very first tour after— I thought I meant more to you than that, that's all. I flattered myself – crazy as it sounds – that I meant a little more than all the others.'

'Of course you did!' I faltered, tears falling heedlessly down my face. 'You meant – you mean everything! That's why I was so empty in the first place! Don't you see? I thought it was over.'

'It is over, Isabel. Even madness passes at last.' And he turned to address the breathless hall, players frozen mid-sentence, mid-phrase – in the trumpet section, by the piano, David motionless against the conductor's empty podium.

'Quite clear to everybody? Any questions, any queries, from the floor? Any doubts that this really is the last turn of the wheel? Because that's what it is, the wheel's last turning. For Isabel I have destroyed the happiness of my wife, lost the respect of my son, and had my work here poisoned for me . . . I thought at least I'd altered her, I thought I'd given her something, a sliver of self-respect, but I was wrong, puffed up with some absurdly arrogant notion of my own influence. She never cared, whatever she might pretend; I was never more than another trophy to hang on her wall, a trophy perhaps a little harder to capture than most. She isn't a whole person; she imagines she cares, but it isn't love, it's desperation.'

William took a breath, and steadied himself; his voice dipping still deeper. 'I've behaved like an utter fool, but – I admit it – I really did love her. I loved her crazy notions, her impulsiveness; I loved her body and that spirit of emotional risk that she carries with her. Love is my excuse, my justification – but it isn't enough, I know; there can be no justification.'

'Oh William, I did love you, I still do, you know I do!' I cried, tears crashing down. I must have looked terrible, but it didn't matter because William couldn't – or wouldn't – look at me. The fight had seeped out of him; he only just succeeded in holding his voice steady.

'No, that's enough. We've had our scene, now we must leave the stage to the other players. I apologise for the intrusion. You may at least comfort yourselves with the recollection that you've been disturbed for the last time.'

At which point David Schaedel intervened. 'My dear friend,' he said solicitously, 'I'm so sorry. Really, I had no idea . . . But you may recall an occasion last year when you surprised me in Isabel's hotel room. I did not wish to hurt your feelings by telling you this before, but she was throwing herself at me, quite shamelessly. This is, I think, a very good example of your point.'

'David,' said William patiently, 'would you do something for me?'

'Anything.'

'Then turn around.'

'Yes, yes.'

'Go back to the podium where Oliver is.'

'Yes, certainly.'

'And finish sorting out the bowings. Will you do that?'

'Naturally,' said David, much puzzled. 'I would have done that anyway.'

'Good,' said William grimly.

Then my desk-partner Caroline put her arm around my shoulder, and I cried and cried.

I couldn't play the concert that night; I couldn't come into work the next day, or the day after that. My friends rang to commiserate; and several abused William for choosing to devastate me in public. I listened, but couldn't respond properly, possibly because in my soul I couldn't blame him. I lay on my sofa and thought about death, the death of love and the death of feeling, and what sweet relief it would be to sleep and to never wake up again. I felt so empty, so achingly empty, that I even dreamed I was dead, that this was death.

I remember looking down from the balcony of my Barbican flat and thinking how easy it would be to slip off the edge, soft air rushing past my skin, like flying. I wouldn't feel the sickening jar of bone crumpling and jabbing through flesh – or so I'd read – because I'd have passed out in mid-air. However, either I didn't quite believe it, or the idea was simply too horrible for me to contemplate, because I stopped eating instead.

I didn't want to eat anyway: all food smelled rancid to me, and the textures vaguely appalled me, meat especially. It was as if I were eating someone's thigh; I found its sexuality as revolting as my own. I hated my body for sending out signals – distress flares – towards Karl; I loathed everything about my body, except what it had once done for William. For days I told friends I'd got flu and ate nothing; finally I phoned Susan in the orchestra office and told her I was still unwell.

'You've been off for almost two weeks. Two weeks tomorrow. Have you seen a doctor, Isabel?'

'It's only a virus.'

'I strongly recommend you see your doctor. You seem to be developing a rather cavalier attitude towards your health.'

'I'll see if I can get an appointment,' I told her, but I didn't. Instead I went back to my sofa and turned up the inanities of daytime television, which was all I could bear to listen to. Music seemed to turn my stomach as much as food.

I refused visitors the third week, and ignored the telephone, the occasional knock on the door. Strangely, I was no longer hungry; and hardly even felt thirsty. About this time I started to have dreams, almost visions. I dreamed that William had broken down the door and was curling his fingers around my fingers, his deep puzzled eyes searching mine. I dreamed about Karl as well, we were all making love together, in a frenzy of

167

orgiastic inspiration. I dreamed about Piotr, who hates all women, but me especially, and I dreamed my death, which would please him at last.

In the end, the door *was* broken down, but it was Warren, not William, who came for me. Unable to locate my landlord, Warren brought the police. Everything seemed unreal by then, the floor bending with the weight of stolid, extraneous policemen, the air flicked sharp from the window someone had forced open. Even Warren looked too solid kneeling beside me – I felt like a ghost among living people.

'This is Warren, Caroline's husband in the first violins,' I told a policeman, who looked mystified. I don't know why I felt I had to introduce them. I tried to stand up, and fell to the floor instead, weakness tipping like a blanket over my head.

'I'm not going to faint,' I said defiantly, but I think I must have, because I woke up in hospital, with Caroline holding my hand.

Her hand was cold; a metallic taste coruscated my mouth and a drip impaled the vein of my arm. I took these facts in drowsily, as if swimming upwards from a great depth.

'I think she's awake,' I heard someone say.

'Why haven't you been eating, Isabel?' Caroline reproached me. I wondered if her face felt as chill and tapered as her fingers.

'It doesn't matter.'

'Why not?'

'There's nothing left of me.'

'No, you're going to be just fine,' said the ever-prosaic Caroline, and I burst into tears.

'I was going to be, before you ruined it!'

Warren crossed from the window. He'd been so still I hadn't even realised he was there. 'I was the one who ruined it, Isabel. If you need to blame someone, blame me.'

I looked at Warren, at his lean thinking face, and knew that he understood. And I couldn't blame Warren, not after everything I'd done to him. He'd made me face what I couldn't bear to face, but I couldn't blame him. Instead I turned towards the wall, wondering how long I could linger out of the world, and whether William would be still be there when I got out.

I came back after a month to a different orchestra. William

had gone, to be temporarily replaced by a Japanese cellist of modest abilities and exquisite looks, whom David maintained (and with some justification, for he had tried) was 'worth a try'. Piotr, who had begun espousing vodka with a dedication worthy of a better cause, had been arrested outside a pub for disturbing the peace. And Roger Ash, put under near-unbearable pressure by the board, had effectively been fired.

This last was the only development to hit the headlines, but it made the first page of the *Telegraph* and *Independent*, and the second of *The Times* and the *Guardian*. Roger's 'increasing commitments elsewhere', and the 'need for new blood' were the official reasons; while Roger's 'slapdash rehearsing', 'middle-brow programming' and 'impenetrable beat' were cited anonymously. It was much discussed, even outside the usual musical circles, but in time the shock passed away, as shock waves must. And when the dust had settled, Roger was in California and Karl belonged to us.

I first saw him again in early April. He was in marvellous fettle, surrounded by his new troops and full of schemes for various tours, recordings, and festivals we were going to do together. To me he was casual, almost offhand.

'You are pleased?'

'Of course.'

'Then you will not miss Roger?'

'I don't think the board handled it very diplomatically, but still, I'm glad. Will you be moving to London?'

'I will, although my wife Giselle refuses to leave Berlin. There are the children, her mother, her friends; these are her reasons . . . Naturally, I will visit Berlin very often.'

The insinuation was too obvious to bear. I interrupted, saying with sudden resolution, 'Karl, what happened in Sweden was my fault as much as yours.'

'You are impulsive: that is not something to regret. Personally I find it charming.'

'No, really, you must listen . . . I've been on my own since, and I have to try to stay on my own. Otherwise I'll never be a whole person – I'll never get over it.'

'Of course,' he said, smiling. 'This resolution does you great credit. We will see, the two of us, how long this idea lasts.'

'Since Stockholm, I've been treated for depression as well,' I warned him, though I hadn't meant to.

'Yes, I was informed of this. You had difficulties; I am most sorry. But you do not want to die, Isabel. The world is full of beautiful places, wonderful paintings, amazing music. We have already too short a time! We should make the most of this time that we have.'

And there was something in me that responded strongly to this, the same incorrigibly optimistic part that believed, in some layer of myself, that William would always come back . . .

And still did believe it, she thought. In the front room, Karl's post-modernist clock chimed four. She was crazy to stay awake most of the night . . . She would play abominably in the morning, even felt a little feverish already.

But her nervous energy wasn't exhausted, any more than her faith in William was exhausted. William would come back; she was still, after all, in need of rescue. She recalled that moment in the Barbican: his struggle not to reach out for her, the effort it had cost him to turn away. Time and sorrow had softened him; perhaps, too, he missed Piotr, the rest of the orchestra. There would be another resurrection, truer and better than the first; Isabel believed in this as passionately as the devoutest churchgoer.

She remembered the first time William had really spoken to her. ('You're caught in a pattern yourself . . . the desire to fail with men, the longing to be used.') She remembered leaning forward in the hotel bar to kiss him – that first moment of utter certainty – and his lightness. ('We will say it was the wine.') She recalled his repeated attempts to warn her off, each attempt less effective than the last, because she belonged to him, had belonged from the first astonished moment of recognition. It only took me so long because I imagined he was old, she thought. For years I was blinded by prejudice and stupidity. As if age means anything! Surely the first rule of adult love is that age means nothing – if there are any rules at all.

She remembered the first night – his hands, sure and warm, his heavy, deep, comforting body knitted with hers – and her drowsy certainty of having come home at last. As if she had loved him all her life, as if every other body had been no more than a shadowy substitute for William's. How he had woken her a few hours later and taken her still more powerfully: a promise, a resolution.

Had they said anything that night? She couldn't remember any words. There was only the night, his lips on her body, and the feeling that nothing that happened, before or afterwards, could mean more than this. Nothing but the night: time translated to the present, the future suspended. And, when she awoke in the morning, nothing at all – for William had gone.

William leaves me whole, thought Isabel. William leaves me whole while Karl consumes me. Karl searches out the darkest corners of my imagination, lives out my most driven fantasies, scorches holes in the fabric. No one else, after William, even makes me feel alive – but still, he doesn't love me. It may even be a kind of sickness.

Over the houses opposite she could see dawn easing over the rooftops, fresh waves of light – seashell-pink, eggshell-blue – drowning the abdicating moon. Tonight there was a concert at the Royal Festival Hall; concentration would be a struggle, but it didn't really matter. Perhaps tonight she'd fly away as she'd always meant to, her illness ended, her new life begun.

The light strengthened, a young and giddy sun spreading shadows carelessly, slipshod lines of blue and black against the creamy façades of the houses opposite. The tops of the trees were suffused with colour, and rustled in the wind. There had to be a way, thought Isabel, closing her diary. It wasn't over yet.

CHAPTER 30

Yet again methinks
Some unborn sorrow, ripe in fortune's womb,
Is coming towards me, and my inward soul
With nothing trembles.

Shakespeare

(from Pete Hegal's diaries)

Beethoven's Sixth is a flawed masterpiece. Its endless phrases are easy to over-interpret; it requires an unlikely combination of lyricism and bravado; and, despite a stirring 'Storm' and some really masterful poetic touches, it's never as surefire a hit with the many-headed as symphonies three, five and seven.

Moreover, it wasn't, and never had been, Leszek's piece. His Slavic morbidity was much better suited to the angst-ridden Scandinavians and brooding Russian romantics; and I'd never heard him come anywhere near the serene sense of line demanded by Beethoven's liquid and meandering slow movement . . . However, I've never met a conductor who didn't secretly feel that he could conduct anything from soup to nuts, and in this mistaken spirit Leszek persisted.

His most recent foray into the lists occurred after a harrowing night flight from Singapore. Gaunt and wan as he looked, I felt it my duty to make one last attempt to head him off from disaster.

'Tell the Festival Hall that we've lost the music.'

'What music is this?'

'Beethoven's "Pastoral". Propose a medium-rare slice of

T-bone Brahms instead. Tell them you're not in the mood. Tell them you promised your mother you'd never conduct the Sixth on the third Friday in a month with an R in it. That crazy accent, those architectural cheekbones – who knows, they might believe you.'

'Have you gone absolutely mad?'

'Call it an instinct. I've got an instinct about it.'

By then, of course, Leszek was simmering nicely. It's my belief that they teach them this on conducting courses. (Hell, they must teach them something.) The lecturer probably kicks off Lesson Four like this: 'Take every opportunity to cow your orchestra manager into submission. Beat early and often, checking your "invective guidebook" for handy insults . . . Don't despair if your English is poor: a ripe vocabulary is bound to come with practice. Never strike a manager with your baton, as the chances are that you'll break it beyond repair. Coffee mugs make suitable missiles (but watch out for those expensive conducting scores!) and excellent results can sometimes be obtained by biting your manager on the leg.'

Whereupon the would-be conductors probably break into smaller groups to practise mug-chucking, innovative tantrums and what experts call the rottweiler grip . . . Leszek, however, was still at the early warm-up stage.

'And I, I too, have an instinct! An instinct for Beethoven, this symphony most particularly! That cello line rising on the last page, the cavorting little asides in the clarinet . . . How do you dare to suggest such a thing? Where do you get the idea – great hulking idiot that you are – that you can sit in judgement on my music?'

Poets and philosophers have insisted throughout the ages that even unrequited love has its compensations. This I take leave to doubt, and never more so than where pieces of music are involved. Leszek may have adored Beethoven's Sixth, but the Sixth had long since pencilled him in as a clodhopping farmer in hobnailed boots, and nothing he was ever likely to do could alter its persuasion . . . Another chronic review would be the least we could expect, but worse than that was the possible effect such a failure might have on Leszek.

It may have occurred to you, while idly perusing these scribblings of mine, that I disliked the dear boy, even detested him . . . Certainly, as with any employer, especially one as ruthlessly arbitrary as Leszek, a modicum of irritation tempered my affection, yet still – 'A was a man. Take him for all and all, I shall not look upon his like again.' An appealing zest informed even his most boorish behaviour, and it was impossible not to admire the sheer verve – nay, I will go farther – the sheer misguided verve of his performances. His was a spirit with a soaring rashness to it, and perhaps a daredevil veneer secretly appeals to us all.

Half a week later we clocked in for the concert. I wandered over in time to hear a dialogue between William and Janice, who was poured into the sort of dress Marilyn Monroe might well have got a kick out of wearing.

'It's not coaching I'm after, exactly,' she was saying. 'I just feel the need to have something to work towards.'

'Why don't you have a word with Felicia?' suggested Will. 'She's much better at that sort of thing than I am.'

'It wouldn't take more than a few minutes,' she urged, and I marvelled – both at her determination and at his resistance. He was unpersuadable, despite the girl's billowing curls, shimmering smile and gravity-defying dress. And she knew it, for he was just proposing someone outside the orchestra when I saw a bolt of livid fury dart across her face. It was unnervingly swift – quenched in the lowering of an eyelash.

I went out into the audience to ponder what I'd seen, and to survey the damage to Ludwig van B. for myself. Then Leszek, hips stringy as a jaguar's, loped on, and Beethoven prepared for his revenge.

Lesson Twenty-seven of the average conductor's course should exclusively cover the advantages of not rushing the 'Storm' in Beethoven's Sixth. It doesn't – it's probably all about flattering monied widows or which low-fat garnishes best accompany sautéed woodwind. But keeping the lid on the 'Storm' is what it ought to cover.

The wisdom of this policy is two-fold: (a) the music retains all its implacable natural grandeur and (b) the players, especially the basses, don't become moody and discontented. Some double basses need jollying along at the best of times, and a rumbling double bass section can sound the knell of revolution.

Naturally these truths (though universally acknowledged) have not prevented conductor after conductor from launching into the 'Storm' as if their Jaguar had just gone phut in Stevenage, and the last train back to civilisation was leaving in half an hour. But it's still rare to find conductors starting the 'Storm' at a moderate lick and whipping it faster and faster.

Now nowhere in the annals of music history is there a record that Beethoven confided to his cronies that a gradual and irrevocable accelerando should prevail, nor is this ever hinted at in the master's many letters and sketchbooks. It is even possible (though I'm frankly disinclined to find out) that what Leszek did that night was a first in musicological history. All I knew was, it scared me rigid.

Because halfway through the 'Storm' I realised that Leszek, appearances notwithstanding, was not to blame. L. Zimetski was no longer in control. That crazy living cello was dictating madness to him.

Leszek's right hand slashed ever faster, and there was a stirring, a perceptible quiver of unease, even amongst the audience. The players couldn't keep up; to give them their due, no players in the world could have kept up. First violin grimaced at first violin; scarlet-faced flute nudged piccolo . . . Suddenly I saw Leszek grip the side of his head, and the faintest trickle – was it sweat, even blood? – torch his collar. I tried to bend round to see Will's cello, but he was blocked from view; and it was a moot point in any case what he or anyone could do. No, the cello was having a temper tantrum, and Zimetski was going to die.

When the crash came, I saw Felicia lurch forward, just a second too late to catch Leszek. He slumped blackly against his stand, the gash in his forehead visible from the farthest stalls. The Beethoven jarred to a stop as if someone had pulled an emergency cord; I leapt on to the stage.

Leszek was unconscious, surrounded by a panicked group of players and a rising tide of commentary. The audience craned around for a better view; while about fifteen doctors, some of whom turned out to be bogus, stepped forward from the stalls.

Leszek looked green; I'd never seen anyone look green before. His eyelids were purplish-blue, but there was an avocado tinge to the rest of his face. I sat there muttering as if he'd died, 'But I liked him, the coffee-chucking Polish nutcase. I really liked him,' while medical opinions proliferated all around.

'Heart or stroke . . . pulse weakened . . . surely anyone could faint in the heat of this stage . . . Losing it, wasn't he, during the last few minutes . . . need to check the blood pressure under proper . . . In my opinion . . . my own judgement . . . For what it's worth . . .'

When the St John's Ambulance people arrived, I was freed to look for William. I found him backstage, savagely shoving his cello back in its case.

'Janice?' I asked swiftly.

'The heat came from behind. But the cello – Pete, I can't describe it . . . And you can't pretend there was anything natural in what happened to Leszek.'

'Will,' I said suddenly. 'You don't think you should have agreed to hear Janice play?'

'You think it might be connected?'

'She was absolutely – incandescent. I think your refusal put her into a vicious temper.'

William shook his head. 'What could she hope to gain by playing for me? Even if I'd got the influence I had in my old orchestra, which naturally I don't—'

'Power might be part of it. Do you want to hear my theory? I think it's an anti-men thing. First she gains some perverse psychic domination, and then the knife goes in . . . Her expression was so unspeakably malevolent – and then it was suddenly wiped clean, nothing there at all . . . Will: she sleeps in his bed at night. What's to stop it ending in murder?'

'I don't know, but mine is a different interpretation. Do you want to hear it?'

'Go on.'

'I'm no expert on the supernatural – didn't even believe in it until recently – but everything I've ever heard suggests a more personal motivation . . . I suspect that Leszek might have offended or upset someone, possibly a relative, a child even, who has since died. Perhaps whoever it is has – somehow – returned, and is looking to exact some form of revenge. Does that sound remotely plausible to you?'

'Pete, my angel,' said Felicia. 'You're wanted.'

Infuriating as it was to be hauled away from Will just as we seemed to be getting somewhere, I was touched to discover that Leszek wanted me in the ambulance with him.

Leszek had a more normal pallor as they helped him into the vehicle. He was receiving oxygen, so he couldn't speak, but I chatted to the medics while his strange, multi-coloured eyes eyeballed me over his oxygen-mask.

'Are you a relation?' one paramedic inquired.

'No, an employee.'

'Broke up the concert early, is what I heard.'

'The sooner every concert breaks up, the better,' I observed, paying due homage to Jane Austen. 'I assume there's nothing wrong with him barring rabies, as usual.'

'He'll be thoroughly checked,' he assured me, without answering the question. Only then did it occur to me to wonder why Janice wasn't with us, and whether Leszek knew more than he was currently in a position to say.

Over the next few days, Leszek was subjected to any number of tests, without result. On the fourth day I cornered one of the hospital doctors and asked him what had happened in the concert.

'It's difficult to describe in layman's terms.'

'Layman be blowed,' I growled. 'Just give me something for the ex-wives and girlfriends, currently telephoning at the rate of three a day.'

The man looked uncomfortable, and suddenly very young.

'The symptoms do not accord with any catalogued disorder.'

I didn't realise until that moment how much I'd been hoping for a logical explanation. I blustered, 'But people don't just – collapse – for no reason!'

'Oh something certainly happened . . . His blood pressure and pulse were deranged, accompanied by some neurological phenomena . . . But it's still a good deal easier to say what didn't happen. Mr Zimetski didn't have a fit, an asthmatic incident, a blood clot, any sort of stroke or even a minor heart attack. Something – we don't know what – simply felled him.'

A good deal sobered, I thanked the fellow and went to view the remains.

They'd put Leszek in a room on his own, bedecked with fresh flowers (the Princess Royal had always liked him). He looked exceptionally Slavic, propped up in bed with some dog-eared scores on his lap.

'Pete,' he said, pronouncing it as 'pit' as usual. 'It is most good of you to come.'

'Not at all.'

'I wanted to see you.'

'S'blood, a natural enough desire.'

'I wanted most urgently to ask you about what you said – a week ago, was it? How long is it I have been here?'

'Three days. What did I say?'

'You said – you said you had an instinct that I should not perform this symphony, the "Pastoral". Call it an instinct, was what you said . . . What exactly did you mean by this? What was this instinct that you had?'

And blow me if I hadn't. I shivered then at my own perspicacity, although in all conscience it was more a turn of phrase, for I'm as fond of a phrase as the next man, and very likely fonder.

'I don't really know. I think – I'm pretty sure I was only kidding. Leszek, may I be frank?'

'Indeed.'

'Why haven't you asked to see Janice yet?'

'I do not intend to answer personal—' he began sharpish, then he seemed to calm down. 'This is entirely unrelated. A private matter.'

'And nothing to do with what happened during the Beethoven?' I asked, watching him closely. For a moment he looked like a ghost himself, those terrible eyes flaring whitely like a frightened horse's.

'Pete, if this is one of your terrible jokes—'

'No joke, I'm afraid . . . Leszek, have you ever – ever offended anyone?'

'I did not ask for you to come in order—'

'Think about it. It might be important. Someone in your past, your family even, perhaps a woman?'

'I am on most excellent terms with my family,' he fumed. 'I fail to see—'

'Just answer one more question, then I'll have done. Does Janice – could Janice possibly remind you, one way or another, of anyone you ever knew before?'

His reaction surpassed my most extravagant expectations. He screamed – literally screamed – as if I'd knifed him, and the nurse who rushed in clearly thought I had.

'Never! Never! Never!' hurling his scores to the floor. A terrifying moment from Britten's *Turn of the Screw* came back to me: that stomach-scooping 'Miles, Miles, Miles.'

'I'm sorry,' I murmured at the door. He was weeping, and the nurse had her arm around him, while the look she gave me would have caused raised eyebrows if directed at a more than usually insensitive sewer-rat.

'Get out! Leave him at once – this minute!'

And I left the hospital, banished for the duration. As the ward sister put it, 'If on the tenth day following, thy banished trunk be found in our dominions, the moment is thy death. Away! By Jupiter, this shall not be revoked!'

Or something very like it.

CHAPTER 31

Marry, this is miching mallecho. It means mischief.
Shakespeare

In the absence of Leszek, the orchestral temperature gradually returned to normal. The accepted version put about was that he'd suffered a nervous fit exacerbated by chronic overwork and jetlag, and such members as suspected differently kept it to themselves.

That August was hot, too hot for the studio work; there was a sultry heaviness about it. William was looking forward to a cool drink in the break when Terence hailed him from the back of the cello section.

'Can I have a word with you, old man?'

Will stifled a sigh. Terence's 'words' were so immensely wordy; nor was William over-fond of being addressed as 'old man'. However, he paused with his accustomed courtesy, cello in hand. Colour still washed over it like waves over a beach: Janice was not far distant.

'What can I do for you?'

Terence puffed slightly, for he was fat and scant of breath.

'I think a lot of you, William, you know that.'

'I'm much obliged.'

'We all do, you know, practically without exception. However, the bottom line is that time doesn't stand still. At the end of the day, we can't recapture the past; what's gone is gone, and none of us is getting younger any more.'

'Sorry to interrupt,' said William dryly, 'but is this yet another attempt to get seating rotation in the cello section?'

'No, no, rather not. Mind, I still think it a sound scheme, but John's views are so hidebound and reactionary—'

'Sorry. Do go on.'

'Thank you. Perhaps you are not aware – or, then again, you may be – of my current feelings regarding my position in the section. There is no doubt that my talents are being under-exploited, unrecognised and undervalued, in terms of the section as a whole.'

William believed that Terence had happened to mention it, now and again.

'Yes, well, I've set myself some new medium-term goals, which, in the fullness of time, may yet address some of the problems I find myself facing on a day-to-day basis.'

William was glad to hear it, and wondered aloud whether Terence had ever considered a career in politics.

'Good heavens, no! I was born to play the cello. My mother discovered this when I was only two. She handed me a toy violin, which I chose to hold uncannily as if it was a cello. This is well documented. No, what I had in mind is moving to a higher position in a different orchestra.'

William warmly observed that it seemed a marvellous plan, and added that he would be delighted to listen to Terence's audition piece at any time that suited him.

'That won't be necessary. My audition piece is Kabalevsky's second, which is unlikely to be in your repertoire; and besides, I have at this point few doubts about my abilities playing-wise. No, what I wanted, if you would be so good, is – in short – a letter of recommendation.'

William listened, alarmed. 'Recommendation! But surely John McDaniel is your most obvious referee. He's the principal; and I'm only number five.'

'True, true indeed, but in the circumstances – may I speak frankly?'

'Please,' said William, seeing his free time rapidly evaporating.

'To be frank then, John and I have radically differing points of view with regard to the multifarious aspects of cello-playing technique.'

'No doubt,' said William hastily. 'But I know he rates your playing highly, and would also be much better placed—'

'Forgive me for interrupting. I have yet to put the full facts of the case before you. In brief, the Orchestra of London is the group in question . . . Now, until last February, is it not the case that you held down the position of associate principal cello in that organisation?'

William admitted the fact under cross-examination.

'And are you aware – you probably are – that one Adam Halloran has since inherited your position there?'

Over Piotr's ever-living body, thought William, and nodded.

'Well, you may not know that Adam Halloran's previous berth, which is to say, the cello four position, has just been advertised. Now *that* is the precise post for which I wish to apply. Under these circumstances, I can think of no one better suited to recommend me than someone who recently left that very orchestra, regretted by all, and who is currently a most esteemed colleague of my own.'

William felt that he could stand very little more verbalising along these lines. Any reminder of Adam's elevation – Adam being sycophant extraordinary to David – always acutely affected him. Hardly surprising that Piotr remained so bitter against him, when his departure had directly led to Adam's elevation . . . And Piotr would absolutely loathe Terence. He would never forgive anyone who had helped to make Terence's transfer possible . . . Though, come to think of it, that outcome might be easy enough to prevent, with a touch of guile. After all, no one was quicker at a hint than Piotr.

'I should be pleased to recommend you,' said William formally. 'And all the best for your audition, as well.'

'I'm glad you mentioned the audition,' Terence pressed on. 'I've been meaning to ask you yet another favour.'

'Yes?' asked William, who had already half-turned.

'You've a particularly fine little cello there, I've often thought so.'

'Thank you. It's – a characterful instrument.'

'In the right hands, it could be really marvellous . . . What I was wondering was whether I might borrow it for my audition. My own cello, as you doubtless know, lacks the subtle variety of tone that I could wish it had. In the long run, I need a really superb instrument, but that's out of the question, at least at this moment in time.'

'Borrow it by all means. I can bring my Lott cello tomorrow.'

'My dear fellow, I'll never forget this. In years to come, in interviews and so on, I will always mention your unstinting kindness to a younger player. It is spelled M-E-L-L-O-R?'

William admitted it, and stood looking after the exultant Terence thoughtfully. He felt like adding that Terence couldn't expect the cello to behave, though it was surely impossible that it should encounter Leszek Zimetski at the auditions for a rival orchestra . . .

He thought: a year ago, I'd have been on that audition panel myself. David, Piotr and me, listening to cellist after cellist, concerto after concerto. It wouldn't have been comfortable – the combination of Piotr's subversiveness and David's obliviousness was never comfortable – but now recollection glossed the memory like the fragrance of childhood happiness.

A week later, Piotr glanced with furrowed brow at the name of the next contender.

'Terence L. J. Hennessy. Sounds like a minor county cricketer.'

'Currently ninth-chair cello in the Royal Sinfonia,' read Adam. 'Recommended – good Lord, David, he was recommended by William. There's a letter from him here.'

'Not William Mellor?' demanded David.

'Yes. Here it is.'

Piotr snatched the letter from David's hand.

'That letter is addressed to the section principal!'

'Very likely. However, I have a strange intuition that it was none the less written to me . . . "Terence Hennessy is a man of many talents" – cryptic, you observe, from the very outset. "He has performed with power and energy in the back of the Royal Sinfonia for some years": in other words, the boy leads from the rear and never plays pianissimo, even by accident. "His commitment and dedication cannot be doubted" – an ambitious little toad, as I suspected. "I am pleased to recommend him to your judgement with regard to the vacant position in the Orchestra of London" – meaning, oi, maties, watch out below. I see all. Do you see all?'

David took the letter, frowning, while Adam objected.

'You'd read things into a shopping list, Piotr. William wouldn't recommend someone he didn't like.'

'On the contrary, I can think of no one more likely to recommend someone he didn't like, especially in these rather equivocal terms . . . William's too kind-hearted to say no to this Terence outsider, but he's too bleeding-heart liberal-democrat to admit that he despises the bastard.'

'Power and energy, commitment and dedication!' repeated David. 'This is a cellist I would very much like to hear. Nor would I wish to discount William's opinion. You know, Adam, I am still very sorry that he felt he had to leave. He was not brilliant – not at all – but he was reliable, a good foil to me. In fact—'

'He had the greatest respect for you, everybody knew that. The trouble was entirely with Isabel.'

'Yes, this is very true . . . Isabel is not as handsome, I think, as she used to be. She has a strange look sometimes, almost sad, and I don't like what she does to her hair, as if she doesn't even care whether it stays up or not . . . But where is this so-fine cellist? He is very slow to appear.'

Terence entered then, ever subtly off-cue. He had slicked back his locks for the occasion, and polished the Italian cello, which glittered like amethyst. His hands looked more corpulent and capable than ever, and his mouth was set in a complacent little line.

'Hello,' said David, extending his hand. 'I—'

'David Schaedel, of course,' said Terence promptly. 'I simply adored your Elgar concerto.'

'Oh, were you there?'

'I was, and, in point of fact, I brought my four best cello pupils with me. One of them said afterwards, with tears in her eyes, that Du Pré herself wasn't in your league.'

'Yes, it was not a bad performance,' said David judiciously. 'I felt perhaps that the beginning of the last movement was too quick. A little quick, I thought I played it, although—'

'The beginning of the last movement,' interrupted Terence, 'had a truly majestic sweep and grandeur. At the end of the day—'

'And it'll be the end of the day, if we don't get on,' said Piotr sharply. 'We're miles behind schedule as it is. What concerto have you brought, Terence?'

'The Kabalevsky second.'

'The second!' repeated David. 'That is most unusual.'

While Terence tuned to the piano, Piotr picked up William's letter again.

Not for Will the word-processor and laser printer. His letter was handwritten in a heavy, upright hand, without a suspicion of a flourish until the whiplike, almost brusque, underlining of the signature . . . Piotr could just imagine Will bent over his desk; his eyes following the curvaceous flight of a blue-tit out of the window. The house would be quiet, except for his fountain pen creaming the paper, empty of wife, son – even the little white dog had gone with these.

Will wasn't used to solitude, thought Piotr. He isn't like me, a maverick, a loner, used to sex on the run and struggling with life. He'd come from a comfortable family and maintained a comfortable home. The wry tone of Will's letter made Piotr miss him furiously. Why had he ever let Isabel drive him away? And the fact that he knew the answer only made his anger burn deeper.

Suddenly he was roused from his reverie. The Italian cello, which had participated willingly enough in the opening of the Kabalevsky, suddenly sprang to life. The instrument sparked as if it had been torched from within; it glowed with a crimson sheen, the crack like lava down its belly. And the sound! – It was a sound that the great Daniil Shafran would have been proud to produce; and on Terence's paunchy face was a look in which disbelief, pleasure and near-terror were finely balanced . . . The little cello was using him, manipulating his muscles to produce what sound it chose: it was malicious, fabulous, insane.

The movement finished, the cello was quenched, strings gradually cooling under Terence's fingers. Shock robbed Piotr of speech, and jealousy silenced Adam, but David Schaedel was delighted.

'My dear Terence, what a sensational tone! What did you say your cello was?'

'No one knows who made it,' said Terence rather thickly. His tongue cleaved to the roof of his mouth; he was breathless with nerves and pleasure. It isn't really my cello, he knew he ought to add, but the words didn't come. He wondered uneasily whether Piotr might know that the cello was William's.

'But where did you find it?' asked David impatiently.

'It – was bought at an auction.'

David strummed the strings but the cello had gone still. 'I don't think we need to hear any more, do you?'

'I suppose not,' said Piotr grudgingly. 'Do you mind if I take a look?'

Terence stood pinkly by while Piotr advanced on the cello. But as he touched the strings, they flared, heating with the speed of a gas fire. He almost dropped the instrument against the chair. It's as if the little brute suddenly – recognised me, he thought.

'Very pretty,' he said meaninglessly.

You're losing your grip, he told himself. One look at Will's handwriting and you're imagining cracks and heat and a sound like a river crashing over cliffs. It's only a cello, only a few pieces of varnished wood, glued up and bound together. And he applied himself resolutely to the c.v. of the next candidate, while David talked to Terence, and Adam Halloran sulked.

CHAPTER 32

Life's but a walking shadow, a poor player
That struts and frets his hour upon the stage,
And then is heard no more.

Shakespeare

Over the months Margot developed a technique of detachment at curious variance to her wholehearted character. There were still occasions when a shrillness in her veins edged her towards misery, but applying herself to a solid problem – balancing her cheque-book, attending to Olivia – rarely failed to restore her equanimity.

And Olivia was always in want of attention. Sporadic, if energetic, in all her enthusiasms, she was currently fixated on the upcoming Euro-elections. Her fervour for the Conservative cause was in no way diminished by the attractions of sitting MEP Edwin Narbold, an agreeable Yorkshireman with an insinuating manner and a melodious voice.

Despite two terms in the saddle, Narbold was pursuing re-election with undiminished determination. He attended dinners, pressed flesh, and took every opportunity to address meetings, believing, and with some justice, that his rich-toned diction was worth any number of votes to him. Olivia often remarked, 'Such a pleasure to hear someone speak English so beautifully! And I believe he's also very clever at French.'

Margot was more circumspect in her admiration. She found Edwin's speeches ponderous, and his compliments (for he always seemed to ask after her) gratuitous.

'I daresay Edwin would be pleased if you came to his

adoption meeting,' Olivia had suggested, but the effort involved dismayed Margot and she could imagine the scene all too vividly. The heavy interior, inadequate heating and tired paintwork of Thatcher Hall; Edwin being pampered by any number of adoring supporters; members discussing 'poor Margot' in deafening undertones.

'Dear ladies,' Edwin would surely begin, before breaking off to compliment Mrs Thornton on his tepid tea. 'Dear ladies – and Group Captain Culbertson, of course – I can hardly believe that it is time to stand before you once again. To coin a phrase, if coin a phrase I must, how time has flown. In Brussels and in Strasbourg, in Strasbourg and Brussels, I have been working on behalf of you, my most loyal constituents . . .'

She had attended too many political meetings, Margot decided, and the night was too mild to waste, the full moon sheathed by diaphanous clouds, and a light breeze riding on the air. She felt a sudden longing to be outside, to experience the soft tang of the last of the summer honeysuckle. The moment Olivia's tail-lights had disappeared down the road she wheeled herself down the precarious slope of the long back garden.

The soil was still soft enough for her chair to leave treadmarks in the grass, but the evening was even milder and more sensuous than she had imagined. Stars were thumbed at clever intervals in navy silk; the air was tangy with the delicious scent of new-cut grass; a fuzzing bee flicked past her face.

Margot forgot her mother, forgot the Conservative Party, forgot everything except the glowing, curtained night. She lifted her arms towards it, as if with one final effort she would catch hold of its mystery – then suddenly she saw him.

Framed in silhouette against Olivia's French windows, a little slimmer, a bit less certain, but William nonetheless. Margot's arms fell, shaking, to her sides. She watched him advance, step by light step . . . But then, he had always known how to carry his weight, and the chrome chair must glint in the light from the French window.

'Margot?'

Yes, I'm here, she wanted to tell him. Wheel me in, reproach me for my audacity. What right have I to sit in the chill of evening, communing with the stars? I'm forty-two, disabled, unloved, alone. There's nothing here to admire, nothing to complement the glowing awakening in the air, the alien fulfilment of the moon.

She could sense him then; her awareness, like a fox's, enamelled by the night; and she recognised his authoritative grip on the back of her chair. If he tells me I shouldn't be here – she thought fiercely, but William had no such intention. The leather grip of the wheelchair represented his only connection with reality. The moon had unspun his brain, and he was a throwback to his heritage – all Celt, all romance and unreason, head braced against the muzzles of the stars.

'I guessed Olivia would be out,' he said, his voice unsteady in the softened air.

How? she wondered. The uncertainty in his voice touched Margot; she hardened herself against it.

'I want to stay outside,' she warned him, resenting his closeness, the command of his fingers on her chair. She felt electrically sensitive to his every movement; she wondered that she didn't feel the earth's crust echoing deep beneath their feet.

'Yes. It's easier to talk in the dark.'

'But there's nothing to say.'

'Even nothing is something, in its way.'

She raged against his understanding. It seemed intolerable that he should dare to understand, even in part, the hideously malformed shapes his behaviour had conjured in her mind. His arms, still strong and well developed, around a girl with a testing face, his body tense with arousal . . . She seemed to recall a similar dream – or had it happened? – in which he had appeared, shadowy charcoal shoulders looming over her bed. But there was something she'd had in mind to tell him, all these weeks and months. She summoned it up.

'There's always a moment when we choose, either to fall in love, or not . . . There was a moment, wasn't there? And you went the other way.'

'There was such a moment, of course. But I didn't recognise it, and anyway, it's long since past.'

His stupidity, which seemed deliberate, infuriated her prickling nerves. She said, 'Nothing passes. It's all baggage we're not allowed to check in. The past becomes ourselves, the very fibrous interwoven marrow of ourselves. We can no more escape that than—'

'So far we agree, at any rate.' And his fingers shuddered on her chair, which resonated with the earth, the serious gestures of the stars. He's seen her, she thought; and perhaps he comes here fresh from tasting the heat of her skin, the salt of her lips.

He thought: of course Margot hated him now – for knowing, for understanding her pain. Pride alone would make her hate him, and even love could stand very little chance against sore branded pride. He had automatically turned her chair.

'Don't direct me,' she said haughtily, and he halted, hands flickering over the handles like an unfamiliar keyboard.

'Do you still want to stay out?'

'Yes.'

He wanted to say, let me get you a jacket, at least, but the motionlessness of her intensity defeated him . . . At this moment she hates everything about me, from my heavy fingers on her chair to my prick, heavy too with hopelessness, tucked deep inside my trousers. I've intruded into her secret misery; and it's far too soon to hope that anything better might come. My instinct was altogether wrong – too rudimentary, too precipitate, altogether too masculine. Women have reservoirs of pain we lack, and deep-seated veins of feeling, like underwater rivers. When the time is right, I'll come back, and screw my every nerve to subtlety . . . When the time is right, if the right time ever comes.

'I'll come again,' he promised, though his voice sounded pleading in his ears.

I don't need you, she longed to say: I don't need anyone, but the words curved over her lips and broke like waves against the top of her mouth. Instead she urged the chair back into the shadows. The stars were unbearably bright once he had gone, and under the earth she thought she heard a murmuring thunder, like underwater springs.

CHAPTER 33

As I did stand my watch upon the hill,
I looked toward Birnam, and anon, methought,
The wood began to move.

Shakespeare

(from Pete Hegal's diaries)

By early October Leszek was allowed to work again. Janice had attended him for most of his convalescence, and all but the most virulent of his ex-wives had visited him at home. Meanwhile the press had obliged with any number of pieces, mainly though not entirely hogwash, about the inhuman burdens of the international conducting circuit.

Though it's a tough life, no question. I mean, just imagine it. Imagine being obliged to fly everywhere first-class and earning thousands of pounds a concert. Imagine the bore of dictating your own musical interpretations to the world's finest orchestras – the sheer daily grind of communing with music of manifold genius. Not to mention the nuisance of having some really stunning women – mainly though not exclusively sopranos – throwing themselves at your feet between rehearsal and concert. Oh, I feel for international conductors, I really do; I cry buckets, most nights, recalling what torture their lives are. Small wonder nobody wants to do it. Small wonder the cry goes up, from every opera house and concert-hall: Would somebody mind conducting this? Doesn't anyone out there want to be a conductor?

But I digress.

Leszek celebrated his recovery by taking Janice to the Bahamas, while the band persevered with a series of talentless guest conductors and second-rate concerts. Boredom and peacefulness were the keynotes, though there were the usual minor dramas – a violist had her instrument stolen, a clarinettist broke a finger in his car door – but then, the absence of those might have been more remarkable.

Eddie Wellington went about looking cherubic and playing devilishly, while William Mellor's little Italian cello went ashen and dark. I knew (because Will told me) that a recent attempt to talk to his wife had been useless. I also noticed that he was keeping Angela at a safe distance – though safe for whom might perhaps be debatable.

The day Leszek was due back, I encountered Janice in the Festival Hall car park. She looked like an advert for something; her firm-toned radiance echoing the Indian summer of early October.

'Had a good break?' I inquired politely. I'd forgotten how purely, archaically beautiful her profile was, but I hadn't forgotten Beethoven's Sixth. I still had nightmares about the screeching woodwinds and murderous double basses of the 'Storm'.

'We had a lovely time, thank you,' she said demurely.

'His nibs well, I trust?'

'Of course,' she said after a little hesitation.

'Not chewing glass, is he? Not conducting ritual sacrifices at the time of the full moon? Nothing, in short, for the average orchestral manager to pine about?'

'I am a little worried about Eddie Wellington.'

I responded gamely, though my heart misgave me. 'No need. The Duke's in fine fettle.'

'Well, he wouldn't know yet.'

'Wouldn't know what, exactly?'

'Pete, Leszek's decided to give him the final warning . . . I simply haven't been able to talk him out of it.'

The day, as foreshadowed, was the sort that makes jaded

taxi drivers whistle. A frisky little breeze just ruffled the Thames while clouds washed over a watercoloured sky. However, this newsflash ruined it for me. Oh, it wasn't the end for the Duke – not definitely – but I could anticipate the upshot all too clearly: the hearings, the arguments, the paperwork, the sheer grinding ill-feeling of it all. I damned and blasted all conductors.

'Perhaps the board . . .' Janice suggested.

'Oh, they'll try,' I told her grimly. 'There'll be a dust-up, no question.'

Janice fished her cello out of her car, while I headed towards the entrance. I was just turning around to add something – can't remember what – when I saw something that dried the saliva in my mouth.

Because Janice, shining and slender as she was, was nonetheless lacking. The cello's elongated shadow darkened the gravel – but Janice cast no shadow at all.

The first thing I did upon reaching the office was to page William. I also left Lenny a message, forewarning him about the crisis in Eddie Wellington's affairs; and then I went out for lunch. I was behind on my paperwork and don't often skive off, but the atmosphere of the Festival Hall was wrecked for me. The notion that I might, around the next bend of a corridor, encounter Leszek – or, still worse, a blissfully unconscious Duke – would have ashed any food in my mouth.

My preferred alternative was a festive eatery in the bowels of Covent Garden. It was there that I spotted Piotr, sub-principal cello and maverick board member of the Orchestra of London. Attired entirely in black, he was surrounded by any number of Equity types, and at first glance I thought he was drunk. He hoisted a glass in my direction.

'No, don't tell me – Omaha beach on D-Day. You were tenth ashore, just behind "Pigeon-Toe" Butler, beating me by two one-hundredths of a second. Well met, sirrah. Permit me to welcome you back to the end of the world.'

'Oh, *do* put a sock in it!' objected a plummily vowelled luvvie. 'You've been doomsaying for yonks and it's getting to be the most frightful bore.'

Piotr ignored him. He was looking at me intently and I realised that he was far from drunk, that he would indeed have given a good deal of money to be drunk. He had hot dry eyes and the loose-limbed grin of a madman.

'Poor petal,' he said. 'You haven't heard, have you?'

'Heard what?' I asked. About Leszek, though I partly detested him – or even William? Why was his tone so personal, so casually merciless?

'You heerd, cowboy. Thissere town ain't a-big enough fer both of us.'

'What the hell are you talking about?'

One of the actors condescended to be explicit: 'It was on the lunchtime news. One of the London orchestras is to be disbanded, either Piotr's or the other lot.'

'But that's crazy – impossible! I'm the manager, for God's sake. I would have heard!'

'Too bad,' said the actor without sympathy, but Piotr was more encouraging.

'Cheer up. I know for a fact that there'll soon be vacancies in a catfood supply depot near Colchester. An easy commute from central London, and the money's good, though there's not much of it.'

I whipped out my mobile and tried the office, but of course it was busy. Every line I could think of was busy. Piotr watched, while the actors, feeling no doubt that the scene, though starting promisingly, lacked dash and grip, began to abuse some casting director. I folded up my phone and turned back to Piotr, who was still leaning against the bar as if too languid to hold himself upright.

'The Arts Council, is it?'

'Would I wilfully mislead you?'

'But I thought they'd chucked that idea years ago.'

'So did I. God bless us all, and Tiny Tim.'

'They'll back down. There'll be public pressure, even questions in Parliament. There was the most terrific fuss last time.'

'There'll be protests, I grant you, but this is a very much craftier scheme – "restructuring", they're calling it. Only one group disbanded and the other on double rations – the Council can't even be accused of actual cutbacks. No, it's Hochler versus Zimetski, cello section v. cello section, eyeball v. eyeball. Bids on the table no later than Jan., decision end of Feb., mine's a vodka tonic.'

'You versus me.'

Piotr waved a deprecatory hand. 'Not at all. Remember, we met – did we not? – at Agincourt. You're built on altogether too hefty a scale to fit into my lifestyle, but I've nothing more concrete against you. As for being the Ranting Sinner's manager – well, it's tough at the top, so they tell me, and even tougher at the bottom. However, there's someone in your orchestra I used to be friendly with—'

'Will.'

'—and if there's one thing I would advise someone never to become, it's an ex-friend of mine. A rotten career move, I call it, and one that his friends should have unceasingly counselled him against.'

'Actually, he was sorry that you hadn't sent your regards, the last time we met. He told me—'

Piotr downed the remains of his vodka so swiftly that his eyes were jewelled with tears.

'I can forgive anything except disloyalty,' he said. 'Even loyalty's better than that.'

'Will still cares about you, I know.'

'Heaven forfend. Just look what happens to the poor buggers Will cares about. Look at Margot, imprisoned at her grisly mother's, and Isabel, stilettoed on the border between sanity and corruption—'

Look at you, I thought, as he leaned across to requisition another vodka. You're wiry as a balcony railing and pale as a banshee; a strong wind could push you over and you're too miserable even to get drunk properly . . . Piotr twisted his glass around and glowered as if daring me to understand.

'I didn't deserve to lose him,' he said, while the voices of the actors rose up in sudden dispute around us. I had to strain to hear his voice, which was ragged with smoke and exhaustion. 'There was an edge, which Will stepped over. I told him it was there, but he didn't listen. I told him, but I couldn't bear it and in the end I pushed. I'll never forgive him for that.'

'For what?'

'For letting me do it. Unamuno. To become a victim is a diabolical vengeance.'

A diabolical vengeance. Piotr was sweating, I noticed, though the day had turned windy, almost autumnal. A little rivulet of sweat rolled from under that black lock across his forehead. There was something inescapably foreign about him, I thought, something alien to (whatever it is) that represents Britishness.

It was as if he had endless layers, and the more layers he peeled off, the more remained. He had so many voices that he sometimes submerged himself entirely, and his intensity was such that he seemed always burning, always consuming himself. I wondered if he'd ever been entirely well, if he would recognise the feeling if he stumbled on it, even whether he wanted to be. Where did Piotr's mockery end and self-mockery start? And where, in the midst of all the play-acting, was the irreducible core of the fellow?

Piotr finished his final drink with disquieting speed, slinging his jacket exaggeratedly over his shoulder.

'Of course, the Royal Sinfonia could always disband, save time and bother. You might recommend this to Zimetski as a course worth considering.'

My mobile – at long last – was ringing furiously in my pocket. It would be Lenny, Leszek, or somebody from the office. My head was still fuzzy with shock and uncertainty, but some impulse of sympathy made me put a hamlike hand on Piotr's arm.

'I'm sorry,' I said. 'I know you've been through a lot already.'

He looked down at my hand as if puzzled to think what it was doing there. 'Hell, don't mention it. What are enemies for?'

Then he was off, moving with surprising agility through the crowd. I picked up my phone and found our worthy librarian on the other end.

'Pete, we need you at the Festival Hall instanter. There have been developments, and Tiger's slipped his lead and is on the loose.'

'On my way.' I snapped the phone shut in my pocket. Phones shrilling all over London, I thought, phone after phone, pager after pager. Pistols at dawn; shoot-out in Arts Council corral. It could be cataclysmic – for the orchestra, for my own employment prospects, for classical music generally. But what I remembered longest was the look on Piotr's thin face when I first mentioned Will's name.

Chapter 34

The enemy's in view; draw up your powers.

Shakespeare

A week later, Paul Ellison rang the doorbell at Hochler's Knightsbridge flat.

'Isabel, hello. I'm not too early, I hope.'

'Of course not. Karl's waiting.'

Paul and I have a history, she had told Karl – though, as histories go, it isn't important. She sometimes wondered whether Paul even remembered it: the smoky Strasbourg night, chandeliers reflecting chopped fragments on to the patio, William emerging from the shadows. Certainly Paul never seemed to recollect it, treating Isabel with the distinct if distant gallantry advisable towards a colleague who was also the avowed mistress of the principal conductor.

Hochler advancing, hand outstretched. 'Paul, my good friend. Thank you for coming.'

They were alike, thought Isabel. Not in appearance, for Paul had a casually sporty air, while Karl retained the meticulous presentation of subtly Teutonic aristocracy. But there was a similar resonance – in beliefs, in attitude – which was probably why Paul had chosen to scheme on Karl's behalf almost from the beginning. They shared an air of mutual self-congratulation: two heads of state, jovial, masculine, exclusionary.

'Paul – gin, sherry or wine?' asked Isabel.

'Thanks – a smallish gin and tonic.'

Isabel had altered, in Paul's opinion, though the difference was hard to quantify. Certainly she didn't look as gaunt as she had when Mellor had resigned, nor as tightly stretched. Yet her beauty had been marred; it lacked the patina that he remembered; she would have escaped it if she could. How old was she, thirty-five, thirty-six? He read escape in her eyes.

The men sipped their drinks in Karl's black-and-chrome lounge. Leave us alone at first, Karl had suggested. Then bring in the canapés, judge the mood . . . After a short preamble, Paul indicated the door, lowering his voice.

'Isabel. Is she completely safe?'

'Safe, my friend? In what sense safe? Women, as you know, are inherently dangerous.'

We have a history, Paul and I . . . Though Isabel had a history with practically everybody.

'I mean the new order of politics, us against the Royal Sinfonia.'

'Isabel is as convinced that we must succeed as you or I.'

'We can't afford leaks, that's all.'

'Leaks? Press leaks? Is that what is worrying you?'

Paul shook his head. 'Karl, I don't know whether you're aware that William Mellor's moved to the Royal Sinfonia.'

Hochler smiled suavely. 'So! At last I understand you. But your fears, I assure you, are quite unnecessary. There has been no communication between them; indeed, I think she has almost forgotten the business. For a while perhaps I thought differently – it was a strange romance – but no longer.'

'Really?'

'He is so much older, and soon he must in any case retire. And besides, she must be angry at him for leaving her – if I know anything of women, she will be angry . . . Besides, between us, there is no possibility that Mellor would have been equal to satisfying Isabel, of that I can assure you. I have conducted him many times, and with some attention. He is without that spark, that insatiate sensuality—No, this affair was an aberration only, when she happened to be alone.'

Paul, though flattered by the intimacy implied by such a

discussion, remained secretly unconvinced. But she's altered, he wanted to say: just look at her. There was a glow when she was William's, the way she moved was different, the snap in her eyes. Now it's as if someone's clapped a lid over her; she's quenched, drained, a snuffed candle.

'Women go with older men for certain psychological reasons,' Karl continued, sipping his wine appreciatively. 'For rather interesting reasons, in my opinion . . . They look for reassurance, comfort, for the sensation of being cherished – even for a belated reconciliation with their own fathers. As you may perhaps know, Isabel has had difficulties with her own father . . . But, as for passion, the kind that you and I would understand – well, that is not the reason. If you could speak frankly to Isabel, I think that you would find she looks on the entire affair as a mistake.'

'Quite,' said Paul, anxious not to disagree. Yet he couldn't help recalling Warren's quiet comment after William had left. ('Is she well? What do you mean, well? She'll never be well again.') Karl, however, elected to dismiss the topic.

'And so! You have the contacts organised that we spoke of?'

'I do indeed; and there's no time to lose. You'll have no worries with Lionel. I only wish I felt as secure of all the others.'

'The special committee has seven members, is it?'

Paul nodded. 'Seven voting members, plus a few advisory . . . Thanks, Isabel. We're deep into bribery and corruption here.'

Isabel sat down, pushing back her soft black hair. Both men glanced at her with more attention than usual.

'Bribery?' she inquired.

'And corruption. It's the Ulverston committee – the one formed to recommend to the Arts Council which orchestra survives . . . I don't suppose you were at music college with Lord Ulverston's youngest, were you?'

'Sorry, no.'

'Ever had a passionate affair with Cecil Murraigh MBE?'

Isabel denied it, whereupon Karl proposed: 'We must use her as saboteur, to captivate Leszek Zimetski.'

'Oh Zimetski's taken,' said Paul, who made it his business to hear everything. 'A new young cellist, Janice somebody.'

'These cellists, they get everywhere.'

Isabel smiled. 'In any case, I doubt whether I'd be of any use.'

Karl slid his hand down her thigh. 'Of course you are of use; you are beautiful and play viola and do marvellous canapés. Are there any more in the kitchen?' And to Paul, in an undertone, 'I don't think we ought to mention the financial side to Isabel. Piotr knows, and you and I. In my opinion, that is quite enough.'

'Absolutely. Couldn't agree more.'

Isabel was more sober on her return. 'It still seems horrible to be plotting against a fellow orchestra. Warren Wilson's got a cousin in the Sinfonia, you know, and Lucy's dad plays there as well.'

'I know some of the wind-players myself,' said Paul briskly, 'but they won't be feeling over-scrupulous about our feelings. At this very moment, perhaps, Zimetski's meeting with Lenny Denver and the rest of their board.'

'Why aren't you meeting with the rest of our board, then?'

Karl Hochler cast a lazy smile towards Paul. 'What is the phrase, that God so loved the world that he failed to send a committee?'

'Piotr's useful,' said Paul. 'He's absolutely committed to destroying the Sinfonia, aside from anything else – but the rest of our lot are simply too dozy to be of much use in a crisis.'

'Piotr? But Piotr's irrational,' said Isabel impulsively.

'Irrational? Don't be absurd.'

'He is – he can be – especially now.'

'Listen, Piotr's the one who thought of – well, several of our riper notions. He's one hundred per cent committed, you can take it from me, and brilliant with it.'

'He is brilliant, but you can't rely on his loyalty. Piotr isn't like other people – he lives by his own rules.'

Paul lost his temper. 'Piotr is absolutely loyal – to the orchestra, and to Karl. What *you* can't forgive him for is for being too loyal to Will Mellor to care a damn about you.'

Isabel flung herself into the kitchen, leaving Karl bemused. Paul said with some embarrassment, 'Sorry, Karl. I didn't mean to upset her.'

'No, not at all. It was most intriguing. Women are un-fathomable!'

'William Mellor was very close to Piotr, in a friendly sense, I mean.'

'This also I recall.'

'Should I follow her, do you think?'

'No, it is better that we are alone . . . Can we really be as sure of Lionel as you say?'

Isabel heard their voices through the door – Hochler's, with its unexpected Germanic angles, Paul's deeper and more insinuating. Politics, she thought, leaning her head against the cool smooth refrigerator. They don't care about me. I'm just a distraction – even an experiment. For Karl, at least, I'm an experiment. He secretly wants to see if I fall apart.

('How much?'

'Depends on reserves.'

'If the Council were to discover—'

'No, it's our best chance. That and the underdog factor.')

Isabel, half-listening, wondered whether Paul's plans, which she didn't understand, were actually legal. Not that ethics had ever troubled Paul. We'll succeed, she decided. The Royal Sinfonia will be too trammelled by decency and doubtfulness. Against Paul's deviousness, Karl's determina-tion and Piotr's sheer verve, they'll stand very little chance . . . What would William do then? Retire early, she supposed, forced into it by his former rival and his one-time friend. She wondered whether that thought would give him pain, or whether it simply wouldn't matter to him – even whether he now regarded the affair as purely unfortunate, purely regrettable.

And yet. It hadn't been so many months since he'd arrived in her Barbican flat, catching her to him, burying his lips in her rich black hair. It hadn't been so many months since she had felt sure and replete, her head feathered across his broad shoulder, and unequal to even imagining a future without William in it . . .

She remembered a rehearsal at Cheltenham Town Hall, shortly after William had resigned. She had been so reckless with misery that her desk-partner Caroline had complained, 'Are you sure you're not pregnant, Isabel? You seem hormonal or something.' While Warren, always alert to everyone's feelings, had taken her aside. ('This will pass, Isabel. You think it won't, but it will . . . And you know Will doesn't deserve punishment.')

All of which she knew to be true, even as part of her soul rebelled against it. He'd left her, after all . . . And even now, a part of her longed to tell him that he was still hurting her, that every day without him still twisted her inside. After all, he had chosen: he'd given himself and taken himself away. Where was the courage in that?

Isabel poured herself a glass of wine. Absence could also be a physical pain: an abdominal constriction, fever stoking the temples, sorrow's grip. Before William, she'd imagined she knew what loneliness was – how absurd that notion seemed now! Sorrow digs a hole for itself, she thought, it reaches deeper and deeper as time goes by. Sorrow consumes us: blood, muscle and bone.

(Karl: 'Will the administration will stand for it?'

'They have to. We're not the only ones with jobs to lose.')

Loneliness is feeling alone while making love to your partner; loneliness is feeling alone in a pub full of friends. Loneliness is waking with sorrow tugging your belly and a constriction in your throat, with tears you'd no recollection of crying astonishing your eyes . . . Loneliness is standing in the middle of the supermarket, suddenly swamped with grief. Taking hold of the cold plastic and letting the ice chill your hand, physical pain as relief, cool plastic against hot heart.

(Paul: 'Piotr's sorting it. That's why he isn't here.'

'Good that you have it organised.')

Isabel brushed her hand over her eyes. Think of something – of anything else: the Arts Council, that mark on the sideboard, the astringent tang of South African pinotage. William's hands serious on her shoulders – no, anything but that. She swallowed too swiftly, wine sparking her throat. If I don't get a grip I'll go under, and I won't, I won't go under. I won't let anyone do that to me again.

A few minutes later she returned to the lounge. The men looked up defensively, but returned her proffered smile.

'Ready for another, Paul?'

'Thanks. You're looking ravishing tonight, Isabel.'

And she was looking better, her colour sparked to vividness by alcohol and resolution. She said lightly, 'Have you sorted everything?'

Karl yawned. 'Oh, I think so. The business side is, in reality, most boring.'

Isabel curved her fingers on his shoulders. Taut, she thought: he's hiding something. And she remembered William's stronger shoulders under her fingers, a little dart of pain. Karl reached up and captured her wrists.

'Stay here and entertain us.'

'Shall I put on some music?'

'Yes, Sibelius. I have been hearing Sibelius all day in my head, the incidental music to *Pelléas*.'

The lingering sadness of the violins resonated out of Karl's expensive speakers. It was his own recording, conducting a fine German orchestra, and one he was secretly delighted with.

Sibelius must have been a depressive, thought Isabel. All that Nordic bombast, and yet such evening sadness too, limitless, plangent. The same song of loss, each time with that bitter-sweet twist . . .

The men were debating the oboe tone preferred in other parts of Europe. ('This Russian timbre I have never come to terms with. Such self-indulgence . . .') Night drew in; the streetlamps gathered strength. Loneliness is remembering the one time you were happy. Isabel lit the candles; the smell of mushrooms, sour cream, sherry, combating her traitorous weakness of heart.

'Stroganoff,' said Paul with pleasure. 'My favourite.'

Remembering.

CHAPTER 35

It harrows me with fear and wonder.

Shakespeare

(from Pete Hegal's diaries)

Only a fortnight after the Arts Council bombshell, the Royal Sinfonia headed off on its annual Greek island extravaganza. Never had the Sinfonia wanted its break more keenly; never had the atmosphere on the plane been quite so blatantly escapist. There was a general feeling of making the most of the moment, for we might soon enough be advertising ('ex-professional, competitive teaching rates') in our local newsagents.

With Leszek left behind, it was small surprise to find Eddie Wellington the self-appointed master of the revels on the plane. He it was who wheedled more booze out of the air hostesses and caroused with the percussion at the back of economy class.

Also among the drinkers, strangely enough, was William. I don't think I'd ever seen him so relaxed. It was as if all his personal tensions had resolved themselves into the communal tension, as if the Arts Council furore had somehow lifted his future out of his hands.

I mentioned as much to Angela, beside me. She glanced at William briefly and, it seemed to me, sadly and then returned to her book.

'It looks more like desperation to me.'

Desperation: it was an odd word to choose! Still, there

was a hectic flush in his cheeks, an unwonted brilliance in his eye.

'Why desperation?'

'How should I know?' she returned, giving me an ever clearer impression that she did. William and Angela, I thought suddenly. They were experienced enough to avoid detection, astute enough to keep their own counsel . . . Angela had that streak of catlike self-sufficiency so prevalent in harp-players, but there was no reason why she should invariably prefer affairs with the brass.

I glanced back at William. What was it about him? Isabel, Angela – and even Janice. He was bending down to hear her over the plane's engines.

'What is it about Will?' I asked Angela.

'If I could explain it, we could all have it,' she returned, not looking up from her book.

'You must have thought about it.'

'He understands,' she said, and I thought: understanding, yes, perhaps. But was it really quite so simple?

'You mean women, I suppose.'

Angela looked at me with her clear Irish eyes. 'Women – of course. But there's more to it than the obvious, physical – much more. Most people don't realise what's happening to them until it's all over. Will knows, every moment, every second, he knows.'

And I knew too, in that moment, a good deal more than she'd probably intended. The catch in her voice, that uncharacteristic hesitancy – of course I knew. Is love a tender thing? I recalled: it is too rough, too rude, too boisterous, and it pricks like thorn. I glanced at Angela, once again bent over her book, electric hair following the curve of her back. Red was what they called it, but red was almost the last colour it was. It was golden-orange, wood-striped, liquid, almost alive.

I thought about that evening in Seville with William – the way he had, effortlessly, drawn me in. And I watched Will's face, exposed yet inward, as he listened to one of Eddie's little jokes. ('You heard the one about the difference between eroticism and perversion? No? Well, with eroticism you use a feather . . . But with perversion you use the whole chicken.')

The beginning of a tour is generally crisis-ridden for the management. Leszek's flight had been rerouted by air traffic control; the hotel had managed to register most of our smokers into non-smoking rooms; while Terence Hennessy opened his door to disclose a naked Greek watching TV from his bed.

'I hope I'm not a prudish person,' he told me, aggrieved, 'but I don't know why he shouldn't wear a dressing gown. It's quite barbaric, in my opinion . . . Not to mention the fact that my key opened both his room and mine! I feel we should protest most strongly to Marios. In the final analysis, the last thing our hosts would want is for crucial orchestra members to be put under unnecessary stress while ostensibly enjoying their hospitality.'

I had dinner in the hotel under siege from these malcontents, and it was almost midnight before I could relax in the knowledge that everyone's passports were in the safe, and that (wherever they might be roosting for the night) everyone was in possession of a valid room. I looked down at the beach, where a few shadows roamed in the dim light.

A dog barked along the coast, and unfamiliar birds – lizards perhaps? – rustled outside my window. The air felt somehow spicier, saltier. It still seemed bizarre that I had woken up in Lewisham, and was about to fall asleep in Greece . . . The air was so seductive that I was lured on to my balcony.

Suddenly I became aware, late as it was, that I was not alone. Several balconies along stood a slim, lissome figure, leaning into the air. As I watched, Janice released her curls on to her shoulders. Then she disappeared in a haze of spangles, leaving only the unblinking stars behind her.

I woke up deciding that I'd drunk too much retsina the night before, and that what I'd seen (or rather, not seen) was impossible. If it was impossible, that meant it hadn't happened; and if it hadn't happened then thinking about it was not only (a) useless, but (b) a chronic waste of human resources ... At breakfast, I heard a rumour about a full orchestra meeting, and buttonholed Lenny to ask if I was eligible to attend.

'Suit yourself. We won't be discussing your salary, that much I can tell you.'

'I heard that dirty tricks were on the menu.'

'All's fair in love, war and arts funding. Besides, the Royal Sinfonia has a noble old tradition in skulduggery.'

So does the Orchestra of London, I thought with misgiving, recalling what Piotr had said. Love, war and arts funding! They were closer, and more twisted together, than Lenny might imagine.

Later that morning the meeting convened on the beach. I don't know whose notion the venue was, but frankly I found it hard enough to imagine the end of the orchestra without the added unreality of a loose-limbed sun and sketchy little breezes.

The sea was insanely blue, the kind of blue with shots of silver in it, and little rippling waves kept coasting up the sand towards us.

Musicians lay on towels, scrounged deckchairs and slouched in hammocks. Angela displayed her slim white legs and arms, but kept her face shielded under a cricket hat. William, in a cool cream shirt, sat beside Eddie Wellington, the latter perspiring freely, for his weight troubled him in the heat.

Lenny's unemphatic voice called the meeting to order, and favoured us first with the official letter from the Arts Council. I found it increasingly hard to concentrate. The sun barbecued my brain, and there was the additional fascination of watching a colony of ants assembling what appeared to be an underground nuclear shelter at my feet.

'... decisions ... priorities ... matter of judgement ...

Leszek's input ... possible longterm commitment to the orchestra ... at the stage of forward planning ...'

They have faith in Lenny, I realised. Some understood better than others – some players are only capable of stringing notes together, ideas only confuse them – but the expressions raised to Lenny's wore a hopeful look, the look of spaniels expecting a walk. He was too cynical to be entirely popular, but then, orchestra chairmen aren't designed to be popular. They exist as an uncomfortable hinge linking players and administration; and politicking soon swamps any untrammelled good nature they might possess.

Eddie yawned, caught my eye and awarded me a dazzling smile. The Duke knew that the situation was desperate, but his natural sunniness prevented him from dwelling on it. When he did get downhearted it was cataclysmic stuff, but, generally speaking, he didn't. Instead he veered from one moment to the next, living entirely in the present, which could be either miserable or ecstatic but was certainly never dull.

At that particular moment the sun was baking his legs, Leszek was in London and Lenny was in command. Eddie had forgotten that he was sitting on the maximum number of permissible warnings and that he – he alone – might be sunk even if the Arts Council did elect to prefer us. Warnings, panic attacks, nerves and downheartedness belonged to yesterday – or to tomorrow. Today was only the sand between his sausage-like toes and the peaceful hum of bugs in his ears.

'Plan of action ... committee to represent longterm forecasts ... policy for the decade ... Before getting down to details—'

Here John McDaniel unexpectedly interrupted. 'Sorry, Len, but before you go any further, I think something should be clarified. Is everyone present actually a member of the orchestra?'

Faces lifted towards mine; I felt a dull flush rising. Lenny said, 'Pete Hegal's been employed by us for more than ten years, counting his time in the second violins.'

'I was referring to Janice.'

Janice was on the very fringe of the group, stretched out in a tiny white bathing suit on a little lilac towel. The sun had already toasted her skin the lightest possible shade of brown, and her hair – not only her head of hair, but every downy little hair along her body – shimmered bewilderingly in the sun. As Shakespeare would have put it, had he been among those present, 'O serpent heart, hid with a flowering face! Did ever dragon keep so fair a cave?' ... Meanwhile Lenny spoke hastily, and, it seemed to me, hectically.

'Perhaps we could discuss that later. Now—'

'I'm sorry but I really must insist,' said John, and I could tell, by the way his feet shifted, that he was exercised. And, of course, he was in the right. Only members should attend such a meeting – though Janice had been guesting for so many months that most people had forgotten she was still on trial.

Janice was focused quietly on Lenny. I half-closed my eyes, and thought I saw a scintillation of light breaking the air between them. I glanced towards Will, who was looking downwards. Look, I wanted to say, but nerves stopped me.

Lenny shook his head irritably, as if trying to shake something from it. He said with unusual sharpness, 'Janice *is* a member of the orchestra, John. She signed her contract last week.'

Janice discreetly collected her things and moved towards the water. I watched the articulated swing of her hips, the casual spring of her stride. She gathered up her hair as she walked, twisting it with a supple motion around her fingertips that irresistibly recalled her loosening of it only the night before. But she left a tornado rising up behind her.

The feeling of the meeting was tempestuous, and overwhelmingly in John's favour. No one could understand how a principal could have failed to have been consulted over an appointment; while the string principals were visibly incensed. Leszek's unilateral action was a threat to their own importance, a downgrading of their jealously guarded influence. I watched them gather together – not physically, but metaphorically; I watched them subtly coalesce while Lenny tapped on his papers. His coolness had returned, but Janice's influence still gripped him. I could tell by the way he stroked his temples, as if puzzled by some soreness there.

'Listen,' he said, 'I ain't any happier than you are about this, John. I did my best to talk Leszek out of it, but well, the boy just wasn't persuadable . . . Besides which I don't believe we can legally object – not as John here chose to give her a trial in the first place. The Union's view—'

'That's not the point! . . . Outrageous! . . . The beginning of the end . . . thin end of the wedge . . . Zimetski's intolerable arrogance . . .'

Lenny let them rant for a bit and then said wearily, 'I respect your objections, believe me – but hell, who sits last chair in the cello section just don't register compared to whether the whole orchestra still exists this time next year. Now can we just get on?'

The mutterings died away into little pulses on the waves, jagged tooths of spray. Lenny continued.

'Now, William, I wonder if you could help us here.'

Will was surprised, I think, but it was crafty of Lenny to shift the meeting's interest to William. He had a reputation, especially among the women, as a vaguely romantic figure, someone mysterious and interesting, because of his immediate past.

'I'm afraid I don't know anyone on the Arts Council,' he said lightly.

'Maybe not, but you know almost everyone in the Orchestra of London . . . Their chairman, for instance. You must have known Paul Ellison for years.'

'Not very well,' said William, remembering Paul's frustration as Isabel had slipped from his grasp that night.

'And Piotr, your old mate Piotr. He's on the board now.'

Will's voice very deep, his face unreadable: 'He wasn't in my time.'

'Still, you must recall some of their longterm planning. That kind of thing could be very useful. We need to anticipate as much as we can of their presentation – and then trump it.'

I saw William, impassive, recross his legs, and understood him as clearly as if he had spoken. How could he be expected to act against Isabel, against Piotr? There was a bleakness in his face that I recognised: the shock of realising, perhaps for the first time, that he and Piotr were enemies, their interests resolutely opposed, one against the other.

Janice was swimming in the Aegean. Her hair was flattened with the water; from behind she looked like a seal. I remembered the shadowless figure in the Festival Hall car park, the terrifying crisis of the 'Storm'. A skittish premonition winged me, but the heat soon lulled it away. The feel of the sand was dry-grained and pleasant, the sun like an arm warm across my shoulders. Drowsily, I thought about William, Lenny, the Arts Council. Then I fell asleep.

CHAPTER 36

O teach me how I should forget to think!
Shakespeare

'The sooner all orchestras shut down, the better. They're all hotbeds of vice, anyway.'

Olivia was referring to an article in the *Telegraph*'s arts section. As the Orchestra of London was mired in debt and the Royal Sinfonia's prospects were not much brighter, the music critic had cleverly proposed an amalgamation . . . Hochler and Zimetski could form a creative partnership, while the dead wood in both string sections could be excised, to the benefit of everybody.

'Dead wood, you see,' observed Olivia.

'They don't mean William,' said Margot, her sense of loyalty stirring.

'They must do. Over forty-five, isn't he? Ought to make way, by rights – give the young ones a chance.'

'They really don't mean people like William. Not everyone gives up practising and waits to retire.'

'Well, an amalgamation would do them no good anyway.'

It certainly wouldn't do William any good, thought Margot, glancing at the rather disgruntled-looking horn section that featured in the photo. Perhaps he would retire, if that happened, if he could afford it. She remembered the night in the garden, his silhouette uncertain against the French window, the feel of his broad hands gripping her wheelchair.

'I doubt that it'll happen,' she told Olivia. 'Orchestras are almost always in crisis, and almost always survive. At least the Royal Sinfonia isn't quite so terribly in debt.'

'I should think not indeed, gallivanting off to Greece the way they do.'

Margot decided against explaining – for the fifth time – that the orchestra was in Greece to make money rather than to spend it.

Olivia had never made any secret of her conviction that William did no real work at all . . . Which wasn't to say he was a bad cellist, because she'd heard him play – rather an appealing sound, she would call it, and she was a judge, singing solo (when the organist couldn't stop her) in her church choir. But still, the cello wasn't a proper job, not a job with any real security, and it certainly wasn't needed by anyone – not like the immigration people for example, or the Church.

Margot put the article aside. What magic to go to Greece, she thought longingly. Long nights in seaside tavernas – the raw taste of wine and olives and those barren, bony hillsides. Lucky William, to have such distractions! Margot remembered running up the craggy steps of the Parthenon as a student. She recalled the stillness of the air, the acrid heat, the grit between her sandals and her breathlessness as she reached the top . . . That was another thing she'd never do again.

Tears trembled in her eyes; she bent her head resolutely over the newspaper. Athens was more polluted now, she knew; and she forced herself to contemplate the damage perpetuated by exhaust fumes and industrial chemicals until her mother spoke again, this time with animation.

'Edwin's coming to tea,' she said. 'I think I might make a sponge cake. Edwin's very fond of sponge.'

'Edwin?'

'Edwin Sutherton Narbold, your MEP. Do pay me the courtesy of a modicum of attention, Margot.'

'I might get too tired,' said Margot, who found Olivia's harping on the Euro-elections very wearing.

'Nonsense. He can't stay long, in any case. Just a short stop and then we're back on the hustings. We've earmarked several crucial roads to canvass tonight, including Rosemary Hill Avenue.'

Margot played little part in the preparations for Edwin's arrival, only gathering flowers from the garden and arranging them, extravagantly but inexpertly, in her mother's crystal bowl. The day was so beautiful that she spent most of it outside, re-reading Jane Austen and feeling the limpid breeze playing around her temples. She was still in a mellow frame of mind when her mother summoned her from the house.

'Margot, darling!'

She thought: odd how I'm never darling unless somebody's by.

'It's Edwin. Edwin's here, dear.'

Edwin stepped forth from the French windows. He was wearing the kind of double-breasted pinstripe no longer affected by anyone beyond top financiers and the dozier segments of what used to be called society. His tie, however, was in the most extreme newscaster mould – thick, wide and saucy, all lavenders and pinks. Margot observed it with amusement.

'That tie will never sell in Rosemary Hill Avenue.'

Edwin smiled. 'Seems to be doing fairly well so far.'

He grasped her wheelchair, propelling her forward. He was subtle enough to know when to release the chair to her own control; on the slope it was helpful for someone to push, but indoors she preferred to be her own agent.

She accepted a glass of wine from Olivia, and decided that Edwin was rather less obtuse than she'd imagined. The suit was fairly grim – though not, perhaps, for the electors he was after – while his modest moustache and receding hairline suited him. What hair he possessed was still mainly dark, and she idly wondered whether he dyed it.

'I spent the entire day on the road,' he was telling Olivia. 'One meeting after another. Then my agent drove us down to his own ward and we spent a dispiriting afternoon tramping around . . . Everyone was either out or anti – one French-hater threatened to set his dog on us. All in all, it was a canvass I'd rather forget.'

Olivia bridled. '*That* ward! A perfect waste of time and energy – I wonder you put up with it!'

'One has to humour one's agent, Olivia. They work so very hard on our behalf.'

Which was true enough, thought Margot, and all for what? Precious little money and no glory to speak of . . . They needed to be still more obsessive than Olivia, who at least divvied up her allegiances – the Church, the Conservatives, and, when so inspired, the Home for Fallen Women. Although any fallen woman who actually fell in with Olivia probably wished that her charitable spirit had taken her elsewhere.

'I feel myself,' Edwin was saying, 'that we concentrate too much on our natural supporters. How I long to reach out to those grappling with poverty and unemployment, those feeling that the European Union has somehow failed them. If only we had more time!'

'You mean, I suppose,' said Margot, as Olivia seemed stupefied, 'that your need to get re-elected prevents you from concentrating on those areas of least support.'

'Exactly. Precisely.'

'Well, *I* think it's poppycock,' said Olivia tartly. 'Some people will never vote properly, however much attention you give them. They read the wrong papers and listen to the wrong people on television; it's like a disease. It's hopelessly idealistic to suppose that more contact will translate to more votes from some sorts of people.'

'True enough. One man's meat is another man's *poisson*.'

'Nothing to do with fish, Edwin. It's a simple matter of electoral integrity . . . There are some people's votes that we should scorn to win.'

'Indeed,' he assented, with a private glance of amusement at Margot. It suddenly occurred to her that Edwin was playing with Olivia, even teasing her. She felt exhilarated by the thought that the Euro MP, though inherently and probably incurably devious, might still possess some secret source of humour.

'More chicken, Edwin?' asked Olivia tenderly, feeling that, having bested him in the exchange, it was her duty to put him at ease.

'Thank you. It's delicious.'

'You'll need to keep your energy going this evening.'

But Edwin was looking at Margot, and she suddenly wondered whether it was a look of some meaning.

A few minutes later, Olivia bustled into the kitchen to answer the telephone. Edwin leaned forward.

'I'd like to talk to you. Some evening, perhaps?'

'I'm afraid,' said Margot lightly, 'that I can go nowhere without Mother knowing. That's one of the penalties of my situation.'

'Do you do nothing on your own?'

I go into the woods when Olivia's out, thought Margot, and sometimes I pretend I'm well and commune with the stars.

'On Thursdays I help at the local Hospice. One of the other volunteers takes me.'

'I'll take you this Thursday.'

'Really,' said Margot doubtfully, 'it's very good of you. But with the election so close—'

'This has nothing to do with the elections. What time are you expected?' And he got out his Filofax to make a note.

Margot told him, thinking: Mother won't like it; she's possessive about her causes. And it's not as if I'm what she would call a proper Conservative . . . She heard Olivia's voice, more precisely enunciated as always when irritated: 'Now Hilda, you've had your say. You can just listen to me, for a change.'

Margot wondered whether she shouldn't unveil the sponge cake, before deciding that Olivia would consider this the rankest betrayal.

Edwin asked, 'Tell me, have you instituted proceedings yet?'

Proceedings, Margot thought blankly – Then colour flooded her face.

'No. No, I haven't.'

'But Olivia tells me that your husband—'

'He had an affair, a serious affair. I found out in February. That's when I left.'

Staccato words, words falling to the floor like tiny nails.

'But it's very nearly October! Have you really done nothing?'

And was that so surprising, after so many years? First people had thought her precipitate in leaving; now she was being accused of being too dilatory in action . . . She shook her head wordlessly.

'Let me send you my lawyer, Simmons, a very sound fellow. He'll have you sorted in no time: house, alimony, the lot.'

I don't want to be sorted. I want – and she suddenly realised that she didn't know what she wanted, that she'd decided almost nothing. All the months of thinking and dreaming and imagining and remembering and, in the end, she'd arrived almost exactly where she'd started from. She might as well have stayed at home, for all the elucidation her gesture had brought her.

'I had to leave,' she said, clinging to that certainty. 'It was a matter of – self-respect.'

'Naturally. But now you have to get the business resolved. Time and tide, you know, time and tide.'

Edwin took her hand; it trembled, a faint rebellious tremble, though whether the instinct came from her or from her illness she could not have said. At that moment Olivia returned.

'I'm sorry, Edwin – shocking manners, I know. I suppose Hilda means well, but sometimes I simply despair . . . Where was I? Now, Edwin, you're going to get a pleasant surprise. I made you a little sweet this afternoon, while Margot was doing the flowers.'

And she unfurled her special sponge like a conjurer, the icing garlanded around the edges like a bridal bouquet.

*

Margot did her best to excuse Edwin's behaviour to her mother, but Olivia remained profoundly discontented.

'That's all very well, Margot, but some of us are putting every moment of our spare time into this campaign – into his campaign, I should say. Personally, I was planning on spending Thursday leafleting Wisteria Close.'

'I don't know why he wants to take me, particularly.' Though there are probably votes in hospices – even some votes in the disabled, possibly . . . Margot had a sudden vision of votes, dangling like apples, ready to be plucked. Olivia sniffed.

'Well, I only hope Bridget's nose won't be put out of joint, good as she is to pick you up week after week.'

Bridget had actually been thrilled at the thought of a Euro MP popping in. It was true that Bridget was easily thrilled – she had once travelled forty miles to see the Queen – but still, she hadn't minded. Margot chose not to remind her mother of this. She had a sudden and shocking vision of Olivia as old, mouth thinning, meagre with disappointment.

Edwin appeared punctually on Thursday and manhandled Margot's wheelchair into his car without difficulty. As they drove off he said, 'Do you suppose Olivia will ever forgive me?'

'She'd forgive you most things, I think.'

'She hasn't forgiven your husband much.'

She said swiftly, 'I hope you haven't asked to come in order to talk about William.'

He glanced at her profile, wind tousling her short curls.

'Not at all.'

Margot rushed on: 'The women at the Centre were thrilled to hear that you were coming.'

'I only wish I could pretend that I was doing it for their benefit.'

The heaviness of the compliment impacted in her ear like a false note on a drum. What was he after, exactly? . . . She wondered whether Edwin was one of those zealots who felt driven to convert everyone to his cause – whether he was clever enough to have divined her innate resistance.

'Actually I loathe politics,' she told him.

'Yes, so do I.'

'What did you say?' she inquired, disbelieving.

He repeated it with gusto, adding, 'International politics especially. After all, at least local councillors can do things, even if they're quite small things. And people who reach the top of national parties also have some influence on events . . . Euro MPs come after the dung beetles, I sometimes think. Earthworms, dung beetles, then Euro MPs.'

'And I'd thought you devoured by a sense of your own importance!'

'One wears a mask for the benefit of the Party drones, Margot, without whom and so forth, God save the Queen.'

'Mother would have a fit!'

'Olivia? I doubt it. Though perhaps Olivia might benefit from a fit.'

Margot couldn't help laughing. Edwin lifted his eyebrows.

'You know, I don't believe I've heard you laugh before.'

'I suppose there hasn't been a great deal to laugh about.'

'But you're better, aren't you? So Olivia tells me.'

'Physically, I'm better – but I don't know why.'

'Perhaps because you aren't struggling any more. You were striving to keep your marriage – for years, perhaps. Now the struggle's over, you can relax.'

'Actually I think the illness is more complicated than that. I think – I think it less human than that. It doesn't seem to respond, as so many conditions do, to internal stress or unhappiness . . . It's more like a small animal, wilful, careless, intent on its own rules.'

'That's a curious analysis.'

'I've grown used to it, to the cycles and the patterns and the rhythms. It's become part of me, grown into me. And, to be absolutely truthful, I don't think I was ever striving to keep my marriage – what a stupid cliché that is! I never realised there was a contest until it was over.'

Margot stopped to draw breath. She hadn't talked so much

or so earnestly since it first happened, she thought. In a way, there'd been no one to talk to. Sam was too much her son; she still protected him, even from herself. Olivia, being Olivia, would never have listened. And the depth of her anger at William was such that it palsied her voice in his presence; William understood at once too much and too little. Is that what I really feel? she wondered: I never knew. I thought my illness something I hated, not a part of me. While of William, perhaps, the reverse was true.

'Here we are,' she said, half-disappointed, half-relieved. 'The Hospice is the building on the right.'

A hospital without hope, with its dew-fresh flowers and feather-crisp beds. The end of the line: that's your lot, frightfully sorry but goodbye. And she wondered for the first time whether she had enough strength of mind to make persevering contact with the dying.

'I can take you somewhere else.'

Edwin's voice, very quiet, and she admitted again that she'd misjudged him. He was a threat after all, this clever, cagey fellow to whom she'd only really spoken once before. His politician's protective colouring had disarmed her into not taking him seriously; Olivia's infatuation had overruled his reality. Yet still the rough hairs on the back of his hands subtly revolted her; he lacked William's quizzical polish; and her physical feelings had been denied too long for her to feel comfortable with their sudden flaring now . . . She felt some resentment, too, at his even daring to understand.

'I can take you somewhere else,' he repeated.

'No. Thank you.'

Edwin obediently swirled his Saab up the drive.

CHAPTER 37

Be thou a spirit of health or goblin damned,
Bring with thee airs from heaven or blasts from hell,
Be thy intents wicked or charitable,
Thou comest in such a questionable shape
That I will speak to thee.

Shakespeare

On the orchestra's fourth day in Greece, William came down early to breakfast. The hotel staff were still setting out the buffet when Janice appeared, wearing a fuchsia sarong over her swimming outfit. She collected her cereal and paused at his table.

'Are you waiting for someone?'

'Pete should be here momentarily. We're attacking the links this morning.'

'Would you rather I sat elsewhere?'

He would, William realised; and he made his welcome the more fulsome on that account. Her wrapped-around beauty stirred his senses – or would any beauty, under such circumstances, have done the same?

'Not at all. Join us by all means.'

Janice slipped her tray opposite, glancing intently towards him. Instinctively, William's hand went to his temple.

She said, 'I woke an hour ago and couldn't get back to sleep. I thought I'd go for an early swim instead. The sun can get very hot by midday.'

'That's why we're playing this morning,' he said, striving to match her casual tone. He fought off what she'd confided; the idea of Janice tossing about in bed was too disquieting. There was a curious drumming along the side of his head . . .

'I was thinking about Leszek,' she told him.

'Tiger.'

'Is that what the orchestra calls him?'

'One of the things. I don't suppose it's got much to do with Blake.'

The poet Blake made no impact on Janice at all – he wondered briefly whether she'd even heard of him. They didn't teach English literature at schools now, not the sort he'd used to love, at any rate.

'I don't know what to do about Leszek.'

'No?'

Didn't Janice realise how, by choosing Leszek, she'd separated herself from the rest of the orchestra? She was contaminated by association; the otherness of his mystique enveloped her too. Voices fell silent when she entered the canteen; subjects were automatically changed. It was the old political story, relived in orchestra after orchestra – join your conductor, lose your colleagues.

'I wanted to ask your advice.'

'My advice is not to ask it.'

The last beautiful creature to ask my advice, he thought – he thought: what a memory to carry. Isabel's look of entreaty, the chequered gold from the reception encroaching on to the veranda . . . He wished his head felt less heavy. Her syllables fell with a hypnotic insistence.

'You're afraid of me, I think.'

'No more than necessary.'

'Perhaps you don't like me much.'

'I try not to judge people. It's my single redeeming characteristic.'

She looked at him, a silvery shadow across her face. And then, in a flicker of an eyelash, he knew. Why had it taken him so many months to recognise? And had she made an error, suffered a lapse of concentration, or deliberately shot him a warning? She shifted in her chair – to his heightened senses the sound of waxed leg on ankle was deafening, the weave of sarong against leather. He looked downwards while the dizziness gradually receded. In some ways, of course, it made it easier; his spirits rose against an identifiable challenge.

He leaned back and sipped his coffee, saying with a rare recklessness, 'Remind me, Janice, which German orchestra did you play with?'

'Regensburg,' she said, unwillingly.

'A symphony orchestra, is it?'

'An opera orchestra. I wasn't there long.'

'You weren't there at all.'

She didn't flinch, but her mouth narrowed.

'I was. Be careful.'

'Why, exactly? Why should I be careful?'

'More coffee, miss?'

The waiter's eyes fastened on Janice.

'No, thank you,' she murmured.

'Sir?'

'You're very kind.'

The waiter served him, eyes captured by the girl. William leaned closer.

'You were never in Germany.'

'I told you once: be careful.'

'But you didn't say why.'

Her lips whitened. 'Too close. You come too close.' And suddenly Pete breezed in – burly and oversized, bringing clearer air like a zephyr from an opened window.

'Morning, all. Sorry I'm late, Will. Do you think we've missed our chance?'

'Not at all. Have some breakfast.'

'This business is well ended. Are you any use at golf, Janice?'

'I don't play.'

No, thought William; golf is a game for gentlemen. On every count, you fail to qualify. Pete, meanwhile, was in cheerful mood.

'. . . much the toughest game in the world. What do you think, Will?'

'I think you should have some coffee.'

The solid satisfying swipe of club on golfball, trees just holding their line against the wind from the Aegean. Will could almost sense them; so keen had his intuition become that he was almost there already. Once he'd sorted out what had just happened – or hadn't happened – he would tell Pete. For now he only craved fresh air: air, sunlight and freedom.

'No, let's scoot,' said Pete. 'For every minute is expectancy of more arrivance, as the third gentleman said.'

CHAPTER 38

'Tis now the very witching time of night,
When churchyards yawn, and hell itself breathes out
Contagion to the world.

Shakespeare

The content of the Greek pops concerts hadn't improved over the years. There were still meandering love songs featuring improbable oboe parts, and predictable numbers in five-eight time, generally about jealousy. The bass lines tended to match the violas', for no very discernible reason, and the violins were still sent screeching skywards during moments of tension.

However, the orchestra was far too relaxed to complain. During liquid evenings in seaside tavernas, members lazily discussed which way the Arts Council might jump, and whether this might be the orchestra's last trip to Greece. But London still seemed a universe away – and a few months like another lifetime.

At the end of one such evening, William and Angela departed the taverna together. Soothed by the scent of wax candles, the tangy smell of vines and olives, they followed the other stragglers back towards the hotel.

'Enjoyed yourself?' she asked.

'Yes. I was just thinking.'

'I thought you were a bit quiet this evening.'

'Am I usually so noisy?' he asked, amused.

'No, but I don't believe you said two words to Janice, even though she was opposite you.'

He glanced at Janice in the group ahead, loose hair starry under the street-lights.

'Why didn't you speak to her?' Angela repeated.

Will paused, suspecting something he felt he had no right to suspect. He recalled Angela's palms on his shoulders, her nipples sharpening against his awakening back – and caught his breath. It wouldn't be right; it wouldn't be fair; but what a comfort it would be! He attempted a normal tone.

'I certainly didn't mean to slight Janice. I was only interested in what Felicia was saying about the ruins.'

But William was not a natural liar, and Angela's doubtfulness revived. She hadn't noticed it before; but perhaps it had never been so obvious before: the way Janice kept focusing on William, the unspoken but vibrant negotiation between them . . . Janice was beautiful, of course, even more beautiful than Isabel, but the thought of them together, of William's strong thighs around Janice's body – Oh, the thought was unbearable! And still more horrible was the notion that William was acting, affecting an indifference amounting to dislike while in reality . . .

Angela paused in order to release a shower of sand from her shoe. William waited courteously, while the others moved still farther ahead of them.

'Will, please. Come to my room tonight.'

'I'm sorry. I can't.'

'You don't want to?'

'I can't,' he repeated patiently.

She digested this, glancing at his set face, eyes hooded in the shadows.

'William,' said Angela.

'Don't,' he said abruptly. 'Don't go on.'

'I have to. I must!'

'Shh! It's half-one! Do you want to get us barred?' hissed Pete irritably, some thirty yards ahead.

'I love you,' said Angela, so softly that the sound rode feather-light on the night breeze. William's hand gripped hers.

'I'm sorry, Angela, believe me. But the truth is that you deserve better, in every possible respect.'

A quick spurt of fear powered her onward. 'It's Janice, I know it is. There's something between you. There is, isn't there?'

'No,' he said with sudden energy, adding under his breath, 'There's something – which I can't explain . . . But there really isn't anyone any more.'

They separated at the hotel entrance: William taking the stairs, Angela choosing to wait for the lift. The others were too tipsy to notice the tears in her eyes; even Pete, for all his usual acuteness, had drowned one too many frustrations in the retsina that night. If anyone had noticed, they would have thought: tiredness, even a good time can tire you. For despite all the unreality of touring in general and this tour in particular, they all knew that real life would crash in on them, in two days' time.

The final open-air concert was over. The crowd was indulgent; one of the pop singers, a tiny Greek with an appealing catch in her voice, won them over completely; and the orchestra had enjoyed themselves. The concert segued effortlessly into the promoter's party, the players dispersed, scattered amongst the crowd.

Stadium lights and a Greek band improvised a dance area on the beach. Audience, soloists and orchestra were united in drinking, dancing, flirting . . . Pete was captured by a lively Greek girl: soon they were gyrating on the dance floor. Angela watched Pete's departure with regret.

'We've had such good times with Pete on this trip,' she observed to William. 'There's always a moment, isn't there, when the tour begins to wind down. Then it's the early morning call and the coach to the airport – and, back home, quiet-eyed people with responsibilities back in their faces, shouldering their luggage and walking away.'

'C'mon Angie; let's dance,' objected one of the trumpets,

pulling her into the mêlée. William watched her go, admiring the way her single coil of hair broke into a thousand curving points of amber light . . . He was attached to Angela, but, recalling the events of the previous night, he found himself half-relieved to be alone.

Among the dancers was a girl – black hair, tanned skin – who acutely reminded him of Isabel. She shot a smile up towards her partner, vividly self-conscious, and William was lost, remembering.

Their first kiss in the foreign bar – that strained encounter in the back of the darkened auditorium – and the crashing silence at the door to her hotel room. In retrospect, every night seemed to coalesce into that first fatal night, each memory into that first memory. Before that night his life had been settled, stable, sailing a recognised route to a known destination, whereas now . . . As the band burst into a livelier number, William wondered whether he would ever feel stable again.

He thought: I should leave while Angela's enjoying herself too much to notice. I'll still be able to hear the sea from my hotel window, saltwater rolling forwards and backwards until sleep flows in.

His resolution taken, he turned to go – yet in that rearing instant, his mood weirdly altered . . . An artificial madness in his veins, Greek music jangling in his bloodstream and his mind bending, almost separating . . . He paused dizzily, itched by a pattern that he couldn't quite recognise. There was something needling just under the edge of his consciousness, something he thought he'd lost lying under his hand.

Janice. He glanced around, and couldn't see her, but somehow knew that she was watching. Every instinct in his heart jerking a warning, he handed his wineglass to a waiter, refusing another.

'My dear chap! Just the fellow I was hoping to see.'

It was Terence, stomach bulging unappealingly out of tangerine shorts.

'Terence, hello. Enjoying yourself?'

'Oh, rather. Lucky for me, isn't it, to be in on probably the last of these binges. Anyway, I've something rather particular to ask you, if you've no objection.'

'Go on.'

'Your Italian cello made quite a decent impression on the audition panel. It might even have helped to get me the trial.'

'I'm glad.'

'Though it's really the player, isn't it . . . Having said that, I was wondering how much you would ask for it, at this particular moment in time.'

'Sorry. Ask for what?'

'For the Italian cello. In case someone – me, just to take an example at random – in case I was to make you some kind of an offer for it in the near future.'

William attempted to apply himself more strictly, despite the tumult in his head. To sell the cello must be a primary aim; and yet the sound, the sound still wooed him. It had played the concert with a yearning beauty that had temporarily assuaged every longing of his soul. Never had it sung so softly, never had its tone been so purely aching, so sorrowful . . . It had that same answering sweetness as Isabel's body in his hands; and he loved it with that same unreasoning intensity, loved it even as he distrusted it.

'I hadn't really thought of selling it,' he said at last.

'No? I'd imagined that, after what you'd said—'

'Let's say I haven't made up my mind.'

'Well, give me some sort of an idea, anyway. Something not unadjacent to its current value as you perceive it. A ball-park figure.'

Dazzled numbers sprang into William's mind. His brain seemed to be spawning numbers, which circled viciously around his head, every number in the world, with zeros tearing after them. Every number in the world, circling, flickering, shadowed by the motion of the drums, the waves' endless whispering, come, come.

'I haven't decided,' he repeated.

Terence, disappointed, changed tack. 'But you don't mind my borrowing it for my trial?'

Where Isabel would see it, and Piotr as well. What would the cello make of Isabel? Would it sizzle, would it shrink, would it explode?

'Of course not,' William replied mechanically.

'You can rest assured that I will do the instrument full justice.'

William turned away without replying. Might the wine be to blame? It had been a good many years since he'd felt this drunk, but he could still recall the challenge of playing quartets against the will of his youthful body, of controlling his fingers against his slippery, ticklish tipsiness. There'd been a perversity of pleasure in that, in commanding his body's control against the grain of his loosening mind . . . But there was no pleasure here. A clash of wills indeed, but the opposition was malevolent, and far too strong. He was playing a chess computer too many levels above his standard. He was being corralled, out-manoeuvred, manipulated.

'Only looking on, Will?'

It was Felicia, Felicia handsome in a flowing emerald outfit he didn't recognise.

'You don't dance, Felicia; you told me that in Spain.'

'When I started something between you and Angela instead.'

He didn't trouble to correct her – and, besides, perhaps she was right. How did such things start? There is always a moment, or so Margot had said. But what if there never had been?

'What happened at the concert tonight?' he asked suddenly, while the sweet sickly feeling tided still stronger.

'What do you mean?'

'The cello, my Italian cello.'

'My dear man, I'm not omniscient. Did it sing, did it dance, did it recite "Gunga Din"?'

'I ought to be able to understand.'

'You're not drinking, is your trouble. Have some wine. It does wonders for the intuition.'

'Perhaps I've had too much wine already. Felicia, do you believe that a cello can be haunted?'

'I do not. And nor, in case you were about to ask, do I believe that little pink men with feet curled like toothpaste tubes are taking potshots at us from Venus. Still, I don't believe in Antarctica either, and the fact that I've inspected Loch Ness without result doesn't prove that the monster wasn't taking a siesta at the time. Do you believe in haunted cellos, and, if so, why?'

Felicia's face, fine-grained, rather angular, seemed to shrink and expand as he focused on it. The band too – the music got fainter and brighter for no reason; there was a rushing in his ears from the synthesizers, from the metallic twanging clashing of rock guitars. And all the while a pull, almost gravitational, towards the navy-silk water, the ice-blue shadows: Come.

'William, are you all right?'

'I don't know that I am . . . I think I'll walk along the coast a bit, and sober up.'

'Mind you don't drown.'

'I won't be long.'

As he walked the sand seemed far away, but sometimes seemed to lurch closer, as the music did, and the opalescent glow from the moon. Occasionally, a ripple of tide, bolder than the rest, would weave itself around the fringes of his shoes; he was aware of crabs scuttling in panic at his approach. The drums still pursued him but he lost the rest: the guitars, the synthesizers, the amplified Greek voices. Smoothed-down sand crunched under his feet like pastry cases.

On its outer edge the pastry gave way to softer grains, and that was where he found her, as he'd known he would, in the near-blackness, curled on a dune. She was silent, but he knew that she was watching him, that she'd been watching him for a long time.

Who is it, he wanted to ask, but he was too drunk, or too

236

truthful, to pretend. In the frail light her pale hair was ignited a fragile blue, taking its cue from the moon.

'I've had enough wine,' he said, with an effort. 'And I'm not in the mood for dancing.'

He heard her laugh, softly, almost privately. Suddenly his legs would sustain him no longer, though at the same time he was perversely conscious of their solid and muscular strength. The moon zoomed in and out of his vision, skimming the waves like a diaphanous sail. The sand under his elbows felt mushroom-soft; a breeze ruffled his thick hair.

She leaned across and pushed it out of his eyes, a gesture that obscurely pained him, though he couldn't recollect why. He ordered his legs to support him but something external overruled; he felt his will buckling beneath him. Not while I've breath, he told himself, but all around was the stealing sweetness of honeysuckle, a dizzying languorous warmth, while her lips breathed music around his ears.

The wrapping scent added urgency to his mind's sick sweetness. Again he attempted to pull himself upright; but his body felt too heavy with longing, the sand too warm. She whispered something under her breath; a language he didn't recognise, perhaps no language of this earth. He caught a word, a name? – not his.

'I don't want this, Janice. You know I don't.'

But it was already half a lie; and his lips already forming rebellious intent. 'No,' he whispered, but the word was drowned in her pale curls.

She pulled him on top of her; he tasted sand, salt, softness. Her body curved little hillocks in the sand; there was sand in his fingers, warm sand between her thighs. She captured his hand and drew it softly along the inside of her thigh, her belly, across that satin underside of breast. Beneath him, she stirred, minutely ravishing every nerve in his body.

Desire like a pain surged through him. His body was pure ache, pure longing; he almost groaned with the burden of its heavy sweetness. It was as if, as if – his mind stumbled, struggled, reached, to make the connection – it was as if the body beneath him was no longer hers but Isabel's.

Isabel. And with that name he suddenly, startlingly recovered all his sweeping sorrow and power. Sorrow pulled him clear, beyond the burden of his longing: sorrow rushed chill clean air into each lulled segment of his brain.

Isabel, and the Mediterranean was clear and salty again; he could stand, he could dictate; desire no longer held dominion. Isabel, and he was released, turning, stretching new muscles over the sand; Isabel, and he was cantering, running for the sheer human pleasure of it, back along the coast towards the music, the drums, the dancers . . . He was running, actually running, as light-breathed and fluent as if he was young again, while the ocean blew salt air into the deepest corners of his lungs. And all the while the rush of sea freshness and the steep silent cry of Isabel along the crest of sand and uninhabited water.

CHAPTER 39

What, still in tears?
Everymore showering? In one little body
Thou counterfeitest a bark, a sea, a wind.
For still thy eyes, which I may call the sea,
Do ebb and flow with tears.

Shakespeare

The gun was otter-sleek, with a slick, metallic sheen. Karl Hochler took aim, holding himself motionless, then fired. The kick-back shuddered his arm but the result clearly pleased him, for he glanced up to the viewers' gallery to ensure that Isabel was still paying attention. At least he remembered she was there, she thought, returning to her book with a small sigh.

It was late and the club almost deserted, though a few dedicated sportsmen were still at work. (Her desk-partner Caroline had protested: 'A gun club! He must have a violent streak.' 'But what a turn-on,' teased Isabel.)

Controlled violence. It was what made his conducting so theatrical; it was in his glance, his signature, even in the elliptical calibre of his voice. His character was seamless, of a piece; Isabel had never met anyone so effortlessly himself, so untouched by mixed feelings, second thoughts or doubtfulness.

She watched his eyes slitting, the gun emptying hotly towards its target. William had once joked, more than half-seriously, 'Never forget that men play games.'

'Ah, the bella donna. Or is that a poison?'

Piotr blackening the gallery doorway with blitzkrieg eyes

and exaggerated gait. Piotr: drunk, or pretending to be – and she could never decide which made him harder to deal with. She felt a spurt of annoyance at Karl for not warning her that Piotr was coming. The Arts Council business seemed to take precedence over everything.

'He's still shooting,' she told Piotr.

'Oh, ducky, *tell* me it isn't true. Whatever will Sidney say? *And* we're twenty mill. over budget already. I said to the producer yesterday, "Jacqui," I said, "Jacqui, my angel" . . . Is the dear boy amongst the cavalry? I don't see him.'

'Second from the end.'

'And all in black, like Olivier doing Hamlet. There's something sinister, isn't there, about a man who prefers to shoot in cold blood? I feel sure that when I murder someone – because, like the great Russian novel, I simply *know* I have it in me – my blood will be hotter than mustard.'

The jocularity of his tone warred with the undertow of his old anger. It came out sharper when drunk, edges torn as a broken razor blade. She asked, 'Did Karl tell you to meet him here?'

'He did. Plans are afoot, the fox away – only a metaphorical fox, of course, as I am opposed to blood sports on principle, and oppose them tooth and claw.'

Never forget that men play games. Karl, Piotr, Paul Ellison – all bound up in a battle which provided their masculine self-importance with a common goal . . . Internal strife, natural distrust, even embedded rivalry – all these were shelved in the cause of the destruction of a common enemy.

'You're very silent, Isabel. Still fretting over the fate of the fox?'

'You forget that I know why you're doing this.'

'So do I. I've got used to eating three times a day. While I could scarcely hope to maintain my reputation for dress sense on a mere fraction of my current salary.'

'You don't fool me,' she flashed.

Piotr glanced at her with a rare attention.

'Dear me,' said Piotr blandly. 'This appears to have the makings of a scene. Is it a scene? Are we talking serious scene here?'

'Oh Piotr, can't you even remember the way it used to be? The way the orchestra felt? How we used to meet for chamber music, the orchestra parties, the laughs we had – on tour, in the pub, after a concert? Don't you remember that night when Caroline announced her engagement, or that Canadian tour when — Oh, I can't describe it; I haven't the words, but there was such a – spirit then! Can't you remember how it used to be?'

Piotr moved uneasily. 'Of course I do, but things were different then. Then the orchestra was secure, Mirabel was alive, and William hadn't — You may deny it as much as you choose, but when it comes down to it, William was at fault, William was the one who . . . And it wasn't as if he wasn't warned. He had warnings enough, from me, from Paul Ellison, even from Warren – God's nightgown! His own eyes and ears should have told him enough.'

'That isn't what I mean! Can't you see what you're really doing? Can't you see that you're all spending every waking moment trying to save us when there's nothing left worth saving?'

'My job springs remorselessly to mind.'

'We've lost everything: our identity, our integrity – our soul! It's sick, the whole orchestra's sick. It simply doesn't – feel – the way it did before!'

'Rot. For a start, orchestras don't have souls, any more than multimedia empires have souls. Orchestras are a conglomeration of the unsuitable and the unspeakable united in a doomed attempt at the impossible. And they're never, by definition, as good as they used to be, like England cricket teams or West End musicals. Well-known recognised fact. Ask any leader writer you like.'

'Have you no sense of loyalty?'

'Loyalty is a concept most commonly used to decry a healthy

self-interest.'

'But you hated Karl before,' she said impulsively. 'And you and William—'

'On the contrary: I never hated Karl. It just took a while for me to recognise his many strong points. You, I seem to recall, spotted them immediately, but perhaps they were rather more – obvious – from the female angle.'

'I remember you describing William as your only brother.'

Piotr's fingers drummed dangerously.

'In common with 79.8 per cent of professional cellists, I confess to moderate neurosis, Isabel, but I'm not quite so mad as to stick by a friend who's just succeeded in kicking my teeth in.'

'But you know better than anyone—'

'I needed him and he left me; I looked for him and he wasn't there any more. And you dare to talk about loyalty! What kind of frigging loyalty do you call that?'

An acidic flush broke over his cheekbones; his eyebrows rushed blackly together.

'Listen, have you ever looked into the soul of someone you loved and realised you'd been completely deceived in them? There's nothing worse, nothing more humiliating, than that. That's what keeps me awake at night, stomach curdling, temperature raging; that's what puts me off my breakfast of a morning. The humiliation that I shared – not my body, bodies are nothing – but my heart's core with someone of whom the best one can say is that he's a dissembler, a charlatan, a hypocrite and a thief.

'Oh, the charm, the skill, the sheer sexual charge of the man! Whom didn't he fool, with his public-school style and his understated charm? He was a gift straight from central casting – handicapped wife included – his serious hands and the way he used to smile, sideways, almost quizzical . . .'

She guessed that he was weeping, crumpled against the wall, hand shielding his eyes, and felt her old kinship flare. Oh, he was wrong, totally wrong, but that hardly mattered. We both loved him, she thought: so many differences but the same kernel.

'We'll never agree,' she murmured.

Piotr wiped his cheek savagely. 'At first I thought his behaviour an aberration. I thought, hell, we all do crazy things sometimes. Then I thought it was all your fault – you'd hoodwinked him – and later still I decided it was a mid-life thing, the sort publicity-minded shrinks spin articles into paperbacks about. And do you know the saddest part? This is the saddest part. When you got back together at the New Year, I actually thought there was something beautiful, something life-affirming, about it; God help me, I even thought it was love.

'I looked down – I'll never forget it – the snow falling, that clean crisp promise in the air. You were locked together, while the wind whipped the snow into waves around you, and I remember thinking, yes, yes, yes, like the end of *Ulysses* . . . All the poems in the world swirling round my head like snow, and I walked miles for the sheer pleasure of feeling the crunch of ice under my feet, knowing that I'd helped it to happen and that it – that it actually mattered, somehow . . . It took months for me to admit how wrong I'd been. William never was who he pretended to be. And all he ever did was run away.'

Isabel couldn't trust herself to respond. The picture he had drawn was too fresh in her mind, the rough feel of William's coat against her neck, the wind thrusting her hair across her mouth, mixing her hair with his kisses. The grey hovering hulk of the Festival Hall, passing cars hissing on damp asphalt, the swathes of circling snow – a moment crystallised by his surrender, in recollection suddenly sweeter and more certain than she could bear.

Karl entered then, greeting Piotr with a handshake.

'Good that you are early! I saw you from below, but knew that Isabel would entertain you.'

And Piotr taking easy command, his eyes perhaps a fraction brighter than usual, but every demon well battened down.

Isabel, less accomplished, pretended to search for a lipsalve in her bag. She heard their voices like a bad recording, isolated phrases veering sharply louder.

'Zimetski's in a bad way. I don't know the full story, but his health's still rocky . . . review in the *Guardian* . . . Lionel on Monday . . . all stitched up, unless . . .' And her own name, arrowing her attention: 'Isabel, may we leave you for just a moment? The bar is still open; perhaps you'd like a little something, my good friend.'

They left her there, still motionless, and suddenly undone by the extent of her desolation. From the gallery came the reverberations of shots from the sportsmen below; this was mixed with masculine laughter from the bar down the hall.

I'm lost, she thought; there's nothing left for me. I'm locked into a meaningless job with people I don't care about and a sadist who treats me as a fashion accessory. My father left me; William left me – everyone leaves me, sooner or later, and each time it happens there's a little less of me left behind.

She could almost hear the voices ('Isabel? Yes, she *was* quite stunning. Gaunt now, of course, and lord does she overdo the make-up, but after what she's been through . . . Do you mean, you never heard about William Mellor? *Such* a pleasant older man – oh, absolutely drove him to it, just couldn't let him alone. And when he left her – of course, nobody could have put up with *that* for very long'). Testing loneliness against the edge of her tongue ('Had her chances, as you might expect, but—'). Hot little tears like tiny fireballs coursing down her cheeks; hot tears drying the smooth surface of her skin.

('Then she took up with Hochler again. Fact, I assure you, though he never even pretended to care about her. No self-respect worth mentioning. What I'll never understand —')

No. Suddenly she couldn't bear to be there another moment, another second. Isabel flew out of the room and down the hall, almost colliding with a massively built sportsman at the front door. She heard a joking 'Hey, take it easy,' in an American accent, and then she was free, lips parted, hair tangled, cheeks fired, gulping down pints of city air. Her eyes, scouring the street for a taxi, attracted the attention of a young man in a convertible stopped in traffic.

'Hello, beautiful,' he said. 'Going my way?'

'Yes,' said Isabel. 'Yes, yes, yes.'

Chapter 40

There are more things in heaven and earth, Horatio,
Than are dreamt of in your philosophy.

Shakespeare

Autumn had arrived in Canterbury. The trees glowed with it, the wind hummed with it, but anyone observing William alighting from his train and taking up negotiations at a taxi rank might have thought him immune to its tangy impulsiveness, its aura of new beginnings. He was wearing a suit and tie; his face was stern, his shoulders tense with resolution.

His taxi released him not long afterwards, the driver indicating a drive across the road. Then there was only the dense peacefulness of the suburb, the rancid squabbles of sparrows, and dust from his retreating taxi.

The Victorian bungalow was set back from the road by some eighty yards, and surrounded by clipped yew that did nothing to lighten the atmosphere. There was a clinically perfect garden – striped lawn, obligatory roses – yet the airless feel extended even there, even to the closed-up, meticulously painted garage.

Suddenly William knew he was being watched. Not through any flicker of curtain or hiss of side-door; he simply knew. The sensation made him feel so peculiarly defenceless that he'd set the bell in motion before he'd decided how to begin, or even recollected the owner's name.

McKinley, he remembered, just as the indoor chain was lifted. Charmaine McKinley, spinster. A shadow purpled the peephole; then the door was creaked ajar, and he followed a small erect figure with a chignon into the front room, where Miss McKinley turned around to face him.

He had expected age, but not this monumental ugliness. Miss McKinley must have been ninety, but he had the impression that she had looked the same for decades. She had blue-white hair, a complexion like yellow chalk, a nose thin enough to cut paper and one eye angled perversely higher than the other. She was so bony that every segment of her skin seemed to skid into crevices and pouches; even her hands had wattles of skin dripping off their edges. She wore a kimono-style dresscoat and her nails were perfect, so shapely and polished that their lush pinkness seemed ironic, a commentary. She indicated a chair while her eyes, the burned-out eyes of the tropics, fastened themselves quizzically on him.

'William Mellor, I presume. An ameliorating, liquid sort of name in my opinion – too many Ls in it. Still, you look a gentleman-like man, of the sort one doesn't see much of nowadays.'

'It's kind of you to see me.'

'I'm never kind, Mr Mellor. I simply wanted to see the kind of man who's still in search of justice.'

William stirred.

'That's what you've come for, isn't it? Or had someone told you how magnificently ugly I am? I have been painted, you know, any number of times . . . The truth is that beautiful people subtly resemble one another; that's the dullest thing about beautiful people. One artist told me I was so ugly that only Picasso could paint me – and that Picasso had done so, without realising, hundreds of times. Do you agree?'

'Perhaps.'

He couldn't tell whether she was offended.

'An equivocal response indeed! You're old enough, surely, to have learned the tyranny of choice.'

William thought of Margot, of Isabel, of the Royal Sinfonia cello vacancy that had allowed him escape.

'Actually, I find most choice taken out of my hands.'

247

'Which is, of course, the coward's usual excuse. You will tolerate my bluntness, Mr Mellor. Age's greatest compensation is honesty – though few enough use it with my peculiar celerity. Would you care for some tea? I haven't any.'

'I'm not thirsty.'

'Still, you may have some coffee if you like. My help is here today, Sarie. She is useless, strikingly useless, but I keep her out of inertia, which is a much underrated virtue, I believe, and practically the only one I still pretend to . . . Sarie, some coffee, if you would be so good. You'll find it well enough made, Mr Mellor, as long as she doesn't confuse it with cocoa, and remembers to plug in the kettle . . . I believe you came about the cello.'

'Your father's cello, I was told.'

'My father's last cello. He had a good many cellos, one way or another . . . My father spent his life searching for the perfect sound.'

'We're all searching for that,' said William with a little smile.

'Don't be absurd.' Charmaine rapped quite sharply on the table. 'Sarie! Have you remembered to plug in the kettle?'

Sarie, a wizened creature of seventy-five, poked her head around the door and nodded thrice.

'She's simple, you see,' said Charmaine, so loudly that William feared that Sarie would hear her. 'A bit touched, if the truth be known. But loyal. Loyalty is worth something, Mr Mellor; loyalty is the only true greatness of which human nature is capable. And mostly, of course, it isn't even capable of that.'

What did she know? wondered William, going hot and cold.

'But to return to the point. You suggest, in your insidious fashion, that you're also searching for the perfect sound. To which I say fiddle – fiddle, tosh and rubbish. You'll forgive an old woman – or if you don't, it's all one to me – but I've neither the time nor the patience to waste poking round the edges of truth. You're satisfied enough with the sound that you make; I can see that in the lines of your face. Well, my father wasn't satisfied. My father was an amateur cellist. Do you know the derivation of the word amateur, Mr Mellor?'

William nodded.

'It comes from love, it means for love. Professionals forget this, if they ever learned it. These days it's all money – money, sponsorship, politics, and similar humbug. But the music knows, Mr Mellor. The music can sense betrayal when it hears it. When was the last time your heart stopped when you heard a breath of music? Were you at music college, perhaps a little later?'

'Oxford. I was up at Oxford. Bach – the double violin concerto, in the Holywell Room.'

For a moment her ravaged face softened.

'Oxford, of course. We have that in common, at any rate.'

For a moment she was silent. Magdalen Bridge at dawn and footsteps on the street beneath the hall windows; the sun arching through the quadrangle and the heavy swish of professorial gowns along the stairs. Then the clock struck and Charmaine roused herself.

'They say, don't they, that the old remember their child-hoods best, and yesterday worst of all?'

'Something like that.'

'Well I remember everything, Mr Mellor. Everything – it's a curse, a memory like mine; it gives me no peace. The war I remember, VE Day I remember, and the day the telegram came about my brother's death, I remember that too. Rommel killed him in North Africa – Rommel personally, as far as I was concerned, Rommel and Hitler between them.

'My childhood I remember – I grew up in the Far East. The Schwedagon Pagoda rising like a giant onion peeled golden over the trees, and the sound of my brother's cricket games near the servants' quarters, where the blackbirds screeched and the king cobras rose up at night to kill our dog. Cobras chew their poison in, Mr Mellor – nothing clean and injected about it, not like a viper. They chewed our dog's hip; we found him in the morning, legs buckled under him, stiff as sheet iron.

249

'And my lovers – I remember them at night. Raymond, who died during the march to Berlin, and Cecil, with a brain tumour that no one could diagnose. My cousin George, with his incorrigible moustache, who proposed to me at fifty – and Colin, who lived with me just after the war, when, believe me, nice girls simply didn't . . .

'They say that elephants grieve, Mr Mellor. The herd returns to the watering holes and picks up the separated, picked-clean bones of their dead, passing them from trunk to trunk in a kind of dance, remembering. I often imagine it – the bones, the swaying ritual, the alien rhythms of animal sorrow. Do you think that image wonderful or terrible, Mr Mellor? – or both?'

'Was it black or caramel-coloured coffee that ye'll be wanting?' Sarie inquired, head around the door. William recognised an Irish accent, which accompanied faded freckles and fragile wisps of hair.

'White, Sarie, white! There's no such thing as caramel-coloured coffee. And I am perfectly aware, too, that bluebells are actually purple, and that there's no real butter in butter-cups . . . Sarie is sadly handicapped by a literal turn of fancy,' she explained. 'I'm afraid you may wind up with no coffee at all.'

William begged her not to mention it. He felt vaguely protective of the crestfallen Sarie – and of Charmaine too. What a macabre name it seemed, under the circumstances, and yet the more he looked at her shrewd skewed hideousness, the more he recognised why an artist might have felt moved to paint her. She reminded him of a horned reptile in the process of sloughing off its skin, but her crêped eyes glittered with more animated intelligence. She leaned forward.

'But to business. Otherwise you'll suppose yourself to have come a fair way to hear an old woman rave about cobras and elephants.'

'Your coffee, Miss McKinley,' said Sarie, stumping in and setting two cups of cocoa before them. 'I hope the lawyer'll take to it finely. Those biscuits'll rise later, sure as eggs.'

'Thank you, Sarie . . . You know that there are words inside the cello. Do you read Italian, Mr Mellor?'

'Not well enough.'

'The words are from Dante.'

'Abandon hope?' joked William, because something in the rinsed-out blue of her eyes unsettled him. Charmaine did not smile.

'The love which moves the sun and other stars.'

Stars. Stars rising before his eyes during *Job*. Leszek whipping up the orchestra, the dance rising tidal from the double basses. The unreality of his situation startled William anew. It seemed so bizarre to be sitting in a house in Canterbury, conversing with a mordant creature out of Picasso's nightmares. He absentmindedly took a sip of his cocoa, which was stone cold.

'Tell me about the cello.'

'I don't know the whole story, Mr Mellor. And I never did believe in justice.'

Charmaine closed her ill-set eyes. It occurred to William that she really was old, fabulously old, and weary enough not to wake up again. Her energy level seemed to have flickered lower, voice slowed to an almost hypnotic pace.

'It is alive, of course.'

Alive. Well, hadn't he guessed as much? The soft pulsing under his fingers and the heat across the belly.

'Where did it come from?'

'No one knows. My father got it in Poland, just after the Second World War – I can't say he "found" it, precisely, because he always maintained that the cello found him . . . It chooses people, Mr Mellor, just as it chooses when to let its beauty bloom.'

William remembered the strange gleam he had first noticed at the auctioneer's; the living sound that had drawn him in.

'At any rate, there was a certain sound he was after – I told you about the sound. It wouldn't be going too far to say it was an ideal, a symbol; something, however obsessively he sought it, that he never thought to capture here on earth. Until he was given the cello.'

'Given it!'

'He always said he was given it. A German prisoner-of-war offered it him for only ten pounds. Well, it didn't look up to much, but even a rotten cello's worth that ... My father missed his own instrument; he was a soft-hearted creature, and the officer was desperate for money. My father took the cello back to his quarters, fitted it up with a roughish type of bridge, and gave it a try.

'And there it was, the sound he'd been searching for all his life. There, in that makeshift practice room at one end of a Red Cross surgery was the first springing of that wild, unearthly sound. My father burst into tears – you can see the marks on the cello still, because tears don't polish off, do they? Too much salt, I suppose, for the varnish. He couldn't stop weeping – or playing, either. And he never went home that night.'

There was a slower rhythm to her words; her eyes were fixed on space. William wondered whether it might be some kind of self-hypnosis – whether part of her tremendous memory might be her intellect, and part down to a skilful stroking of her subconscious.

'How old was your father?'

'He retired just after the war. He wasn't a young man then, Mr Mellor, and, even in his prime, he was never a very astounding cellist. I remember the studies he used to play – Gruetzmacher, would that be the creature? – doggedly going over the high bits again and again, never perfectly in tune ... No, he was a very ordinary cellist; but he only ever played for love, and the cellos always knew.'

'Presumably he brought the cello back to England at the end of the war.'

'Yes. The war was over, my brother was dead, and Mother – oh, Mother was positively distraught. She was a neurotic sort of woman at the best of times, and this was probably the worst of them. Nor was she best pleased to think that Father had spent what spare cash he'd got on yet another cello . . . That was the first time I clapped eyes on it.'

'What did you think?'

'Oh, I thought it a frightful little box, dark, ugly and cracked – you know how it can pretend to go shadowy and dull. I saw it with a friend of my father's – fellow who knew a bit about instruments, and he shook his head as he examined it. "Not worth more than five pound, and it'll cost that just to repair it," he said. But Father just smiled, sat down and played, and the sound – oh, it was bewitching, that night: every colour in the rainbow and the power of a small pipe-organ. I never heard it better . . . Spite, I suppose,' she added, after a moment's pause. 'That cello's never grown up. Sarie!'

Sarie stuck her wispy head around the door.

'Sarie, this coffee tastes quite diabolical. Take it away and do it again.'

Sarie glanced at William.

'Does he know I get the wee pig?' she demanded.

'Of course,' said Charmaine impatiently.

'An' it's drawn up proper, is it? – the bit in the will about the pig?'

'Yes, yes.'

Sarie left, satisfied, taking William's cold cocoa with her.

'Touched, poor creature,' said Charmaine. 'Thinks everyone's my solicitor, and longs for a little jade pig from Taipei, where I lived as a child . . . Oh, I'm leaving it her, as she's such a fancy for it, but she gets very tiresome about it sometimes.'

'Why don't you simply give it to her?' asked William curiously.

'No, no. If I was to give Sarie her pig, she'd only start fixing on something else. Human nature is to blame, Mr Mellor; it's human nature to long for things, and to be dissatisfied . . . Now, my father had brought the cello home.'

'Yes.'

'He never could get it valued, would you credit it? They didn't want to know, the so-called experts in their walled-up offices. No, they shook their heads and pursed their lips and muttered about cracks and bouts and purfling and not knowing whose workshop it might have come from. "A journeyman cello," one of them opined, and another wondered whether a player mightn't have made it himself, and not a proper maker at all. They didn't know then, and they don't know now, do they, Mr Mellor? I forget what you paid me but it was a criminally low price for a sound like that. Though it's a moody, irascible little creature: if it didn't fancy singing, it jolly well wouldn't. I don't expect its attitude's improved since.'

Here she mused for so long that William prompted her.

'Is that all that you can tell me?'

Charmaine laughed, but it metamorphosed into a hoarse cough.

'Forgive me. Shouldn't laugh – how could you know? – but . . . First let me tell you a little about my father.

'My father, Mr Mellor, was an idealist. He told me the world was fair, and I believed him. He told me the sun would rise up every morning, and I believed him. If he'd told me, in the teeth of the evidence, that the sun shone all night I expect I'd have believed that as well. He was a – sunny, open kind of man. He never passed a child without waving to it, and he never met old folks without a smile. I'm not saying he was perfect – he wasn't – but he was the kind of doctor people used to think all doctors were when I was young. Moreover, my father was a gentleman. He doffed his hat. He held doors open. And he was faithful on three continents to my poor mother (who, between us, was a very great trial). Until the cello came.'

'You mean, it altered him?'

Charmaine drummed restlessly on the table, nails clicking like candy-pink scimitars.

'Of course not. How could a wretched cello alter anyone? It's just that the cello never comes alone.'

'Oh God,' said William.

'I beg your pardon?'

'Please, go on.'

'Well! My father returned to England the same month as a new neighbour moved in next door. We met this woman for the first time that very night I told you of, the night when I first heard the cello. It was the only time I ever saw her to speak to, and it was very dark, but I remember her perfectly. She was in her twenties, small – features like chiselled porcelain – delicately, angelically lovely and yet with something faintly corruptible about her . . . The light from the hallway haloed her hair, which was very fair, and lit up the softest pair of brown eyes I've ever seen.'

William gripped his chair. So: she didn't age, or not the way normal people aged . . .

'She asked me at the door if we'd got any milk to spare. I knew we'd a bit left over, but I distrusted beauty – still do – and told her no. She was about to leave, when my father, always generous, came along and insisted on giving her all we'd got left. She leaned to take the bottle from his hand; I saw lights feathering the edges of her hair. And I saw my father's face: strange, open – what's the word I want? – dented, as I'd never seen it before. That's all I remember of that night, but it's also the reason I'll always say that a good memory's a curse, for a man or a woman.'

Her eyes rotated sharply to William's face – he almost recoiled.

'As you'll know as well as any.'

Again he had that sensation of weakness.

'You mean—'

'I do. And my mother – poor foolish creature – my mother died thereafter, by her own hand.'

William swam upwards out of dark water.

'But there's nothing definite to connect the cello with this – young woman.'

Charmaine raised a contemptuous eyebrow. Into the silence stumped Sarie, flat-slippered, laden with burned-out crusts of biscuits and piping hot drinks.

'Now, let's be knowing if ye'll be wantin' aught else,' she

said, nodding significantly at Will.

'Oh Sarie, Sarie, for God's sake, go away!'

And Sarie did, casting a reassuring leer at William as she did so. The jade pig, she mouthed at the door, and he nodded, too devastated to respond.

Sarie shut the door into the silence. Charmaine leaned back. The crooked eye looked shut, but the other was fixed on the carpet. Effort had daubed dots of colour, like badly applied rouge, on both her cheeks, but the rest of her face was bloodless as a mask. She might be ill, thought William with misgiving – even dying.

'Are you sure I haven't tired you?'

'I'm ninety-five, Mr Mellor,' she replied, with a return of her asperity. 'Does it really matter?'

William hesitated. If she should die! And she seemed at the very portals; a fall, a faint, too heavy an effort . . .

'Tell me, would you prefer me to go?'

The lines of her face were grateful, though her voice still subtly mocked him.

'You were beautifully brought up; I'll say that for you. Stay, I'll be with you shortly. You'll be glad to hear that there isn't much more.'

William sipped his coffee, which had a strangely astringent texture – Assam, he diagnosed; a dose of tea thrown in for good measure. Though Charmaine had said that she had no tea . . .

'Forgive me, Mr Mellor. I don't often have a turn, indeed I rather pride myself on my energy, having had only ugliness to boast of all my life . . . I'll be brief, however, and then – with your permission – Sarie will show you out. I'm not such a fool as to decline rest when I need it.'

'You don't need to say much more,' said William gently.

'And what is that supposed to mean, precisely?'

'Only that I – suspect. I suspect that you were your father's favourite, and felt his fall from grace as hard as anyone . . . So that when your father eventually died, leaving you the cello—'

'Ah but he didn't leave it me, Mr Mellor. So far as you surmise, I grant that you're right, grant it freely. I was jealous, furiously jealous; there was a day, walking down the street with the shopping, when I could have – well, well, never mind. But when my father died – liver failure brought on by guilt and drunkenness – he forbade me to have anything to do with his last cello, the cello he'd spent his life looking for. More than that indeed: he explicitly commanded me to destroy it.'

William caught his breath. 'In what terms?'

'Can I put it any plainer?' she demanded.

'No, but – why? For what reason?'

'That it was possessed, of course. Oh, he didn't put that in writing, Mr Mellor. Not after having assured his executors that he was of sound mind; he was not, thank God, such a fool. But that was what he told me privately. "You'll be the last of the family," he said. "See that the cello goes too, I don't care how. I charge you. See to it, Carrie." He called me Carrie; it had a friendlier sound than Charmaine, somehow. But I never could destroy it. I tried, but I never could.'

'I suppose that finances—'

'Finances – fie! Have you ever tried to destroy a cello, Mr Mellor? Have you ever sat, paraffin in one hand and a match in the other, and looked down at a cello so tightly beautiful, so exquisitely real? Have you ever taken a carving knife, a knife created for trimming the thinnest, tenderest slices of duck, and thought to plunge it deep into the belly of a shining, glowing, gleaming, singing cello?

'I never played the cello, Mr Mellor. I played the piano as a child and I played it appallingly. But I could no more murder a cello than I could murder poor Sarie, drivelling on about her silly jade pig. And nor could you – nor could anyone with genuine sensibility, I believe. Besides, I didn't understand. I still don't understand. Do you understand, Mr Mellor?'

'No,' said William unsteadily. 'I can't pretend to completely understand.'

Charmaine had received her second wind. Her eyes were feverish; her fingers, on which the knuckles stood out like a rocky coastline, hummed restively. Yet her renewed energy vaguely disturbed him; it seemed too great for her wiry body, she was an archery bow bent almost to breaking.

'It never went out of tune, Mr Mellor – not for thirty years. The strings didn't snap either. I would take it out, dust it, strum the strings, and close the case. And I would wonder – especially when it moved. For it did move, Mr Mellor – mainly at night. I'd find it waiting for me in the hallway, curled up in the kitchen, waiting, waiting. I'd put it back in the morning so as not to let Sarie know ... And I'd wonder too what had happened to the girl – where she'd disappeared to, whether she was still alive, whether she was waiting – even whether she might be in this house. My blonde cat used to look up at the wall, Mr Mellor – look up at the wall for no reason, shivering and looking, looking and shivering, as if there was something there I couldn't see ... And, strangest of all, I used to hear the cello playing on nights when I was alone in the house. Nothing you would recognise, nothing with a human fingerprint, but its own unmistakable deep-bowed cello-throated sound. Wild sounds sometimes, and sometimes sounds so lost and soft as to break your heart. But when I went downstairs it was always perfectly still.

'Possession, spirits – these are not easy concepts, Mr Mellor. There are still times when I almost doubt the things I've seen, the sounds I've heard. There may be reasons – coincidence, imagination, the all-too-common weaknesses of human nature. Sometimes I'm not surprised at my failure to throw the first stone. The stone was there, as the knife was there, and the bonfire. But I could never throw it.'

'No.'

'My father let me down – he knew it; I knew it. Perhaps, in some complicated way, your father let you down. But if life has taught me any single thing it's this: not to believe in justice. You came here for justice, I know, but all you can take away is

258

a few small grains of truth. It's not enough, God knows, but it is something . . . Put it in your fist, and take it away, Mr Mellor. Perhaps you're strong enough to deal with what I've told you, though I never was. Perhaps even, by telling you, I've helped to fulfil my father's last wish – unless we're mainly cowards, the ugly and the handsome alike. We all know that even truth can be equivocal, after all.'

William stood up. 'Thank you for telling me. I'm sorry that you should have been put through so much.'

Charmaine looked deeply at him, then closed her eyes.

'And I'm sorry it was you who bought the cello. You've had your own troubles; I can see that. You want my advice, you throw it in the river and don't look back. Come and see me again if you like, before the spring . . . Sarie! Come show Mr Mellor out.'

Sarie instantly appeared, without her apron.

'I'll call you,' said William, irresolutely, at the door.

'Before the spring, mind. I won't see out another spring. Good day, Mr Mellor.'

Outside he stopped Sarie to ask, 'Is your mistress ill?'

Sarie shook her head. 'Sure and the cocoa wasn't hot.'

'No,' said William, 'it wasn't.'

'And I won't get me pig neither, not till the spring.'

A flutter of wind ruffled William's jacket. Through the window he saw Charmaine, the loose skin of her forearm flapping like a bat's wing, closing the curtains to the wide front room.

Chapter 41

He took me by the wrist and held me hard,
Then goes he to the length of all his arm,
And with his other hand thus o'er his brow
He falls to such perusal of my face
As 'a would draw it.

Shakespeare

Isabel spent the night in her Barbican flat, which seemed dusty and overfurnished after Karl's. The phone rang with cool persistence around midnight but she made no move to answer it, and whoever it was left no message.

She'd forgotten the blight the weekend always casts in the Barbican, with the residents hurriedly shopping, scurrying into their burrows or disappearing to meet other singles in livelier sections of the capital. They were mostly childless, essentially working people; weekends subtly unnerved them, as light unnerves nocturnal creatures.

One of her houseplants had died, its fingers curled together like the hands of a baby. She cast it out swiftly, remembering the day she had bought it, unable to resist its impossibly pale pink flowers. Finally, with the windows flung open and the flat aired, she sat down at her desk.

After long and painful consideration, she had decided to write to William. She dreaded seeing him without preparation: while the idea of a second public rejection was too horrible to contemplate. No, a reasoned letter would be the best basis for a renewal of negotiations; and, should he still refuse to see her, at least no one would know but herself.

She tore up four drafts, each longer and less satisfactory than the last, before penning the shortest possible note:

William,
I've left Karl. Please see me, even if only for a moment.

She left it unsigned, as she always had; there was an almost sensual pleasure in the recollection. Then she called the Royal Sinfonia office, and learned that the orchestra were rehearsing at Henry Wood Hall. A few minutes later she was on the Tube; she was walking down Borough High Street, past traffic snarled round roadworks, past small cafés and tiny chemists' shops. She felt naked without her viola, indeed she almost regretted leaving it behind, as if it might have provided protective coloration, some subtle justification.

She arrived in Trinity Church Square at midday, breathless with adrenalin and anticipation. The car park, as always, was crowded with musicians' cars, but not the cars that Isabel was used to seeing. A different orchestra: a different world. On the steps of the building, a couple of players gossiped while a girl with striking auburn hair read Charlotte Brontë. Isabel wondered vaguely if she knew the girl, but Angela recognised her in a jerked heartbeat.

'Is the rehearsal still going on?' asked Isabel.

'Yes, only the strings.'

Whatever was Isabel doing here? Could William – was it conceivable that William might have asked her to come? With a rush of relief, Angela recalled that William had chosen to take this concert off. Still, there was a feverish eagerness about Isabel, a suppressed tension that she found disquieting.

When Isabel returned from inside, the glow was gone. She stood irresolute on the top step, twisting an envelope between her fingers.

'Looking for someone?' asked Angela at last.

Isabel glanced down. 'Yes, that is – yes, I am. William Mellor. Do you know him?'

'Of course.'

'We've met before, haven't we? Aren't you a flautist?'

'No, I play the harp.'

'The harp, of course,' said Isabel vaguely.

'Could I tell him you were looking for him?'

Isabel paused irresolutely. 'No. But you might – you might give him this for me. Will you see him soon?'

'Tomorrow.'

Another day's wait. But it would be better than a phone call out of the ether. Isabel handed Angela the envelope.

'Thank you.'

'Goodbye,' said Angela, but Isabel was already halfway across the square, almost running.

Angela glanced at the envelope. There was nothing but his name on the outside, but the envelope was very thin, and by twisting it in the light she could just make out the message, in a flourishing, rather over-feminine hand:

William,
I've left Karl. Please see me, even if only for a moment.

Angela read it, the colour fleeing her face. Karl was Karl Hochler, of course. Isabel had left Hochler, and wanted to see William, for reasons that required no guesswork . . .

One of the brass players asked, 'Who was the looker, Angie?'

'Just someone I know,' said Angela, putting the letter in her handbag.

The looker. Oh, she was still beautiful; Angela was intuitive enough to recognise that the faint premonitions of mortality in Isabel's looks would only deepen their appeal to William. She wasn't a perfected rosebud, as Janice was, but a full-blown rose caught on the cusp of turning. There was poetry in that, poetry in the just-thumbed circles under her dark eyes, a sure, impulsive, immensely human beauty. Her skin, naturally so soft a tan, made Angela dissatisfied with her own rice-paper fragility, and the sweeping fullness of her hair made Angela detest the more languid contours of her own. 'I've left Karl . . .'

What luck that William was absent! Was there a man in the orchestra who could have resisted a look of entreaty from those dark eyes?

The envelope remained in her handbag during the rehearsal. She fingered it when looking for a pencil, when catching hold of change for a coffee. The paper so thin, the writing so flamboyant!

'Thought I saw you talking to Isabel Bonner,' said Pete, at lunch.

'No,' said Angela, without thinking.

'Nay, this is above all strangeness. Upon the crown o'the cliff what thing was that which parted from you?'

'An – adult pupil of mine.'

'Resemblances never cease to amaze me. My own cousin, now . . .'

But Angela's inner dialogue careered on too hectically to attend to him. She longed to tell Pete: You were right; it was Isabel, and she gave me a note for William that I don't intend to pass on. Without any response, Isabel won't have the courage to take it further. She'll think – anyone would think – that he won't see her, doesn't want to talk to her. She'll think he's set his soul against the risk, and he has, I'm almost sure he has. Surely he's got enough to worry about without this.

And the recollection of Isabel, alive and alight, only reinforced Angela's resolve ('I've left Karl –'). The lack of signature, too, disturbed her unreasonably. There was such effortless confidence in it, that the handwriting alone should be enough . . . No, better that he never knew, better that the matter ended here, now, for good. She was fulfilling the office of a friend, by not disclosing the truth to William.

Yet she still had to berate her conscience into submission, to fight the conviction – for Angela was too clever for self-delusion – of her own ignoble jealousy. Wasn't William experienced enough to deal with his own messages? Was it any of her business anyway? Yet she loved him. Isabel wasn't the only one who loved him. She might be jealous, but hadn't fate elected to put the letter into her hands? Her hands, of all the possible members of the orchestra! So she remained, nearly but not completely decisive, and the note remained too in her possession.

In the canteen the next morning, Angela greeted William with unusual warmth.

'Lovely to see you. Coffee?'

'Thanks, I've just had some.'

'I hope you enjoyed yesterday. Were you demolishing a golf course?'

William smiled. 'No. There was someone I had to see, down in Canterbury.'

'A musician?' asked Angela curiously.

'No. A very old lady.'

'How old? Is she ill?'

Before the spring, mind: I won't see out another spring . . . Part of William longed to confide in Angela, but what she'd told him in Greece made him pause. Was it fair to draw her closer to his concerns? Besides, how to explain it? It sounded so unreal.

'She might be ill, Angela. I'm not sure.'

He looked tired, his eyes deeper than usual. Her own name on his lips almost undid her; the letter, folded in her jeans pocket, seemed to heat her groin.

'You don't look well, William.'

'I'll be all right.'

Don't say anything I can't handle, his eyes begged her, and she seized on this as the answer she wanted. In the ladies', she took the envelope out of her pocket and pushed it down the receptacle beside the row of taps. It stayed there until the cleaning lady, complaining about her corns, emptied out the rubbish the next morning.

It was like Karl to require no explanations. He greeted her three days later as matter-of-factly as if she had never surrendered on one of his devices, never been fingerpainted nude for his collection, never disappeared from his gun club without leaving a message.

'Isabel, my dear. I was just looking for you.'

'I'm sorry, I should have—'

'No need. Your things have been sent to the Barbican flat. That is the correct place, I think?'

He means William, she thought, and flushed.

'Yes, thank you. I meant to call, but somehow—'

'Have you been in touch with William Mellor recently?' he asked her smoothly.

'I – haven't spoken to him.'

'Then you have written?'

It was casually, even exquisitely done, but there was an intensity behind it that she instantly recognised. He's always lived off us, she thought; he could bear that I was with anyone except for William.

'Listen, Isabel, I will tell you something, something you should, I think, attend to very carefully. What you need to do at this point in your life is to go back to your father, to make your peace there. You have confused this William with your missing father. You know this, yet still you cling to this fantasy like a little child.'

Denial trembled on her lips, but he went on. 'I tell you this because I like you. You are intriguing; there is such a spark there. You are very alive; this I find refreshing. If you get bored with waiting for this man – who, believe me, will never come back – then call me. Some night, you are alone, call me. No arguments, no recriminations, no histrionics – I do not at all care for histrionics. But call me if you like. I will be there.'

The news filtered swiftly through the Orchestra of London. ('I knew Karl wouldn't last, surprising it went on so long, really . . . Never saw what she saw in him – a sadist, and arrogant with it . . . No, nothing to do with William. She told Caroline that she wants to be on her own . . . On her own – Isabel? Now I really have heard everything.')

And Warren Wilson, taking Isabel aside in the rehearsal break. 'Do you know what you're doing?'

Mad beautiful eyes, he thought; she'd been quiescent for so many months, but he'd always known that she'd fire up again.

'Why, Warren, you hated my being with Karl before,' she teased. William will call tonight, she thought; tonight I'll hear his voice again, deep, a little uncertain . . . Warren cut impatiently in on her thoughts.

'I know you. There always has to be someone. And at least Karl represented some strange, perverted stability, at least he was someone we knew. Also, he doesn't trouble to fake anything; he's got too much confidence to bother to pretend.'

Tonight, she thought; and, at the softening of her expression, Warren seized her shoulders. 'It's no good hoping for that, Isabel.'

'Let go!'

'Have you forgotten February so easily? Are you the only one to know him so little?'

'And love him so much,' she said, very softly. Warren released her, his anger seeping away. There was no arguing with the certainty in her face, and besides, even if she hurt herself – as she was bound to – running like a child after happiness, at least she was back. At least she was alive again, after so many months of listlessness . . . Warren remembered breaking down the door to her flat; her great starving dizzy eyes. He thought: perhaps it was always my fate to save her for William.

Isabel tore home after the rehearsal, but found no message on her machine. To avoid leaving the flat, she ordered a pizza, although when it arrived she couldn't bear to touch it. The day seemed to darken unnaturally early, even for the time of year. From her balcony, the leaden City air seemed suddenly dense, fume-ridden, intolerable.

She had just put the television on to drown out the silence when the phone rang. One ring. Leave it; breathe slowly. Two rings. Breathe, breathe. She caught it on the third ring, her voice flickering: 'Hello?'

266

Caroline: 'Isabel, look, do come round and eat something. I'm sure you've nothing to eat in the flat.'

And automatically: 'No, thank you.'

'What's that? No, she doesn't want to ... Sorry, Isabel, Warren's on at me. He told me you wouldn't want to be bothered, but really, you know, you must eat. The last time this sort of thing happened – well, you remember.'

'I've got a pizza here.'

'Pizza ... frozen, I suppose. Well, mind you eat it. There's some protein in pizza. I'll see you tomorrow.'

'Thanks.'

Isabel stared at the congealing mozzarella, and a spasm of fear shivered her. If he was going to call, surely he would have tried by now. Unless. Unless there was someone else, or Margot was coming back, or he felt simply deadened inside, the way she'd felt herself. Perhaps that was her real legacy: his wife's rejection, fluid death of the soul.

I have to know, she thought, I can't bear not knowing. Anything, even the chilliest possible response, would be better than this wretchedness ... And so, with a courage born of sheerest terror, she did what she'd nearly done – so many times! – since February, and dared press in his Ealing number.

It seemed to take an age for him to answer. She expected every moment his resonant 'Sorry to be unavailable at the moment', but instead there was his voice, very deep: 'William Mellor.'

'William.'

'Oh, God. Let me turn off the radio ... Isabel. What is it? What's wrong?'

His voice, and she was breathless again, nerves colliding with elation. She asked, 'Why didn't you call me?'

'Why should I have called? Was there a message?'

'A note.'

'It hasn't arrived. When did you post it?'

'I gave it to your harpist.'

No end to the dangers of having given way to Angela. No end to the complications. Had she read the note herself, or had she only been shielding him from all that she'd imagined?

'I expect she forgot,' he said, hating the lie, but obscurely wanting to protect Angela. 'It doesn't matter. Tell me why you wrote.'

Easier to write it, as she'd known at the time. Easier than blurting it out on a telephone, than dealing with the silences, the sudden politeness. This silence, however, was equally unbearable. Hadn't she called in order to end the silence, whatever the cost?

'I've left Karl,' she told him.

'I'm sorry,' said William automatically. And he wondered if he might not be a little sorry. Hadn't there been some kind of relief in knowing that Hochler was there for her? She certainly wasn't safe on her own.

'I ran away. I – I need to see you. I must see you.'

As simple as that. And the recollection of evenings in her flat pulled surely at him. Never had his house seemed so sterile, so uselessly, purposelessly spacious, the night so long. He took a deep breath, and said, for no reason, 'You're in the flat, you mean.'

'I need to see you, William. Come tonight.'

William wrestled with his longing. What was stopping him? He was separated; she was single and alone. Was he to be denied all normal feelings, all sexual expression, because his wife had left him? Hadn't Margot forfeited some right to his loyalty? The recollection of Isabel above him, the perfect elisions where ribs slipped into breast, where buttock merged with thigh – and suddenly he couldn't breathe for longing.

'Just this once,' she begged. 'Just to talk.'

'That wouldn't work,' he said shortly. 'You know it wouldn't work. There's only one end to an idea like that.'

She luxuriated in the glorious reassurance that he still wanted her – while he twisted against memory's bewitchment. Never had the idea of making love to Isabel seemed so irresistibly alluring. Absence was allied to frustration, and desire with a feeling (unfair but nonetheless tangible) that Margot, by deserting him, had opened herself up to exactly this . . . But William was mature enough to recognise selfishness, even in himself.

'No,' he said quietly.

'No?' she echoed, a disappointed child.

'Not again. It would only happen all over again. Just remember what it was like before.'

'I remember – every day.'

He struggled against the pulsating waves of his own longing. 'I don't mean – that. Remember what it felt like when I left. Remember pulling ourselves apart, scene by scene, torment by torment. Above all, remember that we can't carry on indefinitely trampling on other people's feelings and our own self-respect. Isabel, you're wasting precious years, important years, on this – infatuation. You must find someone else – younger, but still dependable.'

It was to him a comforting mantra, and had the further advantage of being true; but it only maddened her.

'I love you!' she cried, and in a heartbeat he knew that she had defeated him. All logic, all argument, all the words in the world couldn't hold out against those three, in Isabel's voice. Recklessness seized him, a youthful, effortless ardour. She heard it in his voice, life-affirming, certain, holding out the promise of renewal like spring.

'I'll be with you in an hour.'

'Don't stop for flowers.'

'All right. No flowers.'

'Oh William, you could stay the night! Couldn't you? No one would know.'

The buoyancy in her voice troubled him. Happiness – so precarious a thing; to be able to give or withhold it so terrifying to a man of William's sensibilities. To stay all night: her old dream, to wake with him beside her in the morning.

'Yes,' he said recklessly. 'If you like.'

And he spent the night as he'd sworn he never would, Isabel's tears on his face, her breasts against his back, her hair fuzzed soft and ticklish over his shoulder. No flowers, she had told him, but surely she was her own flower, opening and closing as the hours passed, while he captured her as richly as he'd always used to. And when he thought she was tired, she pulled him between her lips and brought him up again, until the burden of all his longings was lifted, the world's doubts tumultuously expelled. Until time disappeared and sleep claimed them.

Chapter 42

I do beseech you, sir, have patience.
Your looks are pale and wild and do import
Some misadventure.

Shakespeare

(from Pete Hegal's diaries)

It was no use kidding ourselves: we'd had it. The double basses were offering eight to one against Leszek's lasting out the year – offering it freely – while Leszek himself lurched from hysteria to fury and back: at me, at the reviewers, at the whole mad machiavellian world. The woman was eating at him; and if his moods were cyclonic, his performances were diabolical.

In Snape, in my absence, he abruptly departed the stage between movements, hand to his temple, and didn't resume for a quarter of an hour. At the Edinburgh Festival, he paced so listlessly through *Symphonie Fantastique* that a reviewer compared his performance, to the sheep's advantage, with that of an inbred Highland sheep, conducting at sight . . . While two of our trustees were so incensed by Leszek's garbled speech at the annual fundraising knees-up that they called the board to back his dismissal. Rumour suggested, and with no little justification, that Leszek Zimetski and the Royal Sinfonia both would be decently interred almost as soon as the Ulverston commission adjourned to consider the evidence in February.

And what was I, what was Lenny, what was Will doing during this crisis?

Well, not a lot, though Lenny did at least get the official bid forms in to the Arts Council committee. He also flogged his board into attending half a dozen crisis meetings (by then we were in a state of near-permanent crisis), and banged their heads together when they wouldn't agree. I saw the document he hammered out myself, and, considering what they were up against, I've seen mouldier.

They played down Leszek's 'minor health problems', slotted in some jazzy educational tripe, and flash-carded the names of every top international conductor who'd ever (in however misguided a moment) expressed the vaguest wish to conduct us. They also promised, funds permitting, to form innovative cultural links with South Korea. (Korea was big that year, politically speaking.) But Lenny's brightest idea was a themed summer festival juxtaposing Byrd and Birtwistle, which was not only (a) alliterative and (b) British, but had, on paper, the publicity-garnering potential to alienate practically everybody, from the Stone Age, gut-string hamburger-haters to our off-at-the-first-hint-of-squeaky-door-music supporters.

Which was all good, fruity stuff, but there remained enough writing on the wall to discourage a graffiti bug. Those Koreans were animals – anybody's, for the right money – and the agents of most international conductors would consider anything we could afford mere gerbil fodder.

I grieved for Leszek, but much the most terrifying part for me was Will's sudden abdication.

Will seemed to be moving in a dreamworld. He was courteous to the point of painfulness, but remote; sometimes he seemed to hardly recognise me.

'Are you all right?' I asked him, cornering him in a deserted Festival Hall after the troops had fled the scene of the crime. Otherwise, I give you my word, he'd have nodded and walked past.

'I'm well enough, thanks.'

'And the cello?'

'Quiet,' he said, after a moment's thought. 'Satisfied.'

'You were going to destroy it.'

Will smiled. 'I thought that you of all people knew that I don't have courage enough to destroy anything.'

He turned to go, but I stopped him, in a mildish panic. No appetite, weight loss, aberrant behaviour . . . I remembered Greece, Janice – her failed effort at control. I inquired, 'Have you been in touch with Margot?'

'My son has. She's agreed to see me at Christmas.'

Christmas. Less than a month away.

'How do you feel about that?' I persevered.

'How should I feel?'

I grabbed his arm. 'Will, something's changed, I know it has. Has Janice . . .?'

He shuddered deeply. 'No. She's got him to feed on.'

His patience maddened me.

'For God's sake, Will, just – get rid of it! You were going to once, weren't you?'

'Yes – once.'

'Remember what Charmaine told you – and what her father wanted. Will, you know as well as I do what's behind Leszek's trouble. And unless Leszek snaps out of it, he's lost, and we're lost, the entire orchestra's done for! You saw him in Edinburgh. How bad do things have to get before you at least try to do something?'

'There is a reason,' he said, like a seasoned diplomat handling leg-breaks from yapping journalists, 'but I'm not at liberty to tell you.'

I looked at his tired, beautiful eyes, at the slope of his shoulders, at his strong serious mouth, and I intuitively knew. Isabel. Unbelievably, against all likelihood, all reason. I murmured: 'Isabel, it has to be. Love as corrosion.'

Will didn't deny it. Instead he handed me the cello; it quivered darkly in my hands, stirring itself, awakening. And suddenly his quietness terrified me. We're doomed, I remember thinking: it's the king's abdication, the last turn of the screw.

'You can't just – hand it over!'

'Well, I can't do it myself. There was a chance, that night we met Piotr – but if I was too soft then, I'm even softer now. You have my blessing, if it's any comfort to you. You're stronger than I am, and younger. Do it, Pete. Do it now.'

The lights from the stage seemed to dim suddenly against the cello's unearthly glow. I felt it throb in my hand, a vivid, humanly living thing. And, deep inside my head, in the very cornerstone of my brain, I heard hoofbeats starting up, waves pummelling, pummelling inside a heaving sea.

I thought: O all you host of heaven! O earth!

By then the cello was bright enough to cast a shadow beyond William . . . I tightened my grip. What had he said? You have my blessing . . . Do it now.

I didn't rush it. Instead I thought about Leszek, about his old zestful boyishness, about the friendly ritual of taking coffee into his study and having half-empty mugs hurled back at me. I thought about the way he used to conduct – the all-too-human music in his fingers, the caressing expressive finesse-point of his baton. Finally I remembered the scream he'd given in hospital. It sang in my memory like the cry of a broken child.

On instinct, half-blinded, I twisted the cello's back towards me, though, God knows, the back looked liquid too. In my overheated imagination it was gilded like silver in candlelight, while the apocalyptic horsemen kept thudding across my brain. You have my blessing, if it's any comfort to you . . . Will's shadow, immovable: the Commendatore in *Don Giovanni*'s last act. Do it, Pete. Do it now.

I took the foul thing by its neck and hurled it to the floor, plunging my foot inside it, over and over. It didn't crack properly but gave way beneath me, gushing as a body might, sickeningly like a human abdomen.

How long this lasted I couldn't say. There was a perversion in it, not only in the sensation, but in the fractured, cut-glass quality of space, breath, time. But when I backed away, lights splashing on, and the pounding finally fading, I found Will still beside me, and the cello still lying, dark, poised and perfect, by the foot of the stage. Not even a scratch on it. And, in sheer hysteria, I started to laugh.

Will didn't. He bent down to pick up the cello, as if it was his burden and he had to bear it. And in this he was right, of course; if what had happened proved anything, it had proved that we were inside one of those deeply unfair fairytales where only the prince is permitted to crampon the mountain, kebab the dragon and ankle off with the princess. You know the plotline: the squire is always free to have a go, but no business will result, besides which his music will inevitably be represented by a solo viola.

John McDaniel wandered in. Never a typical principal (who specialise, as a general rule, in ruthlessness and verve), John prefers to drift around playing chess in his head. He looked down meditatively from the lip of the stage, as if pinned by an opponent's rook and a bit bemused as to what the upshot might be.

'Ah, Pete,' he observed, 'I've just been having a word with young Janice. Has it ever occurred to you that there might be something wrong with that girl?'

I was speechless, but Will exerted himself enough to ask, 'What makes you think that?'

'We were chatting just now – of this and that – when she suddenly closed her eyes as if something was paining her. At first I thought it might be a fit or faint of some kind, although since leaving her – she recovered after the immediate moment had passed – it occurred to me that a peptic ulcer is rather more likely. I would be sorry to hear that she had an ulcer, at her age. My brother Julian is a martyr to them.'

As if something inside was paining her. I turned round to see what Will made of it, but Will was already gone.

CHAPTER 43

Am not I consanguineous? am I not of her blood?
Shakespeare

'Ah, Lucy,' said Karl Hochler, looking up coolly from his desk. 'I asked to see you on a disciplinary matter.'

Lucy perched uneasily on the nearest chair, wondering whether Karl had observed her giggling at her desk-partner during the concert. His sangfroid had been known to evaporate completely when confronted with such shenanigans, though concentration could also render him near-oblivious. Lucy elected a frontal defence.

'I'm sorry about the bowing in the Schubert.'

'It was not the bowings about which I wished to have this small chat.'

Damn damn damn. He'd definitely noticed Donald, her desk-partner, imitating their section leader from behind. Corpsed, she had, or very nearly . . .

Karl continued, with mock severity (how mock was it, exactly?), 'And what was so amusing? Was my fly undone? There was perhaps some person in the audience that you knew?'

She longed to say, it's just Donald: his droll lugubrious eyes – his cleverness at imitations. Donald could even imitate Hochler, after a fashion.

'Sorry,' murmured Lucy, unwilling to incriminate a friend. How Donald kept such a straight face always astonished her. At the very least, they should have been arraigned in the dock together.

Karl hadn't, in point of fact, noticed anything amiss in the second violins, though musicians, in his experience, nearly always had some misdemeanour or other on their consciences. He leaned backwards.

'Perhaps then you will be so good as to tell your colleagues that you have been most severely reprimanded for this thing.'

Lucy stood up joyously. 'Oh, you *are* a peach.'

'A peach. This is a new expression. What is a peach?'

'An angel. A dachshund puppy. A gin and tonic with a slice of lime in it.'

'Then I am most pleased to be such a thing . . . There is however one small condition.'

Lucy sobered. 'Is there? What is it?'

Karl's eyes raked hers, suddenly, startlingly sexual. No, she thought: this is imagination. There's Isabel, for a start. There'd been Isabel for ages.

'It is I think a very simple condition. That you take off what the British so amusingly call your knickers and sit in my lap.'

He had the most dangerous eyes she'd ever seen, five-hundred-watt eyes. They turned her head to mush and her calves to whipped cream.

'Isabel . . .' she began weakly.

'Isabel and I have parted company.'

How strangely he said it! Cool as you please, and yet, underneath, the merest hint of a genuine frisson.

'I don't believe it,' breathed Lucy.

His voice, precisely clipped: 'I can only assure you that it is a fact.'

'But only William could . . . It can't be; I can't believe it. I was there, that day in February. I heard it all.'

'No doubt. Your situation, however, remains as I have suggested. Or would you perhaps prefer the reprimand, the warning? I expect I could make your life surprisingly difficult if I tried, so arbitrary are the uses of power.'

Lucy caught her breath. There had been a time when she had done her damnedest to manoeuvre this exact moment. There had been a time – a longish time – when she'd wondered whether Karl wasn't playing with her, aware of her attraction, amusing himself by frustrating it. Yet now that he was hers for the asking, she found the idea terrifying – kinky, but terrifying: the slow-pulsed anger beneath those lidded eyes, the careering motion of her heart. Aroused but wary, she glanced towards the door.

'It is locked,' said Karl, watching her. 'It is always locked.'

'Before—' She hesitated, and stopped.

'Before what?'

'When you first conducted us, when I – I mean, why didn't you pick up the signals then?'

He unfolded himself from behind the desk and approached her. As he came closer, the girl became aware of the faint aroma of expensive cigar that clung to him, the voice hot and mocking against her ear.

'If we are going to play games, Lucy, then you must learn my only weakness . . . I am the one who must be in control.'

CHAPTER 44

Sometimes a thousand twanging instruments
Will hum about my ears; and sometimes voices,
That, if I then had wak'd after long sleep
Will make me sleep again: and then, in dreaming,
The cloud methought would open and show riches
Ready to drop upon me; that, when I wak'd
I cried to dream again.

Shakespeare

The news that Edwin Narbold had become 'oh, extremely friendly!' with Olivia's disabled daughter shot speedily around her circle of friends. It was greeted with especial interest by Hilda Somers, who had only recently succeeded Olivia as local Conservative chairman. She lost no time in capturing Margot on the occasion of their November social.

'*So* nice of you to join us, Margot. We *have* missed you recently.'

Olivia bridled.

'Now Hilda, you of all people know the reason why Margot—'

'Oh, a shocking illness, shocking . . . It killed my great-aunt Phoebe, you know, whereupon my uncle became a Christian and never smiled again.'

Margot said that she was sorry to hear it, while Hilda continued, 'As for Edwin Narbold, I *believe* he's a nice man. I hope he's a nice man. He's certainly a sound Conservative – but, as for the rest, one can never tell. Men, even sound Conservatives, are not always what they seem. There was for instance—'

'Truer words were never spoken,' interrupted Olivia, taking a teacup from mild old Mr Bridlington. 'Men are deceivers ever. In the case of my own son-in-law, William Mellor, very few people ever saw through him. To my knowledge, I was the only one who ever noticed that William had an Eye.'

'I never met him,' said Hilda regretfully, managing to imply that, if she had, she would have proved quicker at spotting an Eye than Olivia could ever hope to be. 'But musicians as a class are quite notorious. My cousin's eldest is a contrabassoonist – which is, or so I understand, not someone against bassoons on principle, but a bassoonist of a particular sort . . . At any rate, young Philip was repeatedly denied car insurance by any reputable firm. I believe he finally managed to persuade some fly-by-night outfit to do something for him, but it was an uphill struggle.'

Olivia sniffed. 'When you hear what these orchestras get up to, I wonder any insurance firm would touch them. There was that business in Madrid when one caused thousands of pounds of damage: destruction, orgies – and it wasn't a Spanish orchestra, as you might perhaps expect, but a British group, travelling on British passports—'

'Your son-in-law's orchestra, wasn't it?' inquired Hilda. 'Although standards are dropping everywhere, and I daresay not every musician actually *sets out* with the intention of becoming an alcoholic. I know a couple of piano teachers who are very decent people.'

Other members chimed in, with a sizeable number maintaining that it was all the fault of the schools. 'Now a proper Conservative government . . . started off in the sixties, and went straight downhill from there . . . Oh, pianists are quite a different thing . . . I have no objection to young *girls* learning the piano, but young *boys* – well! Where doesn't it lead?'

And Margot, letting the voices wash over her, was accosted by a peculiar sensation: happiness. She'd forgotten the taste of it, forgotten its illogical, maverick consistency. Happiness was a small child curling his hand inside the circle of your fingers, an unexpected nugget warm and human in your palm. What a perverse creature it was, slighting those who most courted it, alighting on people in the most untoward circumstances!

The appalling decor of Thatcher Hall, the banal arguments – these were all nothing, less than nothing. Margot noticed an oak tree making forest shapes against the window, leaves like monkey-fingers, rust, dark gold, mole brown, while the wind counter-tenored through the loose roof tiles. The evening was at once autumnal and glowing, ripe with promises still unbroken, pregnant with possibility.

She suddenly perceived her anger at William to be both childish and absurd. After all, there couldn't be any orchestra member who hadn't felt at least a passing fancy for another. The stresses of the profession were only too well-known, and William's nature – of all natures – was the warmest, the kindest, the most vulnerable to love. The burden of her anger lifted, startling her with sudden lightness. She thought, how William will laugh when I tell him that I learned to forgive him in the room that the Young Conservatives had painted too virulent a blue, with the November wind whistling through the windows.

'What do you think, Margot?' asked Hilda. 'It's either that, in my opinion, or bringing back corporal punishment.'

'Sorry, I wasn't listening.'

'Well, well,' said Hilda tolerantly. 'I daresay you've other things on your mind. Are you interested in classic cars at all? Someone, I forget who, told me that Edwin is very keen on classic cars. Still, I suppose *he* can afford it.'

They think I'm going to marry Edwin. How surprised they'll be when they learn the truth, that I'm William's, now and always, as I promised I would be. Electrically impatient, she suddenly longed to rush to wherever William was – the Barbican Centre, the Royal Albert Hall – to tell him. I'm sorry, I never saw so clearly before. I'm sorry; I never understood . . . She was swollen with love, half-drunk with it, when she saw her escape route blocked, the doorway filled, by Edwin's long-overdue arrival.

A moment's reflection, and she felt calmer again. Of course, it's partly thanks to Edwin that I've altered. The feelings I have for him – friendship, gratefulness – helped to open me up again. How do you express gratitude like that? I haven't the words. And she turned such a glowing face towards the Euro MP that Edwin paused mid-sentence and lost his line of thought.

He threaded his way towards her as soon as he could. 'Come to the pub with me afterwards.'

'What about Mother?'

'She'll be tired.'

Margot was amused. 'Mother – tired? Still, I suppose she might not mind.'

'Good. I shall be awash in Earl Grey by then.'

'You know you can't win an election without swimming in tea.'

'Which is possibly why the stuff possesses so gormless a taste . . . Mr Bridlington! – you're a lucky fellow! Your wife makes the most refreshing cuppa I've had in ages. Another large one for me, please, if Hilda's left me any.'

I certainly owe Edwin a drink. Besides, it's too late to contact William tonight. Indeed, Margot blushed at her notion of leaving the meeting in order to intercept William. How childishly impatient even adults could be!

A few hours later, in a quiet pub, she listened to Edwin's complaints.

'As for the canvassers, sometimes I think they do more harm than good. A woman yesterday told me, "Well, I don't know as I won't vote for you, though I said I wouldn't. The Tory who came round before was a terror – I never saw such a hat. She was ranting on about this, and gabbing on about that – my husband shut the door in the end and put the telly on louder."'

Margot laughed. She was in the mood to laugh at anything. Where caution had used to temper her behaviour, certainty now made her lax.

'Margot, have I ever told you about my family?'

You know you haven't, she thought. Amused, she recollected his acting: Mr Bridlington! – you're a lucky fellow!

'Well, I don't intend to bore you with them now, except to say that I'd like you to meet them, once your divorce comes through.'

'I'm not getting divorced,' she said with certainty.

'Oh, I know you've done nothing about it yet, perhaps wisely. It becomes a good deal easier once you've been separated for a time.'

'But I'm not getting divorced: I've decided against it. I'm going back to William.'

Edwin was silent – shocked, she supposed. She felt a little quickening at the thought of his possibly being disappointed but really, she'd never promised him anything. How could she? She liked him immensely – his slyness, his subversive intelligence – but the notion of anything further vaguely dismayed her. Politics – what a hypocritical, inconsequential, uncertain style of life! Impossible too to imagine that someone as urbane as Edwin could be completely reliable. Astute as he was at people management, how long would it be before he started to manage her?

He turned his glass around, a tidy circle, and repeated, 'You're not really going back to your husband?'

'Yes.' The moment in the hall: the leaves' soft undersides against the window, the sudden fragrance of happiness.

'Have you told him that?'

'I haven't told anyone. All William knows is that I'm seeing him at Christmas. Sam – our son – insisted on it. Sam wants a family Christmas, midnight service on Christmas Eve, the whole business.'

Edwin's measured silence was beginning to make her edgy. I'm babbling, she thought. What am I meant to say? Is there an etiquette? Many thanks for your kind interest? Is it really quite as simple as that?

'I hope you don't think me rude,' said Edwin, at last. 'I've been thinking. You say that you've still said nothing to William.'

'I – considered going tonight. But he might be abroad, or away. I'll phone tomorrow, if he's in the country.'

Tomorrow. What would it feel like tonight, sleeping, probably for the very last time, in her old white bed? What would the little dog think? Going home, she thought, with an unquenchable thrill of hopefulness.

'Are you sure this is wise?'

'I know what you're thinking,' said Margot quickly. 'It seems like a capitulation. You're wondering what's changed, what's happened, why now?'

'Yes, especially the last. Margot, this is one of the hardest things I've ever had to do.'

'Then don't do it!' she cried, anxious to forestall any declaration.

'Margot, has it occurred to you that your husband might not be at home any more?'

Colour rose from her bones; her mouth closed over the name: Isabel.

'No,' she said. 'No. I don't believe it. It isn't true.'

'I'm afraid it is true.'

'What do you know about it? What could you possibly know about William?'

'I did it for your own good.'

'You did what? What did you do?'

'I had him watched,' said Edwin quietly. 'A private firm, extremely discreet; believe me, he'll know nothing about it.'

She felt winded, but instinct forced denial to her lips.

'Why should I believe you? You might be biased against him.'

'I am biased, and I admit it. I was hoping to enable you to get divorced when and if you decided on it. I never guessed that— But perhaps it's just as well that I did have him checked, under the circumstances. The firm is impartial, of impeccable reputation. You may deny my neutrality, but you must believe their evidence.'

She heard a lawyer's confidence in his tone. Impartial: a

matter of evidence. It was the voice of logic, and alien to everything that she knew.

It sounded so implausible. The notion of detectives (did they really exist?) skulking around the Ealing house, tailing William's old silver Volvo, noting which pub he visited and whom he left with. It seemed the ultimate degradation, that William should be tracked, like a criminal, like a spy. She felt an illogical resentment – resentment at William for being found out, resentment at Edwin for having doubted him. Sam, too. What had Sam told her?

'If you're right then he lied to Sam – to our son. He said he hadn't seen Isabel.'

'When? Recently?'

'Well, not so very recently.'

'This is – recent,' he said hesitantly, and the humiliation of her position struck her afresh. She was back on the telephone to Isabel's neighbour, unable to frame the questions, feeling each word gripping like a pincer, a small, serious shrinking of the heart.

How long had it been happening? Weren't their two orchestras supposed to be locked in mortal combat at the Arts Council? And what had happened to the German conductor? She couldn't bear to ask, and Edwin was far too sensitive to volunteer anything. His sensitivity was like a rash across her wound, an itch across her pain. Tell me, she thought fiercely – spell it out in every demeaning detail. Does she ride him sideways, backwards? Does the light stay on forever? Does she dress up like a nurse and let him screw her on the table?

Edwin reached over, pulling her towards him. Her tiredness and his sympathy were too much: she drooped her head tearfully on to his shoulder. Only a few hours blessedly rolling back the heaviness, before the burden was put back upon her shoulders. Don't I deserve a longer slice of fool's happiness? She slammed the question at God, who made no reply.

Edwin's hand was steady on her arm, a sensation at once

thrilling and repellent. They were still for a long time, listening to far-off laughter from the public bar, footsteps passing in the street.

Chapter 45

Come, come, thou art as hot a Jack in thy mood as any
in Italy; and as soon moved to be moody, and as soon
moody to be moved.

Shakespeare

'We in the Orchestra of London,' David Schaedel told Terence,
'have what I like to call an ideal of sound. This ideal – how can
I describe it? – is at once virile and beautiful, sensual and
subtle. Let me give you a small example of this sound.'

David lurched into the opening of the Dvořák concerto. Few
players paid attention: the flute section was deep in homeop-
athy, while a trombone player sweated through his arpeg-
gios.

Terence alone listened, an enraptured look on his fleshy
face. He was quite skilled at rapturous looks, as his mother
was a painter, and he had often observed the expressions of her
clients who, though charmed, were not about to buy anything . . . Under the circumstances, however, little dramatic
skill was required. Terence was as perfectly convinced of
David's genius as David could wish him to be.

He listened, eyes devoutly closed, while David suffered
through the opening of the concerto. David, however, un-
accustomed to wasting his most eloquent assets, kept his eyes
open. A stunning young Israeli, he generally practised between
three mirrors, observing his play of feature at least as often as
the angle of his bow . . . Indeed, so fruitful had these observa-
tions been that musical opinion was divided as to whether his
most striking talent lay in cello-playing or in cello-posturing.

He whipped the bow off just before the tricky bit on the third page. 'You see? Now that is the precise sound – vital, organic – that I am after. Naturally I do not expect you to manage it to quite the same extent – we do not, you observe, all have the same abilities – but that, that is my ideal. I feel myself—'

'Has somebody died?' This from Piotr, sauntering towards them.

'No, nobody is dead.'

'Then what price the dirge? Why the march to the scaffold? From the sheer horsepower of your emoting, I'd assumed, at very least, that your Mancunian soothsayer had eloped to Buenos Aires with a Scorpio half her age.'

'This is Piotr,' said David with resignation. 'He is a Capricorn, but never serious.'

'We've met,' said Piotr, without enthusiasm. 'Phileas, isn't it, or Horace?'

'Terence.'

'Terence. I knew it was one of those Horlicks-brewing, vegetarian sort of names. You were the punisher with the cruel and unusual cello.'

And come from William's orchestra, which will soon be headed into outer darkness, where there is wailing and gnashing of teeth. And come from William, who's undoubtedly sent me a message of kindly irony and fatherly reconciliation.

'Your cello looks darker than I had remembered,' observed David.

Piotr flicked the strings; the cello flushed from its scroll to its tail-piece. 'Hell, I think it's alive,' he said languidly.

David accepted the cello from the unresisting Terence and sat down to inspect it properly.

'I believe there are some words inside,' he announced. 'Rather hard to decipher . . . Italian words, unless I am mistaken.'

Piotr leaned forward to see, and a haze of stars like snow

shook out of the cello. He stepped back, startled, but neither of the others seemed to have noticed. Drunk, he thought, with a wave of self-disgust. What if this frigging Terence-Horace-Petunia goes back and tells William I'm such a soak I'm seeing stars, spaceships surfing down the slope of the Festival Hall?

'What a very curious front crack,' said David tediously. 'With your permission I will see whether this small cello has the power that I require.'

Stars. Stars, and a ruby-coloured dust hazed with a teasing memory of honeysuckle. A ripe, voluptuous sound that curled under the f-holes and flung itself outwards. A fountain of sound – a sound that carried colours, scents, breezes along it: streams sequinned between shadows, trees erupting the soft wild green of spring.

The two flautists paused mid-sentence, the trombonist stared. Terence crammed his breath like a crimsoning bull-frog; while Piotr swayed as if drink had finally taken his balance away. And David, ugly with avarice, tongue thickened: 'How much do you want for this cello?'

'W-what?' stammered Terence.

'This cello. How much do you ask, in order to buy it?'

'I'll have to check with my – my family. It doesn't really – quite – belong to me.'

'Don't do it, Petunia,' advised Piotr, his heart hammering viciously at him. 'David'll be insufferable if he makes a sound like that, day in, day out. Drowns us all out as it is, out of unadulterated malice . . . Hello, Isabel. And how are you today?'

Isabel stopped in shock. 'You must be drunk.'

'I'm drunk and you're beautiful, but at least I'll be sober in the morning . . . Allow me to introduce Terence, known to intimates as Petunia, who is currently on trial for cello four. Terence, this is Isabel, our ageing if emollient *femme fatale*.'

Terence, doubly dazzled by David's sound and Isabel's eyes, smiled feebly.

David whispered to Terence, 'I have to have that cello, my dear friend. I will send my CD to your family if you like . . . "Popular cello classics, with David Schaedel". Then perhaps they will recognise that I am the worthiest owner of that small Italian cello . . . After that, when I am well-known – very well-known, I mean, for of course I am quite well-known already – I will assist you in every way I can. Believe me, your family will not have cause to repent their generosity to me.'

Terence began to sweat. Isabel's proximity – for never had he imagined William Mellor's former flame so Cleopatra-like – and his nerves about whether or not William would really sell the cello funnelled in furious internal flutterings.

His relief at the end of the rehearsal merged with gratified agitation when Paul Ellison – chairman of the board, no less – strolled over to invite him for a drink.

'Well, that is really most . . . Such a kind attention – and on my first day as well! I hardly know what to say.'

'Yes – or alternatively no – would seem to be called for.'

This from Piotr, scribbling bowings in the part. Terence rallied.

'Piotr's wit is widely recognised. Our mutual friend Mellor once described him in my hearing as the most amusing man he'd ever known.'

'Never met the bastard,' said Piotr.

'Let's go,' said Paul to Terence, giving Piotr a frown. 'I hope you're enjoying your trial?'

'Oh, very much, I assure you. Very much indeed. And I hope to be adding, in some small measure, to the sum of your truly remarkable cello section.'

Paul took Terence to the pub, apologising for Piotr as they went: ' – perhaps a little mischievous, but a valuable member of the orchestral board, and not at all a bad cellist either.'

Terence was only too anxious to corroborate this opinion, along with every other opinion that Paul chose to venture. A word from Paul, he knew, and the coveted number four job might be his – though it would probably be his anyway, should

William be willing to sell the cello . . . Paul bought Terence two double gins and endured any number of references to his cellistic destiny, medium-term goals and career options, before hazarding what he'd had in mind all along.

'Been in the Royal Sinfonia for a while, haven't you?'

'Indeed. Though whenever I've considered my position during that time, I've always felt—'

'You must have attended a fair number of dullish orchestra meetings in seven years.'

'Any number, and mostly very dull indeed. Though the last one at least possessed the advantage of being on a private beach belonging to our Greek sponsor, Marios. A wonderfully hospitable fellow, although—'

'Sounds great,' said Paul without interest. 'I suppose the Sinfonia was rocked at the news of the Arts Council business.'

'Absolutely. Just so. An appalling notion, I call it.'

'What are they thinking of doing about it?'

Terence paused perilous on the brink of the chasm, suddenly conscious of where he was and whom he was with. He hadn't been offered the job yet, and, until he was, it would be suicidal to make the rival chairman party to the Royal Sinfonia's plans.

'What are they doing about it?' he repeated, moistening his lips.

'Yes. Their ten-year plan. Similar to ours, I should think.'

Terence sweated. 'Oh, I should think so. At the end of the day, you know, there's only so much one can do. One's long-term goals can be quite at the mercy of more immediate contingencies . . . However, in the fullness of time—'

'Festivals, themed concerts, expanded educational programmes, I suppose?'

'Er – quite. Just so.'

'I suppose Zimetski's got his finger in most of the pies.'

'Finger in the pies! Ha! Very good! He does indeed!'

Paul paused for a long moment, then sighed.

'Terence, I have to say that I admire you,' he said. 'To be perfectly frank, I was trying it on a bit just now, and I got nothing for my pains. It was just a little test – hope you don't mind – a little test of character. Truth is, lots of people in your position would have given the game away entirely. Loyalty's a rare asset in our line of work, and hell, I respect you for it. Have another drink.'

Terence exhaled for the first time in some minutes. He had proved himself; he could relax. The questions Paul inserted after that were increasingly insidious, and Terence was far too industrious building castles in the air to spot them.

He, Terence (L. J.) Hennessy would almost certainly become number four in the Orchestra of London – probably, in the way of things, spending half his time on the first desk. There, David Schaedel would soon spot his leadership potential, or else (these things inevitably got about) the London Symphony Orchestra would hear about him and make some kind of offer . . . Though by that time, he might be able to contemplate some solo work instead, perhaps with some top-up teaching at the Royal College or Royal Academy . . .

The hum of conversation around them was drowned by the last-order bell. Terence thought: sooner or later everyone finds their true level in life. It was only in the nature of things that some people took a little longer to get there.

CHAPTER 46

Meagre were his looks
Sharp misery had worn him to the bones.

THIRD SOLDIER: Music i'th'air.
FOURTH SOLDIER: Under the earth.

Shakespeare

(from Pete Hegal's diaries)

It was Terence who brought me the news, shortly before the seven-thirty kick-off. I'd been deep in the first violins' work schedules, and looked up sourly as he entered, his flabby face pug-nosed with importance.

'We have a problem in the cellos.'

Now my views on Terence *qua* Terence are rigid and well defined. I have no intrinsic objection to his continued existence, as long as he in turn is willing to exist somewhere else.

Further, the job he was interrupting required considerable concentration and finesse. Probably due to the fact that they've got, on average, about twice as many notes to play as the next most afflicted section, first violins can be very tough cookies. They learn to talk out of the sides of their mouths; they get solid little scabs on the tips of their fingers; they get flint-eyed and case-hardened as Los Angeles cops. I shut the rota book and sighed.

'What kind of problem in the cellos?'

Terence looked gleeful. The bearers of bad news usually do, I've observed, unless it impacts on them too personally.

'John and Felicia haven't come back. They went out for a curry after the rehearsal, at about five-forty. In my opinion . . .'

He drivelled on, but my mind had careered into overdrive. The time was fidgeting around the seven-twenty mark. Ten minutes before Leszek's baton was first raised in anger – and it was far from unknown for a couple of errant principals to swan in at such a juncture, griping about deathly service at the pizza joint or perfect hell parking. Trouble was, I simply couldn't imagine this happening to the players under discussion, whose conscientiousness was near-legendary.

Terence: '. . . while the piece which opens the first half – in point of fact, the first piece on the programme – is the Rossini.'

'The Rossini.'

'*William Tell*,' he finished, disclosing the situation to the dimmest orchestra manager.

Now to many music lovers, this wildly overplayed Rossini overture conjures up no image more arresting than the theme to the *Lone Ranger*. To cor anglais players, in sharp contradistinction, it represents the repetitive-if-fruity tune in the middle. To cellists, however, as it kicks off with no fewer than five cello solos, it is imbued with more fearful connotations – especially for principal cellists, on whom the introduction depends. I swore.

'They've still got nine minutes, I suppose,' observed Terence, clearly gratified by my reaction.

'Nothing, but nothing, would keep John McDaniel from half an hour's warm-up before *William Tell*.'

And Felicia as well. I mourned Felicia, who could dispatch any of John's solos with near-contemptuous panache. There ought to be a law preventing the two principal cellists from currying together before a concert . . . What made the situation still murkier was that our sub-principal was off on maternity leave, while our number four was an aged star with a vibrato like a Mini getting out of second gear. Who ever knew the heavens menace so? I inquired of my immortal soul.

Only then – fool that I was – did I remember William. Will must have done the solo a thousand times while labouring down the rival salt mine; Will could lead anything. Terence's mind, meanwhile, was veering on a separate course.

'Far be it from me to put myself forward,' he said, with an air of modesty which became him lousily. 'But I would like, at this moment in time, to remind you – Pete – in your position as orchestra manager, that I am currently practising this very solo for a performance with the Hatfield Philharmonic—'

There were times when I could bear Terence's conceit, and, conversely, other times. I cut him off in his prime, and charged off to find William.

'Will,' I said, without preamble, for it was seven-twenty-five by then, and I could feel bubbles of perspiration rising. 'Would you object to leading?'

'Not at all.'

'For this relief much thanks,' I told him, breaking into Shakespeare as is my habit in moments of deep emotion.

Terence was still warbling about fullnesses of time and ends of days, but I didn't even hear him. Spotting Janice, I asked her to let Leszek know, whereupon she nodded and departed. I admit – in retrospect –that telling L. was probably my job, but I was curious to survey the battlefield from the front line.

It wasn't easy to find space in the hall, because the piano soloist due to operate on the 'Emperor' was a classic yearling, and every piano student in London had reserved a place in order to praise or bury him. I wound up near the back, and watched the orchestra drift on stage.

There were the first violins, busy sticking verbal needles into each other; while Eddie Wellington blissfully deafened the back-desk seconds with his warm-up routine. Angela's gold-encrusted harp bedazzled under the stagelights as the cellos aimlessly straggled in, still trying to figure their emergency seating plan.

Will advanced quietly to the principal's seat. Some players look different on stage – the most charismatic naturally seize lustre from the light, while others are quietly drained by it. Will merely looked what he was: a big man, distinguished though not young, ready (under trying circumstances) to deliver a solid, steady job. Only the cello – that crazy questing cello – had other ideas. For me, the first note told the story; I needed no more.

As you probably remember, the principal cello solo in *William Tell* begins on a low E and progresses up the register, without so much as a fig-leaf of moral support. I've heard more *William Tell*s than I care to think about, and more low Es than I can bear to remember, but I've never heard a sound like the one Will made that wet November evening. Starting with the softest questioning thrill, it poured out in a wild sonorous richness like a fine wine – here just a masterly touch of hesitancy, there a subtle quickening of vibrato . . .

It was partly the cello, of course, but there was a seriousness about it that was pure William, despite the overflow of feeling. It was as if the cello was dismantling his internal barriers, literally forcing him into being the cellist his innate reserve had never quite permitted him to be . . . While the other cellists, shocked into inspiration, spread their harmonic foundation under his feet.

In the audience, pianists (who had only come to hear the yearling) blinked, battle-hardened reviewers (likewise) lifted supercilious eyebrows from their doodling. The woman beside me let her programme slide unnoticed to the floor, while Leszek swerved, ears captivated by the sound.

It was the kind of moment that makes live concerts superior to any recording, however fabulous. There we were: hundreds of disparate strangers – who had never come together before and would never come together again – all bound together for a startling instant by the invisible strands of that strange, seeking cello.

Finally Will's last harmonic eased into silence, leaving Leszek to chivvy up the allegro. Released, I made my way backstage, where it transpired that John McDaniel was in reasonable shape in hospital. Felicia had rushed him there in a taxi after he'd had an allergic reaction to his curry.

In the interval, Leszek cornered me backstage, in the area infested with players. His skin was taupe coloured; he was lean as a wishbone; his multi-coloured eyes diamonded me.

'. . . First you do not tell me what is happening, then you are wandering around the audience as if, as if . . . Your job is here! Your work is here! You are supposed – you are paid – to support me! How was I to know what was this in the cellos? You think I am a mindreader?'

'Sorry,' I apologised. 'But I did ask Janice to slip you the headline news. Didn't I, Janice?'

But the girl dropped her eyes in a pliant mockery of confusion, and my heart misgave me. Here's an overweening rogue! I thought. A coward, a most devout coward, religious in it . . . Looking back, that was the first time I hated her. Oh, I'd fancied her, worried on her behalf, distrusted her, and more latterly even feared her – but that, that was the moment.

'No,' she told Leszek, with a soft false dip of her lashes. 'I'm afraid it isn't true.'

'What!' This from Leszek, whirling.

'Pete didn't ask me to tell you.' This softer still; and my temper skyrocketed.

'Listen, you don't need to take my word for it: there were witnesses. Will Mellor, Terence – most of the cellos and basses were there. Janice left, at my request, to tell you that John and Felicia—'

'Do you say she is a liar?' roared the mad Pole, his voice accenting itself still more strongly.

The eeriest sensation came over me, an indescribable feeling, as if my temper was no longer mine. I felt myself being twisted into a tight little knot of gusting fury – but from without, rather than naturally from within. Yet there was still some (probably Germanic) determination that stood separate and apart, allowing me to overrule, though my tongue seemed to have mysteriously thickened in my throat.

'My mistake,' I said. 'Janice is right.'

During this little contretemps most of the players had remained: curious, shocked, dubious. Leszek and I had rowed in public before, of course, but in the nature of thunderstorms, 'contending with the fretful elements, bidding the wind blow the earth into the sea'. In other words, two strong men colliding, but with no residue of hard feelings on either side. This was different: they all knew it instinctively, even those who didn't know why.

The hot, stretched silence was broken by Leszek's inhuman fury. 'Apologise!' he screamed. 'To her – and also to me.'

Again, tense, bubbling words pushed themselves against my lips; again I fought them down. I can't pretend that this was strength of character so much as rabid fear. I knew that self-control was my only chance; moreover, I guessed how my determination must be infuriating Janice.

'Sorry, Janice,' I said, avoiding her gaze. 'And I'm very sorry indeed to have let you down, Leszek.'

I could sense the creature's tight-lidded fury, the fury of a small child critically denied some kind of justice. I had the clearest impression of her almost physically expanding, leaving Leszek thinned out, nearly devoured . . . Unwilling to bear the atmosphere a moment longer, I returned to my rotas. Safe, by my troth. But I needed to talk to William.

I found him in the pub after the concert.

'What's all this about you and Leszek?' he asked.

'I've got quite a lot to tell you,' I admitted. 'But let's celebrate your sensational playing first – though you don't appear to be in celebratory mood.'

'No. There's something I have to do tonight.'

I thought first of his wife – and then of Isabel.

'It's the connection I worry about,' he told me, almost to himself.

'What connection?'

'When does an execution become a murder?'

'Murder!'

Will examined his Chablis under the light. 'Destroy is a better expression. I have to destroy the cello.'

I shook my head. 'Can't be done – at least, not physically. I tried it myself, remember.'

'It's possible,' he said apologetically, 'that I'm meant to do it. It chose me, after all.'

And Janice chose him in Greece, I remembered. Still . . . The sound still glowing in my ears, my gut instinct was against.

'Not now, Will. Not after tonight.'

'After tonight especially.'

'Why don't you sell it instead? A principal player, even a soloist, would probably pay any price and thank you for it. Didn't someone from your old orchestra make you an offer?'

'David Schaedel. I turned it down.'

The question trembled on my lips; William answered it.

'You know why, even if no one else does. You know it doesn't come alone. And you of all people know what it – what they've done to Leszek. How in all conscience could I hand it over to anyone, knowing all this?'

'That's true – but could you really be responsible for wiping that tone off the face of the earth? I know I tried, but that was before tonight.'

'I don't know whether I can do it. I only know that it's the right, the ethical thing to do.'

'Thus confirming my suspicion that ethics is only an excuse for doing things as unpleasantly as possible.'

Will smiled briefly. 'Then there's Janice. What happens to Janice if the cello's destroyed? If she dies too, wouldn't that make it, morally at least, some kind of murder? Or is she not completely alive in the first place? If she's only a spirit – but can things "only" be spirits? Isn't the spirit the part that counts? And, God knows, she feels alive enough.'

And it was at this point – the final twist in this curiously vivid, twisted day – that Piotr manifested himself beside our table.

Though not quite the last person I would have expected to see – the orchestral world is a village, with an unusual number of idiots in it – he was certainly one of the last. There was an unwritten rule that this pub was patronised by those who'd played in the concert, whatever concert it was and however rottenly it had been played. And in the current state of tension between the Royal Sinfonia and the Orchestra of London, this was, of course, especially true. Piotr's mere appearance practically came under the heading of hobnobbing with the enemy.

Piotr looked drunk: drunk, fagged or ill, with sallow skin and sunken eyes. He leaned up against our table, and I remember thinking that his neck looked too delicate to hold up the burden of his head. He half-bowed to Will.

'Well met, Guglielmo. I may call you Maestro, may I not?'

William pushed him into a seat, alarmed. 'Sit down, you fool. You look like a famine victim.'

'Bastard,' said Piotr, closing his eyes. 'And to me, who taught you all you know, even to picking apples off a wormy apple tree.'

'Do you want me to leave?' I asked Will uneasily.

Piotr squinted at me. 'Not at all. I forget your name, but your face I remember. Welcome to Philippi.'

'Your names are the same,' said William rather roughly. 'Piotr, this is Pete. Pete, Piotr.'

'How quaint. Life is full of minor quaintnesses, don't you feel?'

'Were you at the concert?' I asked Piotr.

'With bells on, St Augustine. It isn't often I go to a concert, but Karl – Karl Hochler, the man himself – asked me to go to this one. Half our board was there, peppering the audience, snooping. Except for me. I meant to snoop; I rather pride myself on my snooping, but your bloody solo undid me, so I sloped off to the bar instead. Where did you learn to play like that, you bastard? And why did you save it for tonight?'

'You look like hell,' said Will shortly.

'I speak very highly of you as well.'

'Are you drunk?'

'No more than necessary.'

'What have you come for – absolution?'

'You've got that one backwards for a start.'

'You avoid me for ten months; you send me messages of unimpeachable rudeness; then you appear like Banquo's ghost, and sit at my table.'

'I'd prefer, if you don't mind, to be Caesar's ghost. You were my only friend, remember.'

Will's tone deepened. 'I don't own you; I never did. What do you want?'

'Love is an art, Maestro – like music, but harder. Has anyone ever told you that cello of yours scatters sequins like stars?'

It was a bizarre cross-talk act, the dignity of Jove versus the elliptical swipes of Mercury. They made me feel as if I was witnessing a strange love scene. Yet – oddly – rather than feeling closer to Will, I suddenly felt I understood Piotr better. It was as if Isabel and Piotr were the ones I was truly in sympathy with, as if Will's self-control had the effect of separating him from us all. He didn't reply to the shaft about the cello; perhaps he wasn't meant to.

'I only came to warn you.'

'What do you mean?' I asked, but Piotr ignored me.

'Your current weaselly, moth-eaten orchestra's finished, done for, kaput and as good as bitten the dust. It has gone to meet its maker. It is an ex-parrot. And the sooner you clear off the better for those left behind.'

'Why him?' I demanded, as Will remained silent.

'Because Hochler's taken against him,' said Piotr, taking a swig out of my wineglass, and indicating Will. 'Isabel's fault; Karl blames her in-and-out running on him. Foul stuff,' he added, indicating the wine. 'Grainy. Rotten.'

'But what can Will do?' I persisted.

'Oh, he can go down with the ship, if he insists, but I felt I owed him a warning. Because the ship's going down. And because of what he did at the concert tonight. Because he – I allude to that fatalistic, Welsh-begotten, toffee-encrusted, Winchester-and-Oxford bastard – because tonight he made me proud.'

'It had nothing to do with me,' said Will sharply, and then suddenly softer: 'Piotr – it wasn't me. I know it sounds strange, but it wasn't. The cello's haunted.'

Piotr gulped down the rest of my wine. 'Oh Christ, the stuff I think I hear when I'm well oiled!'

Will gripped his wrist, which was spindly as a child's; quick tears sprang into his eyes.

'Let go!'

'You've drunk enough.'

'He gets these delusions,' said Piotr to me, in confidential undertone. 'Sometimes he thinks he's my mother, sometimes an aristocratic Irish setter with great, deep-sunken eyes.'

'If you're doing this to spite me, you'll succeed. Is that what you want to hear?'

'The slow movement of Beethoven's Op. 132 would be infinitely preferable.'

Piotr's face contorted; I feared for a moment that Will, so much the stronger, might actually snap his wrist. 'Will,' I said nervously, but they'd both forgotten I was there.

'Have you no self-respect?' demanded Will.

'You took that too, if you remember.'

'If you cared about me, you'd take care of yourself.'

'What a chronically self-serving piece of pap psychology.'

'Is there anything I can do that won't make it worse?'

'You can stop screwing the tart. Oh, I forgot, that's the one thing you can't do, isn't it?'

Will released his wrist; it looked sickly where he'd gripped it; there'd be a storm-coloured bruise tomorrow. He stood up and looked at Piotr with a terrible ending sadness.

'Goodbye, Piotr.'

Piotr struggled to shape a response, but his voice failed him, face crumpling like fax paper.

William moved heavily towards the door. I followed, but I couldn't help glancing back at Piotr, who had dropped his head inside his arms. Poor Piotr, I thought, and part of me longed to go back, to put my arms around him, and learn to weep.

CHAPTER 47

I shall win at the odds. But thou wouldst not think
how ill all's here about my heart.

Shakespeare

(from Pete Hegal's diaries)

The firing of a full-time orchestra member is a grindingly bureaucratic business. In the Royal Sinfonia, the procedure consisted of two warnings, separated by at least three months, followed by a series of formal hearings before the orchestra board. However, if this sounds organised, even humane, it assuredly wasn't. During the months that followed the first warning, the unlucky member was subjected to the most wide-ranging and exhaustive analysis, anyone who had ever had a grudge against him privately lobbied the board, and his family life deteriorated with shocking suddenness. Meanwhile he was still expected (indeed required) to perform at his peak on every occasion – or face the direst consequences.

Some players can cope. Some – less imaginative, or more arrogant, or simply more determined – can swagger it out, buying drinks, bending ears and organising claques in their turn. But the Duke wasn't like that. For politicking, Eddie Wellington simply had too much heart.

I watched him growing paunchier and more punch-drunk by the concert; Eddie being one of those types that, as misery clamps down, eat more and drink more merrily regardless of consequences. The small pouches under his eyes took on cavernous dimensions; while he played with an increasingly desperate pugnacity. One day his wife phoned me to complain that he was being overworked.

'It's a toughish schedule,' I assured her, angling the telephone so as to inspect the horn lists.

'But really, every day for a fortnight! Can't you pressure him into giving some of the other players a chance?'

Crap, I wanted to retort. The boy was lying through his duty-free. At the moment, the Duke was off more than he was on, mainly because his mere presence tended to send Leszek into road-rage. He must be drinking whenever he was free, presumed innocent.

So I lied to his wife and carpeted the Duke.

'Your wife thinks you're playing every day this week.'

'I had to tell her something, Pete.'

'Where do you go?'

Eddie looked stubborn, and I recalled that night in Madrid.

'She doesn't know, does she?' I said, enlightened. 'You haven't told her that Leszek's trying to fire you.'

'No, I haven't.'

'And have you got any very persuasive reason why you haven't blinking told her?' I demanded, feeling hot and sorry and ready to skewer Leszek with a sawn-off coffee mug.

'I just can't,' said the Duke mournfully. And again I was struck by the contradiction: the tousled, mixed-up boy and the majestic, giant-Redwood-souled horn-player. Where did the one pack up and the other one begin? And why do so many great musicians simply miss out on growing up?

Eddie continued. 'It's my fault, isn't it? I'm not good enough. If I was, he wouldn't hate me.'

I lost my temper. 'Hell, Eddie, doesn't that single brain-cell get lonesome banging around in there? You pumpkin-headed, frog-featured lunatic, that's why he does hate you! Because you *are* good enough!'

Eddie looked up. 'That a fact, Pete? Is that why?'

'Believe me,' I said, keeping it simple. I mean, no point confusing Eddie, in his current state, with Janice and poltergeists and haunted cellos and eyes that shotgunned dizziness into people. The reasons why Janice had it in for (a) Leszek and (b) Eddie were still unclear, even to Will and me, who had at least an inkling. I defy anyone to explain them to your average principal horn – to those gut-rock, passionate, sublimely illogical individuals.

'But Pete, I might lose my job.'

'You might, but it's not likely. Lenny's behind you, so's the Board, and nothing in life is a foregone conclusion. When Leszek hears your Mahler's Five next week, he'll probably chuck the whole idea.'

'The Mahler, yes – I've been thinking about that. To be honest, Pete, the Mahler rather worries me.'

'Duke,' I said. 'Can I tell you a little story?'

'I'm not in the mood—'

'Just listen. I wasted more weekends in my youth than I care to recall at the Royal College junior department, messing about with the violin. One day I was supposed to be having a string quartet coaching, and for some reason I was late. I was buzzing along banging my fiddle against the wall when someone opened a door and I heard a splash of Mahler, can't remember which, coming out of the main hall. There was a sound that just – captured me. And, late as I was, I stood in that doorway until the whole movement was over. The sound came from a solid little pugilist playing principal horn, and I remember thinking, "What a chubby genius. What a blooming wonderful bloody brilliant horn player," and Eddie, that fat little prat was you. So do me a favour and stop drivelling on about a few puny Mahler solos and your future career begging on the steps of the Piccadilly Line.'

'OK, Pete,' said Eddie, looking chirpier than he had in ages.

'Hey, one more thing. Phone the wife.'

'So what exactly has Piotr been doing?' asked Lucy.

'Hold very still, if you please. To my mind there is something – what is the word? – visceral – about a woman holding a gun.'

Lucy complied, while Karl adjusted the camera until it was

only a foot from her face. She was naked; a gun, warmed by the lights, hot between her breasts. It was late evening and they hadn't made love for two days: there was tension between them, palpable as gun-metal. She watched the back of his hands, very close, hairs curling down the sides, a certain purposefulness about them.

'This kind of camera film loses the edges,' he explained, 'not to say, of course, that you have very many edges, especially from this angle. Look up – no, do not smile. A serious look, as if the gun is yours and you might perhaps know what to do with it . . . Better, yes, exactly.'

Lucy's mind was still on an earlier conversation. 'Why did you fix on Piotr in the first place?'

'Piotr is clever and quick, and has no conscience to speak of. Besides, he is on the committee.'

'And he also wants to get back at William.'

'There is some small personal motive there, perhaps . . . Now, farther back, yes, exactly.'

'Do you think they're really back together? Not that they live together of course – they never did.'

'Who?' asked Karl politely.

'Isabel and William.'

Karl became attentive, still and concentrated. Lucy felt a wave of heat rising from him, his voice very low, almost lazy.

'That, of course, I would not know . . . And again, the head just angled back . . . so. Again please, eyes closed.'

The flash went, and again. Such a long time passed that she wondered whether he'd left the room, then she felt his lips shivering the line of her back and wondered how Isabel could have foregone such shocking sureness – Karl's fingers coaxing her body, her nipples hardening with certainty . . . Later she felt his gun muzzle, warm at her crotch, firing.

Piotr crossed one number off his pad and dialled another.

'Paul – the mad mullah, here. Just spoke to Havers . . . No, no problem. He just wants confirmation that there won't be interference from the trustees . . . No, that's what I told him, but he still wants Harriet's say-so . . . Absolutely. Off-the-record, off-centre, oftel, ofwatt, the whole bit. If you could fix that up . . . You too. Make sure the food-tasters beat you to the poisoned mushrooms. Bye.'

Piotr left his desk and poured himself a celebratory vodka. The Arts Council business had proved exhilarating and even illuminating; Piotr had uncovered any number of unsuspected talents. He was adept at manoeuvring, electrical at a hint, and chronically and pre-eminently sneaky.

I'm wasted on these puny orchestral games, he thought. I should be dealing in futures, scrambling multimedia contracts or sending shares bouncing on the Tokyo stock exchange. I should be tiger-hunting in the executive jungle, or angling hostile takeover bids for thrusting young baby-smooth software concerns.

Thanks to me, we've got this chicken sewn up tighter than an Eskimo's papoose. *Merci* to *moi*, we've got this deal watertight, seriously sorted, high-tailed and cooking with gas. And what do I get out of it, I ask myself? A warm handshake, a mention in despatches and, very possibly, a coded vote of thanks at the annual dinner. Then the party's over: get back to your cello section and don't bother to prepare for government. Back to up-bows and down-bows, dictated without due process by a pretentious Israeli in a vile silk shirt . . .

'Hello, Anton.'

The dog crossed to Piotr. Over the months he'd filled out, and the condition of his coat had improved. Only his air of philosophical constraint remained, a dignity all the more noticeable in comparison with more unreserved and excitable dogs.

'You all right, Anton? Or does this perambulatory divination portend some suggestion – however oblique – of walkies?'

You ought to talk to me, Anton. If you could talk I could let the world go hang, and never need anybody. Piotr stared into the unblinking eyes of the dog, allowing the great silky ears to trail through his fingers. Like some woman's auburn hair . . . horrible thought. And William back with Isabel, against all reason – the sheerest brand of near-senile tomfoolery.

'He's gone mad at last; I knew he would,' he told the dog. 'I warned him, as well, time after time I warned him.' But what resonated most were Isabel's words at the gun-club. ('. . . Oh, I can't describe it; I haven't the words, but there was such a – spirit then. Can't you even remember how it used to be?')

Used to be, used to be. The words echoed, vodka-sharpened, in his brain, reinforced by the knowing eyes of the quiet dog.

I don't give a hang, thought Piotr, pushing his drink away with sudden loathing. It's late, but not too late. I'll go to the club, and find someone. A strapping young brickie, perhaps, or an older man wearing his past in his face. Someone – anyone. Anyone to lift the sorrow, for a moment, for a while; anyone to stir the senses, speeding the blood into oblivion. That man with the scar, or the boy with the trim little rear and the vacant eyes. There had to be someone. It wasn't all that late, after all.

Rumours scorch orchestras like bush fires – some swiftly squelched, others secretly prospering – until the forest's edge is reached and the horizon abloom with flame. The latest rumour in the Orchestra of London took a particularly circuitous route.

'You're looking better, Isabel,' said Caroline, adding complacently, 'I always thought you just needed some time on your own.'

But I've never been less on my own. I woke up next to William, watching the dawn sketch in the contours of his face. I watched the rise and fall of his chest, the terrifyingly fragile pulsebeat fluttering his wrist, the minute swiftening of his lashes. I watched the sun uncover every thick lustrous hair, silvered-over and half-crushed by sleep.

And David Schaedel's corroboration: 'Yes, there was a time – you will perhaps forgive my mentioning it – when you looked not at all attractive – quite the opposite, in fact. I remember thinking, "No, she is nowhere near my equal in appearance," as I had sometimes used to think. I told myself, "Poor Isabel, she grows sallow and nervy, like so many English girls." But now – on a good day, of course, when wearing something becoming – you look almost as you did before.'

William, too, had his trials. The day arrived, as he had known it would, when Angela avoided him in the canteen. He forced himself to confront her.

'I'm sorry,' he said quietly.

'She called you.'

'I understand that she also wrote to me, Angela.'

She flashed: 'I thought you resigned in order to get away from all that.'

The mischief started in Spain, thought William. He looked at her Irish-tempered beauty, eyes sore and bright.

'You're right, of course,' he admitted, and, because he was guilty, he took her in his arms and comforted her.

Felicia, always observant, remarked to John, 'Sometimes – only sometimes, mind, and only where women are involved – I think that recruiting Will Mellor was one of your minor errors.'

And John, defensive: 'Not at all; his reputation in that respect is entirely undeserved. The fact that women might be interested in him doesn't mean that— And besides, he's seeing his wife, I happen to know, at Christmas.'

Edwin Narbold didn't call Margot for some days after he admitted having William followed, though the imminence of the Euro-election might have been the cause. Meanwhile Olivia continued to devote herself to canvassing, inspiring her nearest neighbours to spring like meerkats into their burrows at the mere sound of her voice.

Election-night found her stationed in front of the television with her papers, marking pens and swing-charts at the ready. Nothing could have increased her pleasure in the occasion – for, as she put it herself, she had 'fought the good fight' –

except a greater degree of interest from Margot, who had even threatened, on this night of nights, to go to bed.

'Really, Margot! When we shan't know our own result till midnight!'

'The polls suggest that Edwin will win,' Margot reminded her.

'Pollsters are invariably wrong, as you must be aware – and for a very good reason. No really well-bred person would tell a pollster which way they intend to vote, which is why our support is so invariably underestimated. It's such an obvious flaw in the system that I don't know why they don't devise a formula for adding on the Conservative votes afterwards.'

Margot remarked that, if the Conservative vote was inevitably greater than supposed, then Edwin should be even safer than the polls might indicate. Olivia shook her head darkly.

'You forget, Margot, the insidious nature of pollsters. They might have chosen to overrate Edwin's support in order to encourage our people to stay at home.'

'If they stay at home then they can't be very committed supporters.'

'That's true indeed, sadly true. But I'm afraid, Margot, that even the best parties possess some very woolly-minded supporters. There simply aren't enough level-headed people in the country to win an election, which is why the standard of person voting Conservative has become increasingly disappointing over the years . . . The last time I acted as teller at the polling station, I had voters with perfectly appalling accents claiming to have marked their slip correctly. Really, once or twice I hardly knew where to look.'

In the end, Margot stayed – less in order to support Edwin than to distract her mind from what he had told her. She wasn't tired enough to sleep, and her mind was restless. Should she still agree to see William at Christmas? – and, if so, should she admit that she knew what was going on? If she refused must Sam be told the reason? And what about Olivia?

She thought: even at our age it's never only two people; the ramifications go on and on. Workmates, in-laws, grand-children, friends . . . Different levels of involvement, different interests – the pull of the past against the bewitchment of the present.

And she remembered Isabel as she always remembered her: backstage at the Festival Hall, affecting impatience on Karl Hochler's arm, with that giveaway darkness in her eyes. William's grip on her wheelchair; and the German conductor, suave, tactile, his hand just soothing hers. The quartet caught: a fading snapshot, too well thumbed, in the secret album of her heart.

From the television: 'We have Edwin Narbold here, whose result, in south-east London, has yet to be declared . . . Mr Narbold, do you think that the swing we're seeing against the government will affect your majority?'

'Not at all. I have the utmost faith in my supporters. My local teams have all worked very hard and the story on the doorstep has been most encouraging. My own belief is that the story we'll be seeing unfold, up and down the country, will be one of . . .'

'He has faith in his team. Us. Well done us, though I say so myself. And you as well, Margot – after all, you did stuff envelopes that afternoon.'

She recalled it: an afternoon of addressing envelopes, while listening to Hilda being overruled by Olivia. Was this the best that her new life could offer her?

Later: 'Quick, Margot, quick, they're about to give the result. There he is – there's Edwin – in the middle, right in the middle, with the blue rosette. He looks well on television, I think, very well. A fine forehead, really almost— And *that*'s the returning officer, young what's-his-name. Used to sit on the council, but not really our sort. I only wish . . . Oh, we've won! We've won! Isn't that wonderful?'

We've won. It's a team; it's a winning team and we're on it. Edwin graciously triumphant, his voice, well modulated, making a debating point against the local press. Oh it's a party, a side, a group, a team – we won, we beat the others, punch the shoulders, wave the flags . . . The trouble is, I'm not a team person. The only team I ever joined was William's, and that only lasted twenty-five years.

'Well I'm pleased you're happy, Margot, but tears, I think, are somewhat overdoing it. Whatever *would* dear Edwin say? Something droll, I've no doubt. Edwin can be very droll. Perhaps I'll make him a nice sponge, to celebrate. Edwin, in case you haven't noticed, is particularly fond of sponge.'

'I forgot. The Euro-elections, on every channel.'
    'What's to forget?'
    'Everything. I even forgot to vote.'
    William joked: 'The Greens will have missed you.'
    'Well, when did you find time?'
    'This evening, before I came over.'
    'Liberal Democrat,' Isabel mocked him.
    'Reasonably liberal. Fairly democratic.'
    'I'm sure you lost.'
    'So am I. I always lose in the end.'
    'Who's that? I think I recognise him.'
    'He's a London Euro MP. My mother-in-law's a supporter, I think, but I can't remember his name.'
    'He looks rather – formidable.'
    'Nothing like as formidable as my mother-in-law.'
    Isabel laughed, lolling her head back against his shoulder. 'Do you still have a mother-in-law?'
    'I still,' said William gently, 'have a wife.'
    A wife. He remembered with a shock the way she used to turn her head to smile at him, the way she attacked specks of dust on the windows. A wasting disease, some people called it. But what kind of disease was love?
    'Kiss me,' whispered Isabel.
    (Edwin's voice, keenly: 'The story we'll be seeing unfold, up and down the country, will be one of strong and unequivocal support . . .')

William brushed his open lips across Isabel's breast. The contrast between the embossed gloss of the surface skin and the texture of the breast itself always ravished him.

'. . . the kind of Europe, united yet individual, secure yet free, which is the dream of every European from Greece to Ireland.'

I'm still a beginner at understanding, thought William. Because I'm good in bed, women imagine I understand. And because I can sometimes see the end of other people's problems, they think I can sort out my own. The truth is that I can sometimes see a little farther than most people but signally lack the courage to act on what I see. And I grow softer and softer, and more and more incapacitated by pity for people. Making errors like accepting Angela – which only crushed her in the end – and coming back to Isabel, which may yet do the same. Isabel should have married Warren Wilson in her twenties. That was the moment – but such moments only come once, if at all.

'The tragedy of your life is that you turned down Warren Wilson,' he said suddenly.

'And the tragedy of yours is that you were born too sensual to bear.'

('Thank you, Edwin Narbold. And now to West Manchester, where a result is imminent.')

With Isabel, there was always need. Open, passionate, sweepingly affectionate – while Margot was subtler, more reserved, open to inference, negotiation, diplomacy. On the one side Isabel, beating her fists against the world's loneliness: on the other Margot, courageous in her resignation, but lacking that aching warmth of heart . . . Though the question, surely, went beyond simplistic comparisons. How much did twenty-five years count? How many points for a son, for a promise he'd made and meant to keep? Suddenly he loathed himself, for giving way to lustfulness and pity. Isabel's body no longer seemed a tender thing, but lascivious, tantalising, almost evil.

Desperation seized him. He pushed her on to the floor, and for a sickening second it was Karl again, Karl's body manipulating hers, Karl's separation of himself – arid and cool – from the satyr who jerked her backwards, whipping her breath from her body and her arms from her sockets.

William, even in his current mood, did none of these things; he simply became, for a moment, a purely animalistic force. Heavier than Karl and still stronger, he took her with a sadistic anger that somehow cried out against himself, a cry against fate, as if his impulse for revenge was suddenly too strong to control. And paradoxically Isabel felt her body soaring, pulsed against his rhythm, as if stoked by his dynamic into a reflection of his savagery. Breathless and startled, locked in what suddenly felt like a struggle, she found herself searching for William in the loaded eyes of a bitter stranger.

CHAPTER 48

Things that love night
Love not such nights as these. Man's nature cannot carry
Th'affliction nor the fear.

Shakespeare

Two nights later, William awoke with the recollection of a dream misting his consciousness. He turned the clock-face towards him – four-thirty, why did he waken at four-thirty? – aware of memory still tugging at him. Greece, he thought, with a sickening twist of the stomach. Frail moonshine scattered along the beach, and dizziness denting the side of his head. A body shaping a dune and a language he'd never heard before. A language like none on this earth and a name emerging from the sheath of his subconscious. A name that sounded like Mikhail.

Mikhail. How could he have neglected so obvious a clue? He scribbled the name on the pad of paper before he could float back to sleep. Michael – no, surely it had been Mikhail.

He closed his eyes, but his mind was too active, the house too still. He wished he was in Isabel's flat, or back in his hotel room in Greece, the sounds of waves circling rhythmic on the sand . . . Mikhail. It might, of course, be an East European name. Something to do with Piotr perhaps – or more likely – something connected with Leszek. Something connected with whatever had taken the Leszek they knew – combustible but stubbornly likeable with it – and transformed him into this hollowed-out creature, flagellating the music for some meaning he had lost.

She wanted me as well, William realised with rare, undiluted certainty. She tried for me but I was somehow luckier. That night by the sea had been an effort at domination, blood thrashing the temples, the gravitational pull of the water, the call of the waves crying come, come.

William crossed to the window. It might be useful to talk to Charmaine – or to try the name out on Leszek . . . It was icy, the windows already slashed with diagonal bars of frost. Impatience beat at him; night-sense fringed his nerves. If only it was morning, and he could hear Pete's reassuring tones. If only he could ring Piotr – Piotr had used to answer the phone at any hour. But Piotr was gone, estranged from him more damningly than if they too had been lovers – but that, at least, had never happened.

How intrusive night sounds could seem in an empty house! William stood listening to the boiler, faint creaks from the piping. And then he heard it, so softly that he thought it a trick of the wind.

Music.

No, not that, it wasn't possible. He'd left the radio on in the front room; the heating system was decoying his ear; the wind . . . But there was no wind. Instead there was the sound of a cello, a cello with a timbre as thrilling as Domingo's, singing infinitely softly, infinitely sadly. The cello was playing to comfort itself, a voice like no other was singing a song never heard before.

He clenched his fingers on the window-sill, reassuring himself with the texture of gloss paint on wood. He was awake, must be – but he wasn't alone. What had Charmaine told him? Nothing you could recognise, nothing with a human fingerprint . . . Wild sounds, sometimes, and sometimes sounds so lost and soft as to break your heart.

William put on his dressing gown, feeling – however crazily – that he didn't want to appear naked before the cello. Then he moved down the stairs, his ear too captured for his mind to register the accelerating rhythms of his heart.

As he came closer, he recalled what Charmaine had

experienced: the cello perhaps displaced, but silent, dark, dulled, its strings eerily, endlessly, perfectly in tune. And so implicit was his confidence in Charmaine's accuracy, that, despite the witching quality of the music, he only hesitated a fraction of a moment before pushing open the door to the music room.

And the cello still soared, like a tenor inebriated with the towering glory of his own voice. Still it played, shameless, careless, black lights frosted by the richness of it, surer than he'd yet seen it, its colours glossing the air, its sound shivering his eardrum: encompassing, hypnotic, persuasive, untamed. The sound being pulled from deep inside the music: a sound like the waves crying come come.

Giant hands must have been playing it, because the invisible stretches were far beyond the reach of human fingers; and the sound seemed always either louder or softer than humanly, logically possible, kneading his ear, ravishing it. His head felt nebulous as rainwater, the sound's surge tidal, oceanic: the sound rising towards him, come, come. Unable to move, to speak, to breathe – every colour in the world crashing crazy in his ears, lungs bursting, brain blasting, come come. Tears, tears and blood, remember remember: black blood, red blood, come come. Ash-cello mocking; remember, remember, and the shadows thumbing come come. Blood-drums shuddering deep within the mountain and the fountains rising crying come come.

CHAPTER 49

Either there is civil strife in heaven,
Or else the world, too saucy with the gods,
Incenses them to send destruction.

Shakespeare

(from Pete Hegal's diaries)

'An orchestra is a wonderful thing to belong to,' said Lenny, without being struck by lightning on the spot. 'It's full of marvellous musicians playing wonderful instruments, all combining to make the most exciting possible sounds. In a moment – thanks to Seeboard, who have very kindly sponsored this young persons' concert – we're going to play a piece showing off all the instruments in the orchestra. Won't that be just fine and dandy? But first, as you can see, many combinations – or families – of instruments go to make up an orchestra. Which of you can name one of these families for me?'

A boy in the fourth row immediately hoisted his hand.

'The woodwind section contains both single and double-reed instruments, such as the clarinet and the bassoon. The difference in timbre is due to—'

'Fine,' said Lenny. 'Let's start with the woodwinds. First Tony's going to give us an idea of what an oboe sounds like, and then Tony – same bloke, no mirrors – will play the same phrase on the English horn.'

'The English horn isn't a horn at all,' observed the boy. 'Many people think—'

'What an awful lot you seem to know about the orchestra,'

said Lenny, between his teeth. 'Perhaps you should give the lecture, and not me, ha ha. Now everybody, just listen to Tony – there he is, dyspeptic-looking bloke, middle of the band – and try to think about the difference between the oboe and the English horn.'

Later Lenny told me, 'There's one in every kiddies' concert, swear to God. Some precocious little peon, just swiped his grade five clarinet—'

'An orchestra is a wondrous thing, God wot.'

'Lying's part of the deal, same as in your line of work. Now in my wife's job—'

'Sorry to interrupt,' said Terence self-importantly, 'very sorry indeed, but William isn't here.'

In all my puff, I never knew anyone get more of a kick out of bad news than Terence Hennessy. He's like one of those spear-carriers who make a career out of storming in late in the final act to announce that Rosencrantz and Guildenstern have recently copped it. I glared at him.

'What do you mean? He was playing, wasn't he?'

'Well, if pressed, I must admit—'

A hideous thought – call it intuition – grabbed me. 'Yes or no?'

'No, Pete, he wasn't. You see—'

I pulled out my mobile and pressed Will's number. It rang and rang, its meticulous, even tone sneering at me for even trying. I tried Isabel's: the same. The boy was ill; the boy was in trouble; the boy was dead, strangled at night by that breathing, brooding cello.

'Lot of winter flu about,' observed Lenny. 'Last week—'

Interrupting him, I hailed Angela. 'Angela, do me a favour. I can't reach Will Mellor. You wouldn't mind trying, would you, while I get the next show started? The redial button's on the left.'

Only as I put the phone into her unresisting fingers did I remember suspecting that there might have been something between her and William. She took the mobile without comment, but her face narrowed and I saw (like a snapshot) what it would look like in thirty years' time: skin gathered in loops under her chin, plucked and angled eyebrows accentuating the thin lines along her forehead.

When I returned, having kick-started Lenny on round two, she was still trying the number.

'Perhaps he's at Isabel's.'

'No,' I said shortly. 'I tried her before.'

The possibility that he might not be answering occurred to me, but only briefly. There were, after all, such things as session fixers, answerphones, the brutal economic logic of a musician's life. Angela spoke first.

'I'll go by the house myself.'

'No need,' I said, with forced cheerfulness. 'I'll try later.' Only to see, in her clear eyes, knowledge – if not of what I feared, exactly, then of what she feared herself.

'He doesn't live far out of my way.'

Angela was based in north-west London – I couldn't recall exactly where.

I said, with weakening resolve, 'Don't worry,' but she was already at the door. 'Ring me,' I told her, while from the hall I could hear Lenny saying tonelessly, 'Now, the bassoon is a very jolly instrument.'

William woke slowly, tired with a completeness he would not have believed possible. He felt as if he'd been tortured into wakefulness for weeks, his every muscle pulped, as if rhythmically beaten.

He was lying on the floor of the music room, the scent of wood varnish in his nostrils and the Italian cello demurely snuggled inside the folds of its case. The atmosphere, the noises, the traffic patterns, all suggested afternoon to his senses, though the day remained dark enough to count as evening.

It wasn't until he was dressed that he recalled the kiddie concerts at Fairfield. Leszek, thankfully, wouldn't be there –

Lenny ran the kiddies' shows, as a rule – but still, he had apologies to make . . . He was still trying to get through to Pete's mobile when the doorbell rang. Observing Angela, he ran his hand uneasily through his hair, and swung the door open. His voice sounded unused, his mouth very dry.

'Angela. Good morning.'

'It isn't morning any more.'

He couldn't tell whether she was angry, or whether her neutral tone presaged some new crisis.

'Can I get you a coffee?'

'I came to see whether you're all right. Are you? You didn't call Pete.'

William wrestled with the most reasonable lie to make. There'd been a time when he might have considered confiding in Angela, but no longer. How strange that love drove wedges between people as often as it swept them together!

'I'm fine. I'm sorry about Pete, but I didn't sleep brilliantly. I don't expect Leszek would accept so feeble an excuse, but there it is . . . Anyway, no one really needs six cellos for *Carnival of the Animals*. As long as John steers clear of coconut curries, one must be sufficient.'

'You didn't answer the phone,' she persisted.

Had there been, deep in his farthest consciousness, a notion that the phone was ringing? He began to doubt that he had really slept at all. Certainly the heaviness in his head was beyond anything he'd ever experienced, his tongue drugged into sluggishness.

'We've had trouble with the phone ever since the cable people did the street.'

Angela followed him into the kitchen. The house was manicured, colourless and nothing in the least like William. She wondered whether his estranged wife had created the house, or whether William was dismissive of such details as decor and furnishings. He asked her about the concert; then the doorbell rang again.

Isabel: hair tumultuous, pressing her lips to his. 'Thank God!'

'What are you doing here?' He felt a mixture of pleasure and alarm, thinking: Angela, the neighbours, the tautness in his head. It had started to rain with a jagged insistence; her hair was wet, minuscule drops brightening the edges of its blackness.

'Your orchestra manager called me to ask where you were. He tried to pretend it often happened, but I've been imagining – oh! the most horrible things!'

'I missed a kiddie concert,' he told her, throat constricting. 'Nothing to worry about.'

'No, but I was imagining—'

'You shouldn't let your imagination off its lead,' he returned, adding more seriously, 'and you shouldn't have come, Isabel. A friend of Margot's lives opposite–'

She fired instantly. 'How could I have stayed, not knowing? Can't you imagine what I felt? You might have had a burglary – or anything!'

'Even at my age, I'm arrogant enough to suppose myself equal to any number of burglars.'

Angela appeared in the doorway; and Will said hastily: 'You've met before, I think . . . Pete persuaded Angela to come and see whether I was all right. Really, I feel quite embarrassed by the amount of trouble I've caused.'

'Pete was very concerned,' said Angela, flicking a small hostile smile towards Isabel. 'Thanks for the coffee, Will. I've got to run, if you don't mind. I've a pupil at three.'

William saw Angela to the door, returning to find Isabel riding her instinct like a dressage horse.

'Do you know her well, that harpist?'

'Fairly well. Have you got a rehearsal?'

'Not today.'

'Something to drink?'

'No, thank you. William, she didn't give you my note on purpose.'

He wanted to deny it, but honesty owned him.

'I know.'

'She read it. I know she did.'

'Perhaps she didn't need to.'

Dangerously, 'Are you defending her?'

'She thought it would only upset me to hear from you.'

'That isn't the whole story.'

Very quietly, 'Angela's a friend of mine.'

'Friends – no. You've been together – or else she wants you to be.'

'Angela's got admirers young enough to be my children,' he began, with an attempt at a casual tone, but Isabel paid no attention. She put her slim brown hands on his shoulders.

'Yes,' he said heavily. 'Yes, it's true.'

William prepared himself for the scene, the reproaches, Isabel at her most wildly, possessively, innately illogical. He wanted to say: it was on a tour; it was a one-off; it was while I was in Spain with her small white fingers curling sorrow off my shoulders. He thought: when I'm old I'll still remember that night, the soft crunching of Angela's crotch against his buttocks, his side, the backs of his thighs. But he said nothing, because it would deflect nothing, and because he was too purely tired.

'It meant more to her,' said Isabel.

William accepted this truth apologetically.

'I'm sorry.'

Isabel didn't hear him. It hurt – crazy as it seemed – it still hurt that William could behave like other men on a tour. She understood it – but understanding, despite all that her therapist had told her, still failed to carry immunity of prosecution from feeling. However many levels of comprehension she reached, however explicable things might seem, her heart still swelled as wilfully and recklessly as ever.

It hurt, and it would hurt for a while. It might even hurt always. But she couldn't blame him – not after having rushed here in such a state, so she pushed the sorrow down and touched William's arm at her favourite place, where it blended powerfully into shoulder.

'I expect it was her,' she said softly.

'They say it takes two.'

'Not where you're involved.'

He was amused. 'So I'm a complete puppet then.'

'No, you're lethal ... There's something – irresistibly drawing about you.'

He thought: the old Isabel might have reached this point, but only after the most sensational of scenes. Regardless of logic, contemptuous of detail, she'd have blamed him and tormented herself until nervous exhaustion or burnt-out desire impelled her to finish ... Encouraged, he made another decision: he would admit that he'd promised Sam to spend Christmas with Margot.

He had known that the news would give her no pleasure, but was astonished to see swift tears in her eyes.

'But I thought it would be our first Christmas together.'

'Your mother in Gloucestershire ...'

'Oh, she's got my sisters – and my sisters' families, as well. I wanted – oh, William, I so badly wanted to be together this Christmas! And to go to your parents' house – It's Sam. I know it is. Sam's trying to bring you back together.'

He couldn't deny it, with his son's still adolescent-sounding voice fresh in his ears. He said, 'Families always incur some obligations, Isabel. My parents want me to come too – and my little granddaughter.'

It always shocked her to remember his grandchild. She flashed back, 'Prompted by Sam.'

'That may be. But she's fond of me, in her fashion.'

So is Margot, thought Isabel, with misgiving.

'Did Margot ask you?'

'No,' he said, adding with a strict sense of justice, 'But she did agree to it.'

He almost told her about the time he had gone to see her: searching for the glint of her new wheelchair through the garden, wondering if the night, the smoky air, the dizzying last blossoming of summer honeysuckle was real or only an excess of his overwrought imagination. I did see her once, he wanted to say: I interrupted her communion with the stars.

'Please don't go.'

'This is irrational, Isabel.'

'She wants you back, I know it.'

'She's shown precious little sign of it.'

'If you go,' said Isabel passionately, 'I'll never see you again. I won't – I know I won't, I don't know how.'

He remembered the cello's sound shuddering the music room walls, being pummelled to senselessness by the drowning song of the dark-souled cello. What if . . .

'You'll see me at New Year,' he said lightly. 'Now go, before anyone notices.'

She kissed him so expressively that his resolve nearly weakened; but as her battered white Renault disappeared he saw a movement flutter the curtain of the house opposite, and found himself glad to be alone.

CHAPTER 50

CLEOPATRA: If it be love indeed, tell me how much.
ANTONY: There's begging in the love that can be reckon'd.
Shakespeare

'Are you off on any trips soon?' William's mother asked.

'I'm going to Poland in January.'

'That orchestra of yours does nothing but gad about,' Olivia observed, skewering a potato as if it had offended her. 'Why, you were in Greece not three months ago, and Spain before that.'

'The orchestra isn't going.'

'A holiday?' inquired Olivia, in a tone that communicated volumes. A tone implying: earns enough to fool about on expensive treks to trendy places . . . Shocking waste of money, supporting scroungers like that . . . National Health Service . . . cancer charities . . . war widows . . .

'A business trip.'

'Now William, you don't know the first thing about business,' said his mother Vera fondly. 'Much better to stick to what you know . . . Eat up your nice carrots, Emma. They'll make you big and strong.'

'No,' said Emma, three, whose favourite word this was.

'Are you going all the way to Poland on your own?' demanded Olivia, and Margot dropped her eyes. They seemed within half a sentence of Isabel, but William only said, 'No, with Pete, the orchestra manager,' and she breathed again.

William's father demanded, 'What's this? What's this? They keep things from me, you know . . . always at it. That's why my nerves are poorly, I'm convinced.'

'They're talking about William's trip to Poland,' said Margot, adding, 'You must try some of this marvellous gravy on your sprouts.'

'Nobody told me about any trip to Poland,' Hugh accused her. 'I expect it's full of pickpockets.'

'It's full of minor entrepreneurs, like the rest of Eastern Europe,' said William. 'But I'm only going for a couple of days, to Gdańsk.'

'Lot of shipworkers in Gdańsk. I don't expect they get told anything either.'

'A couple of days! How very extravagant!' This from Olivia, busy storing up ammunition. She shouldn't wonder if there was more to *this* than met the eye . . . Poland was a long way to go for such a very short time, and who knew the sexual proclivities of this orchestral manager? Bent as a corkscrew, she supposed, mixing her metaphors with éclat. Probably hoping to lead William still further down the primrose path.

'So is it your business or your friend's that you'll be pursuing?' she inquired.

'There's someone – in Gdańsk – whom we plan to meet, together.'

William's hesitancy didn't escape Margot's attention. She knew him too well to suspect what Olivia did, but wondered at his change of tone. What business could he have in Poland? And why did she sense something unbusinesslike behind it? While some deep-rooted desire to protect him urged her to inquire, 'And what was the weather like in Greece? Wonderful, I imagine.'

'It was pleasant, certainly. Not much work either, on the whole. The music wasn't exceptional, but I'd been prepared for that by – well, by the other members, obviously.'

It astonished Margot, registering the lameness of William's response, that he could ever have deceived her – or anyone of tolerable perception – for any length of time. So: something had happened in Greece, something which in retrospect upset him . . .

'I never heard about Greece,' came in martyred tones from Hugh, just as Olivia began to brag to Vera about her share in Edwin's election triumph.

'No, Vera, it wasn't easy, and I won't pretend it was. There were times – I admit it – when I very nearly despaired. I remember one night in particular, rain like the last trump and the most frightful canvass down Sparrow Drive, where, between us, they don't know Conservatism from a hole in the ground. But we persevered, knowing, as I told Edwin at the time, that every vote counted, and that every Conservative, however slack, would be one more vote on election night . . . We came back bloodied but unbowed, didn't we, Margot? And as I got Edwin a small whisky – he never has more than a finger's-worth, drinks practically nothing – I reminded him that, when the going gets tough, the tough get on their bikes, which he said was a beautiful thought, and very true. Do you remember, Margot?'

'Yes,' said Margot, unable to resist smiling. 'And I recall Edwin's having more than a finger's-worth of whisky, as well.'

William, glancing over, thought how young she looked, her face rose-lit by wine and her curls grown longer and fuller, the way she'd used to wear them. He was reminded of an occasion before they were married: of Margot, her head held at just such an angle, smiling at him privately over a similar family function . . . Olivia, meanwhile, was not amused.

'Nonsense. Edwin is most abstemious. In addition to which, he's the kind of politician who's really needed rather more at Westminster than in Brussels. Not that I mean to impugn our own MP . . .'

'But he can earn more in Brussels,' said Margot mischievously. 'That's the reason – and really, it only shows Edwin's good sense. Why clog the packed halls of Westminster when there are so many juicier perks abroad?'

'I met an MP once,' said Hugh, rapping on his glass. 'And I told him, as well; he got nothing but plain speaking from me. I

329

said the country was going to the dogs, and that the sooner someone got rid of the Tory scum, preferably—'

'Another roll, Olivia?' Vera interrupted. 'They're the shop's speciality.'

'Thank you, no. I have only another half-hour before the late church service. Margot, dear, we must prepare.'

It being one of Olivia's principal objections to William's family that they were not religious in any well-ordered sense, she was all the more distressed by Margot's clear reply.

'William's offered to take me for some fresh air,' she said, upon which Vera eagerly began to detail the best of the local paths, and those least likely to be damp, given time and circumstance.

Olivia, though temporarily stymied, was never silenced for long. She leaned across to William, saying with a good deal of emphasis, 'I only wish *you* had the opportunity to meet Edwin, William. A fascinating mind – and such delicacy! Really, I don't think anything can equal his manners. He insisted on taking Margot to the local hospice, where she helps of a Thursday. They were delighted, as you can imagine, to have their Euro MP pop in to cheer up the dying. Now *that's* what I call true thoughtfulness.'

Her hint wasn't lost on William, though it clearly was on Hugh, who was busy averring, with a strong sense of grievance, that he hadn't been offered a second glass of wine by anyone, in addition to which, nobody ever listened to him, even by accident . . . While William, glancing from Olivia's triumphant face to Margot's averted one, divined something of the truth. So, Margot was admired by Olivia's tame Euro MP! He didn't care much for the thought, but recognised the justice of its irony. Olivia's Euro MP – whatever next?

William fell to musing at the curious way his life had turned in the last two years – ever since that fatal moment, or that combination of fatal moments, with Isabel. The very thought of Isabel was like a breath of sweetness: her irrational simplicities, her emotional directness, the way she moved, with that impulsively self-conscious beauty . . . He heard the bub-bles of conversation rising without registering the words.

Hugh, peevishly: 'As for cheering up the dying, I don't see the point. He'll have only done it for their votes.'

Olivia: 'I wish, my dear Vera, that I *could* stay for the sweet. Nothing would give me greater pleasure. But such a point was made by your vicar of my attending – they quite depend on seeing me, I know. I only hope that some day you – and Hugh, of course – might like to join the Christmas service as well. *What* a joy that would be!'

Sam: 'Tell your grandmamma your new word, Emma, the one you said yesterday. It started with P, didn't it? Can you remember your new word? Penguin. Pen-guin. Remember?'

'I don't know why I'm never told anything. It's not as if I'm not all there, or I ever complain. Doesn't do any good complaining, so I suffer in silence, same as my corns . . . Trouble is, it's always the same old story. It's "Don't tell Dad, he'll only fuss," or "No need to mention it to your father, is there?" Same as pesticides. We all know they're there but nobody really *tells* us about them. Do they, eh? Do they?'

'No, dear,' said Vera serenely, and she continued urging little Emma to try her apple sauce, which was not only wholesome and delicious but would singlehandedly preserve her eyesight from the combined ravages of time and illness. Indeed, Vera seemed to feel that Emma's last best hope of retaining her sight was contained in the very helping of apple sauce currently decorating her plate . . .

Margot was quietly daydreaming. When she was young she'd ridden at a local riding school. She recalled Appuma's fat stupid face and nubbly lips nuzzling her hand for sugar lumps, her own knees gone wobbly from the cantering . . . Now Margot was fantasising about riding away. Wind ruffling her curls, Appuma's coarse forelock skewed in the breeze they themselves seemed to have rocked into motion . . .

In my daydreams I'm always riding away. Why am I never disabled in my dreams? Then she caught William's gaze and suddenly realised that the escape in her eyes was in his eyes too. They stared at each other, shocked as strangers, while noise rose all around them.

There was still enough light afterwards for William to accompany Margot around the fields. He took control of the wheelchair with diffidence, even humility, recalling too vividly his dismissal in Olivia's garden. They travelled in silence, until he thought he detected a sigh. Cursing himself for his awkwardness, he said, 'You seem better, Margot.'

'The shaking's a bit better, certainly. No one seems to know why.'

'I thought your homeopath—'

'Oh, I gave up on all that.'

They passed a rowdy family with young children. William observed, 'Olivia doesn't seem to have mellowed much.'

'She has her own character,' said Margot, almost defiantly. William wished he could see her face. How difficult it was to gauge body language behind a wheelchair! He pushed on along the edge of woodland, avoiding the dampest places.

'What's the point of coming if you won't talk?' he asked mildly. She was suddenly jarred by his mildness; it suddenly seemed a mask behind which he got away with everything else.

'About the same point I suppose as spending Christmas with us – and New Year with Isabel.'

She felt him stiffen. 'Who told you about Isabel?'

'Never mind,' she said, unwilling to mention Edwin. William thought first of his neighbour – of Isabel's recent visit – and then of Piotr, though what motive Piotr might have could only be guessed at. William knelt down to her level.

'Margot, nothing's certain, as far as I'm concerned – or Isabel either. She's never even suggested—'

Well, once, perhaps . . . But William pressed on. 'She's never suggested divorce, and neither have I. Our separation is – and always was – entirely your choice. The moment you decide, it'll be over. Margot, we still have years enough left to start again. You could choose to – today, this very moment.'

Margot had meant to stay silent, but his words so traitorously matched what she'd felt that she said, 'I was going to come back. I was going to call you.'

'What stopped you?' he asked quietly.

She couldn't say, Edwin's detective stopped me. William covered her resistant hand with warm fingers.

'I've told you before. The house is yours as much as mine. Yours to come home to, tomorrow, even tonight. Don't go back with Olivia, Margot – come home with me instead.'

'And Isabel? Are you implying that, should I choose, you'd never see her again?'

His hand tightened on hers. She'd forgotten how broad his hands were, how sure they pretended to be, but their strength reminded her more than anything else of the shock she'd first felt when confronted with his weakness. Perhaps the most terrifying part of the last two years was her growing certainty that she was the stronger, though she'd never meant to be.

'If you came back, I would never see her again,' he told her, though the mere idea tore viciously at him.

'Does Isabel know that?'

'She knows I'm still married; and she must realise I'm not the right person for her to marry. She's always claimed not to care about marriage and children – but still, it must be obvious that this can't go on forever.'

'That isn't an answer, William. Does she know what you've just told me?'

('I'd prefer, if you don't mind, to be Caesar's ghost. You were my only friend, remember.')

'No,' said William deeply. 'She doesn't know.'

Margot looked at his face, eyes darkened and mouth sorrowful, the hair disordered but still thick and shining. This is torture, she thought, and – even though it's his doing – I can't blame him. It hits him hardest, after all. Nobody can hurt us as shrewdly as we manage to hurt ourselves. And there was a perverse glory – something life-affirming – in someone of William's age and character risking body and soul for love. She took a deep breath, and said, 'I think we'd better divorce.'

The shock in his eyes deprived her of breath; the nerves of her hand flickered under the sudden pressure from his.

'You don't mean that.'

'I do mean it. My – condition – isn't fair on you. That can be your excuse.'

'I don't need an excuse, and I don't want a divorce. I want—'

'No,' she said dryly. 'Of course not. You want me to come back so that you can be comfortable again. And you want Isabel, as long as she doesn't imagine anything will actually come of it. I don't know why I ever thought you were different from other men! You're an absolute pattern of male wish fulfilment. They might do a whole textbook on you.'

'You never used to be so – caustic.'

'Comes of living with Mother, I expect. One's sense of the ridiculous becomes fatally sharpened. But also, naturally enough, you want – you need things I can't give you. William, believe me, this must happen to any number of people. There's nothing extraordinary about it, nothing dishonourable – certainly nothing unusual. Very few people can behave nobly indefinitely, and you managed to for far longer than most . . . I'm offering you what you seem to want. Why can't you just accept it?'

'Because I don't want it,' he said with energy. 'I never have.'

'May I ask you a straight question, William?'

'Of course.'

'Do you love her or not?'

William took a deep breath; and her soul rocked, the trees, the family disappearing into specks in the distance. This business will kill me, she thought acutely. I can feel the stress shivering me, jerking the muscles of my heart.

William's voice, very low: 'I love Isabel, yes, but I love you too . . . There were years, decades, when I loved you only, and a time – I admit it – when I loved her more. But choosing between you now would be like choosing between my two arms. Isabel is – Isabel, wayward and impulsive and insecure, while you're sure and mocking and amusing and in touch with reality. You're my life, my past, my truthfulness, and she's the sexy, possessive dynamic I never knew . . . You want a decision; naturally enough, you expect me to choose. But how can you choose – how is it possible to choose, one or the other – between summer and spring?'

Margot was very still; he could feel her pulse stirring under his thumb, skin against skin. How long had it been since he'd touched Margot's skin? He felt boyishly disappointed by her silence. He recalled Piotr ('What have you come for – absolution?') Absolution, retribution: Margot held them both, two cards she refused to play. Though there might be another reason for her refusal . . . He said, 'I suppose what you're telling me is that Olivia's MEP – Narbold, is that the name? – is a factor.'

'She'd like him to be.'

'And he'd like to be himself.'

Her silence seemed a confirmation, perhaps it was. They were passed by a giggling teenage couple, the boy's still-childish hand possessive on the rim of the girl's jeans. William felt the age-old surge of jealousy, recalling the Euro MP's diplomatic deviousness, his suspiciously dark hair. To imagine him with Margot seemed an obscenity, and yet – why not? They had been separated for almost a year. God knows, he'd done worse things in the past year than chauffeuring charity workers to hospices.

He thought of Angela's pointed breasts, of Isabel's mouth, full, rich, demanding, down the line of his back . . . What was Margot thinking? He picked up her wrist and kissed its underside, registering the fragile tunnel just under the edge of flesh. He couldn't tell whether her pulse fluttered, she moved her hand too abruptly away.

'Please don't.'

'Will you leave the divorce, at least for now?'

'I – have to think about it, William. Please. Let's just move on.'

Olivia returned from church in combative mood, and quizzed her daughter mercilessly in their guest room.

'I trust that you intend to be open with me, Margot. We're both too mature, I hope, for prevarication on such a subject.'

'There's not much to tell.'

'I saw him eyeing you across the table. He thought I didn't, I daresay, but I did. And did you notice how he flinched when I mentioned dear Edwin? That got right in amongst him – as well it might – because he's never been in Edwin's league and never will be. Nothing but a two-bit cello-player who, I daresay, has never paid his rightful amount of income tax . . . Did he ask you to come back?'

'Yes, he did.'

'You didn't agree, did you?' Olivia asked anxiously.

'I offered to divorce him.'

'Well! Exactly as I said to Hilda, not two days ago. Hilda, I said, she won't stand for it. No daughter of mine *could* stand for it. Not that it was easy for me, at my time of life, to accommodate your return, but *that* I never regarded. As far as I was concerned, no trouble was too—'

'We're not divorcing, Mother.'

'Pardon me?'

'He wouldn't agree. He – doesn't want me to go.'

'But you just said—'

'I offered, but he refused.'

Olivia seemed divided for a moment between applauding William's taste and observing the mortifying end of all her scheming. Then she brightened. 'He'll change his mind. Time and tide, as dear Edwin always says.'

Margot had no answer to this. She remembered the warmth of his hand – familiar and at the same time intoxicatingly strange – and found herself admiring and resenting his instinct simultaneously. What right had he to gauge so perfectly what could stir a woman? Edwin's hand with its hirsute sides and William's so broad and warm – oh, it was all confusion! Surely there ought to be a point at which the all-clear was blown and life became less complicated?

'None of this would have happened, you know, had William not got an Eye. Years ago, it was, when I first noticed it. Felicity Kendal on the telly, and William — But Edwin, now, Edwin is a real gentleman; Edwin does not, I'm pleased to report, have an Eye. While we were canvassing one night in Crofton – do pay me the courtesy of attending, Margot – we met a really stunning young woman, perhaps thirty, lovely smile, blue eyes, light-brown hair. Handsome is as handsome does, of course – it's put more elegantly in Proverbs, but I've forgotten the wording – but, believe me, Edwin was as distant to her as if he'd seen right through her, metaphorically speaking. Whereas William – well, his eyes simply danced when that actress came on the box.'

'Oh, Mother, really! Most men admire her.'

'Truth is, you'd be a good deal better off married to a man like Edwin. Even if Edwin left politics, there would always be a place for him in his brother's firm. Whereas Richard Morrison wrote in *The Times* that even the orchestra chosen by the Arts Council might not last out the decade, and Richard Morrison is by no means stupid. A friend of Hilda's met him at *Hamlet* and was most impressed with him.'

Margot quietly brushed her teeth and washed off what make-up she'd bothered with, scarcely listening to the ebb and flow of her mother's voice. ('Bridget was telling me about the delight of the hospice workers. Really, I think very few men in Edwin's position . . .')

When all she could think of was William's deep voice and the persuasion in William's warm hands.

CHAPTER 51

Season your admiration for a while
With an attent ear till I may deliver
Upon the witness of these gentlemen
This marvel to you.

O, speak of that! That do I long to hear.
Shakespeare

(from Pete Hegal's diaries)

A cold coming we had of it, for January's not a month recommended for seeing anywhere much, and Gdańsk would undoubtedly have bloomed a good deal more persuasively in the spring. Yet I still carry with me the view of Wisloujście fortress from the river, along with the exquisite Abbot's Palace in Oliwa, both outlined and festooned in snow.

Gdańsk has its elegant old quarters as well, but Will and I had been directed to its most subterranean sector; nor was I reassured when the cabbie, with a look of disdain, asked me to repeat the address.

'This is the place, all right,' I told William, on arrival. 'Four pip emma, lobby of the Hotel Rosenbaum plc, no cheques accepted without banker's card.'

William glanced around the lobby, which had the hungover appearance of a place that only ever came alive after midnight. Stray cigarette butts decorated some of the tables, which were overlaid with a stale miasma of alcohol and sweat.

'American gentlemen play cards, like girls?' inquired the doorman. Will shook his head.

'Sit tight,' I advised him. 'I'll just check whether there's a message at the desk.'

William returned almost immediately. 'Our man's here.'

'Can't be. Ain't nobody around except dead cigarette butts and that sleet-leavened draught from the front door.'

'He's asleep behind the fake rubber plant.'

The aim and object of our trek looked a characterful specimen. Possibly forty-five, he was short but chunky, featuring beefy eyebrows, a little goatee beard and a trim moustache. He sported the only example I've ever seen of genuine hobnailed boots, and had a well-worn pipe propped on the table beside him.

'He doesn't look like Leszek,' I said dubiously.

'My cousins don't look like me either.'

'My dear Will, no one looks like you. The web is woven and you have to wear it. What makes you so sure it's our man in Havana?'

'Didn't you see the snapshot?'

'Only briefly.'

Will produced it from his wallet, and I had to admit that, though taken many moons ago and in a flattering light, it was the same fellow, absolutely.

'How shall we wake him?' Will inquired.

I reached over and shook the bewhiskered bloke on the shoulder. It was only when his eyelids flicked back the curtains that I realised quite how snap my judgement had been about his resemblance to Leszek. He might have lacked Leszek's feline angularity, stressing the fungoid and even primordial characteristics of the clan Zimetski, but the fellow had, without question, the Zimetski eyes. Drooping, multi-coloured, bloodshot, they focused on me until Will took charge of the introductions.

'Sorry to wake you. I'm William Mellor, and this is Pete Hegal.'

The Zimetski eyes sparked. It saddened me to think how many months it had been since Leszek's had looked like that.

'Ha! Mellor, is it? And Hegal? Hegal and Mellor? The pleasure is mine, all mine.'

Upon which we naturally averred that it was all ours, and exchanged any number of handshakes with gusto. Then we gathered around his well-worn card table while Pavlo produced a brandy bottle from a tattered bag at his feet. He had the appearance of a man who regularly produced brandy bottles – part of his product identification, if you will. Will refused, his views on brandy being strictly post-coital, but I obliged Pavlo by saluting our good health. Then I saw him wink at someone over my shoulder, and the doorman wink back.

'You like this place?' I inquired.

'Is a good place for meeting. Private. Has atmosphere.'

There was no disputing either point. Our privacy was such that we seemed to be not only the last people in Gdańsk, but the last people in this section of the universe. As for atmosphere, the *fin de siècle* furnishings, torpid dust and dregs of cigarette smoke spoke volumes. I expected him to inquire about our trip, but he never did, Pavlo being one of those creatures who simply accept that people who want to visit them will find some method of so doing, whether from the nether end of Gdańsk or the west side of Greater London.

'So, how is my crazy cousin?' was Pavlo's first real communication. 'So dramatic as he is! Always either fizzing or dying, dying or fizzing . . . Once he had asthma – a little trouble, half a day, then back to school. However, this was not enough; no, ever after he tells me how he almost died. Ha! True story.'

I was charmed, recalling the operatic description Leszek had given me of his asthma attack – family gathered around the bedside, mother's stifled sobs, the second-to-last rites of the Holy Catholic Church, all followed by a recovery leaving Lazarus simply nowhere . . .

Will only said, smiling, 'You speak English much better than your sister suggested.'

'No, I speak instead American, and I speak it lousily. I was in New York to study – oh, four, five years, I forget how many. Not enough drink, too much hard work and the girls pretty but too religious. So I came home. Your very good healths! Dirt in your eyes!'

'Were you studying music in New York?' I asked curiously.

Pavlo grinned. 'Piano. I study piano to get out of the country. Poland in those days – pah! A doghouse, and you cannot live on girls . . . So I go to New York, the Big Peanut. The Big Peanut, I know it so well . . . Times Square, the Lincoln Memorial, the bridge with its golden gate, the Statue of Liberty – so ugly, and yet, at the same time, so beautiful.'

'Did you enjoy New York?' I asked.

'Lovely players, lovely people; I felt so welcome there. My accent was so "cute"; my name so "cute" – and I was a pianist from Poland. A pianist from Poland, I must be Rubinstein, naturally! But I wasn't. Piano – poof! Conducting – poof! I came back here instead and now I teach. Lots of pretty girls want to learn piano. True story.'

He was certainly droll, but I exchanged a nervous glance with Will as our host downed another dose of brandy. We'd come a long way for precious little if (as seemed only too probable) Pavlo became too plastered to communicate anything.

Fact was, all the letter-writing – three from her, four from me – had been accomplished by Pavlo's younger sister. And the sister not only didn't pretend to know the whole story, but what she knew, she rather doubted . . . In Will's face I read my own worry: that the disapproving sister was in the right – that there was nothing for us here beyond the meandering recollections of a washed-up not-particularly-concert pianist.

However, my own hunch was to dig deeper, and I'd follow my hunches, if not to the ends of the earth, at least to the grungier edges of Gdańsk. I pressed on.

'You grew up with Leszek, I think.'

Pavlo grimaced. 'Same road, same school, same family, and same great-uncle teaching us on his piano. Leszek hated the piano – preferred the violin, always – and I was too lazy. Our uncle used to swipe us on the wrist with a ruler. Wrong note – bang! Wrong note – wallop! Just like a Batman film. Now I have arthritis in the wrist – here – more the right than the left. All for wrong notes! Ha! True story.'

Fact is, we hadn't known where the trail would lead, if anywhere. One night, William had recollected the name 'Mikhail', which Janice had let slip in Greece. On a long shot, I had wormed his brother's address out of Leszek, and the brother had directed me to Leszek's first cousins instead. Pavlo's sister had assured us that – though the story was an old one – Pavlo knew all that was to be known. Recalling this, I asked Pavlo what Leszek had been like as a boy.

'Crazy, always crazy, born crazy like a genius. You know him now; well, he was just the same, there was no difference. No compromise, no patience, no difference! Full of temperament, determination, a truly immovable determination . . . We played music together until I was ten and he seven. We play a little sonata, you understand, but he was rushing me, rushing, always rushing the beat. So I told him he was rushing. Then he threw his violin at me – strings flying, bridge flying – and suddenly a crack in this fiddle, maybe two inches long. It was lucky I had so small a head, to make only two inches! Sometimes I am surprised to live to tell this tale! But after, he would never play with me again: this is true, this story.'

He had Leszek's eyes – the slant, the depth, the flecked subtlety of colours – but quite a different expression, the shrewdly comic expression of a man who took life as it came and revelled in it. The kind to whom rat-race suggested a couple of mugs betting on rodents, the kind who enjoyed what he could and drowned the rest in good brandy. At that particular moment, however, a little shadow crossed over him.

'I do not mind this craziness. It is a good story, to be hit by a fiddle – makes me laugh. But Leszek should have played with me again, he should have forgiven me this thing. And besides, he was rushing the beat; it is the truth; and we all must learn in this life to take the truth. Each allegro had to spin too fast – it was his trouble, always.'

Secretly I agreed, but then attempted to lead the subject closer to our quarry. 'Perhaps Mikhail . . .'

Pavlo laughed explosively, jetting a spot of brandy on to the table. 'You English! So logical – and so impatient! Believe me, my friends, I know what you have come for, and – I guarantee – you will not be disappointed. To prove this: I have with me here a photo, the only one like it on this earth. Behold here my crazy cousin. And behold Mikhail.'

It was a black-and-white photo, worn at the edges from too many fingers. It showed a couple of boys, perhaps seven, perhaps slightly older, proudly clutching their smallish violin and cello cases. They might have been boys of almost any country or any time – the scuffed shoes, the ill-kempt hair, the bookbags slung on their shoulders – but they weren't. The tall one with the too long nose and the gangly legs already had Leszek's rebellious glare. But it was the young and perfected creature beside him – a luminous-featured Adonis despite the falling socks and grubby knees – that shook me. I looked at Will, who nodded briefly. Too close to be real. Too close not to be.

'I look it out for you. So many years since people ask me for this story. So many years since first I found this photo, which I keep for posterity, and also for proof . . . You see the strangeness in this photo? It does not – what is the word – elude you?'

I was too mesmerised by the resemblance to see anything beyond, but Will said very quietly, 'The shadow's missing.'

'Leszek has a shadow,' Pavlo corrected him, a teacher with a favourite pupil. 'Behold his shadow here. But the boy Mikhail – observe! – he has no shadow. Some people think this photo is doctored – and I never had the negative, I can prove nothing – but it is not doctored, you have my word on this.'

I didn't need his word, of course. The Festival Hall car park – that crystal autumn day and the wind across the Thames. The shadow of Janice's cello – and leaning over her shoulder, the ghost of Mikhail. I'd shivered then and I shivered again in that grimy Gdańsk hotel, with Pavlo's pipe smoke spicing my lungs and the ripe, cheap grain of his brandy in my mouth.

'What is the significance of the shadow – or the lack of it?' William asked. Pavlo took a long pull on his pipe. Eventually he stalled.

'It is the way of these things, perhaps.'

'Do you know who took the photo?'

Pavlo shrugged. 'My sister found it in one of Leszek's old schoolbooks. That is all I know about this thing.'

He waited for further prompting, but I was still meditating on Mikhail – the perfect proportions, those silvery forearms – while William seemed lost in his own thoughts. Pavlo resumed with increasing animation.

'This Mikhail – people ask me, who was he? I will tell you. He was an actor, a statesman, a child king. He died a child but he was still a king.'

'In what respect?' I asked.

'In every respect. He played the cello astoundingly. His eyes, his beauty, could light up a room. He could run faster than any of us, play harder – his sheer strength, for his size, was impossible. I myself, three years older and twice his weight – was once wrestled to the ground by this same Mikhail. He had the grip of a wolf. A big wolf. And even boys who would have sneered at his beauty and his music longed for his word, his smile – because he had a strange, mesmerising smile, could make you dizzy, your senses aching . . . But it was always Leszek. They were the two who would never be separated. Their blood was mingled. So many of us had blood brothers,' he added apologetically. 'Young boys the world over, so

344

childish. But here it meant something . . . They even had their own language, like no other.'

'What kind of language?' asked Will, and I remembered what he'd told me about that night in Greece.

Pavlo took a swig of brandy and assured us, 'Not the usual nonsense word-games. A language like music. I used to hear them speak it, in the playground, after school . . . Always there were the two of them: Mikhail and Leszek, though Mikhail was the prince. Leszek was the jester, the courtier, always seeking approval. But also the only one with the secret language, the secret music, the favour of young Mikhail.'

William said, 'Tell us about the music.'

'The music, yes. Well it happened there was a new music teacher at this school – Jewish, very soulful. This man taught not only class music but also chamber music after the school day was over. At first there were many groups – I myself had a little duo for a while – but finally there was just the one. The rest dropped out, lost interest, but not Leszek and Mikhail. They formed a piano trio: two junior boys and this music tutor. All around Gdańsk they played, for weddings, civic functions. There was Leszek on the violin, of course, never very accomplished but with natural verve; the teacher solid on the piano – and Mikhail on the cello, Mikhail who had everything, and knew it. Mikhail, who could take a melody and use it to twist open the lid of your heart. Mikhail with his magical cello, his crazy stretching fingers, and even the boys who usually despise such things were silent when the music crept over the assembly like night mist over the hills . . . True story,' he added, but more as a leitmotif than for any more persuasive reason.

'What was so unusual about Mikhail's cello?' asked William. And only because I knew him so well could I sense what excitement lay behind the question.

'It was a little cello, dark and small, but in power and sound quite simply sublime. It was only seven-eighths size, even three-quarter size perhaps. But the sound – I have no words in

English for this sound. It could project above every other instrument; it could sing down the length of any hall. I used to imagine there was a soul in it, that it breathed like a living thing.'

'What happened to it?' I asked.

'It disappeared when Mikhail died. Some people say it was stolen. I know no more about this cello.'

William was caught up in his own theory.

'Tell me, Pavlo, was there ever a fight, an argument, between Mikhail and Leszek? Something perhaps that Leszek refused to forgive?'

Pavlo nodded slowly. 'No fight, exactly – for of course Leszek would lose it. But Mikhail did do something – this I know – to alienate my cousin. And Leszek can never forgive. It is his only fault, besides this rushing, and a crazy temper . . . Though I love him, my so-crazy cousin. Will you tell him this from me, from Pavlo? That I love him always?'

I reassured him on this point, adding, 'What happened after the split, then?'

'After . . . Well, Leszek refused to play any longer in this trio. And he studied – as if the devil was after him. He finished in my year in the end, three years above his Mikhail. He advanced three years in only one, and never looked at Mikhail again. True story this – but also sad.'

'What about the music teacher?' I demanded. It seemed to me, I don't know why, that the teacher must have had a part to play.

'After Leszek left, Mikhail played alone with this teacher after school. There were stories, of course – who knows now what to believe? Perhaps Leszek suspected that Mikhail had betrayed him with this teacher . . . Perhaps, even, there was something there before. Perhaps this was the real reason. After all, men are men and angels angels, and Mikhail, of course, was neither a man nor an angel . . . I remember one assembly: Mikhail playing the Fauré *Elégie*, and the eyes of the teacher like someone – what is the word? – out of his depth, drowning.

And all the while Leszek in my row, staring before him, not looking, not hearing, not caring that the great roaring cello was singing madly for him. The sound like a waterfall, like a sunset. A cello thumbing the raw core of sunset, light exploding like blood, but finally failing . . . You know this *Elégie* – you can imagine. We are all musicians enough for this imagining.'

There was a silence, broken only by a subdued rattle from the ancient radiator.

'Tell me,' said William gently, 'why Mikhail died.'

Pavlo laughed hoarsely until he began to cough. 'If you had heard even one phrase of this *Elégie* you would no longer wonder! No, instead you would marvel that this child had lived so long, looking at my cousin and receiving such an answer. Hearing such – such passion pour out of this seven-eighths cello and Leszek staring at nothing, only a little frown on his face . . . There is nothing more intense than love choked up inside a child, especially when the child is already half-mad with the music in his ears. You ask how he died; I will tell you. Mikhail died of love, beneath the wheels of a truck, just after the school day was over. I saw it happen, I – Pavlo Zimecki – I was there. I saw Mikhail smile; I saw him lit like gold; I watched him walk out, still smiling, beneath the wheels of this truck. I heard the scream of the driver, the weeping from the girls; I hear it still . . . Afterwards they said how strange that there was no blood, but I knew the reason. Mikhail was not really dead. And he was still smiling.'

'He was lit like gold?' I asked, feeling a ripple of strangeness down my spine.

'Gold,' he assented, but without emphasis, as if he had answered the question too many times before. 'Gold like a flame – not the sharpest blue part, but the middle of a fire, a living gold. I was there. I saw this thing. There was a strange – shuddering in the side of my face, but still, I still recall it. I saw him smile and walk under the great wheels, I, Pavlo.'

'It sounds – incredible,' I objected.

Pavlo shrugged. 'You do not have to believe it. There is no money in it.'

I saw William fingering the table, testing its reality against his broad fingers. Pavlo meanwhile remembered something else.

'You recall the music teacher? The one who taught the trio, and who, later, played with Mikhail alone . . . This man faded away.'

'Cancer?' I supposed.

Pavlo glared at my stupidity, recalling to mind Leszek's fury in healthier times. 'No, no, not at all. He was – eaten from inside; he was consumed. Mikhail consumed him, whether living or dead.'

I thought of Leszek and tingled. I glanced at Will, whose eyes had that hooded aloofness that women found so compelling. He said slowly, 'I thought you didn't believe that Mikhail died.'

Pavlo puffed thoughtfully at his pipe. 'No, I didn't, not in one sense, and this is the reason I believe this thing. I was of course at Mikhail's graveside. Along with all the schoolchildren, I bent down to put this flower there. And I saw what so many missed, but what I will always remember.'

'What did you see?' William asked. He was roped into Pavlo's rhythm by then, a dance, a ritual.

'Mikhail was not in the coffin. His mother thought he was, and his family, but when I saw, I knew.'

'Who was it then?'

'That I do not know, but it was not Mikhail . . . No, this body was no more his than it was my own . . . There was no light, no gold, no smile around the eyes – and no Mikhail. It was a boy, very fair and very good-looking, but I did not know him. He had the look of a small stolen child.'

Stolen! I thought – but Will's mind was bent on the present.

'Pavlo, could – could a spirit still be looking for revenge after all these years?'

'Some things are immortal,' said Pavlo testily. 'This is obvious. Do not forget that hate can be as insatiable as love is. And that the kind of hate that started out as love is the most insatiable of all.'

I heard Will's voice, still deep, still reasonable, my sole, salvageable link with reality.

'Do you imagine it possible that Mikhail's – spirit might still be shadowing your cousin Leszek?'

'It is possible – but not likely. I have not heard of such a thing. My cousin has left all this behind him. I used to think that some day I would hear . . . But that has never happened. I do not think, now, it ever will.'

Will took a deep breath.

'We have reason to suppose, Pavlo, that the boy you knew as Mikhail may be alive, and inhabiting the body of a woman.'

We'd finally startled him. Up till then, I think he'd basically been humouring us. He'd probably considered us a couple of sensation-seeking voyeurs, a branch of some Psychic Phenomena Society with nothing better to do in Gdańsk than to have a drink and marvel at some old ghost stories. Enjoying our attention, he had embellished his character role, with his cunning timings and his 'true stories' . . . But now he suddenly seemed to alter.

He sat straighter; while his mouth seemed to thin beneath his moustache. With ceremonious air, he returned the brandy bottle to the bottom of his tatty bag. Then he looked at Will attentively, almost accusingly, as if he had waited long years for this moment, almost to miss it in the end.

'Leszek. It is to do with Leszek, yes? That is your real reason. Before, I did not understand.'

'We are worried for Leszek,' Will admitted.

Pavlo breathed stentoriously, his eyes fixed on Will's face. He murmured something in Polish, far too swiftly for my understanding. Then he said, 'You are older than I expected. You are pure English?'

'He's part-Celt,' I told him. 'The Celts are always a little magical.'

Then Pavlo did a strange thing. He seized William's unresisting hand and turned it over, the way a woman might, or a madman. His brow creased with concentration, he caressed the palm, smoothing the athletic muscle of the cellist's thumb. It wasn't sexual exactly, but there was something so innately sure about it that I felt a tingle in my own palm, almost a vibration.

After that he somehow hovered – I can't think of a clearer word – his own hand just above William's. The air around us seemed to take on a subtler, lighter hue, as if the husk of pressure had somehow parted, leaving a sheerer feel behind . . . How long this lasted, I can't be sure. Then there was a rush of freshness past my ears; and Pavlo leaned back, looking at Will with respect.

'She has taken Leszek but failed with you,' he announced in clear Polish. 'He – she – has tried to possess you but failed.'

'I'm sorry, I don't speak Polish,' William reminded him, but Pavlo didn't trouble to translate. Instead he said in English, 'You are a dangerous man. Who is the woman?'

'She calls herself Janice,' said William, but he shook his head.

'This much must be . . . You know you hold my cousin's life in your hands?'

'We – have wondered.'

'Though he partly brought this on himself. Is it so obvious that he is ill?'

'Something is certainly obvious.'

Pavlo smacked his hand on the table. 'That it should have come to this! So many years I have wondered . . . And the cello, the cello, too! How many weeks have you had this cello?'

'Since February.'

He shook his head. 'And you are still alive? If you can do this, there may still — But you are older than I expected, and sadder. There is a reason? The woman I saw in the trance, perhaps?' William only shook his head, and Pavlo rushed on.

'English, too – why English? Or why not? Oh, we know nothing, nothing!' He hit his fist on the table, rocking it this time, but he suddenly seemed rather pallid to me, a frustrated and probably alcoholic soul buried too long with brandy and pipe in fusty rooms.

The silence for a moment was so profound I became aware that sleet was piling into slush at the bottom of the window-pane. The radiator rattled, as if startled into action by a passerby. Suddenly Pavlo tapped his pipe on the table.

'Tell me what I can do.'

'Nothing,' said Will deeply. 'If you've told us all you know.'

'No, no! There must be something – something at least to make it easier. My head, my head – I can think of nothing! So often have I imagined this day, but now . . . Ghost stories,' he explained, this time to me. 'People come to hear it, a little shiver – they enjoy this little shiver. Living it – this is a different thing.'

'Could – Mikhail – actually harm anyone besides Leszek?' I asked suddenly, thinking of the Duke.

'My guess is no, not unless such a person came between. But what do I know? It is the spirit of a child, and will behave like a child, a child as crazy as my crazy cousin. Or crazier even, for they were blood brothers.'

I thought of Charmaine. Had her father got in Mikhail's way, or simply been trampled over in Mikhail's single-minded determination to reach Leszek? I thought of the long years the cello had spent winding its way back towards Leszek, the eerie glitter I had sometimes seen – if only for an instant – in Janice's eyes . . .

Pavlo was saying to Will, with unmistakable eagerness, 'And this is something else you must not forget: you were the one selected. This much, at least, we do know. There will be a reason for this, though we may never find it out . . . But

351

remember that you alone may have some power — And as for the rest, whatever happens must happen.'

'How do you know?' I asked, suddenly curious. 'Is that what being psychic means? Whatever you – felt – above Will's hand?'

He shrugged, without interest. 'It is a talent like any other. The Holy Mother knows how I came by it, and, as with all my talents, I use it badly and without application.' Then almost wistfully, he waggled his finger at me. 'Do not forget, Sancho Panza, to put it in the diary. Centuries from now we all get to be heroes.'

I hadn't mentioned any diary, either then or in my letters to his sister, and I decided that all the Zimetskis (or Zimeckis, as they still spelled it in Poland) might be either crazy or psychic. Though, to my mind, the questions still outweighed the answers. What, after all, had Pavlo given us? Coffins with stolen bodies in them, teachers who faded like old photographs, children without shadows and cellos that sang like living creatures . . .

In the end I shook his hand, and went across the road to hail a taxi. Looking back through the sleet I saw a tableau I'll never forget: Pavlo, some inches the shorter, clasping Will's shoulders with both hands, and looking seriously up at him. Rain glossed the top of Will's silver head and sleet or tears ran down Pavlo's face. He was speaking earnestly, but I couldn't hear what he said.

Will was completely silent on the way back, while the taxi ground through the slush and heavy traffic. When we finally reached our own hotel, I asked Will what Pavlo had said at the last.

'He said, "Those who have no shadow have no soul." '

I longed for him to speak further, but Will clearly wanted to be alone. I watched him move down the slick pavement, collar up round his neck, hands deep in his pockets. Those who have no shadow have no soul. We had come a long way for our answer, if that was what it was . . . There was a certain rhythm to it, like poetry, but I found myself shivering all the same, while what natural light still remained was washed away in the grey chill of evening.

CHAPTER 52

Let me play the lion too. I will roar that I will do any man's heart good to hear me. I will roar that I will make the Duke say 'Let him roar again; let him roar again!'

This was the most unkind cut of all.

Shakespeare

There's music that we learn to love, feeling our way towards it year by year, and music which strikes us like a lightning blast, exposing vast acres of countryside for miles around. But there's also music that we're born loving, just as there are places, seen for the first time, which make us catch our breath in startled recognition – a rightness in the senses for which there is no rational, no obvious explanation. Such a work for Eddie Wellington was Mahler's great Fifth Symphony.

Upon his first exposure to the piece, as an incorrigibly wriggly ten-year-old, he became speechless with passionate adoration. On that occasion the Mahler had been attacked by the swashbuckling Bromley Symphony Orchestra, playing for love – and the great over-arching horn calls, the answering plaints of the violins, the spiralling funeral march and the sizzling glory of the last movement fired Eddie's youthful soul like a revelation. And no subsequent performance, however listless the orchestra or pretentious the conductor, had quite managed to destroy its glory for him.

'When I die,' he once confided to Lenny, 'I want Mahler's Fifth played.'

'But we're always dismantling Mahler's Fifth,' objected Lenny, to whom the composer spoke, on the whole, rather less strongly. 'Every season – summer, winter, spring – Mahler Five, Tchaik. Six, and Beethoven Seven – not, mind you, that I object to Beethoven Seven. Oh, I admit, it's your funeral. But when I hand in my own dinner-pail, I want a memorial non-performance of Mahler's Fifth. A season, in fact, completely *sans* Mahler, a Mahler-free zone, in honour of the deceased, one L. Denver, horn-player.'

Second horns, Eddie had decided – though he did some few an injustice here – are always lacking in Soul; and he had taken the argument no further. However, this season was different; everything felt different. For the first time the Duke had observed the master's Fifth on the advance schedule with doubtful heart. For the first time he had muttered to Lenny, 'I just don't know if I'm up to it any more.' Only to hear Len, busy organising yet another emergency board meeting, snort, 'Balls. Bring the house down, won't you, same as normal.'

But Eddie hadn't forgotten Leszek's Shostakovich Tenth, the sick feeling of grasping at something to think of, to stare at – anything to take his mind away from risking tight shivering breaths into his mouthpiece . . . Nor could he forget his upcoming hearing, the hearing at which his job would be, officially, put on the line. I can play the horn, he told himself: it was his mantra, his salvation, but his pudgy fingers felt turgid, his chest tight as armour.

'I don't feel very well,' he told Joyce that afternoon.

'I'm not surprised, considering how late you got home last night.'

'No, seriously. My chest feels funny.'

Joyce put a practised hand on his forehead. 'You're tired, Eddie. Go lie down for a while.'

'It's the Mahler tonight.'

'Oh, good. You'll enjoy that . . . I don't know where I've put that insurance form. You haven't seen it, have you?'

Eddie walked upstairs gloomily, meeting young Harold pelting down.

'Dad, I got a new football, look!'

'Great. Super.'

'D'you want to come try it out?'

Joyce: 'Harold, sweetheart, your father has a headache.'

'Not just now,' said Eddie. 'Maybe in a bit.'

He hadn't got a headache, he thought resentfully, lying on the bed and tracing imaginary patterns on the ceiling. He'd got a soul-ache. His soul was trying to burst out of his chest. He was really losing it this time . . . They'd shut him up in Colney Hatch, letting Harold see him on weekends, with his shiny new football . . . He couldn't regulate his heartbeat; there was a blockage in his lungs, a breathless sickness. He seized his mobile and called Pete.

'Pete Hegal here.'

'It's Eddie.'

'Hello, Duke. What can I do you for?'

I can play the horn, I can. I can play the horn.

'Duke? Still there?'

'Yeah.'

'Well, what is it?'

Luminous, the *Telegraph* called me. Meaning: full of light.

'Nothing.'

'Nothing? Nothing? What – you just wanted to check I was answering my telephone? Sod off, you great clod-hopping imbecile. Some people have to work for a living.'

That evening, as the orchestra tuned up, Eddie realised that his palms were sticky as blood; he felt breathy, light-headed. He glanced around, registering Angela's imperious frown over her harp, John McDaniel's perennially skewed bow-tie – and a curiously intense gaze from young Janice. His colleagues, friends, fellow sufferers – how many times had they all been assembled? Yet the survey, instead of steadying him, for some reason made him feel even breath-

356

ier. He, the Duke, famous for his breath control, celebrated for it! Why the Toadster himself had once told him—

But he realised, with a swelling panic, that he couldn't quite recall what the Toadster had told him. He felt a numbness in the ends of his fingers; his heart hammered viciously; he even worried, with a fearful hounded draining of blood, whether he might not faint. He'd never live that down; the boys would never let him live it down. True, a flautist had once swooned on stage, but at least she'd been pregnant . . . He gulped down a few more breaths, but his lungs already felt full, sickly full, as if there was no space left for breathing. Lenny glanced over at him.

'You up for this, Duke? This is your first-choice desert island disc, remember.'

Eddie tried to respond, but his cheeks were blotchy with misery, and Lenny leaned sharply over to the third horn. 'Hey! Red alert!'

Ian, a young and aspiring star, glared sourly at him over his horn. 'Oh very funny, very particularly amusing, I don't think. Of all the times to try to wind me up!'

'I said red alert!' hissed Lenny; and then, lapsing into his more accustomed style: 'Yes, Cinders, you *may* go to the ball. Reason for same being that E. Wellington has just been transformed into a pumpkin.'

Ian peered round him to see Eddie, fingers dripping sweat off his instrument, eyes staring into the rows of audience.

'Stone me,' said Ian, and then, with growing urgency, 'I never thought – I never even . . . But I never looked at the part, Len, not the first part. You know what he's like – never ill, and loves Mahler like a brother! How could anyone have imagined—'

'Well, you got two seconds to imagine it now, chum,' interrupted Lenny, seizing the Duke's part and nimbly substituting it with Ian's. Ian attempted to steady his breathing. It was happening, it was really happening: every third horn's dream/nightmare, and on Mahler's Fifth of all bleeding pieces.

He prayed: please Lord don't let me crack a note, not a big note, not on the frigging radio. Please Lord let Leszek be sympathetic. Where was that entry in the scherzo . . .

While Eddie looked stupidly at the alien horn part before him. He wanted to say: stop, I can play this, I can always play this! I can play the horn! But the words wouldn't come, nothing would come, and his fingers felt thick and immobile, gripped leaden on the valves of his horn. He looked at Lenny appeasingly, eyes dejected as a beaten dog.

'Relax,' Lenny consoled him, and no one could have told, from the laziness of his diction, that anything was amiss. 'You ain't well, sport; you ain't sprightly. You just leave the heavy breathing to this young sprout here; just for once you sit back and enjoy the ride.'

Part of Eddie heard him, and part heard no more than the faintest crackle of Lenny's deadpan tones merging with the applause, swelling sorely in his ears, that marked Leszek's entrance through the orchestra. He was partly conscious of the minute preparations of his colleagues, of Ian's breathing exercises, of Lenny's watchfulness – yet mainly he was drifting, sounds rising unevenly in his ears, some soft, too soft, and some perilously loud.

He was swimming in the Aegean and the water was pewter, ripples blinding in the sunlight and the seagulls white and grey as the rocks against the horizon. Part of him knew he was drowning, weakening, lungs full to exploding – and part knew and had forgotten to care, a wilful omission. It was more peaceful, not caring . . . He wasn't even conscious of Leszek's glare as he tried to cue him, of his startled bafflement as the first horn part blasted forth out of young Ian's instrument instead.

Between the first and second movements, Leszek shot the horns a look of unmistakable threat, but Eddie didn't notice. He was drifting on the surface of the music until suddenly, in the wild swirl of the scherzo, the Duke awoke. He swept up his horn just before the first obbligato solo, undeterred – perhaps not even noticing – that the first horn part was no longer actually before him. Eyes shut, he was being pulled dripping from the sea, and the Toadster was crinkling his weathered grin at him over the heads of the orchestra. I can play the horn, he thought, in immortal defiance.

The scalding electricity of two horns in unison – Ian's copper to Eddie's gold – startled half the orchestra. Then Ian, at a gesture from Lenny, dropped out, leaving the Duke's tone soaring on its own.

And as they listened they knew it was the kind of sound people only make a few times in a lifetime. Every uncertainty, every sorrow, lifted up in the music – because the music was the root of Eddie's sanity, his salvation buried deep in the soul of his horn. The sound rolled as richly as only a solo horn can, resounding creamy, vibrant and powerful into every corner of the hall. People said afterwards that it was like sunshine after a thunderstorm; some people said it was Eddie's perverse sense of drama rising passionate to the fore; but only Eddie knew it was a miracle, because he'd got back what he thought he'd lost forever.

Lenny switched the music back at the first opportune moment; and Eddie kept the first horn part until the symphony was over.

At the end of the finale, as Leszek urged the orchestra to its feet, Lenny observed, 'Well of all the concerts that I've ever played, that was one of them.'

But Eddie, still not of this earth, was deaf to quips. 'Was I good, Len? Was I?'

'My liege, you were epic. If you don't get a solo bow tonight – well, the audience'll lynch him, that's all. Hell, I'll lynch him myself.'

Leszek was back on stage by then, eyes blazing weirdly, acknowledging the rapturous audience.

'He looks horribly gaunt,' Felicia observed to John McDaniel. 'And what on earth was going on in the horns?'

'The horns?' echoed John. 'Was there something?'

Leszek first chose to indicate the principal oboe. Also called to their feet for solo bows were the first bassoon and the principal trumpet, while Lenny breathed, 'Do it, you bastard, do it.' Then Leszek saluted, to still more tumultuous applause, the principal flute and clarinet. 'I don't believe this,' said Ian, but Lenny's gaze never left Leszek. The conductor was indicating the remaining woodwind, the harps, then finally the rest of the brass together, horns included.

Lenny shot a glance at Eddie by his side, hands hot on his horn, face wooden with misery, and felt his blood pressure pumping skywards. Leszek was shaking hands around the front circle of string-players; he was acknowledging the double basses. His smile was a rictus; he looked ferociously ill, but Lenny was beyond noticing. Eddie's pain, Eddie's playing consumed him, and as Leszek accepted his own personal ovation, Lenny Denver made a vow. Tonight, right after the concert. Leszek would be sorry tonight.

CHAPTER 53

I prithee take thy fingers from my throat,
For, though I am not splenitive and rash,
Yet have I in me something dangerous,
Which let thy wisdom fear.

Why, what should be the fear?
I do not set my life at a pin's fee.
And for my soul, what can it do to that,
Being a thing immortal as itself?

Shakespeare

(from Pete Hegal's diaries)

The post-concert atmosphere is usually one of relief, if not actual exhilaration. After all, even if the concert went badly, at least the tension is past, and escape made possible.

In the case of Eddie's famous Mahler Fifth, however, escape was not possible. Rumours of unease started with the timpanist, who encountered the incandescent Leszek striding off the stage. In common with most timpanists, ours was temperamentally inclined to make the most of a good story, but there was enough likelihood in his tale to alert those in the know.

'Never saw him madder – mouth clamped shut,' whites of the eyes –the lot. It's the Duke – the Duke's had it, RIP, no flowers by request. That's why he missed out on a solo bow, isn't it, stands to reason.'

And those who didn't know why Eddie had been playing the third horn part for half the symphony heard the story related, secondhand, thirdhand, for Lenny was nowhere to be seen.

The circuits of the orchestra were firing – little bubbles and thrills of nerves, of foreboding, excitement, uncertainty.

Meanwhile the queue grew ever longer outside Leszek's dressing-room door – a door that stayed closed for an unprecedented length of time. It was partly the usual: would-be conductors and admirers, acquaintances and students – Lenny and myself. We all waited, in growing restlessness, while new rumours ruffled the surf all around us.

'Won't open the door . . . Whatever next? . . . A body on the other side, like a P. D. James mystery . . . Remember when he was on cocaine? . . . He's finished . . . We're finished . . . It's the dead end of Eddie Wellington.'

Strange as it was, and skittish as we all felt, it was Lenny Denver (of all people) who lost his temper. He tried the door violently, but it was locked fast. I cleared my throat.

'Maestro, excuse me, but there are people waiting to see you.'

Silence was my only answer.

Will joined us. 'Are we sure he's in there?'

'Yes.'

'Alone?'

No one seemed to know, and no one seemed to have seen Janice either. A few audience members, made uneasy by the atmosphere, took their programmes and departed. Others joined in their place, rhapsodising about the Mahler, about Leszek, even, ironically enough, about the horns. Their raptures didn't last long; with the mood of uncertainty, even crisis, affecting even the least observant. I tried the door again.

'Leszek, are you all right?'

'I wait two more seconds,' breathed Lenny, 'Two seconds, then I break down the door. I ain't waiting any longer than that.'

The door opened.

Leszek, framed in the hallway, looked ghastly. He hadn't changed his clothes, though he'd removed his tie and undone the first few buttons of his shirt. His hair seemed darker, as if he'd splashed water on it, and his face was livid, ravaged.

Lenny stepped forwards. 'The committee—'

'Save it, Lenny,' Will urged.

'The committee has just unanimously agreed to cancel Eddie Wellington's disciplinary hearing. On account of the way the Duke played, it was felt by us all that—'

'Not now,' said William, hand on Lenny's string-bean shoulder. Grimly, Lenny shook him off.

'In two words, Leszek: you lose. You ain't going to get your way. It ain't going to happen. After the Mahler there ain't one question left in the board's mind about the Duke. You'll get this in writing tomorrow, and if you don't like it, brother, you can fire the whole board – or the whole orchestra. Hell, you can fire the whole world!'

I'd never seen Lenny so exercised, his stooped body quivering with anger and sweet relief. How Eddie's troubles must have affected him, for their resolution to overflow in such a reaction now! But then I saw too what Will had already spotted, that, if Lenny had reached his own breaking point, Leszek was very near his, and, in his condition, the consequences might be incomparably more serious.

Where was Janice? I couldn't see her in the crowd, though it was fluid: players and onlookers passing and pausing, the very atmosphere sharpening. Leszek's gaze lurched ominously from Lenny to me – swept over the mob scene – and then returned to Lenny again.

'How do you dare threaten me! How do you dare to hound me from my room, to plan and to scheme against me! Out! All of you! Out, out of my sight! Oh God, but the pain in my head, Pete, the pain in my head!'

I was beside him in a moment. Behind us I heard William making a valiant effort at deceit. ('Artistic differences . . . minor dispute within the band . . . terribly overworked.') Then Will and I helped Leszek back into his dressing room and shut the door.

'Stop beating my head,' said Leszek fretfully, glaring into empty space. 'Stop beating. I'm coming. Oh Pete, my head, my head! It softens! Yes, yes, I'm coming. I'm coming, yes.'

I can hardly describe my feelings seeing my old sparring-partner brought so low. I felt sorry, impotent, humiliated, and furious at him for giving way. I could have wept for rage and sorrow, for the familiar yet unfamiliar Polish tones calling me 'Pit' like a broken child.

'Pete, play on the piano!' he commanded. 'In a moment, yes, I come, just one moment . . . Play on the piano, play!'

I don't play piano, never did, not properly. I approached it gingerly, unwilling to refuse, and just fingered a key.

'No, no, no!' he screamed, shoving me aside. 'Play!' And he crashed into some wildly Polish-sounding piece. Perhaps he was creating it as he went along, unless it was being dictated to his crazy brain. It began as some kind of folk mazurka, but then deteriorated into a slouching miasma of dissonance, of misshapen and furious rhythms. Leszek was crouched over the keys, hair splayed around his eyes, and I noticed with a frisson of horror that his fingers weren't splayed about the way they usually were (for he was a pretty poor player himself) but looked curved and expert, with a powerful spread. I raised my eyes towards Will.

'I think this is it,' I said, over the crashing of keys.

And the same look in Will's face that I recognised from Gdańsk, bleak certainty and black resolution. He straightened his shoulders, and moved towards the door.

'Will. Wait!'

He looked back towards me seriously – storing up energy, almost remote from me already – and I thought, I won't see him again.

I thought of Margot – of Isabel – of Piotr's jagged face after the *William Tell*. I longed to stop him from going, but I knew better.

'What do I tell people?' I asked, just to keep him there a moment longer.

His eyes obscurely comforted me, as if he understood all that I'd failed to say. 'As much as they can bear,' he replied, and then he was gone.

The St John's Ambulance people arrived shortly afterwards; they dragged Leszek away from the piano and injected him with sedative. This further collapse would surely doom us in the Arts Council stakes, I realised – but every other thought I had to spare was bent on Will.

CHAPTER 54

Nay, then farewell!
I have touch'd the highest point of all my greatness;
And from that full meridian of my glory,
I haste now to my setting: I shall fall
Like a bright exhalation in the evening,
And no man see me more.

Shakespeare

William left the backstage area, carrying the living cello on his back. He was prepared to meet Janice, but she was gone, or shadowed away – or somewhere else.

The sharp winter air felt refreshing on his face, a little breeze pulling his hair as lightly insistent as a woman's finger. A woman's finger, and ghosts all around.

'Lovely concert,' said a patron, recognising him. 'The Mahler was fabulous.'

William murmured polite acknowledgement; and walked on to where a saxophonist was busking on the steps to Hungerford Bridge. He was playing 'You'll never walk alone' – the contrast indescribable between the night, the unsupported melody and his human unskilfulness. Will could feel tears on his cheeks, tears no wind had spun from him. It was time, but he feared he wouldn't be strong enough. It was time, but music could still prove his undoing. He turned to the busker, making a joke of it.

'This fiver's yours if you don't play till I reach the other side.'

'Och, aye. Mek it a tenner and I willnae play all nicht.'

'A fiver.'

'D'ya care naught fer the sufferings of others?'

William mounted the steps of the scaffold. What was it Mark Twain had said? 'To have to die. It is a strange complaint from those who have had to live.' Death, after all, was the easy part, the release, letting the waters take you. Death alone entailed forgiveness – who could fail to forgive the dead? I too will be released, he thought; but still, every breath in his lungs felt precious, and each step had to be separately willed. Isabel, he thought, and the very memory softened his resolve. Pavlo, Charmaine – he braced himself again.

As he approached the middle of the bridge the cello seemed heavy as a child upon his shoulders. You can't do this, he thought – you're too bourgeois, too tender-hearted. You read the *Guardian* and vote Liberal Democrat. How can you tangle with forces powerful enough to unravel a grown man's brain? Remember Charmaine's father, the first time he played it, how he wept and played all night . . . Remember Janice, blonde hair mixed with sea-salt, the sand grains warm along her back. Remember her radiant softness, her body sweet beneath his, sweeping against the motion of the sea.

Halfway across the bridge and he could feel drumbeats in his temples, a roaring like wind in a shell. A train crossed the bridge, crowded with normal people doing normal things, laughing, eating, reading.

You could be one of them, he told himself. You could sell the cello and forget – But he could never forget, it was useless to imagine it . . . The music knows, Mr Mellor: the music can sense betrayal when it hears it. Charmaine's voice and an entire sea swelling in his ears. The river looked bleak and stark beneath him; he felt the cello tremble on his back.

He put the case down, leaning out across the water. Lights were strung along the river's curve, a few pearls lacking along each pale necklace. The water reflected them only dimly, echoes of themselves made pointillist by the waves. Piotr, always rhythmic: Has anyone ever told you that cello of yours scatters sequins like stars? And Pete: I think this is it.

Time. It was time. He knew it – still, still he delayed.

The Festival Hall, a massive tidal wave of concrete, reared over a moored pleasurecraft, alive with classic jazz and shrill laughter. Beyond, Westminster pointed her crooked witches' fingers into the sky. He heard far-off voices from the boat, ripples from the tidal water, and, farther away, the uneven surf of hissing traffic. There was no one else on the bridge and the busker had been bribed to spare his heart.

Now.

William opened the cello case. The pounding in his ears accelerated, deepening as if every vein in his head was expanding, a glow of heat like a sheen sweeping through his body. Perhaps I too will turn gold before dying, he thought, as he lifted the cello.

Its heat slashed viciously at him, strings like new-kilned steel, but he held it securely. ('And it did move, Mr Mellor, mainly at night.') A bar of pain across his temples and the deepening beating he'd been conscious of before. He remembered Leszek ('My head, Pete, my head') – Leszek's burned-out eyes and scorched-thin body. He would do it for Leszek, for Pete, for Charmaine. He was fifty-six years old; what did he matter?

Now the cello was turning, yielding to his fingers, its neck softening; he'd never seen it so vitally textured, so thrillingly alive. Colour stroked across its belly; and in his ear, the softest cradled memory of its unearthly human sound. The soul of a child, Pavlo had told them. Did he really have it in him to kill a child?

Voices rocked, the waves' hallucination: Piotr, Charmaine, Isabel. Love is an art, Maestro – like music, but harder . . . My mother died thereafter, by her own hand . . . I love you. I love you . . . You take my advice, you throw it in the river and don't look back . . . I love . . . Throw it in the river . . . Don't look back.

I'm not strong enough. Thick weakness cluttered him, sluggish blood stalling his arteries, pain prising the sides of his head apart. At the end of the bridge the traitorous sax had started up again, the fag-end of a disappointing life.

At every inch the cello resisted, those nervous wicked fingers pinching the backs of his eyes. But suddenly a stubborn perversity of courage, layered deeper than he'd ever reached, rose up and possessed him. I'll come with you if I have to, he promised in his soul. After all, it was Leszek's last chance. He had been chosen. Oh God, for love – for love, and Isabel.

In the end, he did it for them all: for Charmaine and for Leszek, for Isabel, Piotr, Margot: in the end he did it for love. The cello was seamed with a final gust of blistering terror but still William lifted it in his grim screaming hands and threw it fifty feet downwards, into the deep red heart of the river.

There was a sound like a thousand cellos roaring, a cry of a thousand broken cellos. He felt the bridge shudder and creak beneath his feet, and then, arms still shaking, he saw the Italian cello sinking, still lit with that diabolical fire: still lit gold, rust, scarlet, and a furious deep-burnished ruby red. A cello-shaped sunset through purplish water, but gradually darkening, shivering into night. Till finally the string of lights lit nothing but the lapping surface of the water; and laughter from the pleasureboat drowned out the dappling waves.

Chapter 55

Thy wit is a very bitter sweeting. It is a most sharp sauce.

There on the ground, with his own tears made drunk.

Shakespeare

David Schaedel sipped his coffee disapprovingly.

'The point is that he is quite selfish, quite purely selfish. That is the only possible reason for this behaviour.'

'You're so right,' said Adam Halloran.

'It's not as if William at his age requires such a cello. No, he requires a mere box for touring, and stumbles instead on an instrument of genius – the kind of instrument that could win international competitions, secure recording contracts, even launch a solo career! It is a crime to waste this cello on such a player.'

'I wouldn't have believed it of William.'

'You would not? Well, I am not so surprised. Between us, he has always been a little jealous of my talent. A little jealousy there has always been. Ever since I was first here – he was then leading, you may recall – he has hidden this jealousy. I do not know if I should tell you this . . .'

'You know where I stand,' said Adam fervently.

'Yes, well, on the Canadian tour last year – you may recall it – there was a swimming party.'

'I remember.'

'And on that very night Isabel invited me to her hotel room.'

'No! Did you–'

'She was begging me to make love to her, imploring me –

until William, of all the people in the world, interrupted us. Of course, I couldn't have obliged her in any case, even though she was still looking her best at that time. It is part of my code – as I tried to explain – never to do such a thing where a member of my section is involved. But William has never forgiven me for this night.'

'But it wasn't your fault, surely!'

'Exactly, my dear friend. What could I have done, more than I did? Was it my fault that she saw me in my bathing outfit? – It was my black one with silver, perhaps you might recall it.'

'You behaved like a prince,' said Adam warmly. 'Turning Isabel down! I wouldn't have thought it could be done.'

'Many people would not have managed such a thing,' David admitted. 'But William was at the time my desk-partner, and, as it happened, it was also his birthday. No, no. The thing was not possible, as I told the poor girl at the time . . . So really, the cello is practically owed to me, when you consider these facts.'

'You were terrific to William when he left, as well.'

'Naturally, I contributed to the car CD player we gave him; as well as giving him a signed photo of myself outside Carnegie Hall. Also, I never complained about my difficulties in finding someone to replace him. You, of all people, know what nervous strain this caused me. Sometimes I feel that there is no gratitude left in the world.'

'I don't blame you.'

'So I told him, "My friend," I said, "it is an uncertain world. Perhaps your wife may divorce you, and you need some money for the alimony. Perhaps, most tragically, you may even get a cancer. If you ever need to sell this cello, count on me. I will be here, ready to buy it, and at a very fair price, because money is entirely secondary, it is the sound alone which matters – " I wonder what exactly is going on over there?'

Subdued if unmistakable excitement had coalesced around Piotr at the door to the canteen. He was holding an *Evening Standard*, which he handed to Warren, before swiftly crossing to Paul Ellison.

'It's in the bag,' he told Paul, over the tumult.

('It's incredible! . . . Hang on, what was her name? I met her; stunning, she was . . . But why? Was it a boating accident? . . . Piotr, did you already know about this?')

Paul was dubious. 'What, just because some cellist drowns in the river?'

'Leszek's cellist, if you please. And they're suggesting suicide.'

'What!'

Warren read aloud, with some distaste, '"Blonde beauty drowned. Royal Sinfonia cellist discovered in the Thames."' He looked at the picture of Janice holding her cello – the melting brown eyes, the cluster of gold frosting her shoulders. Her beauty ached his senses; small surprise she'd found the orchestral world too much to bear.

'Papers'll make a meal of it,' observed Piotr. 'Top conductor's girlfriend driven to suicide, Royal Sinfonia in emotional shambles. Arts Council denies responsibility in the *Independent*. Does the music profession conspire against stable relationships? – *Guardian* health page. Does being beautiful hurt women? – forty column inches in *The Times* . . . Perhaps they'll make a mini-series out of it: conductor loses girl to ocean deep. Wheel on Inspector Morse, complete with synthesisers, violas, morose music. Transpires that Morse had a fling with her mother in his youth and might even be the father. Later on . . .'

David examined the photo with regret. 'She was not at all bad-looking, this cellist. I am sorry I never met her. I wonder why she never applied to my section? I expect she was indeed talented. To me, she has the precise look of a cello-player.'

Isabel recognised Janice instantly as the girl she'd met in the Barbican. Her heart clenched with pity: such a soft, delicate face! Every member of William's orchestra, William's cello section, would be wondering if there was anything they'd done, or omitted to do . . . She kept trying William's home on her mobile, but there was no response.

Paul asked Piotr, 'What will Zimetski do?'

'God knows. But all we've got to do at the Arts Council tomorrow is to show up and run round the track.'

'Have you told Karl?'

'Piotr,' said Susan, the orchestra manager. 'Your neighbour Mary's on the telephone.'

And Piotr's soul ominously stilled.

'Don't take it,' Paul urged. 'We have to decide—'

'I have to take it. Mary looks after my dog.'

'A dog? What do dogs matter at a time like this?'

Everything, thought Piotr, breaking into a run. Had Anton been hit by a car, lost on a walk, actually died? Had his great heart, never strong, finally broken down?

'Piotr here. Quick, what's happened?'

Mary said hesitantly, 'It's not good news, Piotr.'

'Just tell me! Was it a car?'

'No, a heart attack, and he's survived, so far. But it doesn't look good, Piotr, and if there are any decisions to be made, well, I don't want to have to make them.'

Piotr gripped the telephone. 'Are they really talking about – decisions – already?'

'I think you ought to come. I'm at the Royal Veterinary College – you know where that is. Can you come right after your concert? Just ring the bell at the entrance, they said.'

'I'll be right there.'

You can buy love; you can buy a dog. Piotr hurtled down the hall, colliding with his orchestra manager on the way.

'Five minutes,' Susan warned him.

'Tell it to the Marines. I'm off.'

'Piotr, this is a concert we're talking about!'

'You wouldn't kid me? Is the Pope coming?'

'Be serious! What do I tell Hochler?'

'Tell him I'll see him at the Arts Council tomorrow. Tell him this is that favour he owes me. Tell him I'm picking daisies by the side of the Northern Line.'

Susan said doubtfully, 'Illness? Can I say illness?'

'You can. Heart,' said Piotr, with bitter mouth.

He drove through London's backstreets with his finger on his horn, through a roulette of red lights and a galaxy of yellows. Still alive, still alive, with Wagner drowning out the apoplectic responses of other drivers. Alive, still alive, with death in his fists, hot gaze on the road. At one point he brought his hand down so crushingly on the wheel that he felt the bones shiver against his tendons. Was death so churlish as to take back his only comfort?

Of course Anton was a dog, but there was no 'only' in the case. Who welcomed him home except Anton? Who warmed him at night, soft red fur messing the duvet? Who gave him a reason to get up without a morning session? Who else (rising hope in those great tricolour eyes) imparted zany notions of springtime even in winter, inspiriting him into the country, into the fields, into the vibrant rush of sharp fresh air?

He had saved Anton, but Anton had saved him as well – from the despair and misery of losing Will. That a penalty should be exacted on so blameless an affection infuriated him. A few months, a few short months! . . . It wasn't long enough to be fair; it wasn't long enough to compensate Anton for humanity's inhumanity. It was only long enough for Piotr to have learned to miss him. You can buy love, but the price will cripple you. You can buy love, but only for a while. He wheeled up the drive of the Royal Veterinary Hospital with a shriek of rubber on asphalt.

Piotr had been to the College before, but only during normal hours, and in the normal run of events. He'd never had to ring the bell for admittance, nor had the lights switched on for him in the ghostly waiting room. The two enormous dog statues regarded him with equanimity, their hollowed-out eye sockets motionless, lifeless.

They were bringing Anton from the hospital area. At this moment, perhaps, they were waking him in his cubicle. Did the animals stay in cubicles? Did they put them on human stretchers? There seemed something obscenely anthropomorphic about it all. When they brought him to see Anton, however, the dog was in his own basket, his great autumnal head drooping.

'Is he asleep?'

'Mainly drugged,' replied the on-duty vet.

'When will you know what chance he's got?'

'Over the next few days. Then we'll have to decide whether an operation's worth the risk. Might work; you can never be sure – but the odds are against him, at his age. I have to tell you that, in fairness.'

I can relate to that, thought Piotr. The odds have been against me all my life.

'Will he recognise me?'

'Should do. I'll leave you alone for a bit.'

Piotr dropped to the floor, tenderness washing over him.

'Look, Anton. Anton, it's me, the mad Rooskie.'

The dog's eyelid flickered, the tapered elegant tail twitching faintly, auburn feathers across the floor.

'Had a spot of bother with the heart, the lads tell me, on the road to Mandalay. Where, as is pretty generally recognised, the flyin' fishes play, and the sun comes up like thunder outter China 'cross the bay . . . Geography not being Kipling's strong suit, you observe.'

Anton lifted his gaze, and Piotr's soul raved at him. Listen, stoicism's all very well in wartime, but what's needed here is a spot of pep, vim, vigour and the will to live . . . Hang in there, Anton, he urged silently. Don't give up on me. Look, I've been left. You can't teach me anything about leaving. My father left, and my brother, and then my country. My lovers always left – and even William . . . Listen, you're all I've got – you, a few memories, a few pictures on the wall. Somewhere there has to be a limit on how much loss one human soul can be allowed to stand.

And all the while the dog's eyes with a different message.

'You'll get well,' Piotr told him, cradling Anton like a child. 'You'll come through this . . . Then in the spring I'll take you out in the woods again, when the squirrels are back and the wind's creamed as soft as a vanilla milkshake. I'll take you out into the country where you can prick up your ears as if you'd never been put in a home for the souls of lost dogs . . . You just hang on till the spring. Then I'll take you back to the coast again, where I first saw you running, tail like a banner, legs darkened by saltwater. I'll take you to Derbyshire – you'd love Derbyshire, Anton – all hills and wavering rivers, and little brooks polka-dotted with shade and sunshine . . . You wait till the spring, and I'll take you to Derbyshire . . . Oh God! Even a dog deserves more of a life than this one.'

The dog's tail moved again, a feeble swish across the tiled floor. His eyes looked seriously into Piotr's; there was a message in them, but Piotr's eyes were too swimmy to read it. Suddenly a spasm shuddered him, a minor earthquake in his arms; great heart flailing helplessly under his fingers.

'Oh God,' he whispered.

'Oh God!' he roared, and heard the vet pelting back down the corridor towards them.

Aftershocks quivered Anton's lean frame; Piotr hit the dog's chest with his fist, gripping as if by sheer force of will he could free the stumbling, jarring, disoriented heart. A moment later the vet shoved his stethoscope against Anton's deep chest.

'I'm sorry,' he murmured. 'Sometimes it happens so fast.'

Piotr held the dog's head tightly against him, tears plashing the long coat, and a surging misery blistering his soul. The body was limp but still felt hot; he caressed the long extravagant fur, the soft ruffle under the chin.

The vet looked down sympathetically at the skinny little gay with a lock of hair falling into his eyes. Dogs mean a lot to single people. Dogs mean a lot to any number of people. He never got used to losing them. The death of a dog, because of their innocence, was somehow a terrible thing.

'I'm sorry,' he repeated, but the body was still warm and Piotr was still silently trying to say all the things he'd never been able to say to anyone, not even to his dog.

Funny how the owners got sometimes; he was never sure whether or not to leave them alone. Better not to distract, perhaps, better not to break the strange bond between the three of them, life, love and death bound up in the bright fluorescent silence.

I never took you to Derbyshire; I never had time. Sometimes I was too busy even to take you out; I was thinking about getting sex or manipulating someone or simply suffering. But you never complained, you never sulked, you never returned me anything but love. Not since that first moment of recognition in Battersea: yes, that one, the one I was looking for. Anton: my dog.

Some of them take it hard, too hard. It's worse when they don't cry, faces crumpling like broken balloons.

You never had much of a chance, did you? I did what I could; though it wasn't enough, not nearly enough. Anton. My dog.

Probably lonely, poor sod, but what could you do?

Limp body losing heat beneath his fingers . . . Hold on instead to that moment of recognition, of perfect certainty. Turning to the sprite at Battersea: that one, yes – the one on the end. Anton. My dog.

Three a.m. found Piotr parked near Westminster, surrounded by empty Heineken cans, drunk on his own misery. There were fourteen messages on his pager, but thirteen of them were from Paul Ellison, so he tossed it on to the back seat and wandered outside. The House of Commons reared extravagantly over the road, Oliver Cromwell implacably ominous in the orange-yellow light. Traffic swished past at intervals; a policeman paced to keep his blood warm. Piotr paused to watch, swaying slightly, and was accosted by a tramp.

'Any smallish change cluttering up your pockets, sir?'

The policeman interrupted heavily. 'Now you just move along. You just move along there.'

'Beshrew me, a poet,' said Piotr, struck. 'The world is crammed with poets. After midnight, one meets nothing else.'

Piotr wandered in the direction of St John's, Smith Square, kicking the dead leaves out from under his feet. The park was dark and empty. He leaned his head against the chill balustrade while a sharpish breeze tickled the edge of the river. For some reason he imagined lights on the water, the sound of muffled cellos and funeral drums.

He shook his head, which seemed to be rotating of its own accord. What couldn't the imagination do on a February night! Mist and rolling drums, the cry of cellos like seagulls over the water ... The Arts Council ... Leszek ... Paul Ellison.

Big Ben chimed four. Curled in a ball, head on the earth's crust, Piotr slept.

CHAPTER 56

My heart, my rising heart! But down.

Shakespeare

(from Pete Hegal's diaries)

Leszek first insisted on seeing me on the eve of the Arts Council hearing. The nurse managed to persuade him to wait until morning, but it was still early, very early by his standards, when I arrived in Maida Vale.

I hadn't been at Leszek's flat for months, but it hadn't altered much. I inspected the photos while I was waiting. There was a young and gangling Leszek with Barenboim, and a spotty adolescent Leszek with old Pablo Casals. There was Leszek seated awkwardly with his first wife, and standing rather belligerently over his second. (No sign of the third, but then, there never had been.) I recalled a superb studio shot of Janice from my last visit, but this too was missing.

Since Janice's death, Leszek had been heavily sedated: indeed, two newspapers had reported that he was never left unattended. I'd been asked more than once to confirm or deny, and had always loyally denied it; though for all I knew it might be true. Recollecting Leszek's reaction to the Mahler, it didn't seem unlikely. I also happened to know that Lenny had spent the last week redrafting our Arts Council bid to take account of the widely held view of L. Zimetski as a liability and a loser.

The nurse returned at last, looking at me rather oddly.

'He says he won't get better until he's seen you.'

I felt a strange little pull on my heart, and quipped, 'He's got me confused with someone important.'

She shook her head. 'He's not supposed to have visitors, but they made an exception. But you mustn't exhaust him.'

'I can't stay long enough to exhaust anybody,' I said, as we moved down the hallway. 'I'm due at the Arts Council this morning, deciding there how covert matters may be best disclosed, and open perils surest answered.'

The nurse, a severe-mouthed woman of fifty, looked as if she'd never heard of Shakespeare or the Arts Council both, and in the latter respect I envied her. After all, it was probably my last morning in secure employment – the Royal Sinfonia's last, inglorious hour.

'He's sedated,' she whispered, a warning. Then she opened the door.

Leszek looked tired, and he still had that raddled look, but, for all that, he was clearly well again. The grey tinge in his skin had gone; his old snap was back; there was steadiness and even humour in his multi-coloured eyes.

'Pete,' he said, and never had 'Pit' sounded so warmly reassuring. 'I have to thank you – but I do not know for what. I have been lousy – crazy – for so many weeks and months! I do not know what has been happening to me. Please. You understand, I know. You have to make me understand.'

I glanced discreetly at the nurse.

'You. Get out!' Leszek, with a flash of the old impetuosity.

'I would really rather—'

He scowled. 'Out, this moment! Out! Out! Out!'

'He'll be all right,' I said. 'I'll call you if anything happens.'

She departed; and I settled in a chair. Leszek's gaze was fixed on me; and recalling his native impatience I found myself apologising in advance.

'Remember, I don't have all the answers. I still don't know why Eddie Wellington was used, or Charmaine's father – perhaps he was used too. I don't even know what Janice really was—'

'A devil!' he interrupted.

'If Janice was a devil,' I said grimly, 'then so was your friend Mikhail.'

'Yes, yes – exactly! I saw his eyes inside hers – once, I saw them – but then it was too much; I couldn't carry it. My head felt too full to carry it, and too heavy. I cannot describe this to you, how this felt! I—'

I glanced dubiously towards the door.

'If you'll keep calm, I'll tell you what I know.'

Leszek closed his eyes. His face looked thinner, the lines dividing fastidious nose from cheek deeper than before.

So I told him – about the cello, about what I'd seen, about what Will had experienced. I told him about Charmaine, and about my correspondence with his Polish cousins. I was prepared for an outburst then; he was breathing as if he was running, sweat skidding down his forehead.

Whenever I paused, for a moment, for a second, he demanded, 'And then? And then?', with all his accustomed imperiousness. I half-expected some missile or other, but no, he lay listening, as if every ounce of concentration was buried in the tones of my voice, and not a fraction to spare.

'And then? Go on! Go on! What then?'

'We went to meet your cousin in Gdańsk. It was Pavlo who told us what we needed in order to put the pieces together. He told us about Mikhail, the trio you had with Mikhail and—'

'Go on, go on.'

'You mean, skip it?'

Leszek looked deeply at me for a moment, then frowned.

'Some things it is better not to remember. Why do you wait? Go on!'

So had the teacher and Mikhail . . . I longed to ask, but was obliged to obey.

'Your cousin told us about Mikhail's cello – the same cello that William Mellor bought here at an auction.'

'I knew it!' he whispered. 'I knew it was the same. This *Job* . . . They tried to stop me seeing but I always knew.'

'They?'

'They – she – whoever! It is the same. Why do you always keep stopping? Go on.'

'Pavlo also told us about the secret language that you had with Mikhail.'

'Children's games! Go on.'

'He told us about – about when you fell out with him. And about how Mikhail died, that as well.'

Leszek frowned. 'Perhaps there was an accident.'

'Your cousin Pavlo said it was deliberate.'

'I do not know; I was not there.'

I forgot for a second that he was ill, and must be humoured. I said in sheer irritation, 'You do know, Leszek – you must! He left so that he could come back for you. He came back to take you with him.'

Leszek closed his eyes, and for a shattering moment I berated myself: too fast, too much; we've lost him. But when he spoke I knew it was all right.

'Never – never! I will never see her again, never hear this cello storm my beat-up blood . . . Pete, I can begin my life again, this is what it feels like. I have been – how to describe this feeling? – manipulated, obsessed, warped! But now I can be again Leszek. I myself, back in control – you smile, Pete, but you should not smile. I have a temper, yes, but that is part of the temperament . . . Pete, my friend, my dear friend, I don't know how I should thank you. I abuse you, I call you German names, I throw things at your head – and yet still you go to Poland for me – still you seek to undo these things which have been done.'

Give me your hands if we be friends, And Robin shall restore amends.

'It was really Will,' I admitted. 'I'll tell him what you said. I should see him at the Arts Council this morning.'

'He will have also to come to— What! The meeting is this morning?'

'Ten o'clock this a.m.'

'And no one told me, no one faxed me, there was not one message? How did they dare – how could you not have—'

'Oh there were messages all right, but the doctors didn't want to upset you,' I said cleverly. 'I mean, as you can't be there.'

When I left, Leszek was roaring for the nurse. For the nurse and his suit and tie and for the severed head of whoever had failed to tell him that today was the day the Arts Council would decide.

Chapter 57

Brutus, I do observe you now of late:
I have not from your eyes that gentleness
And show of love as I was wont to have.
You bear too stubborn and too strange a hand
Over your friend that loves you.

These are but wild and whirling words, my lord.

Shakespeare

(from Pete Hegal's diaries)

I was late to the Arts Council, though I didn't rush. I knew that Paul Ellison, the Orchestra of London chairman, was to submit their plans and financial audit first, after which Lenny Denver would do likewise on behalf of the Royal Sinfonia. Finally, the committee would adjourn (probably for days if not weeks) before submitting their judgement to the full Council.

The council chamber was set up as if for a *Newsnight* debate. The committee sat in two rows to one side of the chairman's table and speaker's lectern, and there were perhaps sixty observers peppering the hall. Among them I spotted Karl Hochler, spruce and keen-eyed in his pinstripes, not far from Lenny, who was wearing a look of grim determination.

Meanwhile Paul Ellison – a Grade A smoothie – ploughed onward. A lot of their ideas were suspiciously akin to ours – the usual educational gambits, foreign tie-ins, and hints of spreading enlightenment to the masses. There wasn't anything especially gripping about it, but then, we hadn't come up with any clever-clog ideas either. Save Our Souls about summed it up . . . No wonder Karl Hochler had complacent little indentations around his handsome mouth.

Paul Ellison looked to be making a sound impression on the board, and I hoped that Lenny's less polished manner (and rougher-hewn grammar) wouldn't put them off. Perhaps Leszek's belated arrival might create a little stir in our favour, especially as the press had been united in implying that his conducting future lay with a CD-player in a padded cell.

Meanwhile, at the Arts Council entrance, Will met a very dishevelled Piotr.

'What have you come as, a tramp?' asked William roughly.

'Many of the world's finest spirits spend every night on the Embankment.'

'No doubt, but they're usually unemployed.'

'I fell asleep to fragments of ghostly music, and woke to find the sun conjuring pinks and sapphires out of mist and metallic water . . . Do you think I'd ever make a poet, Maestro? Remember, it's in the blood.'

'Go home, Piotr. Sleep it off.'

Piotr lurched up the steps. 'The paternal touch, so delightfully inappropriate. But then, you never specialised in appropriate emotions, did you? Get out of my way, you bastard.'

William said with sudden energy, 'Piotr. Just one moment.'

'You have our ear, petal, but step on it. Had I but worlds enough and time, about sums it up.'

'We both know what's going on in there. This isn't a duel between us; though if it was, you'd be bound to win it. Piotr, we were friends once. Can't you tell me now, before we go in, that we'll be friends again? Can't you at least shake hands before shooting?'

'We interrupt this political broadcast from the smugger-than-thou party to bring you a right ding-dong from the Arts Council.'

'Piotr, Margot's divorcing me.'

'There also seems to be a renewed crisis in the Balkans.'

William powerfully seized his shoulders. 'I'm a failure, Piotr – I'm not worth hating! My private life's a shambles; and my professional life is almost over – I tried to escape, and failed. I tried to be faithful, and failed. Everything I've touched has smashed in my hands. Is it too much to ask, before you help ruin me, that we shake hands as friends? Does the profession really come before everything? Piotr, if you ever cared about – about anything . . .'

Piotr didn't answer. Freeing himself with contemptuous panache, he lurched into the building.

But I only heard about that later on. All I knew at the time was what was happening in the hall, though that was dramatic enough too, in all conscience.

Paul Ellison had just completed his presentation. I noticed William enter as the chairman rose to ask for questions. Suddenly I heard raised voices on the other side of the door.

'I'm sorry, but there's a meeting going on.'

'Behold, my invite. Stand aside, carrion.'

'You can't go in looking like that!'

There was the sound of a scuffle, followed by Piotr's entrance, and entrance is not too theatrical a word. Piotr was wearing jeans, probably quite respectable jeans once you came to know them, but currently earth-covered and sporting a hole in one knee. His shirt was crumpled too, with dirt along the length of one side, while his hair, black and unkempt, straggled damply across his face. He looked like a street urchin out of Dickens, but his expression followed a darker rhythm.

I saw Paul Ellison whisper urgently across to the chairman, while Piotr swaggered down the aisle, swaying slightly.

'Ladies. Ladies and also gentlemen, if any. Welcome to Wonderland. Mind the gap.'

'Who is this man?' Lord Ulverston demanded, so audibly that Piotr himself answered, bowing.

'Sub-principal cellist, Orchestra of London, at your command, m'lud. Also anarchist, homosexual, and sufferer from chronic indigestion. Future career goals include becoming an aspiring poet.'

'Sit down!' snarled Paul, and I saw Karl Hochler turn to regard him with attention. Piotr put his thumbs in his armpits.

'I believe m'lud has asked for questions from the floor. Well I have a question – indeed, I have several. The question of Free Will, for example, is one that has always exercised me.'

Lord Ulverston fumed. 'This man is incapacitated. I must insist that he is removed forthwith. Has anyone a sensible question to ask Mr Ellison?'

Suddenly Piotr's face looked foxy and purposeful.

'I'm a member of Mr Ellison's orchestra – indeed, a member of Mr Ellison's board. I've got a right to ask a question. Haven't I?'

No one seemed in a mood to dispute the point, though I saw one of the committee members reach for a security phone.

Piotr sashayed up to Paul, and Paul, already stiff, looked suddenly embalmed. Hochler too – I saw Karl Hochler age about a decade before my eyes; even the creases on his neck suddenly looked pitiful to me. For myself, I admit, I felt a twinge of burgeoning hope. Awake! awake – Ring the alarum-bell! I thought. There was treachery in the ranks, but it wasn't our ranks. Piotr was cross-examining his own side.

'My compliments, Mr Ellison; I won't detain you long . . . Now, can you deny that you've made private arrangements with no fewer than four of the seven committee members present here today?'

There was a collective gasp; Piotr raised an imperious hand for silence.

'What, silent upon a peak in Darien? We await your response, however turgid . . . Very well, then, can you in fact deny that Havers here and Lionel, to name but two, have effectively been bribed? I should add that, as your ally, sidekick and go-between, I possess more than one item of pretty substantial proof.'

By then there was uproar in the chamber: noise, exclamation, excitement, consternation. Hochler alone remained motionless, a rock in a river of noise. Piotr held up his hand again, and the audience stilled as Paul Ellison licked his dry lips.

'I decline to answer the question,' he said.

'What!' This from Ulverston.

'You don't deny it?' asked Piotr keenly.

'I decline to answer the question.'

'He declines the question,' said Piotr, strutting across the stage – well, it felt like a stage. He tapped the secretary's motionless hand with an encouraging finger.

'Are you taking notes? Take notes, child, take notes! The taxpayer demands his money's-worth. The man on the podium – Ellison, his name is – declines to answer the question. Two Ls in Ellison, capital E, double L . . . And why does Mr Ellison refuse to answer the question? I'll tell you why. Mr Ellison refuses to answer the question because he is guilty as sin . . . only one N in sin. Mr Ellison, Paul of that ilk, refuses to answer the question because he knows as well as anybody that the result of this hearing has been rigged for weeks, if not months. And how does he know? Because we bleeding rigged it . . . Am I going too fast? Do tell.'

'Mr – please! Will no one remove this man?'

Piotr leaned confidingly across to His Lordship. 'Not your fault, m'lud. The best-laid plans of mice and men – do I mean mice? Very possibly not. However, if you want to know the truth, you'll have to ask Lionel about his daughter's soon-to-be-confirmed position as sponsorship assistant to the band. Or quiz Mrs F. J. P. Reinhardt about the tax avoidance dodge her accountant's worked for financing the spring series. Or – a still sounder wheeze, this – you could ask your nephew Joshua, the one whom you invited on to the Council in the first place, precisely how he afforded the Ferrari which

388

Your Lordship's honoured backside graced this very morning.'

Karl Hochler was easing discreetly towards the exit, but Piotr spotted him.

'One moment, please,' said Piotr, his eyes blazing. 'Not so fast, my little pumpernickel. Mr Ellison's guilt is shared, I should say, not only with your correspondent in the field but with Karl Hochler – the distinguished-looking gent in the subtle pinstripe. Many of you will recognise him as the buzzard brooding over the remains on the orchestra's recent CD covers. We three – the rats, they will call us, for centuries to come, in legend and in song – we beavered away to make sure that the right bird won the cockfight. But now one of the roosters is crowing off. Call it conscience, call it honour – you can even call it love – because there's a cello-player in the Royal Sinfonia—'

'Liar!' burst from Paul Ellison. And pandemonium was re-enthroned until Lord Ulverston practised his gavel swipe at the expense of the great oak table.

'Mr – you, sir! Can you substantiate these – these outrageous and unprecedented allegations?'

'Most of them,' said Piotr briefly.

'And will anyone else categorically refute, in whole or in part, these incredible . . . Is this imputed conspiracy to go completely unchallenged? Mr Hochler, surely – Mr Ellison?'

Karl Hochler smiled in a detached sort of way, but Paul Ellison merely glowered towards Piotr, who had slumped in the nearest chair. He wasn't alone in sporting an almost ashen pallor. Looking towards the committee, I fancied I could tell the clean from the unclean by the expressions on their faces.

In the midst of the uproar, Lord Ulverston collected his committee members to one side, and there were expostulations, interruptions, and infuriated disputes. Lionel Swithyns looked to be attempting self-justification, through which an elderly committee member was certainly ticking him off. I caught splashes of dialogue: '. . . man dressed like a tramp . . .

disrepute and dishonour . . . pathetic string of lies!' His Lordship seemed to be putting a very earnest argument to them all, before stumping back to his chair.

Lord Ulverston banged his gavel again, with a good deal of unnecessary force. In mitigation of which it could only be pleaded that he had been tried very high, and that none of the great (or for that matter the good) would be over-enthusiastic about having their bounden duty whipped out from under their feet by an anarchist in an unwashed shirt.

'Your attention, please! Ladies and gentlemen! Gentlemen! I must insist upon being heard! . . . Thank you. After the disgraceful episode we have just witnessed, and the still more disgraceful events which *appear* to have preceded it, I provisionally declare the following. That the Orchestra of London – under its principal conductor Karl Hochler – should be disbanded after the end of next year, and the Royal Sinfonia presented with such assets as it still possesses. I condition that the members of the committee should remain after the members of the public have departed, but declare the meeting otherwise adjourned pending publication of the committee's findings. Good day!'

The meeting didn't conclude so much as disintegrate. Paul Ellison was passionately querying the legality of the judgement, while most of the committee rejoined their acrimonious dispute. In the audience, I saw Eddie pounding Lenny's back until he choked like a string-bean in pain. As Hochler strategically exited stage left, Angela flew up and kissed me.

'It's only provisional,' I warned her.

'I was so sure we'd lost – oh, I can't believe it! It's too good to be true!'

I thought of Leszek, at that moment probably charging towards us in a taxi. I was glad for Leszek, glad for my bank manager, glad for all of us. But it wasn't happiness on the rocks, it was mixed up with all kinds of flavours. Wishing to avoid having my back battered by an exultant Eddie in my turn, I crossed to the solitary figure slumped in his chair – to

Perry Mason, Judas, Philby. I touched his shoulder and Piotr unscrewed an eyelid and peered up at me.

'Why?' I asked. 'Was it really all because of William?'

I heard a commotion; and glanced over to see that Paul Ellison had knocked somebody down. Piotr didn't even look up. Instead he closed his eyes again, speaking dreamily. We were an oasis of quiet in that manic, jubilant, confused and combustible crowd.

'It started with Anton. He died last night.'

'I'm sorry,' I said, at a loss.

'So I drank a bit and drove round a bit and then I walked along the Embankment. I thought about Anton, and what he'd meant, and about William and about everything that happened last year. I thought about Isabel and how stupidly I'd hated her – and about all the grimy, sordid little deals I'd helped to manoeuvre in order to get back at William. There was music somewhere, but I couldn't place it – a strange, broken-up music, as if a cello was singing under the earth.'

'Music,' I repeated.

'I thought it was music . . . In the end I fell asleep by the river. I woke just as dawn was fingering the horizon, neck aching, earth like a slab of ice against my side, but I wouldn't have missed it for anything. You only get a dawn like that once in a lifetime: the winter sun unpeeling shades of translucent violet over the water, buildings unfurling out of a creamy Venetian sky. I can't describe the beauty of it, nor the feeling it gave me – I can't describe the queer, sharp lightness in the air, like the promise of something beautiful . . .

'And as I watched I felt calmness steal over me. You'll think it was the drink, but it wasn't, really it wasn't. It was as if a great weight of anger had been lifted from me, as if I could see the world clearly for the very first time. It was easy then; all I had to do was stay upright long enough to ask the question . . . One question, and you're unemployed; one question, and you're history . . .' He closed his eyes again, as if the light pained them.

'Piotr.'

The voice, of course, was William's.

'You heard my answer,' said Piotr austerely, but his tone had indescribably softened.

'I'm taking you home.'

'He gets these delusions,' said Piotr to me, a last effort at a casual tone. 'Sometimes he thinks he's my mother, and sometimes an Irish setter with great golden eyes . . .' Then suddenly he was crying on Will's shoulder, and the look on Will's face made me suddenly realise – everything. I left them there, wondering what Will's question had been.

The rest was clear enough: the strange lightness in the air, the splintered music, the redeeming spirit which overtook Piotr by the side of the water. What curious chance had taken him to the riverside on that night of all nights! Though who's to say that he wouldn't have scuppered the meeting regardless? I thought: you can scheme as much as you like, but you simply can't budget for love . . . Which was a strange enough realisation to have as Paul Ellison was escorted out by a couple of security guards, and our side gave a fagged-looking Leszek three ragged cheers.

CHAPTER 58

Adieu, adieu, adieu. Remember me.
Shakespeare

Edwin appeared at the door one Sunday evening, fluttering Olivia with expectancy. She hurried in to where Hilda was taking tea, saying, 'Terribly sorry, Hilda, but I'm afraid you must trot along . . . It's Edwin. He's parking round the back – and of course he's really come to see Margot.'

Hilda raised her eyebrows; but Margot intervened.

'Don't go – please. There's nothing particular in this. He's Mother's friend as much as anyone's.'

Meanwhile, it had occurred to Olivia that Hilda might prove useful, though it never seemed likely. Her presence might even create an excuse to leave Margot alone with Edwin. One never knew.

'Very well, Hilda, stay if you must – but please be alert. You know how obtuse you can be. If I give you just the slightest hint, such as, "Dear me, it's getting a bit late," I shall expect you to be off forthwith.'

Margot was in her bathroom, powdering her small and, she considered, very insignificant nose. There was a mournful slope to her eyes which she was at a loss to understand; while her pallor could be described at best as intriguing, at worst as unwell. Contemptuous of her own nervousness, she reached for a previously discarded, rather garish lipstick. It made her mouth look livid, and her skin greenish; she hastily rubbed it off again.

There was something irretrievably ordinary-looking about

her: sweet-faced without beauty, clever-looking without distinction. She didn't look the sort to carry off divorce gracefully; and she tried to remember why she had ever made up her mind to the business . . . It was typical of her current formlessness that last week seemed half a lifetime ago, and her decision little more than a gesture of petulance. Perhaps she had done it simply in order to score off William.

Thoroughly dissatisfied with herself, she wheeled back into the sitting room, where Edwin rose courteously to greet her. Had his hair really darkened in the last ten days, or was it only imagination, a trick of the light?

'Margot. You look wonderful.'

Olivia nudged Hilda meaningly.

'Yes? What is it, Olivia?'

'You were just saying, weren't you, how artistic Margot's patterns were.'

'I was,' said Hilda loftily, trying to discern whether a mention of Margot's knitting patterns might rank as a Hint. 'Margot's got tremendous flair.'

'I hope you've been well?' Edwin asked Margot. 'There's been some very bitter weather.'

Eyes for no one else, thought Olivia, with a stir of triumph. William Mellor would soon realise – if, indeed, he hadn't already – exactly how his treatment of Margot had rebounded against him. In Olivia's mind, Margot was already reigning over a Brussels reception, unobtrusively directing her butler while foreign dignitaries queued to bow over her hand.

What luck that she'd brought them together! And how unusual it was for a man – to put it bluntly – to give brains and character preference over youth and beauty! It was true, of course, that Margot couldn't really be *said* to have much character, but sadly few men could handle a really strong woman. And it wasn't every woman who would have taken the firm line Margot had with William. You had to give her credit, for who'd have supposed that someone like Edwin would have taken such an interest in her?

Hilda, meanwhile, had launched into the subject of farm subsidy. Olivia trusted that Edwin would make allowances for near-total ignorance, for Hilda had never really troubled herself to profit from her friends' expertise.

'If the French only realised—'

Olivia remarked, 'Well, I've never had much opinion of the French, not since they rolled over and played dead in World War II.'

'Really, Olivia! I don't think one can *quite* say—'

'Of course, I was a mere child at the time, but my mother remembers my being quite annoyed about it. "It's all up to us, Mummy," I observed – though of course the Americans did *deign* to join us eventually . . . Still, if you want a decent job done, you've got to do it yourself, as I said to our gardener only yesterday . . . Now Hilda, weren't you going to show me your snaps of Tenerife? Let's pop into the kitchen – the light's better – and I must just check something in the oven.'

Hilda had never even been to Tenerife, and the enormity of the lie rather shocked her. It was in North Africa, she believed – or was it an island?

'Hilda dear!' called Olivia implacably from the kitchen.

Hilda retrieved her bag from under Edwin's feet and made her way to the kitchen.

'There! Now I must admit that you took that particular little hint very adroitly. Let's just have a pleasant chat in here for a while. Only fair, isn't it, to give him every chance.'

Meanwhile, Margot had resumed her knitting. Edwin looked around conspiratorially.

'Have they left the coast clear?'

'Clear? They practically used semaphore.'

'But for how long, do you suppose? Let's slip into the conservatory.'

It was a chilly February night, but Margot made no objection. Inevitability owned her, almost as much as the night she'd spoken to William. And, though she'd never until that moment really believed Edwin to be serious, she suddenly felt quite sure that he meant to propose. She pushed her hair back, nervous as a girl, almost giddy with it. Edwin Narbold – possibly her second husband. Divorce would take a while, of course, but then . . . Well, she would hear him out. It might solve so many problems. If she was abroad, she would escape a good deal. Nothing that William did – even if they actually married – would hurt her quite so terribly.

'Is it too chilly for you?' asked Edwin.

'No, not at all.'

Edwin sat down close beside her.

'I'm sure you've guessed why I came today, Margot. You must know that I go back to Brussels next week.'

She couldn't frame an adequate response.

'Your mother called to tell me that you've finally made up your mind to the divorce. I can only say I'm thankful.'

How typical it was of Olivia to leave nothing to chance!

Edwin continued, 'Yes, I must say that I'm thankful. William has behaved abominably. Bad enough to betray you with this other woman – cheap nights in foreign hotel beds – but really, to return to her again directly afterwards! And I'm very sure that, if you ever did return to him, you would only suffer more humiliation and misery. You'll feel much more secure once you're divorced, Margot. You'll be your own person, as I hoped you might be, because . . .'

Margot fingered the arm-rests on her wheelchair, steeling herself for the second proposal of her life. She was neither young nor beautiful, but someone valued her. It shocked her to realise just how much that assurance could mean.

'Margot, almost since I met you, I've wanted to marry you. Your other-worldly look enraptured me; I could hardly concentrate for thinking about you. And when I did get to know you, I simply couldn't believe my luck. I'd always hoped to find someone with a mind above petty politics, and I'd frankly begun to feel I never would . . . And also, we get on so well, and always have.'

'Yes. We do get on well.'

'Though I have other reasons too, reasons beyond . . . Margot, I want to be perfectly open, perfectly frank with you. I'm an ambitious man, and I worry – that is, I have worried in the past – that my homosexual leanings might some day jeopardise my career . . . Not that anything ever happens, you understand, but it would certainly be better if I was married. I know that you must have sensed—'

'I'm sorry,' interrupted Margot, her head whirling. 'I'm sorry, but you're quite wrong. I never imagined. I never thought . . .'

'Really? With your marvellous intuition? That does surprise me! However, as I said, absolutely nothing – nothing physical – has ever happened between myself and another man. I would never – could never – express myself in that way. Aside from anything else, it's still far too politically dangerous even to contemplate . . . And that's one of the reasons why I want to marry, why I need to marry. Someone intelligent, humane, someone unable – someone who doesn't feel cheated by not having sex. An Englishwoman in the best possible sense of the word, someone I could completely confide in . . . No, please, just let me finish! Margot, you know how much I admire you and esteem you – your character, your sense of humour, your sensitivity. I know it will take some little while for your divorce to come through – and even, perhaps, for you to feel ready – but time makes no material difference. Promise to marry me, Margot, and I will make you the honoured and cherished wife that you've always deserved to be.'

'Never!' she exclaimed. Edwin lifted his eyes, taken aback.

'I'm sorry. I – I don't understand.'

'I could never marry you. Ever. It would be unbearable, impossible!'

'Why? What's impossible about it?'

'Let me make it clearer. A marriage of convenience—'

'Margot! My dear —'

'But that's all it would be, by your own admission!

Convenience and pretence – the politics of matrimony! Don't you see how horrible it would be!'

She visualised all too clearly the emptiness of being his consort – the exquisite, breakable flat in Brussels, the endless entertaining, the restless diplomacy – and the long nights on her own. She would be condescended to by politicians and hangers-on; she would be irritated by their complacency at having encouraged her. ('Not her fault – MS, you know, a shocking case, and they say her first husband behaved abysmally as well . . .') Was she to be manipulated into so 'suitable' an arrangement, just in order to satisfy Olivia's ambitions, to smooth Edwin's career path, and to ease what might remain of William's conscience? Did her own life really mean so little – to her, to everyone?

'I'd thought . . .' Edwin began lamely, and paused.

'You thought I was so accustomed to being used I wouldn't notice. Though I expect it was my fault. I probably encouraged you to imagine – and besides, I enjoyed your company. You made me feel . . .' She longed to say human, but she couldn't. He'd made her feel human once, but now she felt like a vote-winner. Meet my wife Margot, frightfully brave, endearingly unthreatening. The wife? Oh, a real little trooper, never complains, keeps the homefires burning. My wife – bless her – my wife is my strong right hand.

'Should I have lied about my sexuality?' he asked bitterly.

'No. No, of course not.'

'And is it so reprehensible – under the circumstances – to look first for a companion? Or such an insult to be perceived as such?'

She cried out, 'How can I make you understand?'

'Margot, I wouldn't feel so alone with you to come back to, to talk to in the evenings. You don't know what it feels like, living in Brussels on your own.'

'I do understand what loneliness is.'

He took her hand; but some traitorous memory reminded her of William's warmer hand, his silent proposal, fingers trickling along the line of her palm – nerves rushing the length of her back.

'At least think about it,' Edwin urged her. 'Don't give me your answer tonight.'

'Oh, but I have to – Indeed, I must. I can't bear to imagine you back in Brussels wondering whether – Edwin, I'm not proud, but I have enough self-respect to hope to be more than merely useful, an asset on a balance sheet. I was loved once, you see. I do know what it feels like.' Traitorous tears rushed towards her eyes; she blinked them away.

Edwin rose stiffly. 'Then there's nothing more to say – except that I trust you'll have no cause to regret such a sudden and, if I may say so, emotional decision. When I think of this house, your mother, your husband, and what I could have taken you to — Well! Never mind.'

It would look that way, she realised, not just to Edwin but to almost everyone. ('Margot? Well, my dear, it's hard to believe, but she actually rejected that delightful Mr Narbold . . . Oh, wild about her – but no, she sent him packing. No, nobody quite *knows* why . . . A lovely Northerner, so warm and, well, *masculine*, the way so few men are these days . . . What? Nothing to object *to*, was there? Money, position, respect—')

A buoyant Olivia met them at the conservatory door.

'Hilda had to go, such a shame. I expect you're ready for another finger of whisky, Edwin.'

'Edwin's just leaving,' said Margot, and watched Olivia's face fall like an inept soufflé.

'Leaving! But I—'

Edwin, forcibly jovial: 'Meetings all day tomorrow, I'm afraid. Shoulder to the wheel for the country's weal, eh? Lovely to see you, Olivia, as always.'

'But – Edwin!'

'And thank you again for your tremendous support in the election.' He closed his hands over hers. 'You were marvellous. Good night, Margot.'

Margot's response sounded lost and little-girlish in her ear: good night. It might as well have been goodbye, because she knew that she would never see him again. Olivia followed him to the door, then bustled back.

'Well! He left in a rush, I must say. I trust he had no reason to be annoyed at you, Margot?'

'No.'

'I've never known him leave in quite such a – discomfited sort of way. Really, it was as if someone had positively trodden on his feelings. I trust he didn't think that Hilda slighted him, leaving you together as we did. I was hoping – well, never mind. There'll certainly be another time; and he finished his whisky, at any rate. I'm glad I got the Glenlivet in, for I overheard him telling the Group Captain it was the best sort, and I believe he's got a Scottish grandmother on his mother's side.'

Margot felt as low as she'd used to when sitting out a teenage dance. I wasn't rejected, she reminded herself, but without any conviction, for she suddenly felt such an utter failure . . . But now, too, William would know that she meant to divorce him, and his silence implied an acceptance too tranquil to bear.

On impulse she pushed her chair out into the garden; it cost her an effort with the soil so damp, but adrenalin lent her strength to overcome the trembling in her hands. She wheeled herself to the far end of the garden, to where Olivia's 'Margot' shrilled through the night like a message from abroad. There she breathed escape like a runner, watching her quick breaths falter on the air.

CHAPTER 59

So holy and so perfect is my love
And I in such a poverty of grace,
That I shall think it a most plenteous crop
To glean the broken ears after the man
That the main harvest reaps: loose now and then
A scattered smile, and that I'll live upon.

Shakespeare

(from Isabel's diaries)

It was a mad scene. One moment Paul's poised, rather pedantic presentation – the next, sheer lunacy. I'll never forget Piotr's face, his tone. He'd never looked so Russian before, so shockingly alien to me. I tend to forget that he's Russian; that he has two poets for parents, an ancestral excuse for craziness. His entrance, dusty and dishevelled, his voice, first drawling then crackling with cruelty — It was a play, an improvised play, because never for a second did he let us forget that it was unscripted: a highwire act without benefit of safety-net.

The contrast between Piotr and Lord Ulverston, was also memorable. The one cadaverous, taut, impatient as a violin string; the other stolid, ponderous, incurably bourgeois. And Karl's face in the doorway, turning – that lip-curling disdain, almost as if he'd predicted it all along, and was content with observation.

That was the moment I remember: Piotr taunting Paul Ellison, Karl suave in the doorway . . . I wanted to remind Paul: I told you he wasn't to be trusted. I longed to tell Karl:

you never looked sexier than framed in that doorway, eyebrows tilted in the faintest, jauntiest surprise . . . But most of all I yearned to tell Piotr that I was with him. Oh, I knew he was destroying our orchestra and my job, but there was such a rough grandeur about him – such carelessness about his own fate – that it enraptured and even aroused me.

God knows what had happened the previous night – but Piotr, alone of all my acquaintance, becomes still keener-edged when drunk. I've never seen him more sure, more thoroughly himself, than curvetting down that gangway, seizing the meeting by the scruff of its neck and tossing it into history.

Because of William. Because he is – and always has been – in love with William. So much so that he would rather see William's orchestra saved than his own, even though he's twenty years William's junior. 'You heard my answer,' he told him afterwards, and I wondered what the question had been, wondered as I saw William embracing him, so like a father with an errant son. The answer: I love you, in spite of everything. Forgive me my love, my hopelessness. Until I could bear it no more and ran away, the cold wind braced against my chin all the way down Piccadilly.

'Hello there,' said a black athlete in the Underground, and I walked a little straighter thinking: I'm still attractive, I'm not old. After all, I'm the one William chose in the first place – though I knew that in truth I chose him, and that it's only a matter of time before he tells me exactly what he has before . . . He's too old, I'm too beautiful, I need children, Margot needs him.

Because that's the secret, what it always comes down to in the end: who needs him. Which is why even his most selfish gestures are secret acts of sorrow and pity, why he took me in the first place and why he came back, not stopping for flowers — Which is why he is William, after all – William with his final, fatal weakness of heart.

'You all right?' a young girl asks; and I realise that I'm not; that somewhere between Charing Cross and Embankment my heart's burst open, drowning me. Suddenly I'm in tears, sinking against a shop window. A crowd of people gather around; someone puts a Valium beneath my tongue. I recognise the melting chalk taste and swallow it, though my mouth's gone cavernous and dry. The pavement's grime-encrusted; the smell of stale urine competes with Indian spices; someone puts a man's rain-jacket over my shoulders. I feel a hand cool on my forehead and sink with the pleasure of it. I long to sink down into the earth, deeper and deeper until the earth takes me.

When I came to, I was being helped into a taxi, and someone was half-lifting me, not William. That was how it first struck me, as a negative, for I reached out and felt another hand, not his. Not warm enough, not powerful enough – all tendons and bones.

'Warren,' I said, without looking, because Warren was always there in the worst times. When I'm well he's ghostly, distanced, never imposing himself, but when I'm at rock bottom I can almost feel his lean, tensile arms supporting me. He must have followed me from the Arts Council; it was his jacket lying across my shoulders.

'Feeling better?'

'I don't know. I think so. How am I supposed to feel?'

'Better. It's over, after all.'

I remembered then that it was indeed over, that we'd failed. Failed thanks to Piotr, who could never quite be trusted not to do the noble thing . . . I felt suddenly awake, shocked by possibilities.

'We're out of work,' I said, in disbelief. 'The orchestra's finished.'

'Not definitely.'

'What could possibly rescue it now?'

'The decision was only provisional, Isabel. And, even if it sticks, something might still turn up.'

It was unlike Warren to be so positive. There was a sureness about him, a serene security. He wasn't saying it simply to calm me; he believed it; and because he believed it, I could believe it too. After all, orchestras don't often die. Instead they merge, lose ground, alter purpose, change direction. Some orchestras have lived on death row for decades.

He was silent, and I remembered William's face with Piotr weeping on his shoulder. He's beaten me, I realised. It was always an unacknowledged struggle between us, a tussle for William's soul. I'd dragged him down, but Piotr saved him; I'd lost, and Piotr had won.

'Piotr,' I said.

Warren didn't answer, but his eyes were sympathetic.

'I thought he'd win, but not – that way. I never imagined that.'

'No. Though I've never seen Piotr more in character.'

'Do you think he'd planned it all along?'

Warren hesitated. 'You know, I really don't think he had. I think something happened – something jolted him – and the rest was nothing more than his intuitive flair for drama. Piotr never was a sub-principal cellist, not really. He's always had the instincts of a minor and rather terrible Hindu god.'

'But it was only a matter of time before William—'

'William was also in character,' he put in, mainly in order to spare me. He knew that the Arts Council – even Piotr – had only accelerated the end for us, and that this time there was no going back. Once William had tried to end it, twice he had attempted escape, only to return in spite of himself. But this was the end. He was through, through with tormenting his conscience and divvying up his heart, through with giving in to my needs – or even to what passed for his own.

I remembered all he'd confessed about the haunted cello – the effort that business had cost him. Yet, even as he told me, I knew that it still mattered less than his guilt. Guilt about Margot, his mother, his son, his grand-daughter. Guilt, from the beginning, quietly grinding us down.

'I ask too much,' I said, staring hotly out of the taxi window.

'Of William, of course. Always.'

'Not just William – of everyone! Nobody could have given more than he did.'

'William, being William, could have given no less. Though you must have known that at some point he would — But you don't seem to want stability, Isabel. Or else there's something inside you that needs the uncertainty of passion and drama more.'

I hardly heard him. William had once told me, 'The tragedy of your life is that you turned down Warren Wilson.' We'd had a minorish affair in our twenties; later I'd refused to marry him, that was all . . . But it had never so struck me before. Warren, married to my desk-partner, and father to Caroline's child – narrow-faced, poetic, intensely sensitive Warren . . . That Warren could ever have been my salvation still seemed impossible to imagine. No, my salvation was William, and he was leaving me, this time for good.

'I only ever wanted William,' I said impulsively, and burst into childish tears. Though I knew, even as I said it, that it wasn't true. Something inside me, some secret emptiness, courts everyone's approval, even adoration. It's true that William mattered the most, but I needed even more than William . . . In that moment I could imagine all too easily the years that stretched ahead: the men I would, in fatalistic mood, allow to take me at midnight – and the eerie barren feel of the silent mornings after.

Warren put his arms around me and I heard William's voice inside my head. The tragedy of your life . . . but William was wrong – falsely modest, or self-deceived. I knew that the tragedy of my life was unfolding around me, and that its name was William.

CHAPTER 60

> 'Tis one of these
> odd tricks which sorrow shoots
> out of the mind.
>
> *Shakespeare*

(from Pavlo Zimecki to Pete Hegal)

My dear Pete,
I take pen in hand to declare myself most relieved and pleased to hear from you. To know that my poor information was of use is very grateful to me, as you imagine. My crazy cousin writes with too many kindnesses, so let us hope there are no more ghosts! (True story, ha!) It was most interesting to meet you despite these circumstances, and, if ever you come again to Gdańsk, please to contact me once more. With great pleasure, yours very sincerely,
    Pavlo Zimecki

'Karl?'

'Lucy! Where are you now?'

'Still in London, I'm afraid. Karl, I can't come after all.'

'No? And why is that?'

'The Arts Council disaster. It's – well, it's all getting a bit fraught.'

'Is it? But I have been informed that this former sponsor of yours – this Mrs Palmers – is implementing a scheme to save the orchestra.'

'She's certainly trying. Did you never meet her? She used to be Elinor Jay. She was the heiress who almost married David Schaedel a couple of years ago.'

'Indeed? And will she not be successful in this scheme?'

'Nobody knows. We were sure it was over, but now she's come forward, anything could happen.'

'And Piotr? Where is he?'

'Taken leave of absence, but really—'

'And Paul Ellison?'

'Paul's acting general manager. Though, I have to say, there's still a lot of feeling in the orchestra against Piotr – and against Paul and you as well.'

'Naturally,' said Karl, and she could almost imagine him shaking his head. 'The situation is most piquant. That scene at the Arts Council! I would not have missed this for any consideration.'

'It's not that I blame you, Karl, though some people do. I simply don't think we ought to risk a meeting, especially now. Everything depends on Elinor, you see, and she always was rather prudish.'

'Of course,' said Karl lightly. 'And Isabel? How is she?'

'Isabel's falling apart, just as usual . . . Karl, what are you going to do?'

'Well, it is not yet resolved, you understand. However, assuming that my contract can be terminated, I'll probably be going to a chamber orchestra in Rome. I think, between us, I would rather enjoy Rome. There is something about Italy that has always appealed to me.'

'Rome! How marvellous!'

'I have often worked with this orchestra before; and something might very soon transpire. It is all quite secret at the moment, however.'

'I won't tell a soul.'

'Perhaps then you might come to visit me in Rome.'

'That would be magical.'

'This may work out . . . We will have to see.'

'Call me.'

'I will indeed. We will meet again, of this I am sure.'

Karl put the phone down, frowning. A boring creature, this Lucy, though quite clever in bed. Really, it was as well that it was over . . . He ran his hand down the French girl's flank, as she moved drowsily towards him, curling her slender hand around his shoulder.

'He's completely altered,' said Angela. 'Yesterday I actually heard him apologising to Pete. "Pit," he said, "I am sorry about yesterday. I had a most lousy headache." I've rarely seen Pete look so taken aback. Ever since that business with Janice, he's become somehow – kinder, softer-edged. I think she meant much more to him than we ever imagined.'

'In a way, perhaps she did,' said William.

'And Eddie – you wouldn't credit the improvement in Leszek's attitude towards Eddie. You weren't there, but Eddie simply blasted his solo in the Tchaikovsky. I thought, oh Lord, here we go, but Leszek just shook his head and smiled. "You must take *my* beat, Mr Wellington. If you had the stick and I the horn, it might perhaps be otherwise . . ."'

'I thought the Duke was looking pretty pleased with life.'

'I sometimes think he's a – touchstone for the orchestra. When the Duke's all right, we're all right generally.'

They were both silent, until Angela spoke again.

'William, there's something I've been wanting to say to you – an apology I want to make.'

William roused himself. 'An apology? Whatever for?'

'The note that Isabel gave me.'

'Don't worry about it, please. You meant well, I know. I even told Isabel you did.'

'I was so jealous, that was the reason. When she came flying up the steps, she looked so—'

'It's all in the past, Angela.'

'And I embarrassed you in Greece as well. I had some crazy idea that you and Janice – but it was all imagination. There never was anything between you, was there?'

'Not the way you mean,' said William quietly, remembering the night on the beach, the waves' pulsing signals, come, come.

'What worries me is that, all year, I was just one more

408

burden for you to carry. Instead of being content with your friendship—'

'You were never a burden, Angela. In a few months' time, you'll be amazed that you ever felt – anything for me. And besides, it was my fault too.'

And they both recalled, with a quickening of the blood, that night in Spain. Emboldened, she asked, 'What about you? Have you made any decisions?'

'Not yet. I know – I can feel – that this is a pivot point. As if everything in the last few years has been leading irrevocably towards this moment. To stay in the orchestra or retire, to break with Isabel or to endure a divorce . . . I sometimes think it would have been easier, that night on the bridge, if—'

William recalled with a shock to whom he was speaking. He could hardly blame her for wondering, especially with Janice's death so very recent. He finished his drink swiftly. 'Sorry. Didn't mean to bore you.'

'You haven't bored me.'

'I ought to be going, in any case.'

He left with unusual abruptness. She watched him making his way through the crowd, pulling his black coat over his shoulders. The pivot point. What if he . . . but that must surely be impossible.

A new recruit to the percussion section spotted Angela on her own, and took his chance.

'You're Angela, aren't you? I don't think we've met yet. My name's Colin.'

Angela roused herself to civility with an effort. A new colleague always mattered, whatever the circumstances.

'Congratulations on getting the job.'

'Thanks. Can I get you another drink?'

She was a pale, attractive girl, with a wistful face and very unusual auburn hair. He wondered why she'd been bothering with the older fellow.

Angela shook her head clear, and gave him a little smile.

'I'd like that. A dry white wine, please.'

Chapter 61

To me, fair friend, you never can be old,
For as you were when first your eye I eye'd
Such seems your beauty still.

Shakespeare

William left the pub and immediately hailed a taxi. He longed to be somewhere fresh, somewhere where he could think, away from the ferment of London Bridge during rush-hour, the swirling tide of commuter traffic.

'Where to?' asked the driver, pushing back the glass.

'The Embankment, thanks.'

People, hundreds of people, crossing Hungerford Bridge. Women protectively clutching their bags, men striding swiftly, aggressively insecure . . . People: hundreds, thousands of them, old and young, sprinting for their train, late for their appointment, lacking time to breathe, to think, to watch the patterns of the clouds changing over the water.

William wandered past Cleopatra's Needle, admiring its sharp clear lines. How strange it was that Piotr should have been by the river on that night of all nights, Piotr with his streak of heroism, his theatrical lack of inhibition! He watched the shades of water soften as the light faded: metallic rose, silver-blue, pewter.

William leaned over the edge of the water. The pivot point. He had decisions to make, promises to keep . . . But first he had to loosen the grip of the present and the past, to force himself to be sure and logical, the way he'd used to be. He had to convince Margot to take him back – and convince Isabel to let him go. Or else he had to give Margot her divorce and make some kind of commitment to Isabel. That would be the easier path: it had been Margot's own proposal, and Isabel might to some extent be expecting it . . .

He imagined Isabel in his home in Ealing – the heady sensation of coming home to Isabel. He tried to imagine holidays together, the embarrassing if subtly gratifying reactions of strangers to the relationship. They'd been taken for father and daughter more than once already, and that would only happen more often as time went by . . .

Beyond that, there was his family. Could he bear only to learn about Margot's ever-fluctuating condition from a tight-lipped Sam? And what of his mother's misery and disappointment? Her pride in him would be irreparably shaken, and Margot's previous behaviour made all too explicable . . . In his head he could hear the tones of Piotr's contempt, the mockery of his colleagues, even the bewilderment of his little grandchild.

Though other people shouldn't matter, or not so much. It was Isabel who mattered, after all. Isabel, still so youthful, so beautiful – and so passionately vulnerable! Living with Isabel's insecurity, the overtness of her emotionalism, would never be easy. Besides, Isabel would become bored with him. The sexual side would surely taper off; she would surely begin to long for someone younger and more dashing . . . Although might he not be her last best hope for stability? Who was he to deny her that, loving her so much – and pitying her so deeply?

The sun was dispersing, the stream of human traffic just beginning to thin over Hungerford Bridge. Street-lights filtered tangy against the water; while the still-lit windows of office buildings took on a more certain brilliance.

Then there was Margot. Surely it wasn't arrogant to doubt her desire for divorce. Margot had altered since returning to Olivia's. She had reached inward, finding a still-surer strength he'd never supposed her to possess. So unlike Isabel, who was still searching for self-belief – Isabel, still crippled by her desperation to conquer.

No, Margot had offered him freedom precisely because she was complete within herself. He felt perversely proud of her, proud of her resilience, her refusal to feel sorry for herself, her sure clear-sightedness. Proud of the quiet lifting of her head as if to say: I am who I am . . . Margot was someone to be peaceful with, someone to grow old with. He was in love with Isabel, and might always be – but he'd lived with Margot for decades, and she seemed too an immovable part of his soul.

Another train thudded over Hungerford Bridge. The water beneath had turned nearly black, with raucous lights spangled along both sides. There were tears in William's eyes, tears he hastily brushed away. He struggled with the memory of Isabel's dark eyes raised to his, the taste of her lips . . . So many endings! – and none of them lasting. Margot had asked, 'You would never see Isabel again?' But how could he promise? He had promised before, and always lied.

William turned irresolutely towards the Underground station, jamming his hands in his pockets.

CHAPTER 62

His life was gentle, and the elements
So mixed in him, that Nature might stand up
And say to all the world, 'This was a man!'

Break, heart; I prithee break.

Shakespeare

Hilda was taking tea at Olivia's. Margot had just left, giving Olivia just the chance she'd been angling for.

'And now Margot's gone, Hilda, I really must take issue with you. I hear that you've been going about claiming that dear Edwin was romantically involved with my Margot.'

'And?' inquired Hilda loftily. 'You may have forgotten that I was actually here the night when—'

'I can't imagine what occasion you might be referring to, but I am in a position to assure you that any such involvement would have been quite out of the question.'

'My dear Olivia, this is preposterous. I—'

'Besides, Edwin never had any feelings for Margot beyond friendship. That he was quite devoted to *me*, of course, must have been obvious to everybody, but a sequence of constant discouragement finally put paid to any hopes he might have had in *that* direction . . . I'd be most grateful if you could set the record straight on this, for all our sakes.'

For a moment, Hilda was actually too incensed to respond. The idea that Edwin Narbold could ever have been attracted to Olivia quite winded her. Luckily, Margot chose that moment to reappear, causing Hilda to choke back her riposte, at whatever cost to her internal organs.

'The doorbell's just gone, Mother.'

'I heard it,' said Olivia, rising, and only a moment later they heard her voice carrying in every dismayed detail back down the hall: 'Oh! hello. Yes, I suppose so . . . Wait just one moment.'

She hissed, 'Margot, quickly. It's William Mellor. Should I allow him in?'

William. What could William want, except . . . Margot said, very steadily, 'Please.'

Hilda leaned towards Margot. 'This, no doubt, would be—'

Then William was in the doorway, and suddenly the room seemed smaller, dowdier, almost stiflingly feminine. He brought a rush of air with him, shoulders very broad in his black coat.

'Hilda, let me introduce William Mellor,' said Olivia truculently. 'William, this is Hilda Somers, a friend of mine . . . William is a cellist in the Royal Sinfonia.'

'So I'd heard. You're owed our congratulations, I believe. *Your* orchestra seems to have been spared.'

'So far at least,' said William, reaching down to shake Hilda's hand. She was rather struck with his appearance. He was so very handsome, with that soft silver hair and those deep eyes; Hilda wondered that Olivia had never mentioned his looks before.

'Dear me!' she said. 'Margot never told me you were so strikingly – tall – a man.'

'She described you rather better,' said William gallantly. Margot felt a distaste for such charm, though at least William couldn't be accused of scouting for votes. With William it was unselfconscious grace; it was normal for William to make women feel appreciated. As Olivia hustled into the kitchen, William grasped his opportunity.

'Margot, I need to speak to you. Would you mind very much?'

Margot assented, recalling Sam's words ('He wants you

back, I know he does'). She preceded him into the conservatory, resenting the twinge of nervousness winging her stomach. Surely there ought to be an age at which one stopped caring quite so desperately? She wheeled around to face him, lifting her chin with all the courage he remembered.

'I'm listening.'

'Margot, I've decided to retire.'

She was unable to frame an adequate response, so he continued with surer energy, 'I was thinking, if you liked the notion, about moving – to Sussex, perhaps. We could sell the Ealing house and buy a cottage in one of those villages.'

'Sussex,' she repeated.

'Somewhere near woods, open fields, good walking country.'

'And an Irish setter,' she murmured. He lowered himself to the height of her wheelchair, capturing her hand. His voice was very deep, very persuasive, a darker voice than she remembered.

'Margot, you promised once to be my wife till death. Forgive me, and make me that promise again.'

She closed her eyes . . . Curving downs and local music societies, women's institutes and whist drives. Quiet afternoons in the cottage garden; William coming in with her coffee in the mornings. Leaving London, with its traffic and its fumes and all its recollections of misery . . . Leaving London, the endless year over at last. What he was offering was surrender – a straight line between the present and a modest grave with both their names on it. Yet she looked into his warm feeling face and knew she couldn't take it.

'No. No, I couldn't possibly.'

'You don't mean that,' he said, shocked.

'I do mean it . . . It's not that I don't feel grateful to you, very grateful. It's kind and generous of you – and like you to be kind and generous. But I won't have you immolated on the pyre of your own unselfishness. And I can't accept a gift that's no longer yours to give.'

William rose and strode to the window, hand to his eyes. No longer yours to give. Was she right? Had all his torments and doubts meant nothing at all?

She spoke still more softly, but still with resolution. 'You didn't intend it to end like this, I know, but it has ended all the same – and, given that, you owe it to me to accept my answer. Indeed, you owe it to us both.'

'Margot. I must just say—'

His voice suddenly dipped and Margot instinctively cried out, 'Don't! Anything but that.'

Rebuked, head bowed, he asked, 'What will you let me say?'

'That we'll stay in touch. That we'll always be close.'

'Oh God,' he expostulated.

'That it won't – degenerate into bitterness, or hurt Sam more than it must.'

'No,' he said with energy. 'Of course not.'

After more than a quarter of a century. They both felt it suddenly, the failure and the defeat. It had never hit him so surely before. It was as if he had never quite believed that the business had gone so far, though he acknowledged this partly as denial and partly as sheerest arrogance. He fought to keep his voice steady.

'I'll call you soon.'

'Goodbye,' she whispered, offering him her hand, but he was beyond touching it by then, and that word, of all words, beyond his framing . . . She closed her eyes and heard the conservatory door hiss closed behind him, like a long-sustained breath, goodbye. And she felt suddenly cold, as if the sun had slipped behind a cloud, and the wind rising.

Chapter 63

Our revels now are ended. These our actors,
As I foretold you, were all spirits and
Are melted into air, into thin air.

Shakespeare

A week later, William returned to Canterbury. In the months since his previous trip the leaves had unfurled, darkened, crumpled and fallen, the air had softened only to quicken again. However the plot still testified to the skill of Charmaine's gardener, while the dustless timelessness of the place struck him afresh as he made his way up the long drive. He had wondered if there might be a wave of malevolence from the house, but he felt nothing but peacefulness in the cool shade of evening.

He rang the bell and stood back in order to give Charmaine the chance to observe him through the glass. He recalled his last visit so strongly that he could almost imagine her voice grating ('I simply wanted to see the kind of man who's still in search of justice').

It was her Irish maid Sarie, however, who cracked the door open, Sarie who said bossily, 'If you've come on account of the turnips, Mr Wheatley, they're down the side of the house, just as usual.'

'I'm afraid I'm not Mr Wheatley.'

('A bit touched, if truth be known. But loyal. Loyalty is worth something, Mr Mellor; loyalty is the only true greatness of which human nature is capable. And mostly, of course, it isn't even capable of that.')

Sarie peered at him. 'Sure and neither you are. Come in, Doctor. Will ye be wanting soda bread? I've set some out fresh in the pantry.'

'No, thank you,' said William, with a smile. 'Is Miss McKinley in?'

'Aye, so she is, with her flowers.'

'What, in the back garden? It's very damp.'

'No, she doesn't do the garden. 'Tis Timmy does the garden – though he drinks like a wee toad. The cooking sherry as well, unless I'm by.'

William glanced around in perplexity, raising his voice. 'Miss McKinley's well, I hope?'

'Passing well, Doctor, I cannot compliment ye. She's been dead and gone these three hours.'

William felt a little spurt of shock. Touched, indeed!

'Be careful, Sarie. If you say things like that people might believe you.'

'Aye, thankee, I got me pig. Yesterday it 'twas. She gave it me with her own hands and said, "Here you are, Sarie, as I promised ye. Don't ever be a bigger fool than ye can help." 'Tis in me pantry, along with the wee frog and the wee horse. Green jade from China, so it 'tis, and darker than the hills of Ireland. The wee pig brings luck. Would you like to see it?'

'I came to see Miss McKinley,' said William firmly. 'Is she in bed?'

'Oh aye. Smell that wind: it'll rain tomorrow.'

Sarie stumped into the dining room, with William in her wake. There he stopped motionless, shock thrilling the length of his body.

Charmaine's corpse lay on the mahogany table, under a cream-coloured duvet that was dusted with flowers. There were roses with their overblown scent, scraps of chopped-up African violets and holly berries sheared off the bush. The colours – purples and pinks, reds and silvers – had stolen every timbre from her face. It was purely uninhabited, its perversity of ugliness marbled over with whiteness, a final work of art.

Her voice returned to him. ('They say that elephants grieve, Mr Mellor. The herd returns to the watering holes next season and there they pick up the separated, picked-clean bones of their dead and pass them from trunk to trunk in a kind of dance, remembering. I often imagine it – bones curled round trunks, the swaying ritual, the alien rhythms of animal sorrow. Do you think that image wonderful or terrible, Mr Mellor? – or both?')

The flowers were scattered like bones; and he imagined Sarie placing them, with infinite care and an utter lack of natural taste – tea rose on tulip, the torn velvets of African violets everywhere.

'What do you think o' me flowers, then?'

'It's – very beautiful, Sarie. Sarie, does anyone know?'

'Aye, we know naught, altogether.'

'I meant, does anyone know she's dead, aside from us?'

'Timmy saw her fall, but then 'twas over.'

'I'll deal with it, Sarie. Leave it to me.'

('Come before the spring, mind. I won't see out another spring.')

'Sarie. She didn't – leave any messages behind, did she?'

He felt deserted, almost jealous: Charmaine's profile was so precise, her ugliness so rarefied, set off so whitely by the mixed-up embers of firing berries and roses.

'Oh, aye. Writing she was till yesterday, scribbling and banging for coffee and sealing up envelopes with her own hand. Before she called me in about me pig.'

'Where are the envelopes?'

'In the hall, most like.'

William stepped back into the hall, and sifted through perhaps ten or twelve envelopes. The last had his name on it, scrawled in an abrupt and angular hand.

Mr Mellor,
I'm very nearly gone, but I shan't ask you to come and see a dull old woman. All the same, I know what you did, and I thank you for it. You'll be curious how I knew, so I'll tell you. A queer

sharp lightness flooded over the house Thursday week, a gossamer golden shadow, as if spring had come early – then I understood and I was glad. I'm better pleased to die knowing that, where I failed, you have succeeded . . . As for dying, I've little patience with it; it crackles and drags too long. I wish I was already in that other country, where the light is always the colour of spring.

C. McKinley.

William pocketed the letter, and moved back into the dining room, where Sarie, with unexpected gentleness, was brushing a bit of dust off a tea rose. That other country . . . William bent down and kissed Charmaine's still hand.

Sarie: 'Harkee, there's the church bells. Ye'll be off, and I never made your tea, neither I did.'

'It doesn't matter.'

I'll not see out another spring.

'Sarie, tell me. What are you going to do now you've got your pig?'

'It's me collection,' said Sarie promptly. 'I'll be buying a wee cabinet; I fancy pine against the green. It'll be my collection o' jade from Chinaland, the wee pig in the middle . . .'

I wish I was already in that other country.

'Here's my number, Sarie. If anything happens to distress you, call me.'

'Oh aye; the garden'll be well enough, now the weather's turned. Timmy says the frosts is over.'

William stepped out of the house, the door wheezing shut behind him. He stood on the steps and breathed in the soft coda to the day: birds squabbling, the lifted voices of children playing behind the yew in the next-door garden. He was astonished to find young tears in his eyes, as if an illness had passed, a deep joy at the banners of waving trees, blurring shadows, the fragrant promise in the air.

He headed down the drive to the main road. Soon it would be April, he thought, then all the world would explode with the colour of spring.

CHAPTER 64

These violent delights have violent ends
And in their triumph die, like fire and powder,
Which as they kiss consume.

Shakespeare

(by Pete Hegal, March 1999)

I first resurrected my old diaries, you might recall, in order to
try to make sense of Warren Wilson's death. The irony is that I
seem to have made sense of everything else.

Looking back, I find that I can understand much better the
reasons for Piotr's behaviour, and what factors made Leszek
so vulnerable to attack. There were connections I'd never
made, ideas I'd been too personally involved in to consider.
Oh, I still don't understand everything about Janice, about the
cello – but there are surely some things we're not meant to
understand. But Warren's suicide remained a mystery until
yesterday, when I ran into William Mellor in Beare's violin
shop.

Will's been single ever since Margot refused to take him
back, four years ago. She's since married a Bromley head-
master; but Will remained steadfastly on his own.

Not that there haven't been rumours, but I know Will better
than that. I've been down to his place in Sussex – very pretty, if
you like that kind of thing – and we've also had the occasional
lunch in town. He's played in the Royal Sinfonia as well, as an
extra player, though not nearly as often as I've asked him to.

Anyway, I took one look at Will in Beare's, and knew it had

hit him. He carried himself as well as ever, but his face looked bruised from lack of sleep, his great eyes enormous. He grasped my hand almost painfully.

'Pete. Good to see you.'

'I'm sorry,' I said, inadequately. 'I know he was a friend.'

We walked out into Soho.

'Is Margot well?' I asked, for I knew they keep in touch.

'As far as I know; I haven't seen her for about a month. I've only recently got back from America.'

'What! Were you—'

'Yes, I did the Orchestra of London US tour. David Schaedel asked me if I would, because Adam's had tendonitis.'

I whistled. 'You mean you actually went on tour with your old band? Why, you must have been there when— Will, why did he do it? Was he ill, run-down? You were there, you must have seen!'

'Clearly, I didn't see enough,' said Will grimly. We went into a coffee shop, and I ordered two cappuccinos.

'Why didn't his wife go?'

'They thought the tour rather too long to leave the child with grandparents.'

'But if she'd only been there, then—'

'Perhaps,' said Will quietly.

'And what about Isabel?'

'I'll tell you what I know, if you really want to hear it.'

'Go on.'

Will sipped his cappuccino.

'It felt odd, being back with my old orchestra after such a long break. However, tours all have their own rhythms, their own rituals; and in some ways I enjoyed it. I didn't mind the travel; and even the dullest concerts seemed somehow less routine . . . Anyway, in Chicago, there was a semi-official bash. Piotr was looking for action at the other end of town, so I went downstairs on my own.

'The place was crowded with players. There are a lot of new young brass players in the band, nice fellows on the whole, but

I've not got much in common with them. I joined Warren Wilson instead. I'd always had a lot of time for Warren. We were talking about Italy; he had a positive mania about Giotto, we used to tease him about it. In his violin case he's got – he used to have – Giotto copies alongside snapshots of his boy.

'Isabel was with the group near the bar; I'd seen her, and somehow knew that she'd seen me. She was with the younger set – only in their twenties, most of them – and seemed in vivacious mood. I was – aware of her, the way one can be, even while I was talking to Warren.

'Then somebody had the notion of decamping to a night-club. Lucy asked Warren and me whether we were interested in going, but we both refused. I saw one of the trumpeters put Isabel's coat around her shoulders; I saw her looking back at him, flirting, laughing. There was something in her expression that made me feel almost – light-headed, remembering . . . Meanwhile Warren was enthusing about Giotto's famous chapel in Padua. He was supposed to have gone back there in the spring.

'Isabel was one of the last of her set to leave.

' "Not dancing, Warren?" she asked archly.

' "Sorry, not my sort of thing."

'Lucy reappeared in the doorway, calling out to her, "Isabel! Are you coming or not?"

' "Just a moment," she replied, and then to me, in an altered tone, "You won't . . ."

'I shook my head, attempting to smile, for the benefit of witnesses. She kissed Warren rather absently, and then closed her arms around me.

' "Kiss me," she whispered.

' "Isabel, I – no. I can't."

' "Kiss me!" she said, so fiercely that I thought I should comply, rather than make a scene. Everyone was looking – the players in the doorway, the strangers at the bar – not understanding, exactly, but somehow captured by her intensity.

'I gently kissed the side of her mouth, but she pulled me into doing the job properly. Suddenly we were in the snow outside the Festival Hall, we were back in her flat, not stopping for flowers – and for one strange glittering moment there was – oh, I can't describe it, not even to you . . . When I forced myself to stop kissing her, Isabel was in tears. And it was so quiet around us that for the first time I noticed taped music filtering out from the back of the bar.

'She breathed, "Oh, William," and Lucy told the others to go on without her. As for me, I don't think I was really aware of anything except the feel of Isabel in my arms until Warren rose to go.

'I released Isabel instantly and apologised to Warren, as if I'd almost – I don't know why I apologised. Was it politeness, or only embarrassment? He told me it didn't matter, he was going upstairs anyway. "Good night, Isabel," he said gently, but she was looking at me. And I knew – who knows why? – that the struggle was over. Whatever it was had resolved itself, now and forever. I'd never felt such overwhelming certainty, such bittersweet relief. So many years – so many efforts at escape! And it all came down to that strange, certain moment in a Chicago bar, watched by God knows how many strangers . . . The weight of memories was crushing down upon me, but I forced myself to acknowledge Warren, though I hardly knew what I said.

' "Don't set your alarm; it's a free day tomorrow," I joked. It was about the only free day on the tour; David Schaedel had done nothing but complain about it. And he smiled faintly and said, "Yes. Free tomorrow." '

'Free tomorrow,' I repeated. 'So – he'd already decided.'

'I don't know; it might have been a turn of phrase – I might even have misremembered it. The Chicago police kept asking me exactly how he said it, but there wasn't anything that you could pin down. Partly I think it was an impulse – that if I'd been more observant perhaps I could have stopped him – and partly I think he was determined to do it, even that he'd discouraged Caroline from doing the tour in order to take his chance.'

'You don't suppose that Isabel—' I asked delicately.

'That – possibly. We'll never know.'

'And what about – I mean, are you and Isabel—'

'Isabel and I were married last Saturday, in a registry office.'

Married, actually married! I tried to imagine it: Isabel in something subdued with that wild hair and those enormous eyes, Will straight and rather serious in suit and tie. His voice very deep, and their kiss like the kiss that had ended it all – or had it started it? – a continent and six years ago.

William finished his coffee, and the waitress asked if we wanted anything else. I noticed her looking at Will with admiration. Certainly his black raincoat set off his fine eyes and hair to advantage, but I still felt obscurely sorry for him.

Some people are always chosen, I decided – chosen by the cello, by Isabel, chosen to be part of other people's dramas as well as of their own. As if that great casting director in the sky kept thinking, Oh, sod it, get Will Mellor. Will's always box office.

I remembered something else. 'Did I tell you? The Society for Psychic Development got wind of the story of the cello and contacted me for details.'

'I trust you refused.'

'Oh, I refused all right. I couldn't bear to have the whole business pawed over by pseuds and scientists.'

'No, and it wouldn't do Leszek's career any good, especially now it's beginning to take off.'

'I thought of that too.'

We walked out together. Will was silent; while I was recalling the things I'd heard, in the last few years, about the unnamed Italian cello.

Every now and then I hear stories of people who have seen a cello – variously described as ruby, sunset-coloured or almost gold – just under where that pleasureboat sank, a few years back. Some people have even heard, or said they heard, fragments of music.

Personally, I think these tales either pure imagination or exaggerations over-layering old rumours of the truth, though of course one can never be sure. Only once did I think that I might have heard something myself – music under the earth on a soft spring night. Unless it was only the wind across the river. Who knows?